Dead End Deal

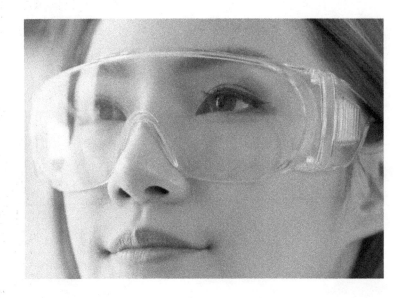

Allen Wyler

Praise for Allen Wyler

Dead End Deal is a medical thriller of the highest order, reviving the genre with a splendid mixture of innovation and cutting-edge timeliness. Neurosurgeon Allen Wyler knows of what he speaks, and writes, and the result is a thriller that equals and updates the best of Robin Cook and Michael Crichton. His latest is terrifyingly on mark, riveting in all ways, and a masterpiece of science and suspense.
—Jon Land, best-selling author of many books, including *Strong at the Break, Strong Light of Day* and *Betrayal*

Dead End Deal by Allen Wyler is a masterful medical thriller, intelligent, ferociously paced, scary as hell, ripping with suspense, and filled with fascinating (and horrific) details that only a neurosurgeon-turned-writer like Wyler could provide. If you like the medical thrillers of Robin Cook or Michael Crichton, you will absolutely love Dead End Deal.
—Douglas Preston, #1 NYT best-selling author of many novels and nonfiction including *The Monster of Florence*, *Relic*, *Extinction* and co-creator of the Pendergast novels

The gritty, graphic details of cutting-edge surgical procedures, capped with an exciting conclusion, should keep fans of the genre riveted.
—Publisher's Weekly

With its lightning-paced excitement and fascinating science, Dead Head has everything you could hope for in a medical thriller!
—Tess Gerritsen, retired physician and author of many bestsellers, including *Harvest, The Mephisto Club* and *The Shape of Night*

Dead End Deal—The Stairway Press Edition

Other titles by Allen Wyler
Changes
Deadly Odds
Deadly Odds 2.0
Deadly Odds 3.0
Deadly Odds 4.0
Deadly Odds 5.0
Deadly Odds 6.0
Dead Ringer
Dead Wrong
Deadly Errors
Dead Head
Cutter's Trial

ISBN: 978-1-949267-77-8 (Print)
ISBN: 978-1-949267-78-5 (eBook)

STAIRWAY≡PRESS

1000 West Apache Trail—Suite 126
Apache Junction, AZ 85120
www.StairwayPress.com

Publisher's Cataloging-In-Publication Data
Wyler, Allen. Dead End Deal—The Stairway Press Edition
1. Neurosurgeon Doctor—Thriller—Fiction. 2. Ruthless
Assassin— Fiction 3. Corporate Greed and Corruption—
Fiction 4. Radical Alzheimer's Cure—Fiction 5. Experimental
Brain Operations—Fiction 6. Seattle (Wash), Seoul (Korea)—
Fiction 7. American-Korean Love story.

About the Author

ALLEN WYLER IS a neurosurgeon who earned an international reputation for pioneering surgical techniques to record brain activity. He has served on the faculties of both the University of Washington and the University of Tennessee.

In 2002, he left active practice to become Medical Director for a start-up medical technology company, Northstar Neuroscience, which went public (NSTR) in 2006. Leveraging a love for thrillers since the early '70s, Wyler began writing fiction in earnest and published his first book in 2005. At the end of 2007 he retired to devote full time to writing and served as Vice President of the International Thriller Writers organization for several years.

He served as a judge for the Hammett Award and has been nominated twice for a Thriller Award. He now chairs the Institutional Review Board at a major medical center in Seattle.

For more information visit www.allenwyler.com

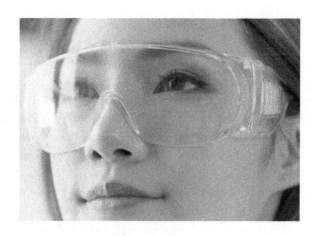

Prologue

Trophozyme Corporation—Seattle, WA

SEEMED LIKE A dynamite idea twelve months ago. Still did, for that matter. But now Marge Schwartz was killing him because of it.

Sweat sprouted across Richard Stillman's forehead—making him worry that any second now a drop would slither into an eye and cause him to blink, but he'd be damned if he'd wipe it.

Besides, with what? The back of his hand?

And if he did that, then what? Wipe his hand on his shirt? How would that look?

No, he had to be tough, cool, unflustered. In essence: in charge.

Schwartz leaned forward on her elbows and drilled him with that squinty-eyed, no-shit-serious look she'd mastered during her take-no-prisoners ascension of corporate ladders.

"The board wants a solid plan to rectify the situation, Richard. Not some grandiose hypothesis."

Easy for her to say—especially with the clarity retrospection brings.

He swallowed the gastric reflux burning the back of his throat and willed himself to appear relaxed. Let her harangue.

After all, that's her job, especially given the financial disaster facing Trophozyme. A disaster for which he freely took responsibility. Yet, he still believed that with enough time, their present track would be profitable. But that required more money and, the way things were going, the company would bankrupt in six months unless he pulled the proverbial rabbit from the hat.

The board members eyed him with various emotions that were easy to read on their faces: empathy from Levy, disdain from Chandler and bored bemusement from Gliner. Warner, well, she was apparently more engrossed in her smartphone than the bloodbath playing out before her.

Schwartz began collecting the various papers in front of her to replace in the manila envelope.

The bitch!

He flashed the vacant, non-threatening smile he'd picked up from their VP of marketing. One he practiced in front of a mirror until he could produce under the most stressful conditions. He scanned the room, making eye contact with each board member—well, except for Warner—certain every one of those smug, egotistical bastards believed they could run the company better than he. Truth be told, their success was due to either dumb luck or magnificent ass-kissing. Or both.

Schwartz raised her lids in exaggerated expectation.

"Well?"

Trophozyme needed a new blockbuster therapy. Their pipeline was drying up. With the patent on their only revenue-generating product expiring in less than a month, their competitors were already licking their chops, gearing up production of a generic substitute while several major shareholders dumped stock. Once the short sellers started...

Schwartz said, "Need I remind you, Richard, you were hired to put our company back on track?"

The board had lured him with a fat signing bonus, high salary, and a group of industry-savvy executives who had no idea where to take the company. To Richard Stillman, the future was obvious: by 2030, thanks to drugs like Lipitor, mortality from heart disease and stroke would be way down, making diseases like Alzheimer's the leading cause of death.

Any company to come up with an effective treatment would be sitting on a fortune. That treatment, Stillman believed, was to implant specially manufactured stem cells into patients' brains to replace dead ones. The problem was the method he picked to grow them didn't work.

Okay, so maybe his first attempt was a bust. But he knew where to get his hands on the right method...

Sweat slithered into his right eye, stinging like hell.

He inhaled and said, "As I've repeatedly advised, we must be patient. My vision for moving us forward remains unchanged. We've had minor setbacks, is all." He shrugged to emphasize the mere insignificance of his mistake. "As my presentation showed, the results of our retinal implant program are excellent."

Two weeks ago his R&D team successfully implanted tissue-cultured stem cells into the retina of three patients with a specific type of blindness. So far, the results were excellent in spite of being too soon to determine if patients' eyesight actually improved.

Aronson, CEO of a major pharmaceutical company, waved away his remark.

"All well and good, but even if this works, it's an extremely small market, nothing that will keep this company afloat. We need revenue or we're out of business."

Stillman squelched a sarcastic reply and settled on, "Everyone understands that, Stan."

You dumb shit.

"What we can't lose sight of is," and chuckled at the pun that no one else seemed to get, "our retinal implant program success will establish the proof of principle to Wall Street. Do that and we leverage the potential that cell implants may have on reversing Alzheimer's."

He said this with the infectious enthusiasm that served him well in securing financing for the previous companies he'd taken public.

Schwartz raised her hand to halt further discussion.

"We're getting wrapped around the axle here, Richard. Bottom line is that during our executive session we made a decision. Six months is all you get." She paused, the room suddenly dead silent. "By then, either this company has a viable therapy or we'll be forced to close down. Believe me, that happens and there'll be no other business on the face of this earth, not even a mom-and-pop 7-11 store in Rwanda that'll touch your resume. *Do you understand?*"

Before he had a chance to answer, she yanked off her glasses.

"Meeting adjourned," she said.

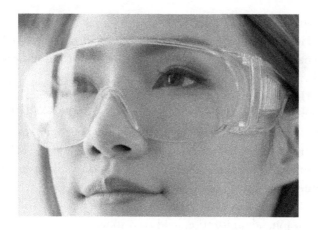

Chapter 1

One Month Later

THE BUZZ FROM the desk phone startled Jon Ritter. The sky was darkening, he realized, and streetlights now dotted the hill across Portage Bay. The phone buzzed again. He swiveled toward the window to watch traffic shoot by on the 520 interchange and picked up.

"Ritter here," he said.

"Hate to bother you, Doctor. Officer Schmidt, campus police. I'm in S-1 and it looks like someone broke into your car. Can you come down and take a look, see if anything's missing so we can file a report?"

Aw, man...

He checked his watch. Already past seven, time to go home anyway.

"Yeah, be right there."

After grabbing his sports coat off the door, he checked to make sure his file cabinets were locked. He decided to pick up Thai take-out on the way home to eat while watching the

Mariners.

He was walking past the secretary's desk when Gabriel Lippmann called out, "Good night, Jon," from the chairman's office.

He glanced into the office as he passed. Typical Gabe. Parked at his desk with stacks of paperwork. Always the last to leave, but never the first to arrive. The only neurosurgeon in the department who no longer gowned up, leaving the younger partners with bigger case loads. In exchange, butt-numbing meetings consumed Gabe's days.

Well, Gabe could have it.

To Jon, administration held zero appeal.

He waved, said "Night, Gabe," and continued out the door.

The elevator rattled and groaned down eight floors to the first basement level, jerked to a stop, hovered a moment before raising a half inch to be level with the hall floor.

Third world countries had better elevators than this.

The door opened.

The car break-in was beginning to seep in now. There was nothing in the vehicle worth stealing, so the act itself was senseless and frustrating. And although the insurance company would pay to replace the broken window—assuming that's how they got in—it couldn't compensate for the inconvenience. More than that was the feeling of personal violation. As a student his apartment had been burglarized twice, giving this an all too familiar feel.

A left turn and a push through the metal security door took him into a tunnel to the parking lot, his footsteps echoing off bare cement. After passing through another fire door he could see his black Audi in the almost empty garage but where was the security officer? Strange, but the car showed no signs of damage either.

Puzzled, he circled the vehicle. No damage, no officer.

Just then a man appeared from behind a round concrete

pillar and aimed a gun at him, his face distorted by what looked like pantyhose stretched tightly over his head, the sight so out of context that it didn't register.

The man said, "Got a message for you, baby killer. You listening?"

Speechless, Jon stared at him.

"Asked you a question."

Jon raised both hands in surrender.

"Whoa, there must be some mistake—"

"No mistake. You're the bloke I'm after. And in case you aren't listening, here's the written version." He dropped a folded paper on the Audi windshield. "No more baby killing. You and your little queer friend are done. Understand?"

"No, I—"

"Shut up. Simple enough. Stop work. Don't and we'll kill you and Dobbs. See?"

A familiar voice called, "Jon? What's going on?"

Jon glanced over his shoulder. Lippmann was exiting the tunnel, heading toward them.

Jon shouted, "Run. Get out of here. Call 911."

Lippmann stopped, looked at Jon's face, then at the gunman, then back to Jon before something clicked and he started to turn. Motion slowed. Dumbfounded, Jon watched as another man calmly stepped from behind a car, raised a gun and fired almost point blank into Lippmann's chest. Lippmann stutter-stepped before going down into a heap.

Jon yelled, "Gabe!" and started toward him when a lightning bolt exploded his head, turning his world into a black void.

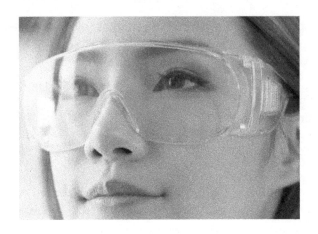

Chapter 2

"FUCK A DUCK!"

Nigel Feist slammed the heel of his palm against the steering wheel. The guard rails of the Alaskan Way Viaduct flew past, Elliot Bay in the distance, putting as many miles as possible between them and the parking lot before the cops started to investigate.

Raymore Thompson said, "Dude, I'm telling you, we had no other choice. The hell we gonna do? Let that fucking geezer call the cops?"

We?

Out the corner of his eye, Feist could see the hayseed wedged between the seat and passenger door, streetlights flashing off his disgusting tobacco-stained teeth. Feist slammed the steering wheel again, just to keep from back-handing the ignorant bastard.

Bad judgment, agreeing to use this shit-kicker tonight.

He knew better than to do it. So why the hell had he?

Fuck!

Intimidate was the mission. Not kill anyone.

"Well?" Thompson asked.

Okay, he could argue the point, but to what end? Raymore was too stupid to understand. Raymore. Who the fuck named a kid Raymore? Sounded like some kind of Georgia Cracker name.

Feist saw the sign for the West Seattle and Harbor Island exits and tripped the turn signal, letting the car drift into the right lane, deciding he needed to tidy up this mess straightaway before Raymore took them both down.

Since resigning as an analyst for Australia's Defense Intelligence Organization twenty years ago, Feist had grown his own consulting firm, a small company specializing in information gathering and disinformation. He never chose sides, simply provided services to anyone willing to cough up his high fees. Clients viewed his results as a godsend. Their targets leveled accusations of industrial sabotage, but nothing they could prove. His reputation included giving clients ultimate discretion. Never had one been exposed nor a project blown. Never had Feist or a client been forced to submit to questioning by a law enforcement agency. He attributed this exceptional record to following a strict set of rock-solid rules specifically engineered to stay out of trouble. The most important of which was impeccable planning—a rule broken the moment he agreed to take Thompson on tonight's job.

Fuck!

To make matters worse, Thompson probably couldn't survive ten minutes of police interrogation without incriminating himself and Feist. Which meant Feist's life was now at risk.

To distract him, get him thinking about something else, Feist asked Raymore, "What do you want to do when you quit working?"

"Huh?"

"Me, I want to retire after maybe a few more jobs, kick back, enjoy life. You like motorcycles?"

"Never much thought about them. Why?"

"Got me a collection of Harleys, I do. Plan to take a cross country Easy Rider road trip on my classic Flathead. Start out in LA, cruise through the south, on up the East Coast, circle back over I-90. Maybe even schedule it for a stop at Sturgis for the festival."

None of that would happen if he got nailed because of Raymore Fuckhead Thompson.

"What the fuck does that have to do with anything?"

"Just making conversation, is all."

Thompson whined, "The dude saw us, man, and he was going to run. The fuck was I supposed to do?"

Feist took the first of two adjacent exit ramps, the road angling down off the viaduct to Harbor Island to his right. Long loading docks, gigantic orange cranes, dented steel containers piled ten high in huge rows, a cruise ship's looming black hull dry-docked three blocks further west, railroad tracks and warehouses in the shadows ahead. The blue Toyota slowed while he scanned the deserted area for the best spot.

Feist said, "Maybe you got a point there, mate."

Thompson nodded.

"Hell yeah, I gotta point," with a note of relief.

Then he muttered something Feist couldn't make out.

Rather than ask him to repeat it, Feist kept scanning the shadows. When he spotted a likely place up ahead, he nosed the rental off asphalt onto chip seal and gravel, slowed further, keenly alert for signs of another person in the area, but it appeared deserted. He pulled along side a dark green SUV and cut the engine behind a squat, one-story, cinderblock building with sooty black windows and an oxidizing aluminum radio mast guyed to a flat roof.

This would do.

"Get out."

Feist stepped out into the smell of diesel and drying barnacles and the steady hum of tires from the West Seattle

Bridge overhead. A boat horn echoed across the harbor. Nothing moved and no one came from the shadows to investigate. No dog bark, no approaching crunch of tires, just the stillness of an industrial area locked up for the night.

"What?" Raymore asked, staying glued to the passenger seat, the whites of his nervous, squinty eyes flashing in the weak fluorescent light.

Feist put a hand on the car roof and leaned into the interior.

"Out. We're changing vehicles. That SUV there?" with a nod, "is what we'll be using."

He walked over to the SUV driver's door and pretended to fumble a key from his pocket.

Raymore whined, "Dude, you didn't say nothing about no change-up before now."

"That's right. I didn't. A contingency plan is what it's called. Not smart what you did, shooting that witness like that. Changes everything. Now fetch our gear and let's be done with it."

Thompson asked, "What gear?"

It took a supreme effort to reign in his anger.

"Don't hear too well, eh? I said to get the fucking gear and stop whining."

Feist watched Thompson pop the trunk and hunch over, look this way and that like a fucking idiot. Before Thompson could straighten back up, Feist tapped the gun to the back of his head and fired. Thompson went limp, half in the trunk, half out. Feist leaned in, nudged the barrel against his temple and discharged an insurance round. Then, lifting Thompson's legs, he rotated the body sideways, dumping him completely into the trunk, and slammed the lid. Standing still, he listened for the sound of feet or tires approaching but heard nothing. Using an oily rag, he meticulously wiped down every spot he'd touched, including common areas he wasn't sure of. After slipping on a pair of disposable exam gloves, he tossed the rag in a dumpster and climbed back into the car.

Feist retraced his route onto the Alaskan Way viaduct, then south to the first SeaTac Airport exit. Drove U.S Highway 99 to a long-term airport parking lot, accepted a time-stamp ticket from a machine, cruised the lot for a spot as far from the pick-up point as possible. He nosed the car to within a foot of the cyclone perimeter fence, set the brake, and stepped out to look around. Only one other person waited at the pickup site. Feist tore up the ticket and stuffed the pieces in his pocket to dump later.

Not much sense in letting anyone know your time of arrival.

Staying in the car shadow, he waited for the van to pick up the other customer. As soon as it drove out of the lot, he walked the street to an adjacent lot where he waited for the next van.

The courtesy van drove him to the airport departure zone, where he rode the escalator down to Arrivals/Baggage Claim. He bought a ticket for an Airport Express to the downtown Seattle Sheraton. Although the odds of a taxi driver remembering him were low, he figured it would be safer to blend in with a group of tired travelers on a van rather than be a single fare in a taxi. Attention to details, regardless how insignificant, kept you from the jaws of the shark.

Forty minutes later, he dumped the keys to the rental car in a sidewalk waste bin two blocks from the hotel.

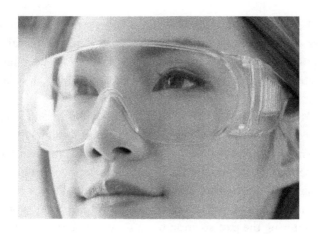

Chapter 3

FBI SPECIAL AGENT Gary Fisher eased the black Explorer past a clot of reporters and looky-loos and stopped next to the narrow guard booth in the center of the road. It had a peaked metal roof and Dutch doors on both sides to handle vehicles in either direction. Fisher lowered the window and flashed his creds at the campus cop leaning out of the booth.

"FBI."

After a cursory glance and a nod, the officer pointed toward the large three level parking garage ahead.

"See where the road splits? Take the lower one down to the second level, go straight ahead. Can't miss it."

"Thanks."

Ahead, the two-lane road divided, the left lanes slicing between the south side of the Health Sciences Building and the top floor of a subterranean parking garage. The right half curved away from the building before angling down into a cavernous cement garage. Following the cop's directions, Fisher entered the second of three levels and immediately saw a mix of University and Seattle Police cruisers thrown haphazardly together, most with their blue lights still flashing, several with doors open, adding a touch of chaos to the image. So far, the campus cops seemed to be doing a good job of keeping TV reporters at bay, but Fisher knew this wouldn't last much longer.

He parked on the periphery of the confusion and scanned the crowd of cops for Jim Lange, saw him talking to two uniformed campus police. He and Lange were assigned to the national task force hunting the Nuremberg Avengers, a group of militant anti-abortionists who claimed responsibility for blowing away two doctors and a nurse from three separate women's clinics during the past six months. A group of grade-A shitheads, far as Fisher was concerned; an opinion Lange shared.

As he approached Lange, Fisher saw a body on the oil-stained cement. His gut knotted. A week ago, The Avengers posted Professor Jon Ritter's profile on their website. But because those shitheads targeted so many individuals and institutions, it was impossible to assess the level of threat to anyone. He suspected that might be their strategy. Seeing a body on the concrete made apparent the difficulty of rooting out these guys.

Lange saw him approach, said, "Gary, like you to meet Lieutenant Helms and Officer Crawford, UWPD." Then to the officers: "Special Agent, Gary Fisher. The one I told you about."

Fisher shook hands and asked Lange, "What've you got?"

Lange nodded for Helms to answer; this was university jurisdiction. Although the campus was within Seattle city limits, the land remained state property with a sovereign police department. The FBI would take control only if this turned out to be Avengers related.

Helms said, "One homicide, one assault."

Fisher's gut knotted tighter.

He asked Lange, "Ritter?"

Lange nodded.

"Yeah, but he's the assault. The corpse," pointing at the

body, "was just ID-ed as a university employee, name of Gabriel Lippmann. White male, sixty-seven. Apparently, Ritter's boss."

Fisher asked Helms, "How bad is Ritter?"

Helms shrugged.

"No idea. Didn't see him. Paramedics say he was banged up a bit when they transported him. Head wound. Probably a concussion."

Fisher shifted his weight from one leg to the other and eyed Lange.

"Who found them?"

Helms jutted his chin toward the blue Caprice police special.

"Guy's over there, in my car."

The three men walked over. A man in his mid-forties was sitting in the back seat, door open, one foot dangling out. Helms introduced him to Fisher and Lange.

The witness explained that when he exited the tunnel from the research building, he saw Lippmann lying in the middle of the entrance, so ran to him but on seeing Lippmann's chest wound, realized he was dead so called 911 on his cell. Wasn't until he was on the call that he noticed Ritter sprawled out several feet away. He didn't remember seeing anyone else in the area but admitted to being too upset to look all that closely.

Fisher thanked him and then he, Lange, and Fisher moved away several feet to talk.

Fisher said, "You know for sure it's Avengers or is Ritter a coincidence?"

Hoping it might be, improbable as that was. Shit! They couldn't guard every person on that list.

Lange said, "Nope, there's a note, just like the other times. Except this one's atypical."

Fisher was about to say something when he noticed a security camera above the door to the tunnel. To date, no one could give a description of an Avenger because their kills were done at long range with a hunting rifle. A video could be a game changer.

With a nod toward the camera, he asked Helms, "That security camera, you view it yet?"

"Not yet. I've been too busy here. But I asked for the feed to be frozen until I get a chance."

Lange hitched up his pants, added, "That's what we were discussing when you arrived. The recorder's at their office. I wanted to wait for you before we took a look."

Fisher had mixed emotions: the last thing he wanted was another Avengers-related murder.

On the other hand, it could be extremely helpful to have an image good enough to enhance into a detailed picture.

Was the resolution of the security cameras here worth a damn?

Assuming, of course, they had been on and recording.

Helms, Lange, and Fisher piled into the Lieutenant's cruiser, Fisher taking the back seat, Lange riding shotgun. Blue misery lights flashing, siren blurting out an occasional yelp, Helms nosed the car through the thickening group of onlookers clogging the parking lot road as reporters leaned in for a look inside the rolled-up windows, hoping to recognize someone.

They followed N.E. Boat Street along the north shore of Portage Bay for three blocks to the Bryants Building, a drab rectangular, two-story clapboard wedged between the street and water. Took the wheelchair ramp to a pitted aluminum-frame glass-door.

Then, with Helms leading the way, they walked single file along chipped linoleum to an overheated room smelling of tuna fish and orange peel, probably from the brown lunch sack lying open down the counter. A long counter ran the length of the far wall and held an aged PC, a flat panel display, and numerous DVD jewel cases. A stocky female officer sat studying the screen as her right hand navigated a mouse.

To Fisher, she looked to be in her early thirties. About the same age as his younger sister, Carrie, had she lived. He caught the similarity between their profiles too, which was kind of spooky. He and Carrie grew up together in a small Tennessee town under the humorless eyes of strict Baptist parents who enforced Bible study every Wednesday evening along with endless bun-busting Sundays on pews hard as granite, during which he played head games instead of listening to how he was destined to eternal hell fire unless he put his faith in Jesus.

Two months into senior year at Chickasaw High, Carrie fainted. The principal pulled Fisher out of class to accompany her to the hospital while the school officials tried to locate their parents. Holding her clammy hand in his, the aid car siren screaming, she'd made him swear to never tell their parents of her abortion. She died from septic shock twelve hours later.

Although he kept her secret, he learned it was performed by a poorly trained midwife in the kitchen of her home because the only clinic in a fifty mile radius capable of providing clean abortions had been shut down six months earlier by hard-line pro-lifers.

The way Fisher saw it, the pro-lifers, not the midwife, were the ones who killed Carrie. When the Avengers case came up, he volunteered for the task force.

He had no problem with either pro-lifers or pro-choicers. Everyone was entitled to their own beliefs. But no one was entitled to ignore due legal process in favor of enforcing their own ideals.

Helms asked the officer at the computer, "What've you got for us, Diane?"

She clicked the mouse.

"Caught the whole thing. Here, watch." She scooted sideways in the rolling chair to give Helms a straight-on view. "I'll start from the beginning."

They huddled around the monitor that showed a grainy wide-angle image of the tunnel entrance and immediate surroundings. She scrolled the time bar at the bottom, found the minute she wanted, hit the pause button, then clicked play.

"Here's where it begins."

In jerky sequence, a man, probably Jon Ritter, entered the field, walking toward the camera. He stopped suddenly. A second man appeared from the opposite direction, his face and hair distorted by something. The masked man aimed a gun aimed at Ritter.

Helms muttered, "That's panty hose, don't you think?"

Lange said, "Looks like."

The first man turned slightly, giving more facial definition. Fisher said, "That's Ritter."

"Sorry about the jerkiness. Runs at only three frames per second," Helms said.

A moment later Lippmann stepped from the tunnel into the garage. Ritter turned around, appeared to yell and wave him away but without audio the scene was eerily silent.

The officer froze the scene, said, "Okay, now watch the left side of the screen. All you're going to see is what looks like a hand with a gun."

A mouse click and the action resumed.

From the left of the screen came a blur of motion, then Lippmann jerked and fell. Ritter seemed to yell and start forward, but the first gunman slammed him in the temple with the butt of the weapon and Ritter went down.

The first assailant exchanged words with the second one before both ran from view.

"See that? Guy's left-handed," Fisher said. Then to the officer, "Can you run it again."

After they'd seen it twice more, Fisher asked Lange, "What about the note?"

Lange scratched his chin.

"Yeah, they left it on the windshield of Ritter's car. But this one's different."

Fisher said, "How so?"

"Didn't claim responsibility. Just gave Ritter an ultimatum.

Said if he doesn't stop work, they'll kill him and Dobbs."

Helms seemed puzzled.

"Mind explaining that?"

Fisher nodded.

"Dobbs is Ritter's partner; they work together on research. The thing that bothers me more is the other Avenger assassinations have been so different, so much more methodical. This entire garage thing is too damn sloppy." He shook his head. "Doesn't add up."

Fisher asked Lange, "You check out Lippmann to see if he has anything to do with anything?"

Lange shook his head.

"You're kidding, right? I haven't had time to take a leak. Speaking of which..."

Fisher was looking at the monitor again, the frozen frame of the second assailant shooting Lippmann. The images could be enhanced but he didn't have faith that the campus police, although part of the Washington State Patrol, had the horsepower to do it to FBI quality.

He pointed at the computer.

"Make a copy for yourself. I want to take the original with me."

As the words came out, Fisher wanted to take them back but before he could Helms shot back, "Don't start that shit with me. We have the capability of enhancing images too."

Fisher considered how best to smooth things over but decided to hell with it.

"Aw, Jesus, here we go. Look, I'm tired and you don't want me to take this to the next level. You do, and you'll lose, and that'll waste everybody's time. We can do a better job with it. You know it and I know it. In the end, isn't that all we want? Right?"

The room fell silent.

The female officer seated with her eyes diplomatically glued to the screen instead of turning to watch her superior officer's face grow deep crimson.

Fisher added, "You got other cameras at the entrance to the garage or the road approach?"

Helms nodded.

"Yep."

"I want the originals of those too. Oh, while you're at it, make yourself a copy of the note they left."

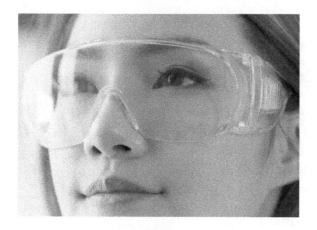

Chapter 4

NIGEL FEIST STROLLED north along the waterfront, past the Edgewater hotel with the huge red neon E on the roof. By now he was certain he hadn't picked up a tail.

At the bulkhead connecting the pier to Myrtle Edwards Park he leaned on the railing and listened to the steady rumble from the massive concrete grain elevator feeding a freighter's holds. Spotlights lit up the ship's rust-streaked hull and he could read the white lettering on the stern: The Voyager. Allegedly from Panama.

Feist didn't believe it. Figured the vessel was probably Russian owned and operated out of Vladivostok. He checked his watch and decided to wait a few more minutes before making his phone call.

The smell of brine and seaweed triggered memories of the two-bedroom flat close to the Cairns Harbour where his old man ran a barely profitable SCUBA dive operation and mum jockeyed drinks for tourists at the local casino. Hated the town. Couldn't wait to escape to see the world. Now he can't imagine living away from the ocean.

Funny, the decisions that chart the course of a life.
He thought back about pivotal moments of his life.

Instead of participating in the high school graduation ceremony, he walks into the small, cramped local Royal Australian Navy recruiting office.

The lieutenant looks up from reading the newspaper.

"May I help you?"

With excitement filling his chest, his mind dreaming of foreign ports, he says, "I want to enlist."

The smiling officer points to a chair next to his desk.

"Well, then, have a seat."

"Feist. A word with you in my office."

Nigel follows the officer into the sparse room.

"Close the door."

They stand facing each other.

"Son, your aptitude test scores are outstanding. I know your goal is to become a naval officer, but have you ever considered intelligence analysis?"

Stunned, Nigel stares at him, his mind flashing through the James Bond movies he loves to watch.

"Well?" the officer asks.

"Are you serious?"

"Would I joke about such a thing? Right, I'm absolutely serious. I'm offering the chance to be an analyst for our Defense Intelligence Agency."

Unaware of the difference between analyst and operative, he immediately says, "I accept."

First day on the job, it takes Nigel only eight hours of plowing through intercepts to realize how mind-numbing this end of the intelligence business is. By day two, he hates the job. But a contract is a contract, and he is a man of his word, so he puts in his time. Not, however, without making the most of it. His position allows him to befriend three field operatives. They,

in turn, teach him the tradecraft of intelligence gathering. Fuck
analysis. Information gathering rules!

Feist checked his watch again. Time to call.

Now several feet closer to the rumble of the grain
elevators, he faced the harbor, minimizing any possibility of
capturing his words with a parabolic microphone. Paranoid?
Perhaps, but attention to detail was the only way to survive this
game. He punched speed dial and listened to the connection
being made.

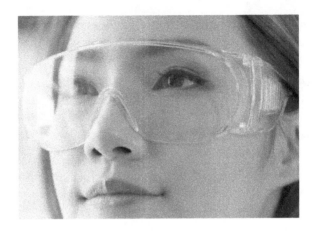

Chapter 5

"OHHH, JESUS, AGAIN?" Nikki Shepherd moaned.

Richard Stillman's lips brushed her navel as his tongue licked salty sweat.

"Mmmmmm..."

Her hands enveloped his shaved scalp when Snoop Dog's *Vato* began thumping from the black iPhone on the nightstand. Stillman hated Snoop Dog. Hated rap and hip hop, but relished the up-from-the-ghetto, bad-ass, nigga gangsta image he so meticulously cultivated.

He loved to spin bullshit tales about childhood struggles against huge sociological handicaps, of growing up dirt poor and black in the projects, sharing a one-bedroom apartment with a sister and grandmother while his unwed teenage mother and vagrant father spent time in the county lockup for dealing crack. That the stories were complete fabrications didn't matter—they were a hell of a lot more exciting than the truth of being the only child of a stay-at-home mom and Silicon Valley software engineer in middle class suburbia. The truth was boring. With a capital B. The gangster image enhanced his reputation for being dangerous.

Snoop Dog continued to rap.

He was expecting a call from Feist, so, as enticing as Nikki's body might be, he probably ought to check Caller ID.

He said, "Hold that thought," and rolled over to check.

Sure enough, Feist.

He muttered to Nikki, "I need to take this," rolled out of bed and headed toward the balcony, one eye glued to her reflection on the sliding glass door.

Loved that body. Too bad she wouldn't divorce that pig of a husband. Not that he had any intention of marrying her if she did, but it'd make these trysts easier to set up. Jesus, if that bitch Schwartz found out he was boning the CFO, she'd need major psychotherapy.

Naked, Stillman faced the sliding glass door to a balcony, the drapes and slider wide open, giving him a magnificent mosaic of office buildings and condominiums, and the traffic twenty-one floors below, leaving him totally exposed to anyone interested in watching him. Like the weirdo who lived directly across the street. His erection pointed straight at the voyeur's brightly lit living room with the Mariners game on large plasma-screen TV. The voyeur—a dumpy middle-aged guy with crew cut—stood at the darkened bedroom window, binoculars glued to them. Dumb shit thought no one noticed, but Stillman usually saw the reflection of streetlight off the lenses. Initially, Nikki had been embarrassed when he watched, but with a bit of coaxing and the passage of time, it morphed into sexual titillation, a major turn on for her.

Cupping the phone so Nikki couldn't hear, he whispered, "How'd it go?"

"Turned into colossal clusterfuck, mate. Your cobber killed a witness."

"What!"

"That's right," Feist said. "Fucking twit shot a witness."

"Christ almighty! Please don't tell me it was Ritter."

Stillman watched a jaywalker dodging traffic as he cut diagonally across the street.

"Right-right, not Ritter. Some old geezer comes out the fucking tunnel whiles we was having our discussion. Asshole said he had no choice. So then I had to bang your boy up a bit."

"Like?"

"Knock him out."

Damn! That could mean anything from concussion to major head injury. Last thing he needed was for Ritter to be brain damaged.

"Goddamnit! Thought I said do *not* hurt him."

"Couldn't be helped. Things went tits up fast." Feist paused. "We was doing just fucking lovely until the geezer pops out the tunnel. Ritter starts yelling for him to run and call the coppers. Thompson shot him, just like that."

Stillman could feel his erection wither, his mind now too distracted for sex.

"This witness—we're not talking about Dobbs, are we?"

"Naw, I said geezer, not fag."

"And Ritter, he'll be okay?"

"Can't know for certain, now can I? But I suppose so."

Nervously, he palmed his shaved scalp.

Wouldn't do to have Ritter badly damaged. Not yet, at least. But murdering a witness...that complicated things, brought more attention to any investigation.

"Back to Raymore...where is he?"

"Fuck if I know. Soon as Ritter goes down, bloke panics. Runs for the car and takes off. Barely got out of there meself before the coppers start showing up. I mean..." He paused. "I thought maybe you'd know where he was. Didn't call you, did he?"

Stillman smiled.

Feist, that lying sonofabitch.

He could pretty much guess what actually happened. By now, the greasy little punk was probably decomposing in the

Cascade foothills. This was even better than he'd hoped for when he demanded Feist take him along. Change that raggedy-ass name from Raymore to No-more.

"Haven't heard a word."

Neither man spoke for several seconds, each waiting for the other to comment.

Feist finally said, "Right. Job's done, then. I expect to find the balance in my account when I hang up. I'll be on me way, then."

Stillman heard water tattooing from the shower. Typical Nikki. Fed up waiting, this was her way of ending the evening. After all, how could a phone call possibly trump sex with her? Even if it was important business. High maintenance, that girl. But he had to admit the sex made it worthwhile. She'd get over it.

Stillman said, "It's been taken care of. But don't leave town just yet."

"Oh? Why's that?"

"I want to make sure Ritter has been persuaded before you take off."

"Had me heart set on vacation, I did."

Jesus, talk about high maintenance. Feist. Another piece of work.

But he couldn't afford to piss him off.

"Once this job's done, you can take vacation any time you damn well please. Look at it this way: if you did your job tonight, you're done. If not…we'll just have to try again. More money for you. That's all I'm saying. Besides, I should know the outcome within a week. At the outside."

"Not if it involves another Raymore, I won't. That wasn't part of the initial agreement."

"Not an issue this time."

And we both know that.

"Alright then, but me fee's double. And that's not negotiable. What's more, change up on me again and I fucking walk. We clear?"

"Agreed. Now, are you clear on what's expected of you?"

"That's another thing, mate…keep up with that fucking superior tone and you can look for someone else."

Feist hung up.

Stillman regretted pissing him off. The last thing he needed was for Feist to walk. Then again, for what he was getting paid, he doubted he would. Stillman dumped the phone into the charger and listened to water spatter against marble. She'll probably stay in there for another ten minutes, the way she loved long hot showers. He considered joining her, maybe resuming where they'd left off. But the mood was gone and when she was like this it wasn't worth the effort to coax it back. Instead, he detoured to the kitchen for the remainder of the cabernet.

Glass in hand, he returned to the open slider but with his back to the view, admiring this magnificent condo. Only 2600 square feet. Relatively small for a penthouse. Tastefully decorated. A stunning understatement of contemporary design fused with the simplicity of stark Asian lines. Muted bold tones, masculine, yet not heavy. Like all of his varied accomplishments, it made a bold statement of excellence.

Yes, he'd done well in life. Last year an article in *Forbes* chronicled his meteoric career, dubbing him The Wunderkind of Startups. Stillman loved that phrase. Such a concise summarization of his record of shepherding a consecutive series of startups from incubator phase through initial public offerings. After the IPO he typically bowed out in search of the next great idea. A *Barrons* article, titled "The Man With The Midas Touch", debated whether his success was due to an uncanny ability to pick winners or such excellent management skills that could turn even bad concepts into gold. He was the man who made the difficult look easy.

Until now.

To say Trophozyme was a mistake wasn't accurate. He still

had a chance to be proven right. After all, the company had two major strengths: excellent people and a valid founding concept. No one could dispute the huge market an effective Alzheimer's treatment would generate. Their lack of success resulted from only one bad choice, and that could be rectified. Culturing stem cells was a finicky process. Culturing stem cells in sufficient quantity to support a commercial therapy simply compounded issues. The solution was stunningly simple: wrench the correct method from the one man who owned it: Jon Ritter. That arrogant prick.

Ritter, like every self-aggrandizing academic asshole he knew, viewed himself superior to the low lives in industry as if industry were a dirty word—an attitude that continued to infuriate Stillman. Ritter had never said anything directly to his face, but he didn't need to. Stillman read all the subtle cues in Ritter' tone and attitude.

Just the thought of Ritter caused Stillman's temples to pound. Not good. He knew his reaction just raised his blood pressure and clogged his consciousness with counterproductive negative thoughts. He chose a spot in the room—a hand-made Japanese ceramic sake set—and concentrated on it, channeling all the negative energy into those simple yet elegant lines, just like the therapist taught him.

Harmony...Form...Harmony...Form....

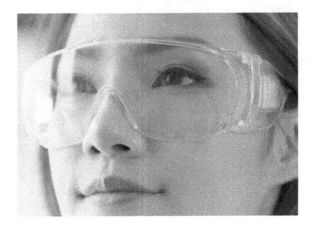

Chapter 6

THROBBING PAIN GNAWED at Jon's left temple as he surfaced from a colorless void into vague awareness. Now he was blindingly aware that both temples were pounding and a railroad spike was being driven into the center of his skull.

Where am I? What's happening?

In excruciating bright light, he squinted out the form of a woman in sky blue scrubs leaning over him pressing an ice-cold stethoscope to his chest.

"Good morning, Doctor Ritter. Take a deep breath," she said, with a perky flip of her dishwater blond ponytail. "Welcome to intensive care. Another breath, please." Her brow wrinkled in concentration as he breathed before sliding the stethoscope further down. "And one more."

Gabe's murder... vivid nightmare or harsh reality?

Wasn't sure. Wasn't sure of anything but the throbbing pain boring into his head. Deep throbbing gnawing pain. Another flash: Gabriel Lippmann sprawled dead on cement.

Without conscious intent, his fingers explored a bulky dressing covering his left eye and temple. Had he been shot too, like Gabe? His index finger gently probed under the edge of the bandage, found a wound with stitches, where even the slightest pressure triggered more pain. He groaned and realized his mouth tasted like dried bat shit.

"Water," he croaked.

"That's good!" She held up a sweating green plastic water pitcher with a white straw with an accordion bend. She held the straw to his lips, said, "Only a few sips at first. You know the drill. We want to see how you handle clear liquids before allowing you too much."

He sucked on the straw, got only a mouth full of air, pondered that a moment before realizing his lips were too dry to seal it. He pressed them tighter to the straw, tried again, and was rewarded with delicious ice-cold wetness. How many times had he noticed those sweating plastic bedside pitchers on rounds without the slightest appreciation for the relief they could give?

She withdrew the straw.

"Hey, easy does it. Not so fast. You need to pace yourself. At least at first."

He let the second dose soak the lining of his mouth before swallowing.

"More."

She permitted another sip.

He took this one less aggressively, gasped, "Thank you." Paused to swallow before asking, "Doctor Lippmann...where is he?"

"Dr. Lippmann?" She said with awkward surprise. "If he's been around today, I haven't seen him."

He couldn't bear to ask. He was too afraid he already knew the answer.

"No, I mean..."

Finally, she broke the uneasy silence.

"Feel up to talking with someone?"

He rolled stiffly onto his right side, hoping a new position might ease the throbbing. Even the overhead lights seemed to hurt.

"Can I have something for pain?"

She checked his IV line.

"Codeine's ordered. I'll get you one."

He nodded, but that only made matters worse.

"Make it two."

She glanced at the door.

"An FBI agent wants to talk to you. He's been waiting since you came out of surgery." Then, with a half shrug, "It's up to you whether you want to talk to him."

Surgery?

He touched the outside of the dressing again and thought about the stitches.

What happened?

"Well?"

Right, the FBI. Would he know about Gabe?

Again, without thinking, he nodded yes, but immediately regretted it. Gingerly, with both hands, he pressed the scalp above his eyes and began to gently massage his head, hoping to ease the throbbing. Then the thought hit him: why FBI? Why not the Seattle Police?

But just the effort of thinking seemed to worsen the pain.

"Yes."

After introducing himself, Fisher said, "Mind if I sit down?"

He stood with a posture indicative of military service at sometime, maybe a foot or two from the bed rail, stuffing an ID wallet back into a navy blazer. Tall, angular, blond crew cut with freckles shot gunned across a complexion that would burn instead of tan.

"Sorry. I'm not thinking. Please."

Fisher pulled an uncomfortable looking wooden chair next to the bed, slipped off his blazer and hung it on the back of it before settling in, as if this discussion would take more than one or two questions.

"I appreciate you talking to me. First, let me say how sorry I am about your injury."

"What about Gabe? Is he okay?"

Fisher dropped his eyes, right hand kneading the back of his neck, searching for words with an awkwardness that made Jon feel sorry for him. He himself had been the bearer of bad news too many times and contrary to popular opinion, it never became easier with experience. Before Jon could say anything, Fisher answered matter-of-factly.

"He's dead."

Gabriel's death was real. No more false hope of a bad dream or that his memory was playing tricks. He wanted to say something, but what could he say? Saying anything would trivialize Gabe's death. Instead, he stared at the ceiling, tears welling up in both eyes. More than a mentor, Gabe had served as a father-figure, his biological father dead three decades ago leaving only sepia-tone memories of fish, diesel oil, and sweat.

During residency, his relationship with Gabe morphed from mentor/student to genuine friendship. Then, three months before graduation Gabe offered him an assistant professorship. He accepted without a second thought about the low salary or shit tasks the senior faculty would inevitably slough onto him. That, he philosophized, was the price of admission to a prestigious opportunity. Gabe helped him establish a lab, compete for grants, and navigate the petty cutthroat politics of university life.

Even more importantly, after his fiancée Emily's death, Gabe helped him survive emotionally. Now Gabe's life had been senselessly snuffed out because of...what, exactly?

What the hell had happened? Why did it happen?

Fisher said, "I'm sorry. I didn't know you were close, otherwise...I'm sorry."

The throbbing in both temples intensified.

"Have they found the bastard?"

"The killer? No, not yet. That's the reason I'm here."

Allen Wyler

Fisher cleared his throat. "Look, I know this isn't a good time. It never is in a case like this, but I need to ask some questions."

Jon nodded.

"If it'll help find those bastards."

The nurse returned with a pill, giving him a good opportunity to compose his emotions and soak his mouth again.

As she was leaving, Fisher said, "Tell me what you remember."

When Jon finished his story, Fisher asked, "You said the one man had an Australian accent. That's pretty specific and could be extremely important. How sure are you it's Australian? Lot of accents sound similar; South African, British, Aussie, New Zealand…"

Jon realized he was clenching his jaw, which was making his pain worse. He tried to relax but couldn't.

"No, definitely Australian."

"How can you be so sure?"

Jon concentrated on replaying the scene bit by bit, trying to find the reason. Then, it dawned on him.

"The Outback commercials. He sounds exactly like that guy, his vowels, the tone of his voice…"

"Okay, good." Fisher made a note of that. "You say he's white. How do you know that with pantyhose over his face and gloves on?"

This was an easier answer.

"I saw his wrist. His left wrist."

"The one with the gun?"

"Yes."

Fisher made another note.

"How about the other guy? You get a look at him too?"

Jon thought about that a moment.

"Yes, but things happened so fast …"

"Also a white guy?"

"Uh-huh."

34

"That a yes?"

"Yes."

Fisher flipped the page, obviously sorting through a list of questions.

"How tall are you?"

"Five-ten."

Fisher made a note.

"Weight?"

"One-sixty-five. Why?"

Fisher paused to jot this down too.

"The whole thing was caught on a security cam, but the angle doesn't give us much to go on for physical attributes, things like height and weight. So comparing him to you helps. You'd say, what, the Australian's bigger than you?"

He thought about too, his finger absentmindedly finding its way under the dressing again. Stitches. Someone took the time to stitch his scalp with small, closely spaced, fine sutures—a plastic surgeon type closure.

Who?

Then another shock: what about other injuries? Like skull fractures?

How long was he unconscious? Minutes? Days?

Fisher seemed to be waiting for…what? Oh, yes, the question…

"An inch maybe…maybe twenty pounds heavier than me. Muscle though, not fat. Definitely muscle."

Fisher scratched the side of his jaw, considering something.

"If you don't mind, I'm going to ask you a personal question."

"What?"

"Dobbs is gay. Right?"

Jon felt uncomfortable discussing Wayne's personal life behind his back. Then again, if it helped the investigation…besides, Wayne didn't hide it.

"Yes."

"And you?"

There it was: guilt by association. Even though this wasn't the first time the question had been asked, it still pissed him off. He resented the implication. Another jab of pain forced his eyes shut, tightening his jaw muscles, making it still worse. He squinted, gingerly fingering the bandage. His head felt swollen and ready to explode.

Fisher asked, "Sorry, did you miss the question? Should I repeat it?"

Fisher, he reminded himself, probably had good reason to ask. Still...

"What's the point? What difference does it make?"

"Could be a huge. Ever hear of the Nuremberg Avengers?"

The name sounded vaguely familiar, but he couldn't place it, and it hurt too much to even try to think of the answer.

"No. Why?"

"You know about the doc who was blown away on the porch of an abortion clinic about a month ago, in San Francisco?"

Now it clicked.

"Oh man, *they're* the ones?" Referring to last night.

"Possibly. Your assailants left a note suggesting that's the case."

"You don't sound convinced." His temple was screaming, making it hard now to even squint. "Besides, I have nothing to do with abortions and I don't use fetal tissue."

Fisher shifted positions in the chair.

"We'll get to that. You haven't answered my question."

What question? He thought back, but came up blank.

"Remind me. I'm not doing so well at the moment."

Fisher looked straight into his eyes.

"Are you gay?"

Oh, that one.

"Thought I answered it. I don't see why that's important."

"Well, it is. The militant pro-choicer doc who ran the abortion clinic was lesbian. Sort of makes me wonder why they came at you. Is this an anti-abortion thing or a hate crime? *That's why.*"

Made sense.

"Okay, got it. No, I'm not gay."

"So, if assuming it was the Avengers, why come after you?"

As if he was supposed to know.

"Hey, don't look at me like that. If I knew, I'd tell you."

The silence was interrupted only by rhythmic beeps of the cardiac monitors in the nursing station and the hollow metallic rattle of cartwheels rolling along the hall.

After several moments Fisher added, "Unless, of course, they're not Avengers."

Hard as he tried, Jon couldn't stop remembering the moment Gabe went down. Over and over again, playing a visual loop he couldn't ignore. Why would anyone kill this gentle man? What had he done to deserve being gunned down in…?

Fisher said, "Tell me again exactly what they said."

Jon raised the head of his bed in hope of alleviating the pounding ache in the center of his skull. Then suddenly remembered a point he forgot to mention the first time through the story.

"He called me 'Baby Killer.'"

Fisher nodded slowly.

"Baby killer? But you're a neurosurgeon, right?"

"Yes."

Fisher lowered his notepad.

"That's what I thought. I don't get it, why call you that? What am I missing here?"

More details started flooding back, Fisher's questions jiggling scraps of memory into consciousness.

"The only thing I can think of is they're confusing my research…"

Fisher readied himself to take a note.

"Yeah? Go on."

"I work with stem cells. But not *fetal* stem cells."

Fisher set down his notepad, sat back, crossed his legs.

"Back up. I need some background information. I have to confess; I've never understood what stem cells are."

Ritter searched for an easy way to explain the difficult concept to someone with a limited background in biology.

"They're primitive cells that have the potential to become any other cell in the body like heart, spleen kidney, bone. They're found at all ages: embryos, children, on up to adults. You have some in your bone marrow right now. But the ones I use are from mice. Not humans."

"Mice?"

"Yeah, it's a long story, but basically, it's a political solution. What we really want to do is use stem cells to replace dead neurons in dementia patients. To a large extent, a stem cell's plasticity depends on where you get them. The ones from embryos have the greatest transformative potential. The ones from a fetus are more limited. Stem cells from adults are the most limited.

"Scientists didn't even know about these cells until 1971 when they found them in mice. Since then, they've been used to treat diseases. Cancer is one. Sometimes a cancer patient's bone marrow can be destroyed by chemotherapy and radiation. The marrow can be replaced by injecting stem cells into the marrow. But here's the problem: the most versatile stem cells come from embryonic and fetal tissue, and some religious groups object to using it and have managed to block their use. Politicians cave pretty quickly when it involves fetuses. We can grow embryonic stem cell in tissue culture, but they've blocked this too. This has really thrown a monkey wrench in several life-saving applications—like growing cultured stem cells into specific organ tissues, a kidney for example."

Fisher seemed to be following.

He said, "Interesting stuff. But you can't grow a brain, can you?"

Jon laughed.

"No. It's easy to grow mice stem cells into cells that appear to be neurons, but the problem is they don't form connections—synapses—that transfer information from cell to cell. That's what Wayne and I've been working on. Just recently we solved this problem with a special mixture of hormone-like chemicals called nerve growth factors that dictate how cells grow. We just recently proved it works in monkeys. So our next step is to do it with real patients."

Fisher thought about that a moment.

"Clearly you have nothing to do with human fetal tissue, right. So why call you 'baby killer'?"

"Only thing I can think of is he had the wrong guy."

"Not if he called you by name, knew your phone number and car and knew where to find you when you'd be alone. Obviously, they've been tracking you. What you're working on, does it have anything to do with babies?"

"No." Ritter laughed at the absurdity. "We're way on the other end of the spectrum. Sure, we use stem cells, but to treat Alzheimer's. Our ultimate goal is to implant mice stem cells in human brains, but we haven't actually done that yet. That's coming. So that's how I know these guys are mistaken. That 'baby killer' thing is ridiculous. Doesn't make sense."

"Okay, so maybe they're misinformed, I'll grant you that, but the facts are: these guys are dangerous and they targeted you. Until we can find out who they are and stop them, my advice is to do as they say and stop your work."

Jon clenched his jaw, driving another railroad spike through his temple. His right eye felt about to explode. He groaned.

Fisher asked, "Say what?"

"I can't shut down my work."

"Why not?"

Jon's anger erupted.

"They killed a man in cold blood for what? Nothing! Shot him down like he was nothing. I'm not going to allow..." Pain forced him to stop and focus on calming down. This was killing him. He muttered, "Besides, it's not simply my decision. It's Wayne's too."

Fisher said, "Word of advice?"

Jon's anger started bubbling over.

"Advice? I don't want any goddamn advice. I want those bastards hunted down and buried in a maximum-security hole forever. I want to see them fry." The headache started sending flashes across his vision. He groped for the call light.

He needed more codeine.

"Aw, shit!"

Fisher said, "Hey look, I know you're angry—for good reason, too. But you need to understand something. These assholes are certified fanatics. And fanatics don't understand the concept of reasonable. That's what makes them dangerous. Do not mess with them. Do what they say. In the meantime, we'll find out who they are and eliminate the threat. Once we do that, you're free to continue working. Okay?"

That did it. Up on both elbows now, Jon raised his voice.

"No, that's not okay. What I didn't mention is that NIH just gave us the green light to do our first patients. You know how long we've worked for this?" He didn't wait for an answer because it wasn't a question. "Ten years! Ten goddamn years! And you want me to throw that away?"

The nurse hurried into the room, arms out, hands waving, "Whoa, calm down," and shot Fisher a withering scowl.

Jon continued, "They killed Gabe, goddamn it! Blew him away like he was nothing more than an inconvenience. Now you want me to turn around and walk away! That's bullshit."

The nurse placed both hands on his shoulders, pushing him gently back against the pillows.

"Please, Dr. Ritter, calm down."

More throbbing bore into him, taking away the urge to scream.

He muttered, "I need another codeine. Make it two."

"I'll get them, but you need to calm down."

She released him and pulled the blood pressure cuff from a wire basket on the wall, wrapping it around his arm.

Jon settled into against the bed while the nurse checked his pressure, the image of Gabe's murder still flashing through his mind. Fisher stood facing the window. Right now, Jon told himself, the most important thing was to nail the sons of bitches who killed Gabriel. Taking out his frustration and anger on Fisher would accomplish nothing.

The nurse ripped loose the Velcro, folded the cuff into a bundle, stuffed it back into the wall holder.

"I'll be right back with your meds."

Jon wanted to say something to Fisher, a fresh start to the conversation, but before the words came, Fisher asked, "Can we continue?"

Jon liked the way the man said it, without a hint of accusation, as if he really did understand his anger.

"Let me ask you something. The way you started out, you sounded like there might be some doubt it's the Avengers. That true? Are you convinced it really was them?"

Fisher seemed to weigh his answer and dropped back into the chair.

"There're things about the attack that don't fit with the Avengers."

"Like?"

"Getting that close to their victim. They've never done that before. The other murders were long-range assassinations with a rifle."

When Jon didn't say anything, Fisher added, "And their note didn't wash."

"Then why think it's them? And if there's a chance it isn't, why tell me to stop working?"

Fisher looked at his shoes a moment.

"I assume you haven't seen their website?"

Website? Did assassins keep websites?

"No."

"Well, they have one. They post potential targets on it. Pictures, personal information, the crimes they claim their targets are guilty of. I guess it's supposed to be a warning of sorts, because when they hit someone, a big red X appears over the picture."

He still didn't get the point.

"Yeah? So?"

"Your profile was posted a week ago."

Jon was stunned. Took a moment for the implication hit.

"A week ago? Jesus! You've known about it for a week and didn't say anything?"

Fisher nodded but didn't look up.

"There's a national taskforce assigned to them. It monitors the site twenty-four, seven."

The pressure in his head came back with a vengeance.

"In other words, yes, you knew about it."

Fisher shrugged, finally looked him in the eye, but without conviction.

"Hey, lighten up. There're over fifty profiles up there."

"Why didn't anyone warn me?"

A fresh bolt of pain knocked him back onto the pillows.

Fisher shrugged and glanced away.

"For the reasons we just discussed, we didn't consider you a high risk."

"I—"

He became speechless, thinking, if he'd been warned, Gabe might still be alive.

He yelled, "GOD DAMN IT! Get out of my sight."

Fisher set a business card on the bedside table, tapped it with a finger.

"Here's my contact information. You're righteously angry. I completely get it. I feel for your loss. But when you calm down, consider two things: the best way to take down Lippmann's killers is to help us. Also, you need to understand—

and this is really important, so listen—the persons responsible for his death know a lot about you. For them to call your office and con you down to the garage indicates careful planning. Bottom line is they know a lot more about you than you know about them. Meaning you're vulnerable. What I'm saying is, don't do anything that'll put you back in their crosshairs. Don't tempt them."

Eyes closed, Jon tried to relax to relieve the pain. Fisher's words made sense, but he didn't want to hear anymore. The bastard knew but never warned him.

"Get the hell out of my room."

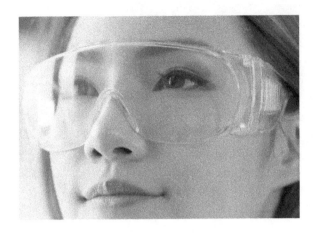

Chapter 7

"HOW YOU FEELING?"

A familiar voice jerked Jon out of a dark, drifting, codeine enhanced state. Squinting, he made out fluorescent light reflecting off a patch of bald scalp. Wayne Dobbs. With a grunt, he rolled onto his left side, sort of, which was limited by the head of the bed being raised.

"Probably about good as I look." He fingered the dressing in the same absentminded manner that, as a kid, he'd played with a loose tooth: repeatedly testing the pain it caused. "How long you been here?"

His head hurt less now, after a double dose of codeine.

"Less than a minute. I was trying to decide if you were just deep in thought or dead. If you're talking, I guess you're not dead."

Jon laughed, which stirred up the pain.

"Aw man, don't make me do that."

"Open your eyes, this is an official consult. Here, look at my finger." Wayne moved his vertical finger to the right then to the left, observing Jon's eyes. Then turned the finger horizontal and moved it up and down. Jon recognized these simple tests.

"Good. Now the hard part. Where are you?"

The question shocked him. This wasn't a joke; Wayne really was checking for any brain damage.

Am I seriously damaged?

"University Hospital."

"What day is it?"

He had to think about that one. The fact that he did was, in itself, startling. As soon as he said the answer, an anxious chill layered in his gut. Was he right?

"Who's the President?" Wayne asked.

Jon wanted to ask if the previous answer was correct but didn't want to appear uncertain, so dodged both issues with, "You know I never discuss politics."

With a frown, Wayne shook his head.

"Well, tell me anyway. I'm serious."

Jon answered.

With a nod of approval, Wayne smoothed a tastefully loud tie against a white French-cuffed shirt, a perfect Windsor knot concealing the collar button, a gold chain restraining the tie. He was one of the few people Jon knew who could wear a double-breasted blazer without appearing overly dressed.

"In case you're worried, you passed."

Jon was relieved.

"Thanks."

Wayne looked down at the floor, the smile gone.

"Oh, Jon, I'm so sorry about Gabe. What a wonderful man. I know how close you were...."

The back of Jon's throat constricted. He swallowed, clearing it.

"Thanks."

Wayne sighed and took the chair Fisher had used just minutes earlier.

"Want to talk about it?"

"Maybe another time, not now." Pointing at his temple, he

asked, "Anything to tell me about what happened here?"

Wayne gave another sigh.

"Sure. The neuro check was for real. Fuller asked me for an official consult. Well, I'm glad you passed.

"The asshole who hit you must've used something other than his fist because you came away with a small, depressed skull fracture and a beauty of a stellate laceration. After Fuller elevated the fracture, DeVito did a plastic closure. DeVito says you should heal up with a minimal scar. Your post-op scan's normal, by the way. No sign of any clots."

Jon fingered the dressing again.

"Yeah, but this hurts like hell."

"Fuller says he'll discharge you later today. I talked to Michael and we both want you to stay in the guest room until you feel you're back on your feet again."

"Thanks. I don't think I'd be very good company. I'll be fine at home. Besides, I need to think about a few things."

"Good company isn't the issue here. Besides, this is a time when you need friends around you. All this," he spread his arms, meaning Jon's situation, "on top of Emily's death. I'm seriously worried about you. I mean that as a doctor, not just because I'm your friend."

"Thanks, but you haven't heard the best part yet. This was no random incident, and the FBI wants us to stop working until they catch the bastards who did this."

By the time Jon finished telling him everything, Wayne was pacing tight circles in the cramped room, ears bright red with anger.

Wayne said, "Unfuckingbelievable."

The pain had returned, and Jon's temples were throbbing. Recounting the story was like putting his head in a vice grip. He grimaced in pain.

Wayne said, "It's bad enough this should happen, but the timing…Jesus, it couldn't be a worse time."

Jon unclenched his jaw, rocked it side to side to loosen up and tried to relax, but his brain was back into an endless loop of: *They murder Gabe, then try to dictate my life. No way will I let them get away with it.*

Well, it wasn't his decision to make alone. Wayne held an equal vote. And Wayne was watching him as if expecting an answer.

Jon asked, "What do you think we should do?"

Shaking his head, Wayne studied the floor a moment and clinked the coins his pocket.

"I…to tell you the truth, this scares me." He looked at Jon. "Scares the shit out of me, actually."

Wayne closed the hall door and continued to pace.

"Let me tell you a story. This happened eleven, maybe twelve years ago, before I met Michael. A friend and I were in San Francisco, down in the Castro district, walking along, minding our own business when two guys jump out of nowhere and get right in our faces, start calling us fags and queers, cocksuckers. You know…all the terms of endearment. I thought maybe we could just walk away without a problem, but my friend knew it wasn't going end so easy. He stared back at one of the dudes, like, daring him to do something. So what's the guy do? Calls him a fucking queer right to his face and tries to kick him in the balls. They both jump my friend, start kicking the shit out of him. In those days we carried whistles for just this kind of thing. I start blowing mine like crazy and Jesus, you should've seen it; guys come pouring out of the clubs and within seconds they were all over those two homophobes, pounding the living shit out of them. And you know what? I just stood there, jumping up and down, cheering, watching the blood fly. I wanted to see more and more until they looked like road kill. There was a part of me just aching to see those two fairy haters stomped into the concrete.

"It was scary, the intensity I felt. I can still remember my reaction the moment I saw that first guy kick Jeff. I thought, 'how dare you! This is our tiny little space, our own neighborhood where we can finally be ourselves. You're the one invading us.' I felt rage. Pure hatred. And let me tell you, I pray to God I never feel that again. The point to this? Well, right now, this very moment, I'm closest to that exact hate that I've ever been since that night. And it scares hell out of me. I don't want it to cloud my mind and cause me to make a wrong decision."

Jon said nothing for fear of interrupting Wayne's story. Of all the life stories they shared over the years, this was the first he heard this one. Jon wondered if maybe it explained why Wayne held a Black Belt in martial arts. He started grinding his teeth, playing with the pain, as if it might focus his thoughts and somehow help him reach the right decision.

Wayne seemed to be winding down and stopped pacing.

"I don't know what the point of my little rant is...other than...those guys we're dealing with—whoever they are—kill people in cold blood. They proved that with Gabe. I'm not so sure I want to mess with them. You?"

Jon avoided answering.

"What do we know about them?"

Wayne looked out the window at the view of the Montlake Bridge, hands in his pockets, playing with some change.

"Not much, I really haven't paid attention to them other than a glance at the headlines. They've killed people. We know that. What more do we need to know?"

Good point. Fisher certainly took them seriously.

"Fisher's not totally convinced it's really the Avengers."

Wayne continued to stare out the window, coins jingling. He slowly shook his head to make the point clear.

"What difference does that make? That's only a name. Whoever they are, they killed Gabe and threatened us, and want us to stop our work. Okay, so maybe we keep ahead of our competition by ignoring them, but what if they end up killing you or me? Would that be worth it?"

Good point.

Still, they'd worked too hard over the past decade to be shut down like this. Especially by someone who didn't understand what they were doing.

"Maybe there's a way to continue without them knowing."

Wayne shot him his you-got-to-be-kidding look.

"In theory. Maybe. But we can't hide what we do. What if they have sympathizers right here in this med school? They could monitor us and we wouldn't even know it."

When Jon didn't answer Wayne stepped closer to study his face.

"Don't! You're still thinking about it, aren't you. Stop it! I'm serious. They have sympathizers all over the place. Just about every pro-lifer on the planet supports them. There's no way we could get away with it. No way."

Jon wasn't convinced. Every obstacle had a solution. The trick was to discover it. There had to be a way to do the human implants without these assholes knowing about it, whoever they were. No one could be everywhere, see everything, unless you were an intelligence agency like the CIA. Even then...

Or was he just being obstinate? Reluctantly he admitted to having a tendency toward oppositional defiance as a personality flaw, an inclination to push against authority, a problem he had harnessed as part of growing up. One facet of being a good scientist was to question accepted theory. But this wasn't science, it was common sense: don't screw around with irrational people...maybe Wayne had a point.

Still....

Jon said, "A reporter called earlier. I didn't talk to him. Maybe I should call him back, make sure he understands we're working with mice and not humans."

Wayne continued to stare out the window and shake his head.

"What good will that do?"

"Just thinking out loud. You know, it bothers me, that

Aussie calling me 'baby killer.' Maybe if I can get the reporter to do a follow up, explain what we're really doing…it's a way to get the word out, correct any misconceptions."

Wayne turned from the window, ears bright red, fists clenched. He threw down his arms in frustration, stood there glaring at Jon.

"What is it you don't understand about the word *no*. Listen to what I'm saying: I'm afraid of these guys. I don't want to mess with them. Easy concept. You shouldn't have a hard time understanding it. I'm not comfortable with anything short of shutting down."

The vehemence of Wayne's anger was shocking, such a marked deviation from his typical easy-going personality. Jon said nothing as Wayne's words echoed in his mind.

What just happened?

Wayne continued to stare at him, hands fisting and unfisting, making damn sure Jon got the message.

Don't! You've been down this road before. Do not say what you're thinking.

Eyes clamped shut, Jon raised a hand, waited a beat.

"Stop. Time out."

The room fell silent.

"Jesus, Jon…I'm sorry."

He waved the hand to silence him.

"Whatever we do, we can't let this destroy *us*."

"I agree." Slowly, Wayne sat back down and crossed his legs. "So what do we do, shut down?"

Their ten productive collaborative years together functioned by consensus, with neither one dominating the other in spite of the fact that the majority of their grant support was awarded to Jon's department. But that was a simple matter of economics: Neurosurgery had a larger endowment than Neurology. In real terms, this gave Jon veto power. Jon knew what he wanted to do, but realized it would take some gentle persuasion to change Wayne's mind.

He said, "We need to think about this. It's more complicated than it may seem. We're dealing with terrorists."

"What difference does that make?"

"Terrorists kill people. That's how they incite terror. But there's not a country or government agency I know of that makes it a policy to negotiate with terrorists."

"I don't see that we have a choice."

"There's always a choice. We can't just stop work because someone asshole demands it."

Wayne looked dead serious.

"Why not?"

Jon didn't have a good answer, and realized much of his resistance was on principle. The Avengers—or whoever they were—didn't have the right! Especially by ultimatum. Pressure began building in his head again.

Wayne said, "I can see you're plotting something, but I warn you...no, I beg you: don't, for one minute, think we can go up against, or even reason with, someone we know nothing about." He paused, cocked his head. "You're not listening to a word I'm saying." He tapped Jon's shoulder. "Hey, I'm talking to you. I know the grant's in your name, but keep in mind that if you continue working the project, you put *me* in danger. This isn't just all about you, you know. It's about my life too. That's what you'd be gambling with. Think about it."

Wayne was just full of good points today.

"I know."

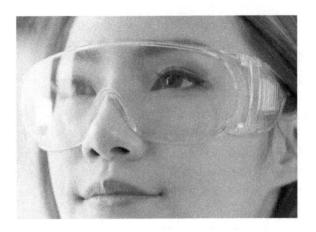

Chapter 8

GARY FISHER WAS checking the reply to his Interpol query when his cell rang. The caller ID showed RESTRICTED so he debated answering, but with all that was going on...he flipped the phone open, put it to his ear to listen.

The male voice carried a slight ring of familiarity.

"Agent Fisher?"

"Who's calling?"

"Jon Ritter."

It took a second to register and then Fisher realized it was who he thought of as only Doctor Ritter. He pushed back from the computer and without thinking picked up his pen and nudged the note pad closer.

"How you feeling?"

"Still numb. The funeral's back in Philadelphia this weekend. That's where he's from."

"Huh?" Then it dawned on him: Ritter was referring to Lippmann. "Oh, right. You going?"

Leaned back his chair and allowed his gaze to wander out the 14th floor window of the Federal Building to a spectacular view of Elliot Bay, Harbor Island, and the massive orange cranes alongside the container ships. Two Washington State ferries passed each other in opposite directions, shuttling cars and passengers between Coleman Dock and Bainbridge Island, and in the background, the snow-covered Olympic peaks across the horizon. A magnificent panorama, especially in striking contrast to the flat sparse land around his hometown.

"No. I wanted to, but Louise, his wife, said only immediate family. We're having a memorial service here at the school."

"I see." Fisher paused a respectful moment before asking, "You think of any new details?

"No. You turn up any leads, anything at all?"

He wished he could say yes, that at this very moment the bastard who killed Lippmann was in lockup with a signed confession on the magistrate's desk. Far from it. They had nothing.

"We're working on it."

"What the hell does that mean?" Ritter shot back, sounding pissed.

The intensity of the remark took Fisher by surprise.

What the hell did he think they'd been doing 18 hours a day since the parking garage incident?

He squeezed the bridge of his nose and tried to massage fatigue from his eyes.

"Look, I—" but stopped to rethink his tone.

Ritter was a victim, why not share some details?

Nothing crucial, just enough to let him appreciate how seriously they considered the case. Besides, there was a chance he'd need his help before things were over. Always better to have allies than enemies.

"We've made some progress. The garage has security video. The stills don't give us as much detail as we'd like, but it's better than nothing and it's a hell of a lot more than we had before. We narrowed down their car."

Where the hell was that cup of coffee?

Ah, on the corner of the desk. He sipped it, grateful for the lingering warmth. Nothing worse than cold stale coffee.

Fisher continued, "According to the time stamp, your assailants entered the garage at 18:13 hours and exited immediately after the shooting. We enhanced the images of the vehicle enough to lift a partial plate and trace it back to a rental agency." He purposely left out the agency name. He didn't want Ritter to start acting like some lone cowboy. "In follow up, I learned the vehicle is due back today, but in all likelihood those shitheads dumped it the night of the assault, so I put a BOLO on it."

"A BOLO?"

Fisher paused for another sip.

"Be On The Lookout For. Trust me; every cop in the area is looking for it."

"I assume you checked into who rented it?"

"Holy shit, why didn't I think of that!"

He immediately regretted his sarcasm.

Ritter said nothing.

Fisher glanced at the display, saw they were still connected, and decided two could play the same game. He had to draw a line here, otherwise Ritter would be riding his ass continually. As he listened waiting for Ritter to speak his gaze went back out the window. He noticed a layer of grime on the outside of the pane.

How'd it get there? Was the air this high up that dirty? And what about the person who had to dangle 27 floors above unforgiving concrete once a year to clean it? No way in hell could he ever do that job. Not for all the money in the world. Not with his fear of heights.

The silent standoff between them was broken when he heard Ritter say, "Oh, that was a stupid question."

Fisher capitulated with, "A male using the name Warren Mattox signed the papers. We ran his California license but of course it's bogus. He paid the deposit in cash and didn't buy insurance. Which I take to mean your assailants knew what they were doing and went out of their way not to leave any sort of trail."

"You talked to the clerk who rented it? Personally?"

Jesus!

"Let me see if I have this straight: you're in charge of the investigation now?" He squeezed the bridge of his nose again and shook his head, more irritated at his own lack of patience than Ritter's accusatory tone. "Yeah, I personally talked to her but she couldn't remember squat about him."

"That's it?"

Fisher pushed out of the chair and arched his back, working on the ache burrowing in between his shoulders.

"No, that's not all. Let me assure you we take this case seriously. Both the University and Seattle cops are also all over it. Last night SPD had two detectives going door to door in your neighborhood asking if anyone remembered seeing anything out of the ordinary the past two weeks. Your assailants knew your routine, so they must've had you under surveillance for at least a few days.

"We went a step further, checked the other car rental companies within a block of the airport. Turns out our guy Mattox rented a different car the previous week. Meaning you were under observation ten days or so. But there's no way of knowing for sure. Satisfied?"

Ritter couldn't possibly know how personal the Avengers investigation was for him, and he wasn't about to explain.

"Yes, that makes me feel better. Sorry if I seem angry. I am. Gabe meant the world to me. I'm having trouble dealing with it, is all...."

Fisher dropped into the chair again, began drumming a ballpoint on a pad of yellow legal paper.

"Understandable. Okay, change of topic. You made a decision yet?"

"About?"

"Shutting down."

Ritter said, "Which raises a question. When you saw me on their website, why didn't you warn me? Give me some protection?"

Here we go again.

Fisher flipped the pen in the air without bothering to catch it, turned to focus on the view again.

"Hey, blaming me for Lippmann's death isn't going to do a damn thing but piss us both off again, so let me put it to you this way: am I'm qualified to do brain surgery?"

"That's ridiculous. What kind of question's that?"

"Here's the point: I'm not qualified to do brain surgery and you're not qualified to run this investigation. So back off and let me do my job. Nobody wants to get these shitheads more than I do. Do I make myself clear?"

Fisher took Ritter's silence as petulant agreement. He mentally patted himself on the back and sipped the dregs of the coffee that had turned cold.

"What I'm suggesting is, until we get the situation cleared up, you shouldn't do anything to provoke them."

Ritter said nothing.

Was he pouting, thinking, or what?

Regardless, he needed to get on with his work, so, said, "I'm late for a meeting. Got to go. When I have something new, I'll call. If you think of anything additional you think is important, call me. You have my numbers. We'll talk."

He hung up.

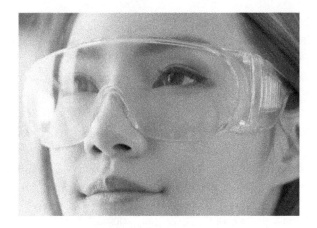

Chapter 9

GODDAMN FBI! JON slammed the phone on the desk.

Five days since Gabe's cold-blooded murder and one fictitious name was the only piece of information the nation's premier law enforcement agency could dig up. Furious, he stared at the rapidly enlarging list of unanswered emails accumulating on the computer, his temple throbbing with each beat of his racing heart. He absentmindedly probed the puffy ridge of scalp where the sutures had been removed this morning. Pressing the wound now provoked less pain than it did in the ICU, which, he supposed, was a good sign, an indication of collagen knitting the edges together. All wounds heal. Eventually. The flesh just more easily than the mind.

His wound began throbbing again, the result of fingering it.

For a distraction, he tried to concentrate on sorting emails, deleting unread the ones he knew were trivial, leaving more important ones to deal with at a time he could concentrate fully. He glanced at the latte next to the phone, cold now, untouched since...? He checked his watch. Jesus, what time had he come back to the office? Sometime after the suture removal this morning, but when exactly?

Being so forgetful these past few days was irritating, this inability to focus on anything.

Okay, sure, he'd sustained a concussion, but still...

Three months now since Emily's death. Now, Gabe, gone too. The two most important people in his life...he felt robbed.

As if this weren't enough, the fucking Avengers were stealing the one remaining part of his life that held any true meaning: his research. This was the activity he buried himself in after Emily died. The place that, in a funny way, he'd felt closest to Gabe. After all, Gabe was how Jon came to be there...

Jon's mind drifted back into history.

Gabriel Lippmann sits across his desk from Jon Ritter, the young medical student applying for residency. Jon is sweating as Lippmann asks why he applied to go to med school.

Ritter laughs.

"Long story. Academics never interested me until I got into med school. Being a doctor hadn't even been a consideration until college. Unlike several of my classmates, my parents weren't docs. My mom and dad ran a fifty-eight-foot purse seiner out of Ketchikan until a storm in the Gulf of Alaska swallowed them up. I was just about to turn nine years old." He shakes his head, thinking back on it. *"No one knew what actually happened because no boat or wreckage, or even survivors, were ever found."*

"So who raised you?"

"My grandparents on mom's side, Christina and Chuck, took me in. But Chuck was a pretty bad alcoholic and died before I turned eleven. When I was fourteen the house burned to the ground. I was in school. Luckily Christina escaped. A fireman pulled her out." Jon shakes his head at his own stupidity. *"I was so stupid, I should've seen it coming."*

Lippmann sits back in the chair, cups his chin between index finger and thumb.

"What should you have seen?"

"Her dementia. The firemen think she walked away from the propane stove with a pot of water boiling on it. In retrospect there were all sorts of little things that had been happening, clues I completely missed, chalking them up to forgetfulness and age. But, I keep telling myself, how much does a fourteen year old know about dementia?"

"Probably not much," Gabe agrees. *"What happened to her?"*

"She was one of the rapidly progressive ones. I had to put her in one of those awful nursing homes. She never forgave me for putting her there. The only good thing about it was she went pretty fast."

Gabe asks, *"This was in Alaska?"*

"Ketchikan. Back then it was nothing more than forty-two taverns within thirty-two miles of asphalt. A costal village with little to recommend it unless you loved hunting, fishing, and fake scrimshaw carvings the alcoholic store owners peddle to tourists."

"It's amazing you got where you are, given that background. But I still don't understand how you were able to afford to go to med school?"

"I figured the only way out of that place and a future filled with nothing but fishing was to get an education. So I got a job at a Dairy Queen, applied to the University of Alaska, Ketchikan, and discovered I really loved to understand—from a physical rather than metaphysical standpoint—why things happen. I really did well in science. I caught a break and lucked into an advisor who suggested med school. I lucked out again when I received a scholarship to the University of Washington."

"What got you interested in doing research?"

Jon hesitates, wondering how truthful to be in this interview. What is it Dr. Lippmann is looking for? He is, after all, one of more than twenty applicants for the single first year slot. He decides to be brutally honest.

"I needed money, so applied for the fellowship. I wasn't really interested in doing research but didn't want to go through another summer of oozing fry grease from every pore in my body. Also," now blushing, *"I thought it'd be a way for you to know me better than just another applicant."*

"So you intended on applying back then?"

Jon nods.

"Yes."

That summer project eventually got written up as a small publication in the journal *Neurosurgery*.

To this day, he can vividly recall the breath-stealing rush from seeing his name printed in an international journal.

His name!

That summer project continued through the following years and summer breaks until graduation. The experience exposed him to a way of life he never imagined existed, a life of curiosity and questioning. He began each unstructured lab day as the first team member to arrive. He'd fire up the espresso machine before starting into whatever tasks needed doing. He worked shoulder to shoulder with other technicians and professors, then spent brown bag lunch breaks in heady scientific debates.

Afternoons flew by, quickly becoming evenings, with no worry as to the hour, as ideas were tossed around, refined, and filed away in excited minds. The intellectual stimulation and camaraderie became an exhilarating elixir, a welcome substitute for the home he'd hadn't enjoyed for years.

He fell in love with the life.

Now, it was being taken from him.

Fucking Avengers.

He brought up Google on the computer, queried, and then watched the screen change to the Avengers website. Just as Fisher had said, the first page listed WANTED targets, the "enemies" of the unborn, as they labeled it. He scrolled down until finding his picture. Another click took him to a list of detailed personal information including his office and home addresses plus a physical description.

Great—making him a target for any wacko pro-life fanatic who deputized themselves in the cause.

What really pissed him off that he and his work didn't use human tissue.

Didn't those crazy bastards understand the difference between a mouse and human?

A telephone ring made him jump, flooding him with a jolt of adrenaline.

He pressed a palm against his chest and drew a deep breath before answering, "Ritter here."

"Jon. Margaret Sorenson."

"Hey, Margaret."

Relief—at what, he wasn't quite sure—swept through him. Meg was the NIH bureaucrat overseeing the human trial he and Wayne were about to start.

"How are things?"

"Not good. I have bad news, I'm afraid."

Her words came across as crisp and emotionless; this call meant bad news, something to do with the study.

A funding delay? That had to be it. Why else would she call?

After a few beats she said, "We're pulling the study, Jon. I'm sorry."

Just like that.

His gut froze. Then again, maybe he misunderstood.

"Pulling the study? What do you mean? Canceling it?"

"Unfortunately, yes."

"Wait a minute, what are you saying? There's a delay in funding or is it terminated?"

"It's cancelled, done, as in it's not going to happen."

He wanted to say that wasn't fair. But when did fairness have a thing to do with federal funding? And, he didn't want to whine.

Still…

"Why?"

Her words carried a hint of compassion this time, like maybe she really did care and was simply following orders.

"I shouldn't have to explain. It's the Avengers thing, you know, the ultimatum?"

Far as he knew, the ultimatum hadn't been released to the press.

"How did you find that out?"

"You're kidding me, right? Lippmann's murder got national coverage."

True, but…to deny that the press knew anything about it would, in effect, admit that it was true.

"Hey, look, we both know how inaccurate the press can be. What the hell does a news story have to do with the scientific importance of a research project?"

Aw, shit, that sounded like whining.

His face warmed with embarrassment.

The crisp efficiency of her voice was replaced by the warm tones so familiar to Jon.

"Cripes, Jon, c'mon, don't make this harder than it already is." She sighed. "You know darn well with the present political climate we want all stem cell funding to fly below the radar. Well, thanks to all the national coverage, you can kiss any hope of that goodbye. You're now being tracked by everyone from the White House to your local crack house, meaning the institute brass doesn't want to risk any political blowback, no matter how small it may seem to be. Especially if, ah, something should happen to you or Dobbs."

"You mean if one of those assholes kills me?"

Goddamn bureaucrats, always covering their back, always worrying about the political implications of every damn decision.

In their hearts they really didn't care if he or Wayne were

shot. Nor did they care about the ten years of work already invested in the project. The only thing they cared about was one or two bad press days from the *Washington Post* and Congress's impression of them.

"Hey, Jon, don't shoot the messenger. I'm as upset about this as you."

He couldn't stop himself.

"Bullshit! Tell me this; did anyone even try to reason with whoever's responsible for this decision? Did *you*? You know how important this study is."

"I do. But, after all the discussions we've had, you know darn well what a political hot potato stem cell research is."

"This is unfair! We finally have a great shot at being able to do something about Alzheimer's disease and you're killing the project?"

"Not my decision, Jon. You don't like it, talk to Murray," referring to the head of the Neurological Disorders Institute. "Know what he'll say? He'll say senators and congressmen don't really give a hoot. It's what their constituency believes that warms their hearts and their constituency believes stem cell research is ungodly. And you know it."

He forced himself to calm down by sucking down a deep breath and swiveling around to admire the view from the window.

"Alright, I have an idea. Since we've already been reviewed and funded, why can't we just delay the actual awarding of the money until next quarter, after things have a chance to settle down and blow over? Then give us the green light."

"You're joking, right? No, Jon, we can't try to fake this. Not with every politician in the beltway looking over our shoulders. We're pulling the study. Forever and ever, amen. End of discussion."

"But—"

No sense arguing, he realized.

"Okay, if you pull it now can we submit the same grant in

three months and get funded?"

"Sure, you can always submit. But I have to tell you, it'll be starting over, so there's no guarantee it'll get funded."

He spoke with a distinct tinge of resignation.

"In other words, we're totally screwed. That's what you're saying."

"Yep. Sorry."

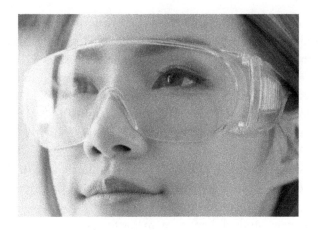

Chapter 10

A FAMILIAR VOICE snapped Ritter out of a deep blue reverie.

"Jon?" Wayne Dobbs stood in the doorway with a white Starbucks cup in each hand. "May I come in?" Without waiting for a response, he stepped into the office and set one of the cups on the desk next Jon's other cup. "Oh, sorry, didn't know you already had one."

"No, that's fine. Finished it an hour ago."

Jon dropped the cold, barely touched latte in the wastebasket. It hit the bottom with a thump too hard for an empty, exposing his white lie.

Wayne cocked his head and eyed him.

"What's wrong, did someone die?" He quickly slapped a hand over his mouth. "Oh, dear…I'm sorry…I didn't mean…"

Jon waved it away.

"I know you didn't. When things go bad, they really go bad. Sorenson just called."

Wayne frowned and carefully placed his latte on the desk.

"And?"

Jon told him the bad news, that their project was dead. Wayne sat there inspecting his thumb nail, turning it this way and that, ears bright red. When mildly perturbed, Wayne became sarcastic. When outraged, he usually settled into eerie silence. But his ears were the best mood barometer.

Jon broke the silence with, "I've been thinking."

Wayne shot him a tight-lipped questioning look.

"About?"

"Maybe I could talk to Richard Stillman, see if I can persuade him into funding the work. Do the trial with Trophozyme. What do you think?"

Wayne studied him a moment to gauge his degree of seriousness.

Then, with a laugh, "Even if I thought you were serious—which I don't—I'm not sure you could handle it. Given your history with him, and all."

"As far as I see, it's our only option."

Wayne picked at his thumb a moment.

"Maybe, but do you seriously believe that arrogant prick would be gracious enough to do something like that? By that I mean, help us out without gloating or rubbing our noses in it?"

"Yes. If he thought it might help him and Trophozyme. Besides, we're big boys. We can take some gloating if it gets the work done."

Wayne shook his head and crossed his arms.

"I don't know...the bad blood between you two..."

"There's something I didn't mention."

"I don't like the sound of that," Wayne said.

"Don't worry, it's nothing that affects you, but it is relevant. About five months ago he invited me to have lunch. I told him if he wanted to talk, it had to be here in my office. Surprisingly, he agreed. He came over, we talked and he offered me the job of Chief Medical Officer."

Wayne's eyes grew wide.

"At Trophozyme? And you didn't tell me?"

"I figured I'd never work for him, regardless of how big the salary or what signing bonuses he put out there to entice me. So I didn't even ask any particulars."

Actually, he told Stillman he'd worked too hard at becoming a surgeon to now leave clinical practice for a life of 100% lab rat, that the present university position allowed him to practice neurosurgery in addition to running a lab. Yet he hadn't been completely truthful with Stillman. Putting aside the personal animosity between them, Jon's real reason for rejecting the offer was the strong prejudice Gabe instilled in him years ago, that corporate biomedical researchers were not real scientists, they were nothing more than businessmen in disguise. That their ardent claims of wanting "to improve people's lives" basically served as just a smokescreen for their real motivation: to make money. And lots of it. Nothing more, nothing less. Capitalism at its finest. He agreed with Gabe and wanted no part of Stillman's world. Early on, when Jon made his first presentation at a national meeting, Stillman stood up and embarrassed him, Gabe's prodigy, in front of the audience, making public their mutual disrespect.

"Why are you telling me this now?"

"Because he acted different than I'd ever seen him, at least to me, he did. He seemed to sincerely want him and me to start over, maybe establish a good working relationship. The point is, if we can't find a safe way to continue our work and move it over to real patients, ten years of effort is going straight down the drain. Can you really accept that? I know I can't."

Wayne made a fist and then opened his right hand, watching the movement, seemingly fascinated at all the little muscles involved in the action.

Without looking up, he muttered, "No. No, of course not. But if that snake agrees to do it, you know damn well there's going to be a hidden agenda…some way to screw us that we haven't even considered. It's not like the guy's a philanthropist. So, tell me this: what's in it for him that would make him want to help us?" He sighed and waved off the question. "Forget Stillman. The question is: do you really think you could live with yourself if you went into industry? I, more than anyone, know your prejudice on this issue."

Good question.

Jon sipped his new latte and considered the answer. Hard as it would be to climb in bed with Stillman, he couldn't see any other way to salvage the past ten years.

"I don't see that we have another option. Hey, if you got a suggestion, I'm willing to hear it."

Wayne returned to studying his thumb nail.

"Okay, but what about the Avengers angle? Sure, you can always say we complied with their ultimatum by shutting down *our* lab, but the note made it pretty clear; it said to stop work. It doesn't give a lot of semantic leeway. I can't see how moving to Trophozyme removes the danger."

"Here's the thing...what if we can do it without anyone knowing?"

Wayne gave a sarcastic grunt and shook his head.

"Impossible."

"No, no, listen. What if we shut down the lab and move the project to a place the Avengers wouldn't know about?"

Wayne shot him a look of bemusement.

"You're joking, right? From everything I've read, and that's a lot in the past twenty-four hours, they have sympathizers all over the world."

"True, but what if we did it in Korea?"

Wayne's face froze momentarily, eyes locked into his, questioningly. Then he got it.

"Jin-Woo?"

Jin-Woo Lee. A neurosurgeon who spent a six-month sabbatical in Jon's lab learning tissue culture techniques. During that time the two men developed a friendship.

When Wayne didn't answer, Jon became impatient and frustrated. He'd expected Wayne to jump at the idea, but instead ...

"We don't have much time. Yes or no?"

Wayne blew through pursed lips.

"You're serious."

"I take that as a yes."

Wayne swallowed and looked at his nails, then back at Jon, gave a slight nod.

"In for a pound or whatever that ridiculous expression is. But I want it on the record I'm not wild about the concept."

"Good. I've already set up a meeting with Stillman for seven tomorrow morning. I called Jin-Woo and pitched the idea. He's going to call me back in," checking his watch, "about ten minutes. I booked a flight to Seoul for day after tomorrow."

Wayne shook his head in amazement.

"You really *are* serious. What about this," sweeping his hand around the room, "your job? Setting up a trial over there will take time. Can you arrange to have that much time off?"

He smiled and absentmindedly fingered the wound again, rubbing along the healing suture line.

"With my injury, I'm good for a thirty day leave of absence."

Chapter 11

AT PRECISELY 7:00 AM., Stillman exited the elevator onto lush carpet of the lobby of the building in which Trophozyme offices were located.

He definitely would've preferred for Jon Ritter to come to his office during regular business hours, say, after 9:00 o'clock, so he could make self-righteous prick wait fifteen minutes in the outer office in full view of staff, just to drive home the point he was the one in charge and Jon was now dependent on him. But Ritter had insisted on meeting early. Surgeon's hours.

The good news was, by accepting such an early hour he would be making a concession, which in turn, would give the impression of flexibility. Truth be told, with his condo only a block away, most days found him in his office by now anyway. Being the first to arrive each day gave him an uninterrupted block of time to scan the latest news and prepare his schedule before the constant onslaught of unanticipated interruptions and meetings turned any semblance of an orderly schedule into havoc.

Ritter was already waiting in the lobby, white Starbucks

cup in hand, studying the building directory. At the sound of the elevator door, he turned with a hopeful look on his face.

In spite of this newfound hope, he appeared haggard: sagging facial muscles and dark circles under the eyes. Stillman couldn't suppress a hint of satisfied smile. Jon Ritter, the holier-than-thou academician, didn't look so goddamn smug now. Not the same sanctimonious prick who, a year ago, stood up at the North American Stem Cell Symposium to challenge Stillman in debate. He remembered all too well the embarrassing sting of not being able to answer Ritter's hyper-technical, nit-picking questions. Questions only a lab tech might reasonably discuss. Running a company didn't give him the luxury of wandering the halls to visit labs and learn about every employee's job. That style of management was, in his opinion, micromanagement, and he had more productive ways to spend the precious minutes of his already heavily scheduled days. So, yes, Ritter might be an expert on growing cells in petri dishes and flasks, but the prick didn't have a clue about the skills needed to grow a fledgling company from nothing into a red-hot Wall Street IPO.

Well, time to eat crow, Ritter.

Stillman smiled.

"Right on time. Promptness. I like that."

Ritter offered his hand.

"Thanks for meeting with me."

Stillman graciously motioned him onto the elevator, punched 5.

"Trophozyme has three through five. My office is on five."

The elevator door rattled shut.

Stillman eyed Ritter's clothes, a professor cliché if ever there was one: gray slacks, navy blazer, white shirt, rep tie. Ninety percent of the neurosurgeons he'd ever set eyes on lived in those preppy blazers with the gold buttons as if it were some uniform. Today, Stillman wore understated corporate casual: a black Ermenegildo Zegna long-sleeve, form-fitting crew-neck sweater, chosen to emphasize his well-developed pecs, light weight black wool slacks, black, well buffed Ferragamo loafers, a black faced stainless steel Movado Museum Dial on his wrist.

If you knew what you were looking at—which Ritter obviously didn't—his selection made a statement of superior taste and class. Casual elegance, he believed, blended him into the start-up company culture while simultaneously elevating him above common employees.

Both men faced the door as the cage moved upward, Stillman thinking, *My my, how things change.* Five months ago, when offered a generous salary, fat signing bonus, and stock options, Ritter turned up his nose. It hadn't been the refusal per se that pissed Stillman off—it was the *way* Ritter did it: without a moment of hesitation. As if he'd been offered an intravenous dose of Ebola virus instead of a well-paying, once-in-a-lifetime career opportunity.

Even more grating was Ritter's unspoken attitude. As if he, Stillman, was some kind of leper instead of the leader of a biotech company.

Well, look at you now, Mr. Arrogant Holier-Than-Thou Academician.

The temptation to utter those exact words was almost too much to resist. Instead, Stillman simply savored the delicious irony unfolding before him.

Off the elevator, down a hall, Stillman led Ritter single file past a series of work cubicles and an empty conference room. He turned left through a doorway and motioned for Jon to follow.

The moment Jon walked into Stillman's office, and his eyes registered the interior, he stopped, amazed at the elegance. The size wasn't impressive. On second glance, the square footage seemed rather modest. But a wall of floor to ceiling windows provided a stunning view of Lake Union and Capitol Hill, a dramatic backdrop to a sleek stainless steel-framed, glass top desk, probably a limited edition from a rarified German industrial designer.

To the left of the desk a round conference table with four chairs. Rap music—a total disconnect from the office's otherwise sophisticated image—pulsed softly from a sleek black stereo. Compared to the university, or offices in incubator companies, Stillman's was in another universe.

The wall opposite the windows held framed newspaper articles and a massive shelf filled with trophies, some apparently crystal, glass, or clear acrylic, one shaped like a seven-inch Washington Monument. Jon took a closer look.

"Tombstones," Stillman said.

"Tombstones?"

"That's what some people call them. Go ahead, pick one up."

Jon took the one shaped like the Washington Monument. Lighter than expected, making him think acrylic instead of crystal. He peered through flawless material at lettering etched on the back surface in stylishly clean font—Maximum Velocity, 2010.

"It's an industry tradition to award trophies to team members as a way of celebrating a significant milestone. A financing perhaps. Maybe an important patent. That particular one commemorates a very difficult genetic sequencing one of my companies commercialized."

Jon replaced it on the shelf.

"How many companies have you been with?"

"Since when? Graduate school?"

That surprised Jon.

"I didn't realize you went to graduate school."

Stillman made a point of making certain people heard his pull-yourself-up-by-the-bootstraps black ghetto survivor success story.

Stillman smiled.

"Ph.D. in biochemistry. Berkeley."

Very impressive, Jon was forced to admit to himself—especially given Stillman's impoverished roots. Clearly, he'd misjudged the man. Why? Professional jealousy? Because of Stillman's smooth flair for business? Because of Stillman's financial success? Because Stillman's strengths were Jon's weaknesses? Whatever, he felt guilty and petty for it.

"I didn't know that."

"There're probably a number of things you don't know about me. But to answer your original question, Trophozyme is the sixth."

"How many as CEO?"

Stillman laughed, as if becoming more comfortable with what both men had anticipated would be a difficult discussion.

"Four."

Jon made a quick calculation. Given Stillman's present age and the assumption he entered college at eighteen, subtract the number of years to make it through grad school, this left an average of approximately four years per job. Not the same institutional dedication of academics.

Without thinking, he said, "Isn't that a lot?"

Immediately, he felt another pang of guilt.

Why be so critical of the man?

Stillman laughed good-naturedly.

"For a man my age? Not really. I know what you're thinking, but we all have very different goals and styles. You're the staid career university professor with ivy growing up your body. Nothing wrong with that. On the other hand my thing is start-ups. Your goal is tenure with your picture on a wall of the faculty club. I want a successful IPO after which I hand over the reins to someone else while I search for the next good idea. We have very different goals, is all."

Jon had to admit he was right. They viewed careers from opposite poles. At a loss for something to say, he swept his hand toward framed newspaper articles on the wall.

"Tell me about these."

Stillman's eyes twinkled with satisfaction.

"Accolades and battles. And only battles won, of course.

Wouldn't do to advertise one's losses, would it?" He turned to face Jon again. "I know what you're thinking and you're right. It's egocentric and gauche to display these."

Jon felt his face burn.

"I...wasn't thinking that...at all."

Stillman laughed.

"Sure you were. And you're right, of course. It is. But you have no comprehension of what it's like to grow up in a poor, black, working-class family. Oh, hey, don't worry, I'll spare you all the crap I know you really don't want to hear. But the thing you obviously don't understand are the obstacles I faced growing up. You didn't have mother who couldn't grasp the concept of taking on a five-thousand-dollar student loan—one that would more than pay itself back numerous times—to send one of her sons to junior college. Or a father so threatened by the mere thought that his son might do better than he..." He raised a hand and paused. "Forgive me. I'm doing just what I promised myself I wouldn't do. The point is, until you've grown up in that environment, don't dare diss me for indulging myself with this wall of accomplishments. Think what you may, Doctor Ritter," his smile gone, his face stone cold serious, "but don't dare criticize me."

Jon's face grew hotter from a mixture of embarrassment and shame at misjudging him. He scrambled for the right words to apologize but came up empty. Stillman turned to his trophy wall again and pointed at one of the frames.

"This particular article?"

The Wall Street Journal, Jon realized.

"We were competing with a much larger, better funded company. A real David and Goliath battle. And just like David, we won. Not only that, but we sailed through the FDA, hitting the market two years earlier than the competitor. With a far superior product, I might add. Now that, my friend, is something to be proud of."

Jon vaguely remembered hearing the story—the kind that

rapidly becomes biotech folklore to be told as a case study over a beer or two at national meetings.

Stillman gave Jon a friendly punch in the shoulder.

"But you didn't come here to talk about me. Come on, over here, sit down."

They took opposite sides of the table and settled in.

Stillman started with, "First, let me tell you how sorry I was when I heard of your fiancée's passing."

A lump formed in Jon's throat.

"Thank you."

Stillman's sincerity further stoked Jon's guilt.

Maybe the guy was okay after all.

"Are you aware that NIH awarded us a grant to implant a small number of Alzheimer patients?"

Jon assumed he did, because, after all, this was public information easily picked up by a Google alert. Surely Stillman closely tracked every morsel of news about competitors he could get his hands on.

Stillman gave an approving nod.

He began twiddling a pen between his fingers, moving it from one to another, then back again like a baton twirler, never bothering to look.

"So I heard. Congratulations." His eyes narrowed. "Your monkey data hasn't been published yet, has it?"

"No," he said with obvious pride. The paper would be a blockbuster. And for a moment he savored the pride Stillman must have felt as Jon admired the trophies. "We intended to release it as the first step in recruiting for the human trial but then…well, I'm sure you heard about the attack and Gabriel Lippmann's murder?"

Stillman let the pen fall to the desk, shook his head woefully, and dropped his eyes in sorrow.

"I did. A tragedy for all of us in science. But I'm especially sorry for you because I know how much he meant to you, getting you started and all."

Jon swallowed and interlaced the fingers of his hands, one into the other.

"The police think it was the Nuremburg Avengers. You know about them?"

"I've heard of them."

"It's difficult...they—the Avengers that is—threatened to kill Wayne and me if we didn't stop work immediately."

Stillman pushed up from his chair, closed the office door, and came back around to sit on the corner of the desk.

"Wow, that's a pretty heavy threat. What are you going to do?"

"It's a pretty difficult situation. Those guys are fanatics. No telling what they might do, but I'm not inclined to risk anyone's life to find out."

Stillman rubbed the side of his nose.

"I don't blame you."

Jon was about to get to why he was there when Stillman said, "The job offer's still good, if that's why you're here. Join the Trophozyme team. Same goes for Wayne Dobbs if that's an issue. Do that and we'll support your study in a heartbeat."

There it was; exactly the attitude he hoped for, just not exactly the right offer. He wanted their financial support, not employment. He grappled for a way to explain the difference without sounding ungrateful or rude.

"I'm not ready to give up being a surgeon quite yet."

Stillman nodded thoughtfully.

"So you've said. Okay then, how about this: sell me your technique. Let me assume all the risk. This way you can remain a surgeon and I'll see it that your contributions to science continue along the path you've always intended."

Jon didn't even consider the offer.

"Look, you know it's not for sale. This isn't about money," then thought, *what exactly* is *it about?*

With a puzzled expression, Stillman cocked his head.

"Maybe I'm confused. Why are you here?"

Jon decided to stop being paranoid and just lay out his plan.

"Here's the deal: I want Trophozyme to fund a small clinical trial, exactly as planned. But instead of doing it here in the States, do it offshore."

"Offshore?" Stillman slid off the desk, dropped back into his desk chair, palmed his shaved scalp. "Interesting idea. Hmmm…interesting. You obviously have some place in mind. Where?"

"Korea."

"Korea." Stillman tilted back, eyes toward the ceiling, steepled fingers gently tapping his lower lip. "Why Korea?"

"Because I have a friend there, another neurosurgeon. He also has a lab very similar to mine. We've collaborated before, so I know his set up. It'll be perfect."

Stillman nodded.

"Apparently you've thought about this. What exactly do you have in mind?"

Jon's gut knotted. This was the part that killed him.

"We, meaning Wayne and I partner with Trophozyme on this."

"Partner with Trophozyme…hmmm…" Stillman stroked his scalp again. "That's pretty vague. Be more specific on exactly what that means."

"You fund the cost of the trial and I'll find a way to execute it."

Stillman laughed and picked up the pen again.

"Damn it Jon, do I look like a fat old geezer with twelve reindeer who lives in the North Pole?"

Jon wasn't sure how to answer.

Stillman said, "I'm going to be perfectly blunt. What does Trophozyme get out of this?"

"My formulation."

Around his fingers went the pen again.

"That's not very specific, Jon. What exactly does that mean? The entire formulation written out in recipe form?

Licensing rights? What? You need to lay it out for me."

Jon realized he hadn't thought this through nearly well enough. Not in the sense of a business contract. And this, he realized, was just another indication of how foreign these negotiations were to him.

"Exclusive licensing rights."

There, that sounded about right.

Stillman laughed again.

"I can see you don't know much about deals. You're a professor. That means the university probably owns everything you discover. Unless, of course, you have a prior agreement with them. So the question is, who owns your technique, you or the university?"

Sensitive subject. And the only bone of contention with Wayne.

"I do."

Stillman's eyebrows went up.

"What about Dobbs?"

"No, it's totally mine."

Stillman seemed to be genuinely surprised and viewed Jon with what appeared to be new respect.

"And he'll go along with this, ah, plan?"

"Yes."

"Interesting." Stillman let the pen fall on the desk, tilted back in the chair and wiped his scalp once more, "The Koreans, huh," then shook his head. "I'm going to be perfectly blunt with you. I don't trust Koreans one iota. Never have. Never will. This buddy of yours, what's to keep him from screwing us and stealing the formula? We'll end up with nothing and they'll walk away with your technique. We can't risk that."

"Already thought of that. The only way to assure they don't, is for me to personally do every step of the work. No one will have access to anything proprietary and I'll make sure nothing leaks."

Stillman thought about that for several seconds.

Allen Wyler

"Long as we're being blunt, let me say, you're asking for an investment of at least a million to fund work you've been told—by a group of crazies, I might add—to stop. Under threat of death." He paused. "Say I put up the money and they kill you? Then what?" He turned both palms up. "I'm out the money and the results. I take risk in business every day, sure, but this deal? Man, I have to tell you it just doesn't seem like the kind of risk I want to take."

Much as he hated to admit it, Stillman had a point. One option was to give up. The other option was to find a deal that would work for them both.

"What do you suggest we do, then?"

"There are two risks I need to mitigate. The first is that something bad happens to you. The second is that something bad happens to the study."

"The study? Like?"

"What if, one of your patients—God forbid—dies as a result of the implant, then what?"

"It's a small enough study that only a few people will even know about it. If things were to go bad, the results would never see the light of day. But that's not going to happen. The implant worked in monkeys, so it's going to work in humans."

"Okay, so we could cover our tracks, but that still leaves me out a million bucks."

Jon asked, "What do you suggest?"

"I have to get something out of this. You have proprietary techniques that would be useful to me. If things don't go well, then all your methodology reverts to me. How does that sound?"

Jon hesitated a moment before agreeing.

Stillman said, "Which brings us back to what happens if you never return from Korea?"

Jon saw no other option.

"If that happens, the technique reverts to you."

Stillman seemed to think about that a moment.

80

"If you're willing to bet your life on this, I guess the least I can do is help, so here's what I can do: Four patients. A small feasibility study—one that can be used to move forward with the FDA—is all this can be. As insurance on my investment, here's how we'll do it: document your technique completely as if you were publishing it. Once this is done, we place the document in the hands of a trustee. This can be an institution or a person who is not affiliated with either of us. It could even be a safe deposit box, if that makes you more comfortable. If, for any reason, the trial goes bad and/or you don't return from Korea the technique reverts to me."

"But what about Wayne? He's put in as many years into this as me."

Stillman sucked his cheek, thinking it over.

"What happens to Wayne if you drop dead walking out of this office?"

Jon hadn't considered that.

"The technique would go to the University, I guess. I haven't thought about it."

"You're risking your life. I'm risking a million dollars. What's Wayne risking but some time in the lab he's been paid for? So this is my best offer. You want to take it or not?"

Jon saw no other way.

"I'll take it."

"Good. How long will it take for you to write up the methodology?"

"That's essentially done."

"Who would you suggest keep a copy of it—a sealed copy—until you return?"

"Wayne. Is that acceptable to you?"

Stillman nodded agreement.

"Start making the arrangements with your friend in Korea and I'll have our lawyer draft the agreement."

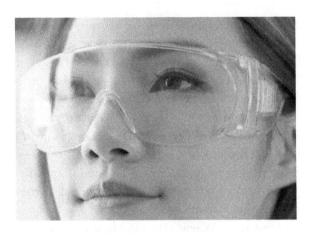

Chapter 12

AN ADRENALINE HIGH buzzed Jon as he drummed the steering wheel in time to an up-tempo jazz piece on KPLU, the local NPR affiliate. The sunroof was open to a pleasant 70 degrees, the air thick with exhaust fumes from the long backup of vehicles waiting for the University Bridge to lower.

Guilt wracked him for originally misjudging Stillman and being so woefully unprepared for such an important meeting. Perhaps the asshole wasn't such an asshole after all.

Once Stillman realized what a bind they were in, he'd helped engineer a solution. He very well could have left them twisting, which, he had to admit, he would've found tempting if the roles were reversed. But he hadn't. Now he felt grateful to the man he previously despised. Never again would he harbor such resentment to another human being and vowed to be more open-minded about people in the business end of science.

Should he reconsider Stillman's job offer to work for Trophozyme? It seemed to be still on the table. Maybe working for him wouldn't be so bad after all. Full time research would mean giving up surgery, but hey, no more operating room would mean a huge decrease in his level of stress. That wouldn't be so bad, now that he thought about it. At this stage of life—mid forties—he should consider lessening the pressure that neurosurgery placed on him. There were, after all, numerous studies to show how chronic workplace stress decreased longevity. Maybe after this project was over...

As the draw span began lowering, several drivers fired up their engines, bringing him back to the immediate issues. Once again, he mentally reviewed his to-do list; myriad little things, like following up with Jin-Woo for a budget, finding his passport, throwing some clothes together, on and on...but the big issue was how to actually do the implants and remain below The Nuremberg Avengers' radar. And this raised the issue of email and phone security. He needed a secure method of communication, something the Avengers knew nothing about. Perhaps a new cell under an assumed name? Or was this being overly paranoid? Maybe he should ask Fisher to help on this.

While leaving Stillman's office, the reality of what he was about to do began to sink in: he and Wayne would be flying directly in the face of the Avengers' ultimatum. Moving the experiment to Seoul didn't change the fundamental issue. He was willfully placing their lives in danger. How could he be so selfish?

He picked up his Droid, thought, *reach Stillman and call the whole thing off, no harm, no foul? Leave everyone safe. It's not worth the risk.*

The car directly ahead moved. Jon dropped the phone into the passenger seat and shifted from PARK to DRIVE and followed, the simple diversion causing him to reconsider yet again. They would, after all, be working in Korea. Only three or four people would know...were the Avengers really so well connected they could find out about it?

If everyone involved kept quiet...he'd talk with Jin-Woo again and emphasize how important secrecy was...but, hey, was iron-clad security really possible in a university setting with so many people around? There were so many ways to slip up, if they weren't extremely careful. Hospital personnel like admissions clerks, surgery personnel, countless others, would be involved with getting patients in and out of the hospital.

Meaning, he and Jin-Woo needed to come up with an original way to disguise the surgery so only he and Jin-Woo and the patients themselves would be aware of what was really happening. That would be extremely difficult.

Suddenly the list of problems needing to be dealt with ballooned, spawning more issues to solve during the flight over. Jin-Woo would have to handle Tyasami security...

He picked up his Droid again and dictated another note to himself. Was there any way to discreetly learn if The Avengers had an active cell in Seoul? Would Fisher know? Would even a discreet inquiry be enough to tip his hand? Had to think about that...so many things...

And what about Yeonhee? Did she still work in Jin-Woo's lab? Was she involved with someone? What would she feel like to hold in his arms? To kiss? To...

Where did that come from?

He quickly tried to suppress the answer but couldn't. And once again felt a tinge of shame for the attraction he'd felt for her while Emily was alive.

But Emily isn't alive. Wayne's right. I need to move on with life.

The car behind him honked. He realized he was blocking traffic.

Stillman scrolled through the directory for Feist's number and dialed. Took ten rings before the Australian picked up.

Lowering his voice, Stillman said, "Good thing you stuck around. Turns out our friend hasn't given up. He wants to move things to Korea."

"That a problem? Least he's not doing it stateside."

Stillman glanced at the door again, a double check to make

certain it was tightly closed.

"The objective of our little venture was to shut him down so he'd sell me the technique. That doesn't mean take it offshore. He obviously didn't get the message, so you'll have to, ah, reemphasize it."

"Right. Got it."

"This time make sure he gets the message."

"Korea, eh? Don't much fancy their food, mate. They eat dogs, don't they?"

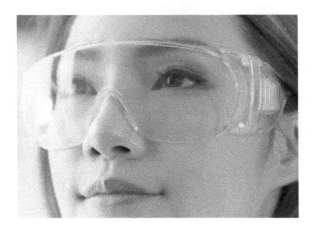

Chapter 13

FROM INSIDE THE darkened rental car parked a half block away, Nigel Feist watched Jon Ritter's house, a small two-story clapboard on a modest lot of mowed grass and shrubs in need of pruning. *Dutch Colonial,* was a random bit of trivia that popped into his mind.

12:12 A.M. The last light, an upstairs bedroom window, went dark an hour ago.

Should be sleeping by now.

Feist slipped from the car, hoisted a small black rucksack over his left shoulder, quietly locked the door, and was across the deserted street, past a line of parked cars and, without making a sound, into the shadowy driveway in less than 30 seconds.

He tugged pantyhose, similar to what he used in the parking garage, over his head, tore out two eye holes, and double checked to make certain his custom flat black .22 caliber weapon was inserted firmly inside his belt in the small of his back and hidden under a loose-fitting black sweatshirt. Black jeans and black Nikes completed his outfit.

He moved along the driveway to Ritter's back door, set his rucksack on the porch, worked his fingers into Latex exam gloves, removed Night Owl Optics 1.0X Night Goggles from his rucksack, slipped them on and tightened the headband and chinstrap to be stable, yet comfortable. Waited sixty seconds for his eyes to dark-adapt before switching them on. One final adjustment to the angle of the lenses and everything previously black became shades of green. The door lock was a Yale, nothing exotic or problematic, certainly nothing a security-conscious person would opt for. He quickly sorted through a set of picks and found the right one, slipped it into the lock, twiddled it until the tip resistance caught, then rotated the shaft. The deadbolt clicked.

Feist reassembled the pick set, stowed it away, and hoisted the pack over his shoulder. Entering the kitchen, he left the door open in case he had to exit in a hurry, although he couldn't imagine that would happen.

Jon snapped wide awake from a dreamless sleep, his heart hammering in his breast. Some primitive region of his brain was signaling that something was very wrong.

What?

He listened hard but heard only a soft swoosh swoosh swoosh of his pulse in his left ear. Yet still knew a sound had awakened him.

What?

There! A subtle creak. Nothing obvious. Then a rustle. Something out of synch with the usual random ticks of a house cooling at night. Suddenly it registered: someone was inside his house.

A jolt of adrenaline jangled his limbs.

Get up! Don't get caught defenseless.

He rolled left, slid out of bed, stood, mentally scanning the shadowy dark room for a weapon, his mind visualizing every detail not visible. One pass, then another. Saw nothing worthwhile. Almost frantic now, growing more aware of his naked vulnerability as each second blew by.

There!

In the glow of the clock radio was the dim outline of the phone. He grabbed it, thumbed the ON button. The beep was as loud as a thunderclap.

He was raising the phone to his ear when a metallic sound came from downstairs. Palm muffling the dial tone, he listened more closely but heard no other sound. Finally, put the phone to his ear but the dial tone was now longer there.

"Light sleeper, are you, mate?"

He jumped, glanced at the phone in his hand. He'd recognize that voice and accent anywhere—the man from the parking lot.

The voice in the phone said, "Don't suppose you've noticed the little red light goes on when the phone's in use. That's the reason I knew you picked up. Pretty canny of me, eh mate? Figured you was calling 9-1-1, I did. Was I right?"

Jon stayed frozen, phone to his ear, unable to say a word.

"Hear you ain't taking us too serious, that you might even be planning to do something stupid. That true, you that stupid?"

Could he be reasoned with?

Worth a try.

"Listen to me. I have nothing to do with fetal tissue or abortions. Nothing at all. You have me confused with someone else."

Then he remembered the heavy flashlight in the bedside stand. Not much, but better than nothing.

"No confusion at all, mate, none at all. Consider this your final warning. Keep at it, someone's going to die. You needn't want that to be you, would you?"

Jon was quietly sliding the bedside drawer open when the phone went dead. Three seconds later the front door latch clicked. Jon quickly re-established a dial tone punched 9-1-1, told the dispatcher he had a house intrusion in progress, gave his address, dumped the phone in the charger, grabbed the heavy flashlight and moved to the open bedroom door. The man might outweigh and out-muscle him, but at that moment Jon felt he had enough raw adrenaline-fueled rage to beat the bastard's head to a pulp.

Pulse pounding, breaths coming too hard, he crept past the door and listened. He heard only the soft hum of the fridge one floor below, the silence heavy and profound, like the forest when birds suddenly stop singing.

Now what?

He crept into the hall.

At the top of the stairs, he listened harder. Still nothing. Maybe the Aussie was gone. Still...Jon crept from the landing down one step, then two, another pause, more silence. Three steps from the bottom he paused again to scan the immediate area in the weak streetlight through the windows and the half open front door. A slight breeze chilled his arms. The Aussie had obviously left, leaving the door open. Jon exhaled relief, went to the threshold, looked out at a car driving past. No one out on the sidewalks.

The instant Jon closed the door he sensed someone next to him.

The Aussie said, "Over here, mate."

Suddenly, the room lights clicked on, blinding him. A bolt of lightning slammed his flank, exploding nausea and pain into his gut, doubling him over. With a gasp, he dropped to his knees and gagged back vomit.

The Aussie knelt down, face to face with him but with pantyhose squishing it into a fleshy blob.

"Got ourselves a big fucking problem, you and me. Told you to stop work but you don't fucking pay attention, now do you?"

The pain and nausea continued, making it hard to hear the words, much less pay attention to their content. Jon gasped, unable to move or defend himself.

Is this how I die?

"Final warning, mate. Do not persist to fuck with us. You should know you can't bloody well let out a silent fart without us knowing. So don't even try. DO I MAKE MESELF CLEAR?"

Over the pain, Jon sucked enough air to wheeze, "Fuck you!" then rolled onto his side, his eyes level with the bottom stair, expecting a kick in the side, covering his head, but nothing came.

After a few moments, he opened his eyes. Strange, he expected to see feet in front of him. He rolled over to look in the other direction, but he was alone. Struggling onto wobbly feet, he staggered to the porch to sit and wait for the cops.

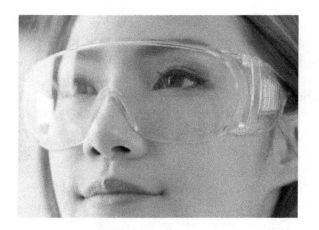

Chapter 14

INSIDE THE DARKENED Taurus, Nigel Feist watched a blue Caprice park in the bus stop directly across the street from Ritter's house. A man stepped out, slammed the door, walked briskly across the street to Ritter's front door, leaving the car blinkers flashing.

A copper.

A metallic blue SPD cruiser had arrived a half hour ago, making this new arrival most likely a detective. Feist speed dialed.

Stillman's sleepy voice answered.

"What up, dog?"

"All done. I reckon he got the message this time."

"Anything I need to know?"

Feist laughed, assuming this was Stillman's oblique way of asking if he'd killed him.

"No. Everything's the way you want it."

"Excellent."

"Appears I'm done, then. But just to make sure, I'll standby for a day or two. You should know for certain by then, from the sounds of it." Hated Korea, he did. Didn't much fancy chasing Ritter across the Pacific to Seoul. Preferred to end this nasty business right here and now. Aggressive, pushy little buggers, them Koreans. The Jews of Asia, they were. Worse than the fucking Chinks when it came to business. No ethics, the whole lot of them. "And just so's we're clear, the meter's still running for every day, right-right?"

"Christ, Nigel. Try thinking of something other than money for once in your life."

"Right, I'll use you as me fucking role model."

Feist clicked off and dropped the phone back on the seat.

Time to get some rest.

Special Agent Fisher said, "One more time. Run through his exact words," before taking another sip of overcooked 7-11 coffee.

The paper cup gave it a bitter cardboard flavor that was just shy of disgusting. But it was caffeine.

He and Jon Ritter were sitting in the front seats of Fisher's blue Caprice, across the street from Jon's house, while an FBI technician finished examining the back door and kitchen for fingerprints. Green glowing digits from the dashboard showed 5:11 AM. The sky hinted an impending dawn.

Dog tired, Jon decided the terrible coffee was only worsening the sourness corroding his stomach, so he replaced the cup in the holder. An oily sheen shone on its surface reminded him of the news clips of the Gulf disaster. He noticed his fingers trembling and rubbed them against his jeans to stop it, but the shaking remained. Probably the result of a perfect storm of fatigue and caffeine on top of having the shit scared out of him. To say nothing of a huge heap of angst at the apparent ease with which the Aussie entered his house in the middle of the night.

If there was ever a case for owning a dog…how long had the bastard been there? Jesus, he could've crept the stairs and

*put a bullet through his head. But for whatever reason, he
didn't, preferring instead to play mind games with him. Why?*

"Jon?"

Fisher just asked a question, he realized.

Which was another thing…the FBI not warning him…

"What?"

"Take me through it again. What caused you to wake up?"

Ritter palm-wiped his face and blew an audible breath.

"I don't know, a noise maybe. Something. I've been
through it so many times I don't know for sure. I woke up, was
all. And knew someone was in the house."

"And when you heard his voice, you knew it was him?
Same guy as before?"

"Yeah."

Jon massaged his temples and pinched the bridge of his
nose, yawned and rubbed at the fatigue irritating his eyes.
Maybe catch some sleep on the flight to Narita, take along some
Ambien just to be sure, although he hated those mental cobwebs
it left behind.

Fisher said, "I don't get it. Why threaten you the second
time?"

Jon found Fisher's need to rehash the same damn questions
over and over irritating. They weren't covering anything new
and the interview was quickly becoming a waste of time.

He shrugged.

"Like I said last time you asked, I don't know. And the
more you push, the more I'll probably fabricate."

Well, it was the truth.

"See, that's not the feeling I get. There's something going
on I don't know about. What?"

*And there it was. The fandango they'd been dancing since
Fisher's first question. Tell him about Korea? Maybe it wasn't
illegal, but it was bound to piss off the FBI agent. He didn't need
that on top of everything else. But how did the Avengers learn
about the plan with Trophozyme? Was his office bugged? Shit.*

Better to confess to Fisher than be killed by one of those crazies.

Jon glanced out the smudged window at a slice of Puget Sound sandwiched between two houses, with the sky indistinguishable from water, both still black, the picture reminiscent of Ketchikan. If he were ever asked to describe Hell, he'd say take a look at Ketchikan and you'll have it. No way in, no way out, other than boat or airplane. At least that was it when he lived there.

"We're going ahead with the study." He thought about the next forty-eight hours and amended the statement with, "Maybe."

"What!" Fisher did a double take. "This little detail just happened to pop into your head now, after going through this, what, three times?"

"Hey, lighten up. I'm purposely keeping it quiet."

Jon explained the possibly of implanting four patients in Seoul, well away from the Avengers' radar.

Fisher sat wedged in between the seat, door, and steering wheel, half sideways, one arm over the wheel, the other over the seatback, staring at him hard.

"Are you out of your mind? You seriously think you can pull off something like that without them finding out? Didn't tonight's little episode teach you a damn thing?"

Too tired to argue, Jon wearily hung his head.

"Okay, sure, I'm out of my mind. Call it whatever. But you'd make the same decision if you were me. This is my whole life. Everything. For ten years I've lived it. Wayne too. We bled every ounce of energy we had into this project. I can't just turn my back and walk away. Especially now, with Gabe's…"

He choked on the word, murder, and swallowed, unable to actually say it.

Fisher's oppressive silence made Jon feel the need to buttress his defense with, "In four months I've lost the two people who were most important to me. So yes, I know the risks but I'm willing to take them."

He glared at Fisher until another wave of exhaustion swept through him, making him turn back to the view out the dirty window.

One of the FBI techs approached the car from the house and Fisher whirred down the side window.

"Find anything?"

The woman spread her hands in a hopeless gesture.

"Lifted several prints, but I doubt they're anything other than his," with a nod toward Jon. Then she made a *DING* sound, said to Jon, "You're free to move around the country," turned and headed to her small black SUV.

Jon asked, "We done here?"

"Not yet. Obviously, he knew about your plans. How?"

"I didn't say he *knew*. At least not directly. But he certainly implied it." He reconsidered this. "At least, I didn't get the impression he knows for sure. I got the feeling he was guessing."

"Bullshit. He knows. Why else come here?" Fisher scratched the stubble along edge of his jaw. "The point being, you and Dobbs talked about this at work, right?"

"Yes."

"Okay then, if it's okay with you, I want to sweep your office. If we find a bug, we might be able to do something with it. Find out where it came from."

"That's the first constructive thing you've said all night. Fine with me."

At least they'd be doing *something*.

"One more thing. You have any training in self-defense? Military, anything like that?"

"No, nothing."

Unlike most of his high school buddies who used time in the service to figure out what they wanted to do with their lives, Jon went straight into the University of Alaska, med school, on through residency, never questioning his career vision.

"All the more reason to back off. You're a sitting duck."

Jon checked his watch.

"I've got a flight in a few hours, and I haven't even packed yet. Mind if we continue this conversation some other time? Besides, I don't know for sure if my friend in Seoul will even agree to do it. That's the reason I'm going over there. I should have an answer in a little over 48 hours."

Fisher was drumming his fingers on the dash now.

"Does your cell have global roaming?"

"Yes."

"In that case, I want you to stay in touch. Keep me up to date, I'll do the same with you. In a situation like this, knowledge is power. Believe me, we're on the same page. I want those shitheads out of action as much as you do. Okay, we're in agreement, you'll call?"

Jon nodded and offered his hand.

"Sorry about earlier. This whole thing has really upset me."

Fisher shook his head but stuck out his hand.

"I understand."

Jon angled across the street toward his house, a modest, two-story structure with a driveway to a detached one-car garage in back. Bigger than the Ketchikan home he grew up in. More expensive too, even factoring in inflation. But not even close to the cost of the waterfront homes on the opposite side of the street.

From the corner of his eyes he caught a flash of red as taillights vanished around the bend in the road, then heard footsteps approach and spun around. His neighbor Linda Rodriquez was padding across the yard, right hand hugging the lapels of a heavy blue bathrobe to her throat, the other hand stuffed into a pocket. Slender and attractive, maybe two years younger than he, she carried herself with the stoop of a woman who never adjusted from an abusive husband years ago. She was now single, he knew, because she'd made a point of letting him know.

"Jon, everything okay? I saw all the lights on and all those people…"

"Yeah, everything's fine, Linda."

He glanced at his house, anxious to go inside, hoping maybe she'd get the message of being in a hurry. The sky becoming lighter shades of gray with the approach of dawn.

"You sure?" Her gaze dropped to the sun-parched grass in need of mowing. "If you want, I could scramble us some eggs, make some coffee, that is unless of course…"

Aw, hell…

"That's really sweet of you Linda—I appreciate it, but—"

"Oh, that's okay," She offered before he could finish, her head seeming to hang a little lower now. "Just a suggestion. I thought…"

He started to reach out to touch her arm in a not-to-worry gesture but caught himself, knowing she'd take it to mean something more than intended. He started to say he was leaving town and would be back but caught that too, a paranoid area of his mind warning to tell no one, even someone as benign as her. He immediately felt foolish for it, but…

"How about we go out for dinner one day next week? Try that new place off Alki way?"

She immediately brightened and looked up hopefully.

"Sure. That'd be great. What night would work best for you?"

Oh, man, why'd I have to say that? Now look what you've done.

"Tell you what. I'm leaving town for a few days. Not yet sure how long. Soon as I return, I'll check the calendar and let you know."

He fingered his scar again, playing with a persistent dull pain along the healed suture line.

Her smile evaporated, embarrassed by her obvious eagerness and the rejection in his reply.

"Yeah, why don't we do it that way." She glanced at her feet in an awkward pause. "Okay. I better get back before I freeze to death." Then, with a brave smile, "I'll wait to hear from you."

She turned to return along the same route she came.

Jon kicked a pebble off the narrow concrete walk and turned back to his house.

She knows you don't want to take her out.

Then flashed on Wayne's encouragement to start putting his life back together; start dating, get laid.

He shook his head and headed inside to pack.

Nigel Feist watched Ritter climb the steps to the back of the house before starting the car. He'd head back to the motel to wait to hear if the warning produced the result. A gut impression said he'd be flying to Seoul in a couple hours to finish the job. But he'd been wrong before. Maybe it wouldn't have to come to that.

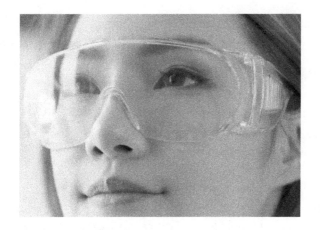

Chapter 15

STILLMAN'S 2PAC ring tone competed over the hum of his electric razor.

Who the hell would call this time of morning?

He hurried from the bathroom to silence the damn thing before Nikki started yelling for him to answer it. She was already sitting upright up in bed, short spiky blond hair flattened on one side, her beautiful breasts fully exposed, giving him an expression that...

He muttered, "Sorry, Cash."

The nickname he only used in private. One she loved.

He checked the display, saw JON RITTER, and answered.

"Yo, Dog, what up?"

Without consciously thinking, he began rubbing his freshly shaved scalp, checking for missed stubble and found a patch. Then moved to the window sliders to admire the city as Ritter told him about the Aussie, about how the FBI seemed ineffectual, about how the Avengers seemed to *know* he didn't intend to stop work on stem cells. He admired Nikki's reflection as she walked naked into the kitchen. A moment later, heard the familiar rattle of coffee beans pouring into the grinder.

When Ritter finished, Stillman asked, "The guy that broke in, did he mention Korea specifically or did he only talk in generalities?"

"No, nothing about Korea."

He smiled and was careful to not let the grin creep into his voice.

"But he knows you're up to something."

"Yes."

Then, throwing a very serious edge, said, "We can always cancel, you know. You're the one at highest risk. Your call," figuring cancel would be the last thing Ritter would want to do.

"No. I just got off the phone with Wayne. We don't have choice. We have to do it. But Fisher raised a good point. How did the Avengers know? He wonders if my office might be bugged. I gave him permission to check it out. Maybe you should do the same. I'm sure if you call him, he'll send someone over."

Stillman turned to watch Nikki lean against the kitchen counter, arms folded over those perfect breasts, long legs crossed at the ankle, the fading tan line triangulating her waxed pussy. The sight provoked warm tingling in his crotch.

Soon as he hung up...

"Good idea. But I'll have a private security firm do it. Not that I don't trust the Feds, it's just I want it done as soon as possible. Speaking of which, you all packed, ready to shove off? Don't forget your passport."

"What are you now, my mother?" Ritter gave a nervous laugh. "Yeah, it's in my coat, along with my ticket. I've double and triple checked. As far as packing, I still have a couple hours before I need to leave for SeaTac. I'll throw some things together soon as I hang up."

"Don't forget to check in often. Call me on the cell. It's always with me and turned on. Even in the can."

He laughed, trying to sound as if he were keeping it light as a macho way of covering up real concern, when in fact, his only real concern was getting Ritter to tell him the tissue culture method, no matter what he had to do to get it.

Back in the bathroom, Stillman was touching up the stubble on his scalp when Nikki's reflection appeared in the mirror, mugs of black coffee in each hand. She paused to admire his muscled back and perfect butt.

Without turning he said, "Hey Cash."

"Hey baby."

She set the one of the black mugs of black coffee on the black granite counter next to the recessed black sink, leaned against the wall, her own mug held in both hands. He dumped the electric razor back into the charger and picked up his mug. Too hot to drink, so he put it back on the counter. With his warmed palm, he cupped her breast and rolled the nipple between thumb and index finger.

"You really think Ritter's technique is going to do the job?" she asked, all too aware that talking business during sex was a turn on for him.

Earlier, he debated telling her about the Korean trial but finally decided there was no way he could avoid it. As Trophozyme's CFO, she'd eventually sign the checks to cover expenses. He simply neglected to mention employing Nigel Feist to make certain he got Ritter's tissue culture technique no matter what. Not that he didn't trust her. It was simply that there was absolutely no reason for anyone other than Feist to know about it.

Even Feist's fees came from personal funds. Although expensive, he considered the high fees simply the cost of an investment guaranteed to yield huge returns. Considering the number of shares of the company's stock he owned, it would parlay into a small fortune. His only misgiving was having shifted his entire portfolio entirely to Trophozyme stock.

On one hand, with the stock price in the toilet this past

month it'd been a hell of a buy, considering what would happen to the price in a few weeks. On the other hand, he'd sunk every dime of his personal net worth, and then some, into it. Leaving him slightly queasy for breaking such an elementary rule of investing. Even children knew the old adage to never put all your eggs in one basket.

Unless, of course, it was a sure thing because of having the ultimate insider information.

Once he had stem cells that could be safely implanted into human brains to reverse Alzheimer's Disease, his stock would be worth a fortune. Making this opportunity the one exception to the rule.

Uh-oh...Nikki was waiting for an answer.

He said, "Yes. I do."

"How can you be so sure?"

She spread her legs slightly, giving him a full frontal, making it apparent her interest in his answer was less important than his reaction to her body. As his eyes wandered down to her labia, the tingling between his legs increased. As he continued folding her nipple, she walked her fingers from his chest to his abdomen.

"Because he showed he could successfully implant monkeys. That pretty much assures it'll work on humans."

"All that has shown," Nikki's hand caressed his erection, "is they can stuff a glob of stem cells into a monkey's brain. That doesn't prove it'll do diddly squat to someone with Alzheimer's disease."

She was right, of course. But her point was nothing more than a technicality. Enough business for now. He effortlessly picked her up and set her on the counter where the ridge of her spine and a flare of freckles across both shoulders reflected in the mirror.

"We're going to do exactly what NIH wanted him to do. Prove it in humans."

He began flicking his tongue from her belly to the crease

between her legs.

Supine on a hotel bed, head on a stack of pillows, the iPad propped up on his thighs, Nigel Feist studied his hand. On-line poker was his way of relaxing before sleep. Sitting in the rental car surveilling Ritter's house all night on top of an additional twenty hours of work was taking its toll. More so than in his younger days. Just another sign of retirement being in the cards for him.

His cell rang.

He rechecked his hole cards—a pair of 8s—before glancing at caller ID. Fuck! Mister Richard you-can-kiss-my-ass Stillman. The fifteen seconds warning flashed on the screen: bet or automatically fold.

Fuck it.

In spite of holding what was probably a winning hand, he picked up the phone, said, "Go ahead."

With mild disappointment, he watched the final three seconds expire, effectively folding his hand. Texas Hold 'Em. Loved the game, played daily as a defense against the mind-numbing hours this job usually required.

Stillman said, "Your plan didn't seem to make the desired impression. He's leaving for Seoul. Same flight as previously."

"Fuck a duck! What's wrong with the bastard?"

Feist swatted away the iPad and swung his legs over the side of the bed. He wore camo boxers and an olive drab tee shirt.

Feist grabbed his Patek Philippe Calatrava from the nightstand, ready to strap it on his wrist the moment the call disconnected.

Wouldn't do to forget it, now would it?

Not the most expensive in his prized collection of fifteen watches. In contrast to his heavy Rolex Submariner, the Calatrava was thin, feathery, and elegant. The dial showed 10:03 AM, meaning he'd have to haul ass to reach SeaTac for the flight.

But before packing, he'd check the account to be sure that snake Stillman made the deposit.

Feist cleared his throat, said, "Alright then. Just so's we're straight on this we're at the end game now, right? No more warnings. This is it. Right-right?"

He pictured Stillman in black pants and black mock-tee, looking like a fag German industrial designer. He wondered if his *black is beautiful* concept carried through to his apartment? Black toilet paper, black sheets, an ample supply of black condoms.

What a piece of work.

"The one caveat is to make sure the Avengers get the credit."

Nigel disconnected, unplugged the phone charger and threw it in his rucksack, decided to wait until making it through security and securing a boarding pass and seat assignment before checking his account, but he'd damn well check to make sure the money was there before boarding the flight. Besides Stillman wanted this done so badly he wouldn't try to stiff him. And Stillman damn well knew the consequences if he did.

A heavy drizzle completely saturated the oil-stained gravel parking lot, rapidly enlarging puddles here and there. Underneath the eve of storage shed roof, Fisher turned up his raincoat collar before dialing Jon Ritter's cell. To his left, an eight-foot-high cyclone fence topped with razor wire encircled the lot. Directly ahead three uniformed poncho clad Sea-Tac cops with clear plastic hat protectors guarded a cordoned area around a rental car, their squad car's blue misery lights flashing.

"Jon, Fisher. I realize you're in a hurry, but I need to give you a quick head's up. Still on the one o'clock to Narita?"

"I am. Why?"

Fisher wiped a drop of water that blew into his eye, flicked it off his finger.

"We found Lippmann's shooter."

"How?"

"The rental car was found in a long-term parking lot out by the airport. Someone noticed a smell and recognized it for what it was. They had the SeaTac police pop the trunk. He was in there shot through the head."

"Good! Who is the son of a bitch?"

Fisher glanced at the crime scene the cops were guarding until the King County coroner could remove the body.

"We got lucky. He had his wallet on him, and we ran the name through NCIC. Turns out he's a small-time punk, name of Raymore Thompson. The bad news is he's decomposing in the trunk of a rental car."

Ritter sounded disappointed.

"He was shot through the head?"

"Yup. Two shots, execution style. From the looks of it, I suspect your Aussie friend of the Avengers is responsible. The bad news is we still don't have a lead on where that guy might be. But we now have a name associated with him. Nigel Feist."

"Whoa, how did you figure that out?"

"We got some more enhancements back on one of the cameras in the parking garage. We were lucky enough to have a shot of them just prior to slipping on their stockings. The quality was good enough to run it though Interpol in the assumption you're right, that he's Australian. Got a hit back for Feist. Interestingly, he owns a home in Los Angeles."

"What makes you think Thompson shot Lippmann?"

"We don't. Not for certain, but the car he was found in is the same one the surveillance camera picked up entering the parking garage. This isn't enough to even take to a grand jury, but it's a start."

Fisher recognized the medical examiner van bounce over a chuck hole, heading toward the car with the open trunk.

Ritter said, "I just hope you're right, that Thompson was the guy. If so, he got what he deserved."

"Hey, I'm with you on that particular sentiment. Change of

subject. A word of motherly advice. Be careful. Remember, those shitheads have extremely good intel. If you're not careful, they'll know exactly what you're doing. You listening to me?"

"Yes."

"Okay then, I just did my job by warning you. What you do at this point is your business. In any event, stay in touch. I want to hear from you regularly. Got it?"

"Yes, mother."

Fisher cracked a smile.

"No joke, Ritter. You're messing with some serious shitheads here. Don't forget that."

After hanging up, Fisher debated whether to walk through the rain to meet the ME team or stay where he'd be relatively dry. Looked at the rapidly increasing puddles and decided to stay under cover and make another call instead.

Special Agent Ross Harding answered with, "Yeah, Gary, what is it?"

Harding had the perfect appearance for an undercover operative—the farthest thing from a law enforcement officer you could get. None of the usual macho mannerisms, none of the arrogant self-assurance, no bluster. The perfect picture of a generic male of indeterminate nationality and a profound lack of flair. Not overly masculine but not gay. A guy who considered being well dressed a pair of new Levis and an Old Navy sweatshirt. You would be surprised to find no calluses on what looked like a working man's hands.

Fisher said, "We're right. He's on the United through Narita."

Harding answered, "I'm ticketed."

"Excellent. Got additional information for you, a lead on the Aussie. Name's Nigel Feist and, interestingly enough, he really *is* Australian. So Ritter nailed it. What's more, everything about him fits the details of the parking lot. I emailed you a picture a few minutes ago, so it should be in your inbox."

Fisher already had Feist's face and physical description

memorized so rattled them off: 42-year-old Caucasian male, six feet, 190 pounds, short cut brown hair, intense green eyes, muscular. No identifying scars. Born Cairns, Australia. Tats on both arms only. No ink elsewhere and none of it the amateur prison crap.

He added, "The most important thing you should know about him is he's one smart sonofabitch. Do *not*—I repeat, not—underestimate him. Right out of high school, he signed up for the Royal Navy. His scores were so off the chart they offered him a job in the Defense Intelligence Organization as an analyst. While there he developed covert skills. Soon as his contract was up, he resigned to start a private intelligence gathering company. Specializes in industrial espionage and dirty tricks. Word is he's quite good at it. He's suspected of being behind two assassinations but there was never enough to even hold him on a seventy-two hour. Point is he's never left enough trace to be seriously questioned although he's been under suspicion numerous times. At the moment, he's our man until proven otherwise."

"Understood."

"If he is an Avenger, I want his ass. If he isn't, I still want his ass. My gut tells me he probably doesn't give a shit about abortion one way or the other and is doing their work for hire. It's that simple. Bottom line: nailing Feist is your first priority on this trip. Protecting Ritter is secondary. We get Feist, we get our first big break in nailing the Avengers. Got it?"

"Loud and clear."

Fisher checked his watch.

"Better get your ass in gear. Don't want you to miss that flight."

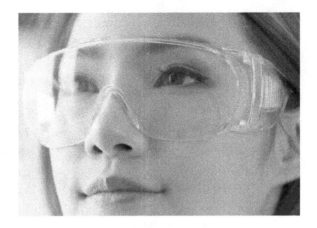

Chapter 16

HAIR TURBANED IN a white terry cloth towel, Yeonhee Lee climbed out of the large marble soaking tub onto wet white tile. She pulled a large bath towel off the stack on the table, shook it out and wrapped it around herself, tucking in the top to keep it in place.

At the moment, she was the only bather this evening, leaving the rest of the sauna deserted of customers. Only two sun-wrinkled attendants remained.

Funny, the differences in language, she thought.

Koreans refer to public baths as saunas. Americans consider saunas more along the lines of the Scandinavians, a cedar room with dry heat for sweating.

She'd taken a leisurely soak and would now get a massage—exactly what she needed after a tense day. She always looked forward to tub time as a way to free her mind and contemplate various issues.

Especially recently.

She was pleased to see none of her girlfriends here. Tonight in particular, she wanted time to herself to relax and think.

Jung-Kyo kept increasing pressure to become engaged. Knowing him, an ultimatum would not be far off. Then what?

She padded into the other room where the massage therapist waited, lay down on the slab of marble and tucked her hands under her right cheek.

The therapist asked, "Anything special today, or just the usual?"

"Maybe a bit extra on the left side of the neck."

A knot, from bending over the lab counters so much these past few days?

The therapist's hand began running up and down her back, adjacent to her spine.

"Your boyfriend still pressuring you?"

Yeonhee sighed.

"I don't know what's wrong with me. Any girl would consider him a great "catch." He has a high paying job as a Vice President with Hyundai. Comes from a good family. Handsome. Dresses well. The list goes on and on. No question he'd take care of my mother."

The therapist's fingers homed in on a knot in her trapezius.

"He sounds wonderful, what's the problem?"

"I just can't seem to tolerate his…chauvinism. I noticed it on our first date, and it drives me crazy."

"Like what?"

"For one thing, he spends all his free time with his buddies, weekends golfing, evenings out drinking when he should be with me."

"That's what Korean men do, Yeonhee. Your girlfriends, I bet they would put up with it if they had a chance for a man like him. What makes you different?"

A topic she'd thought about several times and ascribed to her time at UCLA and in Seattle. Western men were very different than Koreans.

They treated women better—something her girlfriends didn't appreciate.

She simply shrugged and said, "I'm not sure."

"Then maybe it's just not the right chemistry to get married?" the therapist said.

A half hour later, in the dressing room, Yeonhee unwrapped the towel before a full-length mirror to inspect her body.

Too fat?

She turned, looked over her shoulder at her butt. Sagging? Time was passing. Men liked younger, firmer women. Though only in her early thirties, as far as female competition was concerned, she was definitely on the down slope. Plus, there was only so much time to devote to working on your body. Even the gym and the spa could only do so much....besides, her day job took time.

She wished her boobs were bigger. She hadn't really wanted big boobs until she got to UCLA. There it seemed as if every LA girl had a thin waist, big tits, tight buns and a tan, and it made her jealous. Sort of. What she lacked in a gorgeous body she made up for in her face. At least that's what she'd been told. To her, it seemed too round, like a full August moon.

Did Jon Ritter find her attractive? She hoped so. He certainly was. Not that it would lead to anything. She felt a tingle of excitement at the idea of working next to him again. But the other voice in the back of her mind whispered caution. She'd been attracted to him when they worked together before, when he was engaged to Emily. Then he was already taken. Sad.

Why couldn't Jin-Woo be more like him?

Seattle had been a difficult time for her, being away from friends and family, and Jin-Woo so persistent about trying to sleep with her. Jin-Woo wanted more from her than being his lab tech, even to the point of acting jealous.

He had the nerve to suggest he'd leave his wife for her. How ridiculous. Yes, there was a small bit of attraction to him, but the most important thing was that if he was willing to cheat on his wife then, she would never be able to trust him if they ever did develop a relationship more than work.

She suspected he regularly cheated on his present wife, so why would she be silly enough to believe he would be faithful to her? He'd cheat. There are some things you can't change in a person. Fidelity being one. And she didn't want a husband out running around with other women.

Was this being silly and naive?

She moved to the locker room and slipped the key from the coiled pink elastic band that left a temporary little mark around her wrist. Time to get dressed. Morning would come soon enough, and she was expected to be in the lab by 6:30.

While dressing, she thought again of Jon, about what it might be like now that he was no longer attached to Emily.

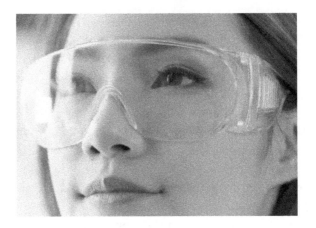

Chapter 17

A FLIGHT ATTENDANT glided down the aisle checking seat belts and seatbacks. Thankful to finally be underway, Jon up ended the flute of champagne, savoring the tingling effervescence at the base of his tongue. A good buzz just might allow two or three hours of sleep—a perfect way to burn up those interminable hours of constant engine noise, a time when passengers watch movies or sleep and bored flight attendants gossip in the galley or flip through dog-eared magazines.

The smiling flight attendant took his champagne flute with, "I'll bring you another, soon as we're airborne."

"Do I look *that* nervous?"

Her smile brightened.

"No. But you seemed to enjoy the last one so much I thought you might like another," and continued for the galley.

The jetway withdrew, exposing a train of empty baggage carts and a trio of ear-protected workers sauntering toward the terminal. The plane jerked backward as the overhead video started playing the familiar United Airlines melody. Jon pulled his Kindle from the seatback pouch and got ready to settle in for the long boring hours ahead.

Three pages later Jon got the feeling of something wrong, a premonition of sorts. Or maybe of being watched.

From overhead came, "Flight attendants prepare for takeoff."

The engine whine increased as the Boeing 777 lumbered through a left turn from the taxiway onto the runway. The feeling wouldn't go away.

Was an Avenger on this flight? Were they following him? Maybe even Feist?

Panic squeezed his heart.

Engine thrust increased, masking voices of the conversations around him, hurling the huge jet forward, slowly accelerating, then the 777's nose lifted, breaking tire contact with the runway and suddenly cutting decibels of noise to the constant rumble that would encase him for the next third of a day. The feeling didn't go away now that they were airborne.

Now what? Pick up the Airphone and call Fisher? And say what, exactly?

Get a grip. Chill. Think.

He took in a deep breath and dried both palms on his thighs.

Think!

His heart pounded. A band of tension tightened around his temples.

Jesus, they know!

A soft ding.

The seatbelt sign turned off while the angle of climb lessened. Jon unbuckled, stood, stretched, nonchalantly stepped into the isle, stood for another undecided moment before heading toward the rear lavatories in spite of being in Business Class.

He walked slowly down the aisle, scanning the passengers for someone who might cause even the slightest vibe of familiarity.

In the cramped lavatory Jon studied his healing scar without seeing it, the routine inspection now an unconscious habit rather than true interest, thinking, *get a grip.*

You're being paranoid.

Back in his seat, Jon ordered a double bourbon, hoping to calm his nerves.

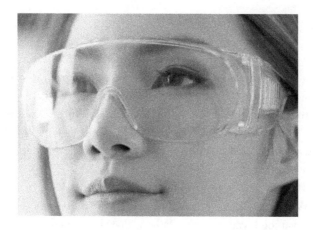

Chapter 18

Narita Airport

JON STEPPED INTO the narrow aisle and arched his back, trying to stretch out aching muscle tightness from sitting in an uncomfortable seat for so many hours, then waited for the cabin door to open. He massaged his temples, the skin oily slick after hours of warm recycled air.

Too tense to sleep, he'd spent eight and a half hours watching two mindless movies and reading. Yawning, he knuckled both eyes, the lids feeling as if lined with sandpaper.

The cabin door opened, allowing impatient passengers to surge out into the jetway. Bag in tow, Jon moved with the pack until he was able to break into a stride in the wider passage up to the arrival terminal. A few feet past the gate he stepped aside and pretended to read the signage while inspecting the stream of deplaning passengers. Again, no one radiated any vibe of familiarity.

Jon fell back into the flow of passengers and continued toward the connecting flight but couldn't shake the feeling of being watched.

Thirty minutes later he waited in line at the boarding gate, eyeing other passengers, looking for someone paying attention to him. He knew he was being paranoid, yet…he kept coming back to a soldier in fatigues slouched in a row of molded plastic chairs. Big, husky, shoulders like the killer's, but his brush cut hair was blond, not black, not…not what? Something about the soldier resonated.

What?

Whenever he was looking elsewhere, the creepy felling of being watched came back. When that happened, he quickly glanced at the soldier, but each time the soldier was occupied elsewhere. Again, a chill snaked down his back. Yeah, the soldier bothered him.

Finally, the attendant at the jetway door picked up a microphone and announced boarding for First Class. Jon was relieved to be moving again.

In his peripheral vision, Nigel Feist watched Jon Ritter scan the crowd only to settle on him again. He read the uncertainty in Ritter's gaze, figured he must be thinking, "Is that him?"

The beautiful thing about sitting right out in the open like this was it lent a touch of credibility to his disguise. Just another GI returning to active duty in South Korea. He casually checked the heavy stainless-steel Citizen on his wrist. Cheap-ass watch had to be at least ten pounds heavier than his real timepieces, but it too, added a touch of authenticity to his cover—as did the engraved stainless-steel Zippo in his pocket along with the Marlboros he didn't smoke.

Attention to detail often was the only difference between success and failure in an operation.

Feist checked the time. Five minutes until boarding. Fucking brain surgeon didn't have a clue.

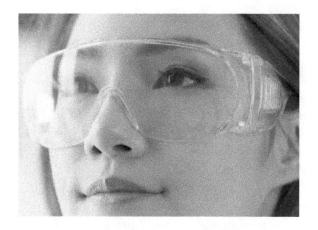

Chapter 19

Incheon, South Korea

JON STOOD IN one of four switchback lines to passport control booths, the rows defined with red strap-tape tightly stretched between chrome stanchions, three for Korean nationals, one for non-Koreans. Not nearly enough to efficiently handle the number of people. A digital clock on the wall behind the booths showed 16:30 hours, Sunday evening. What would that be in Seattle? 8:30 Sunday morning, he thought without conviction. For some reason, the International Date Line made the calculation more difficult for him.

"Next."

He stepped from the scuffed red line on the floor to the booth, handed the officer his passport.

The officer ran the edge with a bar code through a reader, asked, "Nature of your trip?"

"Business."

The Korean appeared deceivingly bored in spite of an unmistakable intensity in his eyes.

"How long?"

Jon really had no idea. Depended on what Jin-Woo might say.

"A week, maybe two."

"Where are you staying?"

Jon flashed on Fisher's warning: *They have sympathizers everywhere. Be careful. You never know who you're talking to, even with friends.* An Immigration officer as informant....yeah, it could work. Lie? Chance it? Do they ever check?

He chose a hotel at random, "The Ritz-Carlton," not knowing if there even was one in Seoul.

The officer grunted, flipped through the passport pages searching for a suitable spot, stamped one, slid it back under the Plexiglas.

Jon fell in behind a ragtag line of passengers heading along a windowless hall to Customs.

Would Yeonhee be waiting with Jin-Woo?

He smiled at the thought.

Another official waved him past the checkpoint without a second look and he continued on toward two opaque glass doors that slid apart with a hiss of air, depositing him in a teaming arrival lobby. He immediately recognized Jin-Woo's full-moon face bobbing above the crowd, craning to spot him. Jon waved, caught his eye, and looked for Yeonhee next to him but she wasn't there. Jin-Woo broke into a broad smile, hand extended.

"Good see you, My Teacher."

"Thanks for meeting me."

Driving all the way out to the airport to meet him was a big deal and an imposition, but one Jin-Woo gladly offered now that the international airport was located miles west of Seoul, near the city of Incheon. The old Kimpo airport was closer to Seoul but much smaller, making the increased volume of international traffic impractical.

Jon said, "This is all I have. No need to stop at baggage claim."

"This way, then."

Jin-Woo led him from a crush of milling travelers, past car rental and currency exchange booths, through another set of automatic glass doors into heavy humid smog as the wavy remnant of an orange red ball started to disappear behind a building. A black Hyundai waited at the loading zone, the driver snoozing comfortably at the wheel. Jon threw his bag into the trunk, then slipped into a pleasant, air-conditioned chill and black leather. Doors slammed, seatbelts clicked, a moment later they were heading toward the airport exit.

Jin-Woo gave the driver an order in Korean before turning his attention to Jon.

"We have much to talk about during the drive. I will take you to Walker Hill Hotel." Before Jon could reply, Jin-Woo patted Jon's arm. "It is hard, I think. Your loss of Emily. My heart is heavy for you."

"Yes, it is. It's hard getting used to life without her."

Jon turned toward an endless series of aluminum light poles flashing by, his eyes misting over in one of those emotional moments that seemed to float just below the surface of consciousness. He'd built up defenses to deal with the loss, but there were other times, like right now when the mention of Emily's name hit him square in the face and thinking about her death triggered tears. Lately a new twist to this emotional yo-yo was making him even more despondent when he thought about her. He was aware that his memories of her were blurring around the edges and he had to concentrate to recall small details in her face. The mole on her neck just underneath her right ear. The speckles in her green eyes.

To break the awkward silence, he asked, "How is Sunhee?"

Jin-Woo's wife.

For the next ten minutes they chatted only about personal items and avoided discussion of the clinical trial. After a pause Jin-Woo leaned closer to Jon and lowered his voice so the driver couldn't hear.

"To do your project without committee supervision is very dangerous for me in Korea."

In most medical centers, any form of human experimentation, like drug studies, must be overseen by an internal review board. For obvious reasons, Jon and Jin-Woo agreed to not risk the exposure of submitting a protocol for review.

"Look, if——"

Jin-Woo held up a hand, cutting him off.

"I only say this because I understand you wish this to be a very silent study. No one in the medical center is to know."

Jon cast a quick glance at the driver, hoping to send Jin-Woo the message to drop the subject until they were really alone.

"Exactly."

Jin Woo followed Jon's look at the driver and then leaned even closer.

In a whisper, "Then you must realize such a thing is impossible without help from someone high in administration."

A bad feeling burrowed into Jon's gut.

"Meaning?"

"Our CEO, his father has Alzheimer's. I had words with him last night. All very quiet. His father will be one of the patients."

Jon couldn't tell if this was a question or statement. Most of all, he didn't know anything about the man—basic details like if he would qualify for the protocol. But the way Jin-Woo said it, it was important to include him.

He straddled the fence with, "I don't know. I know nothing about him."

Jin-Woo sliced a hand through the air for emphasis.

"No. You do not hear me. He will be a patient or there will be no implants."

Jon wanted to remind Jin-Woo how much was riding on the outcome of the trial, that clean data requires careful screening of subjects, especially to verify their diagnosis. Just because a person may have signs of dementia didn't mean they have Alzheimer's disease. But hell, Jin-Woo knew all this. Instead, he nodded.

"Got it."

Jin-Woo added, "There are many reasons for this. One is, to work in my lab, you need security pass. He can arrange this immediately. Otherwise," he glanced down at his folded hands, "it will take time."

"Okay."

"Excellent. In the morning I pick you up and we go to Tyasami for an interview. No decision is made without his approval."

Jon wasn't convinced he entirely understood.

Why couldn't Jin-Woo arrange a temporary security pass for him? Why the interview?

He wasn't comfortable with this arrangement, but by now Jin Woo was scanning emails on his phone, and it seemed the matter was settled. The car interior grew silent, and Jon was feeling more and more uneasy.

Although he trusted Jin-Woo, how could he trust the CEO, a man he'd never met? Did this represent a weak point in their security?

Nigel Feist gripped the handlebars and leaned over the tank of the black Hyosung GT650 motorcycle.

Fucking Korean piece of shit.

A nothing bike compared with any of his Harleys. A disposable bike, one you rode on a trip, then dumped. The only good thing about a Hyosung was its cheap price.

He wore black gloves, black leather coat, black jeans, black turtleneck, full-face black helmet with a black duffel strapped to the rack and a black rucksack on his back. He cruised easily through traffic, tailing the black Hyundai. He thought about the image he presented. Stillman would probably get a hard on, what with all this black. But the reason for it was simple: people noticed red or yellow cycles, especially the gaudy ones tricked out with tons of chrome. But a totally black machine could zip past and hardly be noticed and never remembered.

Although the Hyundai carrying Ritter remained several cars ahead, Feist focused on the taxi.

More specifically, the lone man in its back seat.

Feist didn't worry about losing Ritter because if forced to guess where he'd stay, he'd put his chips on the Sheraton, the hotel closest to the medical center. And if that turned out to be wrong, he could always surveil the medical center until Ritter showed up.

No, his primary interest was the passenger in the taxi. Feist first noticed him on the Seattle-Narita flight because the bloke so obviously had an eye on Ritter. If it had ended there, he would have thought nothing more of it. But then the bloke ends up on the Seoul leg too. Okay, sure, people heading to Seoul commonly connect through Japan so the odds were in favor of a few passengers being on both segments. But the man followed Ritter right on through baggage claim, on out to the meet with his slant-eye friend. Now the bloke was in a taxi tailing them.

Why?

Two options popped immediately to mind: the publicity surrounding Lippmann's murder increased Ritter's attractiveness to the Avengers, meaning they'd pop him here in Seoul. The second, more likely scenario, was the FBI could be using Ritter as bait to nail an Avenger. Either way, his presence made the job trickier—a wrinkle he'd have to sort out before doing anything with Ritter.

A doorman in a well-tailored grey uniform opened the car door for Jon.

"Welcome to the Sheraton Walkerhill."

The stately old hotel sat atop a park-like hill overlooking the Han River, the Tyasami medical complex easily seen on the opposite bank. The driver popped the trunk for the doorman to unload Jon's wheelie.

Jin-Woo walked Jon to the revolving door, said, "Sorry I cannot go to dinner tonight, but after such a long flight you need rest. Tomorrow morning. Eight o'clock. I fetch you for your meeting with the CEO. Sleep well."

From the parking lot, Nigel Feist watched the slant-eye's Hyundai pull away from the hotel as Ritter disappeared into the lobby. He now knew where Ritter was staying, which meant he probably knew where the bloke tailing him would be.

Book a room or go elsewhere?

Problem was there were no other hotels in the immediate vicinity, making surveillance problematic. He parked the motorcycle and headed for the entrance to the Sheraton.

Chapter 20

FROM PREVIOUS STAYS at this same hotel, Jon knew he needed to insert the key card into a wall holder just left of the door jamb in order to activate the electricity. Although this conserved energy, it left the room without air conditioning or circulation for whatever time elapsed since the last person was inside.

When Jon opened the door a wall of stifling stale air greeted him. The moment he slid the key into the holder, the A/C powered on. A quick check of the thermostat showed 36 degrees Celsius—whatever the hell that converted to in Fahrenheit. He simply set it for 22, a figure that memory said seemed about right, and resigned himself to broiling before the room drifted down to a tolerable temperature.

He tossed his wheelie on top of the first of two queen beds, kicked off his loafers, threw his blazer on the other bed, opened the drapes, and unpacked. Finished with that chore, he stood at the window admiring the lights of Seoul. He should be hungry but wasn't. Instead, his stomach was sour and his mind sticky with fatigue.

How long since he'd slept well? A week?

He stripped, stood in the hot shower for ten minutes, toweled off, wrapped himself in a white terry cloth robe and returned to the bedroom. With the room temperature now at a more tolerable level and the layers of dried sweat washed away, he felt refreshed. Mentally, however, he couldn't shake a vague fear in the pit of his stomach. He inspected the minibar, selected the two bottles of Jack Daniels. The miniature ice tray was, of course, empty. Seemed like too much trouble to walk the hall searching for an ice machine, so he upended both bottles into a glass, took a swallow and enjoyed the satisfying burn at the back of his throat.

He took the glass and cell phone to a chair beside the window, settled in, programmed the international prefix onto the phone numbers for Stillman, Fisher, and Wayne, and tried to figure out what time it'd be in Seattle.

Did it really matter? Hadn't they said to call, regardless?

He downed another sip before the first call connected to Fisher.

Jon asked, "Anything new to report?"

"No. How about you?"

Jon hesitated.

Would it seem paranoid? Probably, but he had to mention it.

"I know I'm just imagining things, but I swear I felt like someone was watching me."

"Huh!"

Jon didn't like the sound of that.

"What's 'huh' supposed to mean?"

"Could be a couple things. Maybe it's only natural, considering what's happened. Or maybe the Avengers are following you."

A jolt of anxiety surged though Jon, tingling his arms and making him short of breath. He glanced at the door.

Was the deadbolt on and safety chain fastened?

When Jon didn't answer, Fisher said, "There's a solution, you know. Go out to the airport and hop on the next flight back. Don't screw around taking chances. If one of those shitheads is tailing you it can only mean one thing: you're in serious trouble."

Damn, he was hyperventilating. He upended the glass and swallowed, hacking at the burn along the back of his throat. He wiped his lips with the back of his hand. He didn't need this kind of pressure right now.

"I need to go. Sorry to wake you."

"Think about what I just said. Think about it real hard."

There was no more bourbon in the wet bar, so Jon dumped a scotch in his glass, returned to the chair by the window and stared at the lights stretching into blackness, thinking about Jin-Woo.

Something about their interaction...something different, something subtle. Or was he so weirded out over this Feist thing that he was imagining things that didn't exist?

Man! His brain hurt from all the angst. He needed sleep. Things always look better in the morning.

Call Wayne first.

Wayne said, "Where are you? Sounds like you're still in Seattle."

Jon was rotating the glass, watching the amber liquid swish around the side.

"In Seoul, about ready to crash."

"We all set?"

There it was, a perfect opening to the subject.

He spoke as neutrally as possible to gauge Wayne's reaction.

"No. Jin-Woo says that in order to get me a security pass I need an interview with the CEO. It's scheduled first thing in the morning."

There was a slight pause.

"Are you kidding? And what exactly are you supposed to

say you're doing there?"

"He knows. Jin-Woo told him. He said he had to involve him to short cut a lot of red tape and get me a security clearance for the lab. But as far as anyone else is concerned, the story is we've worked together over the years and I'm here to help him figure out some lab issues."

"Fine, but I thought we were trying to keep you low profile."

"I know. Look, I don't like it either. But Jin-Woo's ass is out in the breeze on this. He's worried."

"How so?"

Jon sipped scotch.

"I'm surprised you have to ask. He's doing this without any IRB oversight," referring to the Institutional Review Board that is required before any human experimentation. "He can get totally hosed if someone blows the whistle on him. I don't know exactly how the system works over here but it's conceivable he could lose his license. Although he hasn't come out and said this, I think he figures if the CEO has been informed, he's covered."

Again Wayne hesitated.

"But?"

Jon paused, searching for how best to describe his anxiety but came up lame, so opted for, "He's acting a little weird." He decided to not mention the feeling of being watched. "Just fatigue, I guess."

Wayne wasn't convinced.

"You sure?"

"Yeah. It's just that I'm beat. Catch you tomorrow."

Jon debated touching base with Stillman, decided what the hell and dialed. He told him about the meeting with the CEO in the morning and also described Jin-Woo's plan for how to get the patients admitted and scheduled for surgery without raising suspicion.

A few minutes later he broke a ten milligram Ambien in half and chewed it into a pulp before smearing the paste over his gums with the tip of his tongue. The alcohol would accentuate the drug, putting him out for at least four hours—six, if lucky—in spite of the time zone difference.

With the room bathed in shadows and dim city light, he slipped into the bed closest to the window and tried to relax and wait for the Ambien to work its magic.

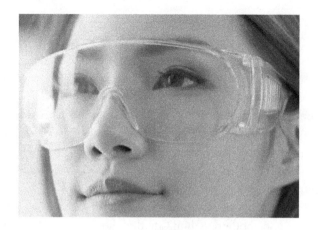

Chapter 21

AFTER DISCONNECTING from Ritter's call, Richard Stillman continued standing at the glass slider, looking out, absent-mindedly tapping the phone against his palm.

Start the day or go back to bed?

Twenty-one floors below, the patches of mercury vapor light reflected off puddles that had formed earlier in the night. He watched a lone man walk an arthritic dog to a square in the sidewalk where a tree struggled to survive, and wondered what their story was.

How many years had they lived together? Had he raised him from a puppy? How did it feel to have a pet? Was the man married or was the pooch his sole companion?

When growing up, friends had pets, but he never did. Not even a hamster or parakeet. And for a split second he felt a tinge of self-pity for himself, missing out on such a common part of childhood.

Did that contribute to his not wanting kids and this resigned satisfaction with single life? Was this normal? Was he abnormal?

Too many questions. Might as well start the day.

Carefully, he replaced the phone into the charger and made certain the charge light glowed green before heading to the bathroom. Stripped, and ready for the shower, he gripped the edge of the Jacuzzi tub and, toes on the floor, began fifty angled pushups. Same routine every day, even days he also worked out at the gym. Pushups, he believed, were the single best exercise to keep shoulders and pecs toned. Always accentuate your best physical assets was one of his tenets, and broad shoulders were definitely on his list.

2Pac began rapping from the dresser.

No one bothered him at this hour without it being extremely important.

Curious, yet irritated at the interruption, he checked the display, saw Feist's name, so answered with, "Yo, Dog, what up?"

"A bit of bad news, I suspect. There's another bloke been tailing your friend since SeaTac. Might a started before then but don't know for sure. Don't much fancy that. Do you?"

Hmmm…absentmindedly he palmed his scalp, checking the stubble, processing this new wrinkle.

"Are you absolutely positive?" Didn't make much sense, unless…"

"No question in my mind."

Stillman sucked his upper lip, sliding his lower teeth back and forth over it.

Could it possibly be the Avengers? Could some weird freaky thing happen, like one of those lunatics took the website posting seriously? Man, wouldn't that be something!

Three weeks ago he'd had Ritter's profile posted on the site as the first step in setting this entire scenario in motion and to give Feist's threats authenticity. Maybe now…

He asked Feist, "Male or female?"

Not that that would tell him much.

"Bloke."

Had to be an Avenger. Which could present a huge problem if the whacko were to execute Ritter before the cultures were finished and the patients implanted.

"Just talked to Ritter. Have any idea which hotel's he in? Didn't think to ask."

"The Sheraton across the river from the medical center. The slant-eye dropped him there from the airport straightaway. In his room, he is. Been there since check in."

Well, that's a relief.

"Where are you?"

"Got me room right next door to his. Stroke of luck, that was."

Until the patients were implanted, he wanted Ritter alive and not interfered with.

"Good thing you called, I have some fresh information for you. They're planning on two separate surgery days, two patients each day, all scheduled as DBS implants."

"How about talking fucking English, mate."

"Stands for Deep Brain Stimulation. But that part really doesn't matter, just find a way to know what surgeries Dr. Lee schedules. Any patient with the diagnosis of Parkinson's Disease is probably one of ours. That's how they plan to get the operating room time without anyone knowing what they're really up to."

"Hey. No need to be so fucking condescending."

Stillman shot an angry glance at the iPhone but reminded himself how much he needed Feist's services. At least for now.

Soon as this was over, however...

He swallowed his irritation and, as smoothly as possible, said, "Forgive me, didn't mean it to sound that way."

Asshole.

Feist said, "All right, then. What do you want done about the tail?"

"It's worrisome. Very worrisome...could be an Avenger. You've seen him. What are your thoughts?"

He could pretty well anticipate Feist's answer but wanted him to be the one to say it first.

"Could be," Feist said, sounding noncommittal. "No way of telling just yet."

"Then, use your judgment and take care of it however you think appropriate."

"Right."

After disconnecting, Stillman pumped out an extra twenty pushups—putting a little extra into it. Much as he disliked the Australian, he considered himself fortunate to have someone with his skills working this. Unforeseen problems could derail even the best thought-out plans. He had to give Feist credit, though, for picking up on the tail.

On the other hand, Feist was being paid top dollar to execute well.

Good was supposed to be good, that's why it was called good.

Strange how these things happen.

Because of posting Ritter's information on a website, an Avenger was actually pursuing him. And now, Feist was actually getting paid to protect the pompous asshole—at least until the study was complete. In the meantime, Feist would take care of it.

Laughing and shaking his head at the irony, he stepped into the steaming spray of water.

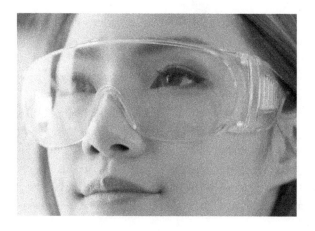

Chapter 22

JON SNAPPED WIDE-AWAKE. The horizon was growing lighter, making the shadows angling over the walls disappear.

The digital clock radio showed 5:03.

He rolled over to face away from the window and shut his eyes again and thought about his impending meeting with Tyasami's CEO. Once that thought focused his attention, no way he could drift back to sleep.

Yeah, he understood Jin-Woo's explanation for the need to meet, still…he didn't like it…

He rolled onto his back and stared at the ceiling to think about it.

Once, as a kid, he and a friend shoplifted a couple of paperback books from a drugstore. Not because they wanted to read them—in fact, they didn't—they just wanted to see if they could get away with it. He remembered the churning weightlessness in the bottom of his chest and tingling in his fingers in the moments before actually slipping the books under his coat and crossing the threshold between thinking of a crime and actually committing it. The same anxious feeling wormed its way through him now.

And it wasn't just the risk of the Avengers knowing about his work here that bothered him...it was seedy the way he and Jin-Woo were going about it. Although the patients would know what was being done, there would be no ethics board oversight. They wouldn't actually be breaking a law by implanting their stem cells into the patients' brains. The nature of original medical research requires physicians do things to patients that have never been done before. That's why it called "the first time." Just wasn't ethical, the way they were going about it.

As an aftermath of the Nazi war crimes tribunal, international standards for human research were established. To meet this standard, the patients would be fully informed about what Jin-Woo and Jon intended to do before they signed a consent.

So it wasn't what they were about to do that bothered him—after all, before his work became a political hot potato, the NIH loved it—it was having to sneak around like CIA operatives in order to do it, leaving him feeling slimy and guilty.

He sat up and rubbed grains of sleep from the corners of his eyes. Might as well get out of bed and start the day. He flipped on the electric tea pot, showered, wrapped himself in the terrycloth robe and used the room's complimentary high-speed Internet to check email. This took only fifteen minutes off the clock, making it seem like forever until THE MEETING.

He tried to work on a paper he and Dobbs intended to submit to *Science,* but couldn't focus. After thirty minutes of unsuccessfully editing only one paragraph, he gave up and swapped the computer for the television and CNN Asia.

Second after second ticked by at glacial speed.

For five minutes he waited at the red velour cordon separating the dining area from the lobby. At precisely 6:30 a hostess in a red and white *honbock* unhooked the sash, officially opening the cafe for the day, and led him to a small table next to the wall, set down a menu and asked if he wanted coffee or tea. He ordered coffee and the traditional Korean breakfast of kim chee, rice, fish, and pickled veggies.

In spite of being hungry, he couldn't eat, so ended up only drinking three cups of bitter black coffee with a taste that was more like Nescafe than his usual Starbucks.

By 7:35—twenty-five minutes early—he positioned himself just inside the front door where he could watch the circular drive for Jin-Woo. Too early, he knew, but Asians consider punctuality a sign of respect. Jin-Woo always arrived at least five minutes ahead of schedule, so Jon wasn't about to have him wait at the curb. Besides, he couldn't bear another minute killing time in the room.

At 7:51, Jin-Woo's Hyundai crested the drive and pulled in behind a black limo in the process of loading luggage. Jon was out the hotel door and into the passenger seat before the doorman could react. With nothing more than a good morning nod, Jin-Woo started driving them back down the winding road of Walker Hill.

Jin-Woo led Jon through a tall double door into an air-conditioned room with a high ceiling, wood paneling, thick carpet, and a withered, gray-haired woman behind a desk.

After a nod at Jin-Woo, the secretary muttered a few hushed words into the telephone. Then, with a bow, ushered them into an adjoining office with parquet floors covered by beautiful oriental carpets. A short bald man stood with one hand on an imposing mahogany desk. The CEO wore an impeccably tailored gray suit with a starched white shirt and prep school tie. Jon estimated his age somewhere in the mid-forties, which would put his father, one of their patients, somewhere in his sixties. Jon was surprised to realize that he hadn't asked Jin-Woo the man's age. The CEO greeted them in Korean, then waved them toward two couches on opposing sides of a hand carved teak table.

Jon and Jin-Woo dropped into the nearest couch, the CEO settled into the one across the table and crossed his legs in a straight back posture that struck Jon as somewhat feminine. The CEO and Jin-Woo began chatting in Korean while casting occasional glances at him, which Jon found unnerving. This continued for several minutes until suddenly the CEO stopped talking. Several seconds of silence ticked past, making Jon wonder if he was supposed to say something now that both men were looking at him expectantly.

Jon turned to Jin-Woo, "Something wrong?"

Jin-Woo exchanged a few words with the CEO before telling Jon, "He asks if you had a pleasant flight to Seoul."

Jon smiled at the man.

"Yes."

Jin-Woo asked, "He wants to know if your accommodations are satisfactory?"

"Yes. Quite satisfactory, thank you."

"I explained this is not your first trip to Seoul and you have visited my laboratory before, and I have visited you several times to watch you operate and to learn from you."

As Jin-Woo spoke, the CEO studied Jon with a dead-pan expression, which only stoked Jon's anxiety. What was he thinking? Most unnerving was not having a clue if the guy understood English.

Was this some sort of test of character?

Jon said, "Please tell him how impressed I am with his medical center and the quality of staff here."

The CEO pushed out of his couch, opened a desk drawer and came away with a small box wrapped in sky blue paper—the same blue as Korean Air jets, the national color—with a silver ribbon and bow. Smiling, he bowed and presented the box to Jon.

"A gift to you," Jin-Woo explained.

With a bow, Jon accepted it, "Thank you."

Shit. Should've known this might happen. Why didn't I think of this and pick up a gift at the hotel?

Too late now.

Jin-Woo pulled a thin, wrapped package from his coat pocket and handed it to the CEO with a bow and a few words, then turned to Jon and said, "We go now. He thanked you for the gift."

That's it? The interview's over?

Jon hesitated, embarrassed and confused.

What do I do now?

Jin-Woo gave a gentle tug on his sleeve.

Without a word, he led Jon through the outer office to a hall with the bank of four elevators, Jon hurrying to stay alongside him.

"What was that all about? I thought we needed to discuss the study and his father. Thanks, by the way, for covering me. What was it you gave him?"

"A pen." Jin-Woo punched the DOWN button. "He makes decision later today after he and I talk." He made a show of checking his watch, which didn't do a hell of a lot to convince Jon the interview went well. "I have much to do today. I will meet you at your hotel, six o'clock. I will make dinner arrangement."

The elevator to their right dinged and the door slid open.

Jon stood with one foot in the elevator, the other in the hall blocking the door from closing, fighting growing irritation at not having the slightest idea what just happened or would happen later.

"Wait-wait-wait. What just went on in there? I thought this was supposed to be an interview. What was it?"

"That was the interview." Jin-Woo repeatedly punched the button for the lobby level and motioned Jon into the cage where an elderly woman stood watching them. "I will organize the taxi to take you back. Please wait for my call."

After hesitating a moment, Jon realized there was nothing more to do, so reluctantly stepped in and released the door.

"At least give me some sort of hint. Is he for or against this?"

Jin-Woo shrugged.

"I do not know. He and I will talk at two. I will call after."

Jon's gut knotted.

Nigel Feist bowed to the chief of Tyasami security, a dour pit bull with wire rim glasses, no fat, and the attitude of a Paris Island Drill Instructor. "Captain Sun, thank you for taking time from your busy schedule to meet with me."

Sun returned a curt bow, and said, "My pleasure," and inspected Feist's bogus FBI credentials.

With a nod of approval, he handed back the wallet.

Feist pointed at the open office door.

"Mind if we close that? What I need to discuss is in strict confidence."

"Yes, of course." With the door shut, the small, utilitarian office seemed to close in on Feist. One gray metal desk with nothing but a handheld radio in a battery charger, a matching metal bookcase full of books and folders, a desk chair, a straight back visitor chair. "Please, have a seat."

Seated, Feist leaned forward and lowered his voice.

"What I am about to tell you must remain in strict confidence. Do you understand?"

"Certainly."

"We have reason to believe an American doctor named Jon Ritter is planning to conduct a series of experimental brain surgeries here with one of your surgeons, Dr. Lee, Jin-Woo." Feist adhered to the Korean custom of putting the family name before the first name. "The surgery is so experimental Dr. Ritter was forbidden to do it in the United States."

Sun appeared confused.

"I am sure you are mistaken. I do not believe this is allowed here."

Feist nodded solemnly.

"You're right, of course. Under normal circumstances, it would not be. However, our intelligence source believes Dr. Lee plans to schedule them under false pretense so that they would appear to be routine surgery for Parkinson's disease. Once the patients are in surgery they will, instead, do the experimental part."

Sun's brow furrowed even more.

"Why do you tell me this? I have no control over medical issues, just hospital security. Your concerns must be discussed with the appropriate department head, the Chief of Staff or Medical Director, someone like that."

"Under normal conditions, that's exactly what I would do. But before I dare risk damaging Dr. Lee's excellent name, I need to confirm that the information is correct. What we do know for sure is that Dr. Ritter arrived in Seoul yesterday and was met at the airport by Dr. Lee. Our intelligence cannot yet verify when exactly the surgery will take place, but I suspect that detail will be decided within a day or so. What I need is for you to monitor Dr. Lee's hospital admissions and scheduled surgeries. Let me know immediately what surgeries he schedules. If I see what appears to be the experimental ones, I'll discuss the matter with the Chief of Surgery. May I count on your assistance?"

Sun didn't hesitate.

"Yes, of course. We always help the American government."

Feist stood.

"Excellent. I'll be back in touch. And please, let's keep this very confidential. I would hate to be mistaken and damage Dr. Lee's excellent reputation, especially as it reflects on Tyasami Medical Center."

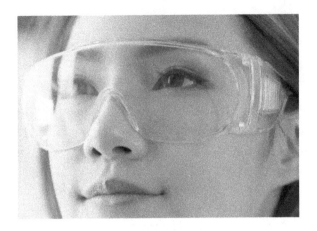

Channel 23

JON WAS BACK in his room at the Sheraton by 10:30—with nothing to do but wait to hear back from Jin-Woo and try to contain his anxiety. He tried reading but couldn't concentrate on the words so finally threw the Kindle onto the other bed, propped himself up on pillows and turned on the TV. Not much to see other than what seemed to be Korean soap operas. No English programming, not even CNN Asia.

Finally, he went out for a stroll around the hotel and then killed some more time having lunch at the coffee shop. The meeting between Jin-Woo and the CEO wasn't until two o'clock but Jon was back in his room by 1:30. He sat at the window looking at the view, waiting long minutes for the phone to ring.

Finally, when it did ring, Jon had it against his ear before it could ring again.

"Yes?"

Jin Woo said, "I will fetch you for dinner. Five thirty. Okay? You will be ready?"

"Yes, but what about the decision? What's happening?"

"Can't talk now. Five-thirty. In front of the hotel."

Jin-Woo hung up.

Shit!

Jon dropped onto the bed and rehashed the exchange. Did Jin-Woo's tone imply anything? No. Now he had more time to burn and really had nothing to take his mind off how slowly the minutes passed. Well, he'd rather be moving than sitting here staring out the damn window. A moment later he was out the door.

He started off by wandering around the expansive marble lobby but realized there was nothing much to see on this level. The lower level contained a variety of shops he wandered through regardless of the merchandise. But he wasn't a shopper and had exhausted them all in ten minutes.

He strolled outside into a warm sunny day and followed the meandering drive downhill to a residential neighborhood where he dawdled away another twenty minutes wandering side streets. As the minutes passed, his anxiety slowly morphed into a fatalistic *que sara sara* mindset.

After all, he'd done everything within his power to keep his research alive. At this juncture, its fate was truly out of his control. Continuing to worry would be counterproductive, accomplishing nothing while stressing him more. Realistically, considering all the complications over the past few weeks, he was lucky to be alive and in good health. For which he was truly thankful. The time passed.

Showered and dressed in a black blazer and lightweight mock tee, Jon exited the hotel lobby to await Jin-Woo at the loading zone curb. A doorman approached to ask if he wished a taxi. Jon declined, thanked him and moved further along the circular drive to wait. Two minutes later Jin-Woo's black Hyundai glided to the curb.

In the parking lot, Nigel Feist straddled his rented motorcycle and watched Ritter exit the sliding glass doors to the loading zone, exchange words with one of the doormen, and wait.

Two minutes later, a black Hyundai arrived with a woman in the back seat. Feist recognized the driver as Dr. Lee. He started the engine and slipped on his helmet.

Jon reached for the passenger door when he noticed Yeonhee smiling at him from the backseat. Two years ago, she and Jin-Woo came to Seattle for a six-month training stint in his lab. At the time, Jon wondered if they had a thing going but never asked in spite of his curiosity, especially because of meeting Jin-Woo's wife at a symposium a year earlier. Jin-Woo had made it known to Jon that in spite of being married, he had a girlfriend.

Yeonhee was as stunningly beautiful as ever with large almond eyes, oval face, and black hair pulled into a relaxed ponytail. In the lab, Jon had often seen her wearing glasses, but tonight she didn't, opting, he suspected, for contacts. From the moment they met, he'd been attracted to her but never acted on it because he was dating Emily at the time.

As he opened the door, she leaned forward and held out her hand. "Hello, Jon."

He smiled and shook her hand.

"Yeonhee," then, "Jin-Woo," and slipped inside, thinking her handshake meant Jin-Woo brought good news. Maybe.

Don't get too optimistic, pal.

Beaming, Jin-Woo extended his hand.

"Good news. CEO says okay. Tonight we celebrate."

Yes!

Jon slumped into the black leather, took a deep breath, held it a beat, slowly blew out.

"Thank you," A feeling of huge relief and joy surged within him. Finally, he and Wayne would have a chance to learn if their ten years of hard work would pay off. He turned to Jin-Woo and repeated, "Thank you."

There's no way to let him know how much this means.

As he drove the windy two-lane road down Walker Hill, Jin-Woo said, "I bring Yeonhee so we can start making plans on how you want to begin in the lab tomorrow morning. We will celebrate, sure, but we have business too."

Jon simply nodded, his mind fully preoccupied, listing all the preparatory tasks that needed to be finished in the next twenty-four hours before they could actually begin transforming cultures of stem cells—the ones that would be implanted in the brains of their patients.

Feist secured the chin strap of his helmet, kicked the stand up against the cycle, and waited, the engine vibrating gently against his thighs and up through his tailbone.

A moment later, Ritter's tail, the suspected Avenger, pushed through the lobby doors and hailed a taxi. Then they were scooting down the curving road like a caravan: Ritter in the slant-eye's black Hyundai, the Avenger in a taxi, and Feist on his cycle.

Jin-Woo became uncharacteristically silent as they drove, probably, Jon figured, distracted by thick rush hour traffic. At the bottom of the hill, they turned toward the downtown business district of serious-looking buildings and neon.

So far, Jin-Woo said nothing about their destination, but at this point it didn't matter; Jon was content to gaze at the passing scene rather than forcing conversation. Dinner would be devoted to planning the tasks to be done tomorrow.

Seoul's sidewalk scene appeared similar to any major U.S. city at this time of day as commuters made their way home for the evening. A man in a blue suit and black attaché case hurried into a subway station. A withered, *mamasan* shuffled along the sidewalk, shoulders sagging from bulging grocery bags in each hand. A street vendor was hawking his wares.

It dawned on Jon then that his silence might be considered rude, so said to Yeonhee. "How have you been?"

Before she could answer, Jin-Woo jumped in with, "She is engaged to a big guy with Hyundai."

"I am not!" Yeonhee grabbed the corner of Jon's seat and pulled forward, closer to the separation between the front seat head rests. "He's just a guy I see."

"But a serious guy?" Jon asked, surprised at his tinge of jealousy.

Where did that come from?

She leaned left to make eye contact with him between the seat backs.

"I am sorry about Emily."

Jon noticed she had almost no accent, probably from having spent so much time in the States.

"Thank you."

He caught the same scent she wore in Seattle. It triggered memories her of working next to him, all the stolen little glances at the curve or her neck, the concentration furrows across her brow, wisps of black hair she repeatedly swept behind an ear...

During college and residency years, he'd been involved with a consecutive string of women, none of the relationships lasting more than eight or nine months. The reason for the break ups segregated roughly into two bins: she wasn't what he was looking for, or she interpreted the long hours he needed for studying as delegating her to a runner-up status in his list of priorities, so she dumped him. And the ones in the second group had been correct. In a way.

Good grades—the caliber required to succeed in the extremely competitive environment—didn't come easily for him, so work did trump relationships. But at a price. Because fourteen years later, after finally graduating residency, at a time in his career he could finally stop studying his ass off, he had become jaded and cynical, believing that women were attracted to him now only because of the status and earning power neurosurgery brought. So he gave up looking for a permanent relationship, opting instead for a comfortable single life of superficial relationships that satisfied the basic need for sex and companionship.

Then, two years ago, Emily Miller changed his life. By the end of their first date he was smitten. Within weeks they were seeing each other exclusively, then became engaged. And for the first time in his single-man career, he'd found a woman he would be happy marrying. Then a drunk in a Toyota Tundra blew a red light and T-boned her Corolla, leaving her dead on arrival at Harborview Trauma Center.

Jin-Woo turned right, into a narrow alley, drove a half block and stopped beside a glass office building with a Japanese restaurant on the first floor. A smiling valet opened Jon's door and said something in Korean. A greeting, most likely, so Jon stepped out and nodded. Yeonhee joined him.

Jin Woo motioned them to a second, inconspicuous glass door to the left of the restaurant.

"Not there, here."

In the shadows at the far edge of the small parking lot, Feist dismounted, engaged the stand and exchanged his helmet for a New York Yankee baseball cap.

Staying in the shadows of a brick wall, he watched Ritter, the unidentified woman, and the doctor walk from the car to a door. The taxi following Ritter stopped further down the alley and cut its headlights. The Avenger slipped out and waited for the cab to leave before moving into the shadowy corner of the parking lot.

Feist unwrapped a cigar, clipped the end, and began to chew it, his mind sorting through various options.

After kicking off their shoes in a small lobby, Yeonhee, Jin-Woo, and Jon took a flight of stairs to the second floor where a Korean hostess in a slinky maroon dress met them.

She bowed and exchanged a few words with Jin-Woo

before leading them along a narrow hall to a sliding *shoji* screen. With another bow, she opened the screens, exposing a small private *tatami* mat room with an Asian style dining table in the center.

After Jin-Woo took the head of the table, he motioned Jon to sit on his left and Yeonhee on his right.

As soon as they sat, a waiter placed a large bottle of beer in front of Jin-Woo who promptly filled Jon's glass. Then Yeonhee poured his, before filling her own.

Jin-Woo raised his glass, said, "*Kanpai!*" using the Japanese toast. "To a successful project."

"Kanpai!"

They clinked glasses and sipped.

Immediately, various small dishes of *kimchee* and other food Jon didn't recognize began arriving. Jon realized he was starved and started in.

How long had it been since he really enjoyed a meal?

Talk turned to the clinical trial and the time-crunch they faced. The first task of the morning would be for Jin-Woo to escort Jon to Security for an ID card. Once that was finished, Jon would begin by multiplying the stem cells that would become neurons once implanted into the patients' brains. Laboratory stem cell cultures require twenty-four hours a day attention, especially if they are to become neurons.

The cultures must be kept sterile, and because they are being grown without a normal blood supply, they need to be maintained in a 95% oxygen environment, which makes transporting them difficult. Making matters worse is contact inhibition, a phenomenon that stops cells from growing if they touch each other. To prevent this, clumps of cells need to be gently broken apart by sucking them into a pipette and then releasing them back into the growth medium.

All this was running through Jon's head when Jin-Woo's cell phone rang. He excused himself from the room, leaving Jon and Yeonhee in awkward silence.

Finally, Jon asked, "This guy of yours, tell me about him."

She blushed and lowered her eyes to the slice of *kimchee* held between the tips of her chopsticks, then slowly replaced it in her rice bowl, set down her chopsticks and folded her hands in her lap.

"This is a problem, you see…he is an executive with Hyundai. He is what my girlfriends call a 'good catch.' He wants to marry me, but I don't know…"

"You love him?"

She immediately shook her head, paused and looked him in the eye.

"How about you? Have you found someone or is this still too soon after Emily?"

Why did the question embarrass him?

He stalled by exchanging his chopsticks for a sip of beer.

"Wayne keeps encouraging me to start going out again, says I need to put that part of my life back together, but I don't know…there's this neighbor…I know she's interested…" He looked at the bowl in his hand, replaced it on the table, "I asked her out but with what's going on, I haven't had a chance yet."

He glanced at the door, looking to see if Jin-Woo was headed back in.

When he didn't see him he said, "May I ask you something?"

She blushed and nodded.

"You may. And I may choose to not answer."

"Do you and Jin-Woo," with a nod toward the door, "have something going?"

With a dismissive laugh, her blush vanished. Again, she looked him in the eye.

"I'm sure people wonder because we work so closely together, but no."

"Did you? When you were in Seattle?"

She sighed, dropped her eyes, and after a moment shook her head.

"No. It was hard at the time because I was lonely and didn't know anyone in Seattle and it was difficult for me speaking English all the time. With him I could speak Korean, which was a relief. But I really didn't want to get involved with my boss. And I know he has girlfriends. A lot of Korean men are like that. It is accepted behavior. But I can't accept that."

Jon decided to change the subject.

"Your fiancé...tell me more about him."

She picked up her glass of beer and sipped, taking more time than needed.

"His name is Jung-Kyo, so you can call him that if you prefer. I don't know if I'm going to marry him or not. If I do, it would help provide for my mother. She lives in the town I grew up in, Kyonggi-Do, a city south of Seoul."

"So your father, is he not around?"

Yeonhee gave a bitter laugh.

"He moved out when I was thirteen...to live with a younger woman. He and my mom never really divorced, and he never assumed financial responsibility for us. It's always been up to my mother to support us. She does peoples' laundry for money."

Seemed like everything he asked became uncomfortable. He tried for something less emotional while still wanting to learn more about her.

"Us? You have brothers or sisters?"

"I have an older brother, but he can't really help out because he has severe psychiatric problems. He's calm one moment and then can be enraged the next. It makes it so no one will hire him. I have a younger sister, but she married when she was sixteen and is a baby machine—four children. It's hard for her and her husband to provide for their own needs.

"I wanted to stay at home and help mom, but two weeks after I graduated high school my brother went crazy and came after me with a butcher knife." She shivered and paused to rub her upper arm. "I made it to the bathroom and locked myself in.

The police came and took him away for a few days, but mom would never press charges because he's okay when it's just the two of them."

Yeonhee got a distant look in her eyes.

"I realized I couldn't stay at home any longer, so I came to Seoul to live with a girlfriend. I was lucky, found a job as a lab assistant. It paid enough money for me to start university. I still send money to my mom every month."

"Have you ever asked your father to help out?"

She looked him in the eye.

"I will never communicate with him. Never. Two weeks ago my sister called. My father's in hospital. Liver cancer she said. He's going to die within two or three months. He's my father and I know I should go see him, but I just can't do it. Not after what he did to us."

Jon decided to change the subject.

"When we finish this project—"

The door slid back open, and Jin-Woo stepped in.

"Sorry. That was the hospital. I had to take the call." He settled down on his cushion. "Where were we?"

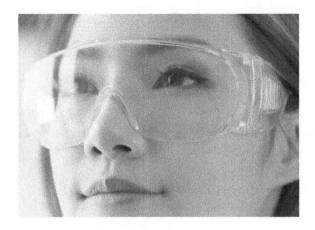

Chapter 24

AT THE FAR END of the parking lot, Nigel Feist chewed slowly and deliberately on an unlit Maduro torpedo when Ritter exited the restaurant followed by the doctor and the girl.

Quickly, Nigel dropped the cigar into his pocket for later.

Rather than pay attention to Ritter and his friends climbing into the Hyundai, Feist watched the other bloke. There he was, still cloaked in shadows. Then Nigel was moving, heading straight toward him, hand pulling the guitar string from his pocket, both ends twisted into loops around wooden pegs, the perfect weapon to sneak past TSA inspectors to assemble on site.

Feist slipped between two cars, coming up fast behind the Avenger, then looping the garrote around his neck while buckling the man's knees, he dropped him down behind another car. The man struggled but everything happened so fast, he never had a chance.

Nigel crushed his windpipe before he could even make a sound. Nigel held tight, fighting the struggling Avenger, keeping him back on his heels while his fingers clawed at the wire he couldn't loosen. Nigel listened for the crunch of gravel that would warn him of anyone approaching, as he patiently waited for his victim's brain to die.

Finally, the man became motionless, but Feist kept the wire taut for three more minutes. He wanted to make sure he didn't leave this guy alive. While he held on, he listened to traffic and the random sounds of a densely populated city.

Finally, he removed the wire, quickly rewound it and stuffed it back into his pocket.

Nigel found an unlocked car further down the alley, opened the back door, dragged the victim over and slid him onto the seat. He fished out the dead man's wallet and angled in the dim streetlight for a better view.

Aw, fuckin' Christ. A fucking FBI agent.

He just offed an agent of the fucking U S of A. Stunned, frozen in place, his mind raced through ramifications.

Fucking think!

Witnesses—any witness hanging around?

Carefully, he scanned the surrounding office buildings and was relieved to see most windows dark. But on second thought, for someone to see him down here in the shadows, their interior lights would have to be off, so blacked out windows didn't mean shit. Someone could be calling the coppers this very second.

Christ, don't just stand here.

Heart pounding, Nigel slid into the driver's seat and shut the door.

Fuck!

If the car belonged to a restaurant patron, the valet would have probably slipped the key above the visor. Ran his finger along the edge and sure enough, found it. He paused to think through his next move. Killing was not a part of the job he fancied. Hated it, in fact. But occasionally it was necessary to achieve what he was being paid for. But only after methodical planning.

With this one he'd been forced to ignore this rule. First,

Raymore's senseless execution of Lippmann. Now this. Navigating a sea of bad luck was what he was doing. Made every damn move on this job riskier, testing the boundaries of good fortune, putting him at high risk of exposure. Killing a fucking federal agent could be an absolute game-changer. Certainly it could bring a shitload of grief down on him. He needed to do something quickly, but very carefully. This fucking job was spiraling out of control.

Hold on! Think. What the hell was this bloke doing here?

Didn't seem likely the FBI would assign an agent to *protect* Ritter. More likely they'd use Ritter as bait for an Avenger. That had to be it. Meaning his murder could be made to look like...

Nigel scanned the immediate surroundings one more time, concentrating on anything that could incriminate him. He saw nothing, thought about it one more time, just to be sure.

No, nothing.

He glanced around, thinking, anything else to worry about?

Certainly didn't see anyone who might be a witness, but couldn't tell about the surrounding buildings. He'd waited in the alley long enough to be confident it was deserted except for the valet who spent most his time inside the restaurant. He popped the car trunk, wrestled the FBI agent into it, then was on a main street driving to no place in particular, just racking up miles between him and the alley. Four blocks later he tossed the shredded cigar out the window.

Sweating still, heart pounding, he tried to suck saliva into his mouth. No go. Dry as the Gibson Desert. Killed a fucking FBI agent, he did. There was an upside to it, he thought. A stroke of luck, spotting him, for if he hadn't, no telling what might've happened.

Time to quit, mate. Time to leave the business while you're ahead.

Fuck Stillman's money.

Neither political nor religious, Nigel worked only for the

money, taking any client who would pay. As a child, his family had struggled financially, leaving him to believe you best estimated a person's wealth by the location of their house. The wealthy built on the hilltops with panoramic views. The poor rented in flood plains with a view only of the neighbors' loo.

Growing up poor left him with a huge hunger for money, but not to the point of greed. Greed, he believed, was a major cause of bad judgment. Despite his financial advisor's words, he had enough now to live in a modest home on Mulholland Drive, a collection of expensive watches, and a garage filled with classic Harleys. In fact, right now he longed to be home instead of in fucking Seoul working this fucking job. Fuck the risk. Fuck working for buggers like Stillman. Soon as he got back to LA, he'd roll the flathead out of the garage and begin the cross-country motorcycle trip he fantasized about all these years.

Assuming of course, he could dump this fucking FBI agent and avoid capture. Survive this one last job and be done with it.

Feist turned off a busy street into a residential neighborhood of row after row of cookie-cutter concrete apartment buildings, each one distinguished from its neighbor only by a large block letter and number on the upper right-hand corner.

Very few windows glowed at this hour of night. Feist figured a big-assed complex like this would be a perfect place for a parked KIA to go ignored until the trunk stank enough to draw attention. Might be a couple days. By then he'd be long gone and done with this fucking job.

After wiping clean all interior and exterior spots he might have touched, he locked the doors and started walking in the general direction of the business district. Three blocks later he dropped the car keys in a drainage ditch. He'd cover at least two more miles before flagging a cab to take him to the center of town.

From there it would be easy to double back to the restaurant and retrieve his piece of shit rental cycle.

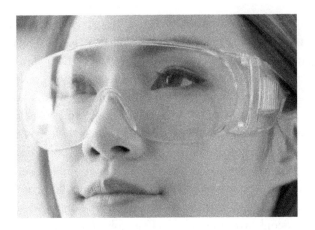

Chapter 25

THE INCOMING CALL on Stillman's cell didn't identify
the caller, so he figured it had to be Feist. He stepped to the
door to his office, scanned the area of cubicles in the immediate
area to confirm they were empty, and his secretary hadn't yet
arrived.

Satisfied, he closed the office door before answering with a
simple, "What up, dog?"

"Ran into a bit of a snag, mate."

"Hold on." Stillman angled the Venetian blinds to minimize
the risk of being lip read by someone with binoculars in a
neighboring building. "I'm back. What kind a snag?"

"You dead certain this connection's secure?"

Stillman laughed at Feist's paranoia, but at the same time
he appreciated it. It paid to be cautious when it came to these
things.

"Yes, but just to make sure, no names."

"All right, then." Feist hesitated. "That tail on our friend? A
government man is what he was. Federal."

"What?"

"A fucking FBI agent, he was."

Several things flashed through Stillman's mind, all competing for dominance. He paused to sort them out, selecting the most important.

"You said *was*. The use of past tense, is that intentional?"

"Right-right."

"Government, huh. You say FBI. You sure about that?"

"Oh, yeah."

Stillman thought about that and smiled. This could be a very good sign. The FBI would be tailing Ritter for only one reason: they swallowed the initial bait planted the night of Lippmann's murder. Perfect. The Avengers would be blamed just as long as he and Feist were careful enough to leave nothing to point back to them.

"Does that surprise you?"

Feist hesitated again.

"No. But what it does do is increase the risk of this job. And the bad news for you is this means a twenty percent surcharge that's neither negotiable nor delayed. I want it paid up front, now, meaning it appears in my account before I do any bloody more work."

"Understood." Stillman's smile broadened. *The extra cost? Chump change compared to what the formulation would net.* "I'll wire it immediately. Same account?"

"Right."

"Settled. New subject: you good to go as planned?"

"If the payment's in my account, I am."

"Excellent. Stay in touch."

Stillman set the phone on the desk and leaned back in the swivel chair. A week at most and, if things went a planned, Ritter's clinical trial would be a disaster, something the Koreans would never let see the light of day, and Ritter's technique would be his. When the time was right, and that would be soon, Trophozyme would apply to the FDA for the first-ever human stem cell implant to reverse Alzheimer's disease. He expected to get quick approval. After all, he would argue, it was previously reviewed and accepted by the NIH. This would place Trophozyme in the forefront of a huge lucrative market. Too bad Ritter hadn't jumped at the chance to be Chief Medical Officer. Would've been nice to have him on the team. Oh, well, we all make mistakes that ripple through the rest of our lives.

This, in fact, could be a pivotal point for my life.

Stillman grinned at the thought.

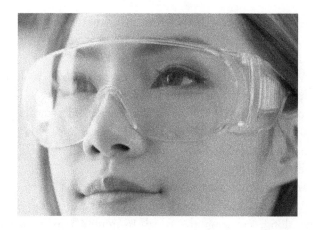

Chapter 26

JIN-WOO WAS ALREADY outside in his idling Hyundai when Jon walked out of the hotel lobby at 7:02 the next morning. As Jon climbed into the passenger seat Jin-Woo wished him good morning. Jon detected an unusual note of excitement in his voice, a departure from the usual monotone.

Jon awoke two hours earlier in spite of downing an Ambien before slipping into bed. It wasn't just the time zone change that accounted for the premature awakening. The anxiety over what they were about to embark on began yesterday, intensifying with each preparatory step completed. The stomach butterflies had been in full force when his eyes abruptly opened at 5:00 AM.

Today they'd start the cultures.

Two days from now, they'd implant the first two patients, The surgery would probably be the easiest step in the entire experiment. The most difficult part would be waiting the next four months before they could do the first tests to evaluate any change in the patients' dementia. Right now, he needed to stop thinking about the future and focus on all the little details leading up to surgery. If things went as they usually did, once they actually began culturing the cells, his anxiety would be pushed aside by his intense focus.

As they drove, Jin-Woo seemed more animated, quick with little nervous laughs and small attempts to crack jokes in spite of the cultural differences in humor. His looser mood helped ease Jon's edginess. More importantly, it helped convince him that Jin-Woo would put forth the same effort as Wayne.

How could he ever repay him?

Rush hour traffic was relatively light, allowing them to breeze along, covering the usual 15-minute trip in just over eight. Jin-Woo drove into the huge concrete garage behind the medical center, parked and led Jon through a damp musty basement to a windowless steel fire door.

From there they took the stairs to the first floor, went down a hall, turned right and were at the front door to Security. They entered a small reception area. Behind a laminate counter stood an officer with nicotine-stained teeth and a bad brush cut.

After a few words from Jin-Woo, the officer raised a section of counter and motioned Jon to follow him to a small room with a straight-backed chair. Immediately behind the chair was draped a blue sheet as a backdrop. Jon sat. The officer checked the display on the digital camera, adjusted Jon's head slightly before snapping a head shot.

Within a minute, Jon's face was embedded on a bar coded plastic ID card dangling from a lanyard, the entire procedure consuming less than five minutes. This security card provided Jon access to all areas, except a few restricted regions within the medical center, day and night.

While retracing the path to the garage, Jin-Woo explained, "This card is your key to the entire building. You must wear it at all times. If you not have it on, where security can see it, and they see you, they will make you to leave building."

They cut across the garage to an unmarked steel fire door into the largest rectangular building of the medical center complex. Embedded in the cement wall to the right of the door jamb was a card reader with a glowing red LED. Jin-Woo nodded at Jon's ID card.

"Go ahead, try it."

Jon swiped the card through the reader slot. A slight pause, followed by a metallic snap of a lock, the red LED turned green.

"See. It works."

The heavy door opened into an echoing, concrete hall with the disgusting smell of animal feces and dried food pellets. A half block of concrete hall took them to a no-frills freight elevator protected by a heavy steel mesh door so well counterbalanced Jin-Woo could raise it easily with one hand.

Once inside, Jin-Woo lowered the door and pressed 5.

As soon as they stepped off the elevator, Jon recognized the entrance to Jin-Woo's lab two doors down. To the right of the door jamb was a stainless-steel plate, speaker, number pad, and a glowing red light. Jin-Woo punched six numbers into the pad and hit the # sign. A computerized voice responded. Jin-Woo spoke slowly and clearly into the speaker grill. The door lock clicked.

"Voice recognition," Jin-Woo said proudly. "Very good security, I think. I installed it two months ago. We will program your voice soon as cultures begin."

Jon entered a spacious laboratory with temperature-controlled air carrying the hint of disinfectant. An impressive setup, lavishly outfitted with state-of-the art equipment greeted him: spotless black soapstone work counters, gleaming chrome and stainless-steel fixtures, six-foot high freezers, centrifuges, microscopes, computers—all the toys a well-funded neuroscientist could ever ask for as well as a status symbol of Jin-Woo's standing in Korean scientific circles.

Jin-Woo proudly showed Jon his supply of stem cells and the vials of various nerve growth factors to be combined to force the cells to eventually become neurons.

"I think you will find everything you need. You start. I will come for you at six, take you back to Walker Hill."

The plan was to work round the clock with one person always in the lab to prevent contact inhibition and perform the other routine chores that couldn't be confined to the hours of a standard workday.

Jon watched his friend leave and heard the metallic snap of the lock, immediately encasing him in heavy silence. For a moment he stood still, absorbing the sleek impressive laboratory, savoring the milestone so long in coming.

Along with this heady elation, fear began deep within his stomach. By nature, he wasn't a gambler, preferring to be relatively conservative in just about everything that influenced his life. The person to always do the responsible thing, to start saving for retirement as soon as his training ended, and his first real paycheck arrived.

At this moment, all his career chips—the accumulated worth of a dedicated professional reputation—were being risked on the outcome of this trial. The gravity of the course he was about to take became almost paralyzing.

Where to start?

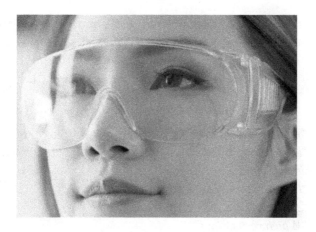

Chapter 27

AS YEONHEE LEE sat in the speeding subway, she felt a combination of anticipation and anxiety.

Her excitement was pleasantly titillating but made her mouth unpleasantly dry and her palms tingle. The anticipation of working in the same lab with a world-class scientist was, in itself, exciting.

Knowing she would be standing shoulder to shoulder with *him* gave her an extra layer of excitement.

She knew what it would feel like and wondered if he felt the same. She thought about the way her heart beat faster when they accidentally brushed against each other in the close laboratory quarters.

Did he ever wonder what was beneath the shapeless white lab coat?

Is he a good kisser?

But she had to concentrate on her work. For the next four weeks she needed to devote one hundred percent of her energy to the laboratory project. Jin-Woo made that clear. And because he was her boss, she would do it. But she also knew how much this project meant to Jon. And that, more than anything, cemented her commitment. But already Jung-Kyo was acting like a spoiled little brat. She though back to last night, when within five minutes of walking into her apartment, her phone rang.

"Where have you been?" Jung-Kyo asks.

"I told you. I had to go to dinner with Dr. Lee and his American friend."

"Had to? He said he'd fire you if you didn't?"

"No, but it was expected of me."

"Which restaurant?"

"Is that really important?"

"Oh, so you don't want to tell me. Is there anything else that happened last night you don't want to mention?"

"What are you implying?"

"Why so defensive? Are you hiding something?"

He was already jealous of the time she spent with Jin-Woo. They'd fought about it before.

"You fuck him, don't you."

"Believe what you want. I don't care."

"Why don't you just tell me."

"I need to hang up. I have a busy day tomorrow."

Did he really expect a girl her age to be a virgin?

Did she ask for a detailed list of every girl he'd ever slept with? Or the various things they'd done in bed?

As long as it wasn't her best friend, she couldn't care less who he'd slept with.

The airbrakes hissed for the Medical Center stop.

With her mind still caught up in personal issues, she flowed with the morning crowd onto the subway platform and then, in a clot of other workers, toward the escalators that would carry her up to the huge plate glass doors.

She pressed the button, spoke her name into the speaker,

heard the metallic snap of the lock.

A moment later she was inside, face to face with Jon.

Jon was checking email when the lock snapped, and the door opened and Yeonhee entered.

She smiled at him.

"Morning, Jon."

He responded with, "Morning," and immediately felt awkward, like a teenager.

She let the door close and lock automatically, quickly exchanging her black raincoat for a white lab coat, then came over to where he was working, her hands in the coat pockets, face serious, ready to begin work.

"You already started the cultures, I see."

"Yes."

She stood next to him, studying the flasks he just finished preparing, her familiar scent triggering memories. He studied the wisps of black hair loose around her right ear, and resisted the urge to reach out and touch her.

"Have you posted the schedule?" she asked.

He routinely posted a schedule on a clipboard near the counter for pipetting the cultures for the duration of the experiment. Whoever was responsible for the task on that particular shift initialed the sheet each time they completed it. He was impressed that she remembered such a little detail and took it as just one more indication of how meticulously she worked.

"Over there," pointing at it. Then, without thinking, asked the interrupted question from the other night. "When this is over and we have time, would you like to have dinner with me?"

She smiled broadly.

"Yes. I would like that."

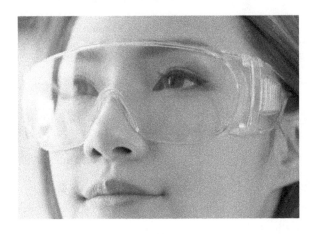

Chapter 28

JON PICKED UP the square, black, carbon fiber frame that looked like the skeleton of a box big enough to fit over a person's head.

He steadied it as Jin-Woo positioned the holes at the bottom corners over the patient's head. An hour earlier they'd implanted the first of their four patients. The surgery sailed along, without a problem, increasing Jon's confidence that the technique itself would not influence the outcome of the trial.

Jin Woo marked a dot on the scalp directly under each of the four fixation points with a sterilized felt-tipped pen. Four blue dots, two on each side of the head just above the eyes, the other two just behind the ears. They worked in one of the medical center's three MRI rooms, both surgeons in bright aqua blue scrubs, their watches, keys—anything metallic—locked securely in Jin-Woo's desk drawer. Even their credit cards— with magnetic strips on the back side—were stored well away from the scanners' strong magnetic fields.

The patient—the CEO's mildly demented father, a bald man with buck teeth—was on the MRI table under general anesthesia, his head supported by a small pedestal to allow the two surgeons to bolt the carbon fiber frame to his skull.

By acquiring a series of images with the frame rigidly attached to his head, the sides of the rectangular frame would be used to compute an XYZ trajectory to targets in the brain. Then, after drilling small holes through the skull, they would insert a small diameter probe to their target to deposit the stem cells that, hopefully, would become neurons. Theoretically this replacement brain tissue would resolve some of the Alzheimer's symptoms.

"You can remove it now," Jin-Woo said, reaching for a syringe of local anesthetic.

With the frame clear of the patient's head, Jin-Woo numbed the skin at each blue dot so the sharply pointed screws could be painlessly tightened into the man's skull to hold the frame rigidly.

Jin-Woo picked up a scalpel, muttered something to the anesthesiologist, and made a tiny stab wound at each of the four numbed injection sites.

Then to Jon: "Hold the frame, please."

Jon held the frame in position while Jin-Woo used a torque wrench to seat the four screws into bone, rigidly securing it to the skull.

Done, Jin-Woo muttered, "There. All set."

An MRI taken with this frame attached would then be used to plot the path to the injection site.

Jin-Woo inspected his work, nodded approvingly.

"We will get an MRI now."

Jon dropped into a chair to watch and wait. In a few minutes the second patient would be injected, then two more the day after tomorrow. If this worked, thousands of people just like his grandmother might be spared slowly atrophying lives in disgusting nursing homes. The ultimate test of his career's work was now underway. This realization almost overwhelmed him.

As he waited for the machine to crank through the images,

his initial relief and awe began to be eroded by fear. What would happen if a strange, unforeseen side effect occurred, like the implanted cells turned rogue and became malignant tumors?

Was that possible? Could he live with it if something so bizarre and unanticipated really happened?

Fear blossomed into panic, stealing his breath.

That doesn't happen, that doesn't happen...

Still...

Jin-Woo did a double take.

"You okay?"

Jon waved the remark away and tried to distract himself by watching the scanner on the other side of the control room window.

"Yeah, yeah, just...jet lag."

Jin-Woo leaned closer, squinting in the dim room light.

"You look pale."

Another wave of anxiety swept over him.

"No, no, keep going."

Jon watched the technician position the patient on the tray that slides into the tubular scanning gantry. Satisfied, the tech slowly moved the patient into the huge donut-shaped MR machine. Once completely inside, the tech hung the IV bag on a plastic stand and the anesthesiologist did a final check of the settings on the non-metallic anesthesia machine. After the crew was convinced they were ready, everyone left the room to begin the imaging.

Minutes later pictures of the patient's brain with attached frame began appearing on the control room monitor. Image quality was excellent, making the job of pinpointing the implant areas easy.

Jin-Woo muttered something to the technician.

Then to Jon: "We will go to surgery now."

The MRI files, transferred from scanner to the operating room via a fiber-optic network, arrived before the two surgeons.

Jon tapped the touch-sensitive control screen, moving from one "slice" of brain to the next, searching for the area to inject the cultured cells. Without a Korean medical license or hospital privileges, Jon could not participate directly in the procedure, so they operated under a verbal understanding: Jin-Woo did the actual surgery while Jon "made suggestions" or answered critical questions.

Hopefully, the other members of the operating room crew wouldn't realize Jon was the mind behind Jin-Woo's hands.

Jon flipped between the present image and the immediately preceding one, switching back and forth. Finally, he pointed at the screen.

"Here's your target. Might as well inject the remainder right here," indicating a region just behind and above the roof of the eye sockets.

Jin-Woo muttered approval, typed a few characters on the keyboard and magically a straight white line appeared, starting at the target site and continuing out through the top of the skull to intersect the carbon fiber frame, forming the X,Y,Z coordinates and trajectory.

Jin-Woo called out the coordinates and angle in English along with the depth from the skull to the target site as Jon wrote them on paper. As a fail-safe to make certain no targeting error occurred, a third observer verified Jin-Woo's figures matched those Jon transcribed. Jin-Woo drilled small holes in the skull through which the narrow cannula would be inserted into the brain.

Finished, Jin-Woo began suturing the small wounds, leaving Jon with nothing to do but sit in the chilly OR and watch—a role he hadn't played since residency. As he waited, the earlier anxiety crept back...only this time not so much fear as premonition...of something bad about to happen, causing him to reconsider....

Wait a few more days before implanting the next two?

Maybe even wait a couple months? See what happens to the first two before proceeding? Perhaps call Wayne to discuss it?

Heavy fatigue settled over him seeping into his joints, sagging his shoulders. Maybe jet lag. Maybe the culmination of ten years of work. Maybe both, rolled up into one heavy shroud. Whatever the cause, he became incredibly weary.

Jin-Woo's hands worked quickly, laying down double square knots, snipping off excess suture so that ends slipped below the surface of the scalp.

He mumbled something to the anesthesiologist before turning to Jon and saying, "His vitals are perfect. We have no problems."

A moment later Jin-Woo withdrew the black carbon-fiber frame from the patient's head, officially completing the second surgery, half the study. He slipped the mask down off his nose and grinned at Jon.

Thirty minutes later the two stood at Jin-Woo's locker pulling the sweat soaked scrub shirts over their heads.

Jon wondered if he dare call Wayne with the good news that both patients were awake now and doing well, but decided not to. Years of practice taught him to wait hours before declaring a case out of the woods.

"It goes well, I think."

Jin-Woo smiled and tossed his wadded-up scrub shirt at a laundry hamper. It sailed wide, landing on the floor a foot from the target where it would remain until a janitor cleaned up. Every surgery locker room Jon ever saw began the day neat and tidy, only to end up looking like a disaster relief station.

From his narrow metal locker Jin-Woo withdrew a white dress shirt with the loosened necktie still under the collar and began slipping an arm in.

"We meet for dinner later?"

Jon hesitated, the fatigue and fear still smoldering inside. Somehow celebrating seemed...premature?

Courting bad luck?

He leaned against a locker, massaged the back of his neck and once again mentally reviewed the surgeries. Everything seemed to go perfectly, yet…probably best to lay low for the evening. Not that he was superstitious…but he needed some down time anyway.

"Thanks, but think I'll just hang out at the hotel, go to bed early. These last couple weeks have been," he stopped short of saying murder, "hell. Want to catch up on some sleep, do some reading."

Jin-Woo shrugged on his suit coat and shot his shirt cuffs.

"You sure? We can make it short. Get you back early. No girls. Just us."

Jon reconsidered. The cultures for the next two patients were scheduled to start first thing in the morning. Tonight would be devoted to relaxation and rest.

"Naw. Thanks. Go ahead."

Chapter 29

NIGEL FEIST SLIPPED into the dimly lit room and moved quickly to the bedside. The patient lay flat on his back, snoring softly. He removed a syringe from his white lab coat, uncapped the needle and inserted it into the injection port of the IV line.

One gram of potassium chloride—enough to cause a cardiac arrest.

And because KCL was a normal blood electrolyte, its presence would go unnoticed during a routine autopsy unless the concentration was specifically tested. Even then, it would be hard to detect. And since the IV was already in place, there would be no tell-tale needle mark. He injected the bolus as rapidly as possible. The patient groaned from the sting as the salt burned through his vein, but by then Feist had the needle capped and back in his pocket. He placed his hand over the patient's mouth to stifle the groan. A few seconds later the old man was dead.

Then Feist was out of the room, across the hall, and into the second patient's room.

Jon became vaguely aware of the phone ringing. He reached for it and slammed his knuckles on an unyielding surface. Another ring. Up on his right elbow now, he glanced around the dimly lit room. Faint city streetlight filtered through the gap in the drapes, reminding him that he was in a Sheraton in Seoul.

A call? What the hell?

He rolled onto the opposite side, checked the glowing digital clock. 1:57 A.M.

The phone rang again.

Shit!

Middle of the night calls were never good news, especially with fresh post-ops in hospital. But they were Jin-Woo's patients, so no one should call him. Unless, of course, it was Jin-Woo with bad news. Bolt upright, he stared at the bedside phone, too paranoid to lift the receiver. Only Jin-Woo, Yeonhee, Stillman, Wayne, and Fisher knew he was here. A call from any of them could mean bad news.

Another ring.

Could be a wrong number...

The premonition hit the moment his fingers touched the phone.

"Hello."

"Sleeping well, mate?"

What the fuck?

A bolt of fear and panic struck.

Can't be.

Feist continued, "Your patients doing well, are they?"

Jon opened his mouth to answer but stopped.

Was Feist just fucking with him or did he actually know?

"Don't play dumb, mate. I'm talking about them geezers you and your little slant-eye mate did surgery on today. Hold on a moment, I reckon that's an inexactitude and I should really be calling it yesterday seeings how it's past midnight and all, right-right?"

Jon's mind blanked with fear. Feist *knew*. He goddamn

well knew.

How?

They'd been so careful…then remembered Fisher's warning. And the GI at the airport.

"If I was you, I'd surely want to know how them patients of yours are doing. Indeed, I'd be right worried, I would. What with all you got riding on 'em."

The phone went dead.

Gut churning, Jon cradled the phone. And realized he was holding his breath.

Now what? Call the hospital, check on them?

That's what he'd do if he were in Seattle, but Tyasami Medical Center, Seoul? Probably wouldn't work. Most of the nurses didn't speak English well enough to handle a surprise call from a doctor they didn't know, especially this time of morning. Jin-Woo would know.

He flipped on the bedside light, reached for his wallet and pulled out the scrap of paper with his cell number, and dialed.

Jin-Woo picked up with, "Jon?"

"Where are you?"

"Hospital called," Jin-Woo spoke in gasps, his English choppy from stress and agitation. "I drive there now. The patients…something wrong. Bad, I think."

"I'm on my way. Where should I meet you?"

"Don't know. Patient's room, I think."

Jon threw on the same clothes as yesterday, flew out the door and down the hall where he furiously punched the elevator call button over and over, as if repetition would make it arrive faster.

A cab idled a few feet from the hotel entrance when Jon blew through the front door. He threw open the passenger door, asked the young driver if he spoke English. He did. Jon said to take him to the medical center, an emergency. The driver took him seriously, peeling rubber out of the stately circular drive.

The deserted windy street took them to the bottom of Walker Hill in record time, but they hit a red light and stopped. Jon glanced around. No headlights anywhere. He reached between the seats, pushed the driver's shoulder.

"Go! Go! Emergency."

The driver glanced right then left then blew the red light.

How did he know? What have I done? Aw, man, those poor patients.

Jon's gut felt sick with nauseating guilt, just shy of vomiting. Fisher warned him, damn it, goddamned warned him.

Fisher. Call him.

Wayne too.

He patted his pockets.

Shit!

Forgot it. It was still back in the bathroom charging in the only 110 volt outlet that accepted US electrical plugs.

Then they were crossing the bridge over the Han River, moving fast, the medical center looming ahead. A moment later the taxi entered the empty circular drive and screeched to a stop outside the dark front entrance, the meter showing 15,000 *won*. Jon threw 20,000 into the front seat, scrambled into humid night air, slammed the door. The automated glass doors didn't open so he tried the manual one to the right. Locked.

Shit!

The cab had already left.

A glowing red dot on the wall next to the door caught his attention: a card reader.

There you go!

He reached for the badge on the lanyard around his neck and came away with air.

Aw, shit, did he forget that too?

Wait a minute…when did he last have it? Couldn't remember. Matter of fact, couldn't remember taking it off when he returned from the hospital earlier. But he must have.

Shit!

He pressed his face to the glass and peered in at the dimly lit deserted halls in hope of spotting someone who might open the door for him but saw only spacious marble floors and columns.

Fuck-fuck-fuck.

Wait a minute, the ER. Go there.

He started running the path that bordered the main building, worried about the time his stupidity was wasting. Should've known the front door would be locked. Why didn't he tell the cabbie to take him to the ER? Rounded a corner, saw the brightly lit ambulance bay with a glowing backlit sign in Korean characters. The automatic doors parted with a soft hiss as he approached. Five feet inside a security guard in olive drab paramilitary fatigues raised a hand for him to stop.

Jon blurted, "I need to find Doctor Jin-Woo Lee. He's here in the building on an emergency."

The guard studied Jon a moment before asking something in Korean.

Jon shook his head.

"You speak English? I don't speak Korean."

The officer waved over a nurse, said something to her. She smiled at Jon, gave a quick bow.

"Yes? May I help you?"

He was looking past her for signs to lead him to the elevators in the front lobby, but all signage was Korean characters.

"I need to find the neurosurgery ward."

She stood with hands clasped together at her waist.

"I am sorry, but these are not visiting hours. You are not allowed in."

He glanced from her to the guard, back to her.

"Please, I'm a doctor. I need to see Doctor Lee."

"I am sorry, but you are not allowed in now."

She gave another bow, ending the conversation.

"Goddamn it, page Doctor Lee. Now!"

The guard eyed him while speaking rapidly into a microphone clipped to his epaulet, then stepped directly in front of the nurse, blocking Jon from further entrance into the main hospital. He said something Jon didn't understand, then stood eye to eye for a moment. Suddenly the guard shoved Jon's chest, windmilling him backwards.

Jon regained balance thinking; *little fucker's stronger than he looks.*

The nurse put a hand on the guard's shoulder, spoke to him, then said to Jon, "The police are called. Either you leave now or you will be arrested."

Chapter 30

MAD, FRUSTRATED, NOT sure what to do next, Jon barged into his hotel room and flipped the wall switch.

Nothing.

The door clicked solidly shut behind him. Suddenly he was encased in dense darkness made worse from just leaving the hallway. He froze, the hairs down the back of his neck tingling with instinctive animal fear.

Was Feist here?

The call to the hospital…Feist knew he'd come…

Turn around and leave?

No, that would mean turning his back to the room. He dropped into a crouch, ready to spring at the slightest sound or perceived movement. And waited.

Slowly, his eyes adapted to the weak light, bringing with it familiar shapes: the beds, the dresser, the partially open drapes. Were things as he left them? He didn't see what might be the shape of another person in the room.

Aw, shit, the room doesn't have power without the card key in the holder.

Embarrassed at his paranoia, he cracked the door enough to insert the card. Immediately, the room lights flickered on, blindingly bright. With one hand still cautiously holding the door open, he scanned the room one more time. Just in case.

No, no one else here.

His cell was where he remembered putting it. But his ID...wasn't. Did he have it when he came back to the room? Had to think about that...he took it off when he hung it in Jin-Woo's dressing room locker, but did he put it back on after changing from scrubs to street clothes? Couldn't remember, probably because the act was so trivial it didn't warrant a memory. Still...not knowing left an uneasy queasiness festering. He glanced around the room, checking details, looking for things out of place.

The cell showed two missed calls, both from Jin-Woo. He highlighted the last one, punched SEND, walked to the window and opened the drapes wide. Something about the expanse of city lights and empty streets felt calming. Slightly. The connection clicked through.

Jin-Woo sounded breathless.

"Jon!"

Jon didn't like the sound of his voice.

"The hell happened?"

"Both patients dead."

His stomach dropped out. Both knees weakened.

"Dead?"

How could that be?

"Dead," Jin-Woo repeated.

He leaned against the plate glass for support as fireflies danced across in his vision.

"How? I mean, what happened?"

Jon could hear other excited voices in the background of Jin-Woo's end of the conversation.

"I do not know."

He took a deep breath and dropped heavily into the club chair, knocking over a small table in the process.

"I tried to—"

"The police are here. Asking many questions. I don't have answers."

Feist. Had to be.

"What—"

"They demand immediate autopsy."

"But—"

"I call back."

The line went dead.

Paralyzed with disbelief, Jon tried to process Jin-Woo's words, his mind flooded with questions, each fighting the other for dominance. Maybe it wasn't Feist. If so, what could possibly have gone wrong? The patients were doing so well when he checked…bullshit, it had to be Feist's work.

Fuck fuck fuck!

Fisher needs to know.

He scrolled through the programmed numbers, highlighted Fisher's cell, thumbed SEND, listened to the hollow echo of cyberspace, until Fisher picked up. Jon started straight into the story: Feist's call, the trip to the hospital, Jin-Woo's report. Fisher listened without interrupting. When Jon finished, Fisher backtracked through the sequence, point by point, making sure he understood exactly what happened. Not that the story was complicated.

Fisher said, "Okay, look, right now my big concern is to get you home safely. Feist is fucking with you, killing those patients. Fifty to one you're the real target. What I haven't told you is I have an agent watching your back. Had him on your flight over. Right now, he's your immediate asset. Here's what I want you to do. What time's it there?"

Jon checked the bedside clock radio. 2:59.

"Early morning, about three."

"Guy's name is Phelps. Gene Phelps. I'll get hold of him

soon as we hang up and have him come to you. What's your room number?"

Jon's mind blanked.

"Hold on," and checked the number on the phone. "Seven thirty-five."

"Seven thirty-five. Got it. I'll send him up soon as I reach him. In the meantime, get your ass on the first flight out of there. Doesn't matter if it's Chicago or Atlanta, just get the hell out of Korea. Phelps should be up there within a half hour. I'm sure you're not going to have to leave before then. He'll stick with you all the way out to the airport. We can handle this better if you're on US soil. Understand?"

Jon thought about the patients, their families, Jin-Woo and Yeonhee.

"But, I can't just leave."

"Think not? You want this fucker to off you next?"

Point well taken.

Still…he was torn.

Just leave without a word?

Fisher, obviously sensed his indecision.

"Think I'm joking? Let's review what just happened. Your friend Lippmann is shot to death while some shithead's telling you he's going to do the same to you if you don't shut down. So, what do you do? You go right ahead and do what he told you not to do. Tell me: what're the odds two patients just up and die within seconds of each other on the night of surgery?"

Fisher was right, of course.

"I know…"

Fisher continued, "Feist called you, for christsake. Knew where you were and your room number. It should be clear to you: unless you want to be next, get your ass on a flight out of there. You're dead meat until you're home."

"Okay, okay." Jon's mind was beginning to function again. "What about Wayne?"

"Don't worry. We'll look after him."

Jon scanned the room, mentally packing. He could call Jin-Woo and Yeonhee from the airport.

"The guy's name again, the one you're sending up?"

"Phelps. I know I don't need to tell you this, but don't open your door without checking who's there. Oh, and don't put your eye to the door's peep hole without first turning off the room light. Got it?"

Jon reached Wayne at his office and broke the news.

It took a moment for Wayne to totally process it, but when he did, he said, "Holy shit."

Jon told him to get out of the lab.

"Go home. But before you do anything, check in with Fisher. I'll feel a hell of a lot better if he knows where you are."

"What about you? What are you going to do?"

Jon agreed with Fisher's plan.

Okay, sure, he'd feel guilty for leaving Jin-Woo to deal with all the blowback, but realistically what good could he do other than provide moral support?

He certainly had no influence with the Tyasami hospital administration and, in fact, had been doing research in an institution where he held no privileges, so that point might work against him.

He said, "I'll get hold of Jin-Woo and let him know what's happening. I'm worried for him. Then I'm out of here first flight I can get."

Wayne sighed.

"What a mess."

"I know. Sorry, if I knew—"

"If you need me for anything, I'll be home soon as I can get there."

Jon tried Jin-Woo's cell but it rang through to a recording in Korean. Because the female voice spoke a language he didn't understand, he couldn't be sure he'd reached the right number, so called again. Same voice, same recording, so this time he left a message for Jin-Woo to return the call. He stood at the window to organize his thoughts.

When would Phelps arrive?

He opened the United Airlines website on the laptop but couldn't find a way to rebook an existing ticket, so powered off the computer. He remembered a leather-bound portfolio of important numbers in the center drawer of the desk, found the direct line for United Airlines and called, but after ten rings it rolled over to a recording. He tried Jin-Woo's cell once more. Again, no answer. He thought about calling Fisher but had nothing new to say. Plus, he didn't want Fisher distracted. Instead, he paced and waited for Phelps.

The phone rang. He jumped on it.

Fisher said, "Haven't been able to get hold of Gene yet, but I'll keep trying. You booked a flight out of there yet?"

"No. They're not answering the phone. But I checked on-line and nothing's leaving in the next couple hours anyway."

"Just go to the airport and get re-ticketed at the counter. Soon as I reach Gene, I'll call you. When he gets there get the hell out of there."

Jon hung up, checked the clock again. The minute hand didn't seem to be moving at all.

Why wait for Phelps? Why not go ahead and shower, shave, and leave?

Freshly showered and dressed, he tossed his clothes and shaving kit into the suitcase without bothering to fold anything, then returned to the window to fret. He really should tell Jin-Woo he was leaving. After all, he, Jon, was ultimately responsibility for the disaster he now had to deal with.

He dialed the number, but once again it rang through to the answering service. Not answering calls really wasn't like him. Even when tied up in surgery, Jin-Woo had the circulating nurse answer his cell and relay messages.

He called Wayne who was now at home with Michael.

Knowing he was safe made Jon feel better. Slightly. Then checked his watch again.

Where the hell was Phelps?

He began to wonder how *did* the Avengers find out? He and Jin-Woo had been so careful to disguise their actions. The patients were admitted under a false diagnosis, the surgeries scheduled as Parkinson cases. The only people who knew what they were really doing were Fisher, Stillman, Wayne, Jin-Woo, Yeonhee, and Tyasami's CEO. Unless of course the CEO told someone.

But that didn't make sense. Jin-Woo? What would he gain from that?

Yeonhee? Same thing.

Wayne? No way.

Stillman? No, that didn't make sense. He was the one....

Or did it?

Chapter 31

BY 5:45, JON was coming unglued. Jin-Woo hadn't called and wasn't picking up his cell. Nothing from Gene Phelps, and not even a call back from Fisher.

Screw it. Leave.

Couldn't tolerate being holed up in this damn room one moment longer. He needed to head for the airport and make flight arrangements at the counter.

Time to go.

He put his hand on the doorknob but didn't open it. Was Feist outside, waiting for him? He turned off the lights and peered through the security hole at a distorted fish-eye view of empty hall. At least, that small area was empty.

But what about down the hall in the elevator alcove?

Jesus, get a grip.

He took a deep breath, opened the door and was down the hall pulling his suitcase, just short of running. In the lobby he approached the reception desk manned by a pimply thin young male with thick black horn-rimmed glasses. The man bowed.

"May I help you?"

"Can you rearrange airline reservations?"

The guy appeared lost.

"Rearrange?"

Jon tried to explain but the receptionist didn't understand.

With a smile and a bow, "One minute, please," and vanished through a discreet door in the darkly stained walnut paneling behind the desk.

A moment later, a plump middle-aged woman with a round head, square glasses, and short black hair emerged through the doorway. Her speech carried a slight British accent.

"May I help you?"

Jon asked the question again and to his relief, she nodded.

"Yes."

He slid his ticket across the black granite counter.

"I have an emergency at home and need to move my return flight up to today, soon as possible."

"Certainly. I will see what I can arrange. Please, have a seat in the lobby." She swept a palm toward a grouping of ornate red velvet chairs. "I'll fetch you as soon as I have an answer."

Unable to sit, Jon paced, stealing glances at the two doormen waiting patiently outside, ready to open a car door or hoist luggage into a trunk. The sky hinted of impending dawn.

The smiling woman waved him back to the counter.

"Mr. Ritter?"

"Yes?"

"At this moment I am unable to obtain a confirmation for you, but there is a possibility of a flight to Seattle this afternoon, leaving at seventeen hundred for Seattle through Narita. Is that agreeable?"

An eleven hour wait. Seemed like an eternity now that he was anxious to leave. But he reminded himself, sitting in an airport lounge was probably safer than waiting here.

"Nothing sooner?"

She shook her head.

"Not unless you wish to fly through Chicago."

"When does that leave?"

"Fifteen hundred."

Two hours earlier but ultimately it would result in a Seattle touchdown hours later than the direct flight.

"No, that won't work. What about San Francisco, Portland, Los Angeles?"

"All booked."

"Okay, I'll take the Seattle flight later today."

She began typing on a keyboard. He watched, unable to keep from glancing over his shoulder to scan the lobby for Feist, Fisher's warning eating away at him.

He asked her, "How soon will you know?"

Eyes on the monitor, she said, "Most likely it will take an hour or so," then glanced at a delicate gold Seiko on her wrist. "Our café opens at six thirty. That is not too far away. I suggest you have breakfast and when you finish, check back with me."

Jon scanned the front doors again, coaxing himself to calm down, aware that he was only making the anxiety worse.

"That'll work. I'll be back."

Which was worse, waiting here, out in the open, or back in his room?

Might be safer to just pack and get out to the airport, but he had a few things to tie up before he'd leave.

"Very good, sir."

Back in his room, suitcase next to the door, Jon flicked the TV to CNN Asia on the off chance of catching a story about the dead patients but they cycled through the same old stories and video clips as earlier. Feeling the need to talk to a friendly voice, he called Wayne.

"There's a good chance I can change my ticket to this afternoon. I'll let you know soon as I find out."

Wayne said, "Want me to pick you up at the airport?"

"No," Jon tried for a joke, "Michael might get jealous."

"Ha! Dream on."

The room began to shrink, become too hot, the air too

stale. The receptionist was right, the restaurant would be the better place to wait. He told Wayne he'd call with the flight number and left the room without bothering to look through the security hole this time. The way he felt now, it'd be better to encounter Feist and just be done with it.

An attractive waitress in a sky blue *hanbok* and woven sandals led him to a table for two next to a window with a view of the parking lot and garbage cans at the back of the hotel. She handed him the ubiquitous steamy towel roll and gave him a choice between the standard breakfast, the buffet, or items from the menu. He opted for the standard Korean breakfast and coffee. She bowed and shuffled away with the flat-footed step so common to women who grew up wearing sandals.

Minutes later, she returned with a breakfast tray and coffee. He drank the first cup and a refill but only poked at the rice, *kim chee*, and fish in spite of an emptiness in his stomach. After the second cup he decided he really couldn't eat, put down his chopsticks, and paid the bill.

Back at the registration desk he took his place in line behind three guests checking out. He caught the eye of the woman who had helped him before. She smiled, raised an index finger in the universal sign to hold on while she finished dealing with next person in line.

Jon stood nervously drumming his fingers on the granite counter, stealing an occasional glance at the revolving door in spite of knowing Feist wouldn't do anything here in the open lobby. More likely, if he were to do something, it would be in his room. Which was all the more reason to head to the airport now. He glanced at his watch again, but the minute hand seemed to be at the same spot as the last time he checked.

The assistant manager disappeared into the room behind the counter and reappeared a few seconds later, all smiles, his United Airlines ticket folder in hand.

"Doctor Ritter, I was able to confirm the change in flights.

However, I was unfortunately unable to obtain an aisle seat for you. A window seat was the best I could do. Does this meet with your approval?"

He wanted to hug her.

"Perfect. Thank you," and slid the ticket folder into the breast pocket of his blazer.

"Will you be checking out now or later this morning?"

He was already sliding his Visa card across the counter.

"Now, thank you."

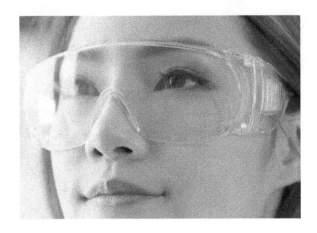

Chapter 32

A MUTED DING announced his floor. The elevator stopped its ascent and the doors slid open for him. He planned to stop at his room only long enough to grab his luggage and return to the lobby, catch a cab to the airport. Once there, he'd confirm his seat assignment, then spend the rest of the morning and afternoon waiting in the Business Class lounge for his 3 PM flight. He would be safer there. Or at least having other people around would make him *feel* safer.

He turned left into the hall to his room and stopped. Three doors away, two police officers stood outside an open room. His room, he realized. The officer furthest from the door noticed him, reached out and tapped the other one on the shoulder. The second officer turned to look.

Shit! Why would cops be in my room?

Idiot. They want to question you.

No, that didn't feel right, there more to it…their posture…something in the first cop's expression.

Too late now to turn around.

That would certainly appear suspicious. Question was, did

they recognize him? Four doors past his room the hall turned left, eventually dead ending at a fire door to a stairwell. Could he bluff and walk past them?

Jon continued forward, hoping they'd interpret his hesitation as nothing more than surprise at the encounter. The first cop watched him approach, not moving from the center of the hall, forcing Jon to slow. Then, at the last moment before Jon would be forced to stop, he stepped aside. Jon took the opportunity to steal a quick glance at his room. A stocky Korean, with the face of a bulldog, a military brush cut, and a poorly tailored brown suit, stood just inside the door facing the bathroom, cell phone against his ear. His peripheral vision must have caught the hallway motion, because he to turned to look directly at Jon's face. A flicker of recognition registered in his eyes.

Jon continued walking without slowing, made the corner and sped up, heading straight for the metal fire door with a glowing green EXIT sign overhead. He started trotting, hit the horizontal push bar on the door and let momentum carry him through into the landing. Then was flying down stairs, covering two flights before he stopped to listen for pursuing footsteps. Heard only eerie hollow silence and his heavy fast breathing. Sucked down a deep lung full of air, palm-wiped his face, deliberately slowed his breathing and tried to steady his shaky legs.

He took another moment to straighten his blazer and finger comb his hair before opening the door to a hall identical to the one he just left two floors above. Trotted to the elevator alcove and punched the call button, waited a beat, punched it again even though it was glowing.

Shit! Come on, come on!

An Asian male pulling a suitcase entered the alcove and stood next to him. Jon clasped his hands together to mask the shakes. Heart pounding, Jon patiently waited, ready to bolt at the first sign of...

Shit. Come on, elevator.

An eternity seemed to pass before the ding finally came as the light above one of the four doors lit up. A moment later the door opened to an empty cage. Jon allowed the man to enter first, followed him in and faced front, saw he'd already pressed the button for the lobby level.

So far, so good. Maybe the cop really didn't recognize him. Maybe their presence in his room wasn't all that ominous. Maybe he could get to the airport and the hell out of Seoul. But none of that would happen unless he left the building immediately. Fisher's alarm and insistence he leave town kept reverberating through his mind. And his missing ID card was bothering him greatly.

All he had to do was make it out of the lobby and catch a cab to Inchon airport. To hell with his things that remained in the room. They were the least of his worries and all easily replaced. He checked the inside blazer pocket and was comforted to find the ticket safely tucked away.

The door opened. He stepped out first, moving as quickly as possible without attracting attention, on into the lobby heading for the front door.

Fifty feet from freedom, a hand clamped onto his arm as a voice said, "Doctor Ritter?"

He jerked his arm to free it, intent on ignoring the voice, but the hand seemed to have a death grip on him.

"Doctor Ritter!"

For a split second he considered lying. Instead, he turned to the voice and came face to face with the bulldog in the poorly tailored suit.

"Yes?"

He released Jon's arm and held up an ID.

"Inspector Park, Seoul Metropolitan police. You must come with me for questioning."

For two long seconds he sized up Park's face: hard, determined, prematurely sun wrinkled and brown, as accusatory as his tone. He glanced at the ID filled with meaningless Korean characters and a picture. Official looking. For whatever that was worth.

"Questioning? For what?"

Park's breath reeked of garlic and tobacco.

"The deaths of your patients."

Those five words carried alarming incrimination. No fucking way would he go anywhere with Park. Then again, what options did he have? Couldn't run. Could he call Fisher and have him talk to Park? And say what, exactly?

Try to bluff? By doing what?

Besides, Park saw him pass the room moments ago, so how could he explain that?

Figured his best bet was getting a shot at the airport, so said, "I just heard about that. But you're mistaken. They're not my patients. They're Dr. Lee Jin-Woo's. In fact, he just called, wants me there immediately. That's why I'm in such a hurry. So, if you'll excuse me, I'll be happy to talk with you later."

Park's eyebrows raised in mock surprise.

"You just heard about their deaths?"

Two uniformed police materialized from nowhere to close ranks with Park.

Heart pounding, Jon swallowed his next words. Park seemed to know he just lied. How? An icy cloud blew through his intestines.

What did Park know that he didn't?

They stood looking at each other, Jon trying to appear as calm as he possible could.

Park narrowed his eyes, said, "I don't believe you. You come for further questioning."

"Sure. Glad to. But first, how about one hour at the hospital? Doctor Lee wants me there. As I said, once I finish there, I'll gladly come in for questioning."

One hour and he'd be on the next flight to fucking Botswana if that was the first one out of Korea.

Park nodded, as if affirming an impression rather than agreeing.

"Then I have no choice but forcibly hold you on suspicion of two counts of murder."

"Murder?"

"We do not know this for certain. Not yet. When our medical examiner finishes, we will. Okay, so you come now."

Park grabbed Jon's arm, jerked him toward the hotel entrance with surprisingly force for a man his size.

Jon dug in and tried to pry Park's hand away, but his iron grip tightened. Jon was finally able to wrench free, but the two uniformed officers were on him, pulling both arms behind him. Jon glanced around them to see who was watching, thinking if he raised a fuss, maybe...

"Get your hands off, goddamnit," he yelled. "I'm a United States Citizen. I demand to speak with the Embassy."

Park and the uniforms shoved him toward the door, throwing him off balance, only the officers' grip keeping him from falling.

Park said, "No. We talk. You call no one."

Two additional police rushed through the revolving door to help. Park barked a word and the officers stopped dragging Jon.

Park stepped in front of Jon, held out a hand.

"Your passport."

By now a small crowd of guests and employees were glued to the scene but from a safe distance, no one willing to interfere.

Ignoring Park, Jon turned to the onlookers.

"I'm a US citizen. Someone please call the Embassy for me." Then, to the desk clerk: "Give them my name. Have someone come to help me. Please."

Park said something to the newly arrived officers, and one reached into Jon's blazer pocket and came away with his passport and airline ticket. Then Park dramatically patted him down, clearly playing for the audience.

Again, Jon frantically scanned the crowd for someone

willing to help him, but no one moved. A few hotel employees looked away.

Jon called, "Someone help me. Please."

Park tauntingly waved the passport in front of Jon's face. "You have no choice."

He nodded for the cops to continue dragging him toward the door.

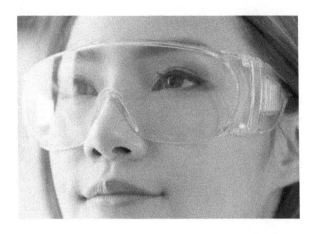

Chapter 33

THE CAR'S A/C either didn't work or was purposely switched off with the windows closed, turning the interior hot and muggy, making the black vinyl upholstery stick to Jon's skin with every move.

The back seat reeked of garlic, body sweat, and old vomit. Jon hunched forward, elbows on knees, to keep his back off the seat. He asked Park several times to tell him the grounds for being held on suspicion of murder, but Park remained impassive in the passenger seat, saying only an occasional Korean word or two to the driver. An attitude, Jon suspected, was deliberately orchestrated to piss him off.

Well, it was working.

He figured any show of the intense anger boiling inside would only feed into whatever mind game Park was playing. What bothered him most was the gnawing suspicion that Feist somehow set him up, and that he'd fallen for the trap. If Park only intended to ask him a few questions, why take the passport? Why treat him like a common criminal? Thankfully, he hadn't been restrained with flex ties or metal handcuffs. He wasn't sure he could tolerate that without going batshit.

He flashed on the TV series *Locked Up Abroad*. He had seen trailers for it but never the actual show, yet even the trailers were sufficient to leave little doubt that huge problems could arise from being arrested in a foreign country. Although he'd been deceptive about the intent of the surgeries, he hadn't murdered the patients. Sure, it would be a bit awkward explaining the deception part, and the other...well, Park could talk cop-to-cop with Fisher to resolve whatever misunderstanding there might be. He almost talked himself into relaxing. Almost. Still...

A maze of congested streets, drab concrete apartment buildings, and a patchwork of small shops sped past. He didn't know a thing about how the Korean legal system worked. He'd heard news stories and seen movie depictions of egregious civil rights violations in various Asian countries.

Did those include Korea?

At the time, he hadn't paid that much attention, for some reason assumed they related mostly to China. Now he wasn't sure.

With each passing second, his fear grew stronger. Maybe he really was in serious trouble. After all, like Fisher said, two dead post-op patients certainly raised suspicions.

But of what?

Hadn't Park mentioned waiting for the autopsy, so nothing was for sure yet?

Yeah, but he used the word 'murder.'

He'd call Fisher. Fisher would vouch for him.

The unmarked police car dipped down a ramp into the Seoul Metropolitan Police Agency then nosed into a slot in a garage half-filled with other police vehicles. Jon followed Park to an elevator, the uniformed cop/driver bringing up the rear. They entered the cage and rode up six floors where Park led him along a worn linoleum hall to an eight-by-eight foot room of beige walls, recessed fluorescent lighting, three mismatched chairs, a scarred Formica table bolted to the wall and one tar-coated ashtray. The humid warm air reeked of stale nicotine, staler sweat, and raw fear.

The door slammed leaving Jon alone.

He tried the doorknob. Locked.

Of course.

A rectangular mirrored window was recessed into the wall on his right. Park would be watching, he figured, purposely making him wait in an attempt to increase his anxiety. Well, hell, it was working. Unable to sit, he paced in tight circles, working through an explanation of the surgery. Checked his watch again. Jesus, if this went on too long, he'd miss his flight.

Five minutes crawled past.

He continued circling, unable to relax.

The door opened and Park stepped into the cramped room. Jon checked his watch again and discovered he'd been waiting thirty goddamn minutes. But he reminded himself, he still had enough time to easily catch his flight.

Park slammed the door, pointed to a chair, said, "Sit."

An order instead of an offer. Park hooked a thumb over his belt, pulled back his suit coat exposing an empty hip holster. With his other free hand, he slapped a sheet of paper on the table.

Jon ignored the paper, said, "You said you had questions. Go ahead, ask whatever you want. I have things to do today."

"Your purpose here in Seoul, Doctor Ritter?"

The words sounded more of an accusation than a question. He didn't like the tone with which this interview was starting. It made him considered his answer carefully. Probably best to stick closely to the truth without divulging any additional information.

"Well?" Park asked.

"I already told you. I work with Lee Jin-Woo on some collaborative research. We've worked together for years. Go ahead, ask him. He'll verify it."

Park's eyes bore into him.

"Doing what exactly?"

"Like I said, research. He's worked in my lab in Seattle, and I've worked in his here before."

Parked leaned against the door, a subtle reminder that he held the power over who could open it and when.

"What research?"

"Does it matter?"

"I don't know if it does until I hear your answer."

Shit.

Less than a minute and this was already tedious.

"We work with stem cells.

"And do what with stem cells?"

Jon looked at Park's cold, unblinking, irritatingly righteous eyes.

"Why am I here?"

Park smirked.

"I ask questions. You answer. What you do with stem cells?"

Jon realized the tactic: piss off the interviewee, making it easier to blunder over lies. But he really had nothing to lie about. Well, except the surgeries. He blew a long breath and palm wiped his face.

"Our ultimate goal is to find a way to cure dementia. You know what that is?"

"Why were you in Tyasami last night?"

Jon started to deny being there but caught himself. He *had* been. Momentarily. Just never further than the Emergency Room.

"I wasn't *in* the hospital last night."

Which, if taken literally, was true. He didn't elaborate.

Park appeared skeptical.

"You were seen there."

"Yes. I was outside the hospital, but never was able to get inside. I took a cab from the hotel to the medical center but the guard in the ER wouldn't let me enter."

"Why not?"

"Because I didn't have my ID. I think I left it there yesterday."

The questions coming rapid fire now, Park not giving him a chance to think about answers.

"What time was this?"

Jon remembered seeing the bedside clock when reaching for the phone. Add the time to dress, catch the cab...

"Sometime after two...two-fifteen, maybe, something like that. Yeah, two-fifteen sounds about right."

His tone now sarcastic and drenched in doubt.

"But you didn't have ID?"

"Right. I, eh, left it somewhere. I don't remember exactly where."

Park appeared even more doubtful than before.

"Look, this is simple enough to verify," Jon said. "Find out which guard was on duty last night and ask him. There was a nurse there too. She translated for the guard because he doesn't know English very well."

The weightless in Jon's gut intensified. Park clearly wasn't buying it. Mind racing, he searched for other details to validate his story.

"Oh, here's another thing: I spoke with Dr. Lee moments before leaving the hotel. Check the phone records."

Park poked a finger at him.

"*Before* that. Where were you?"

Jon licked his lips, checked his watch again.

"Asleep. In bed asleep. Why?"

Park's eyes bore into him.

"Then how do you explain the computer records that show you entered hospital at one twenty-two?"

"What records?"

"Security system records. They show you entered through front door at one twenty-two."

The missing ID.

Shit!

He tried to swallow but his mouth was dry. He was sweating, his heart beating wildly, all obvious signs of stress which Park surely noticed. He held up both hands in surrender.

"Whoa...stop. I told you, I lost my ID. I couldn't have used it. Listen, there's some background you need to hear about this that will clear things up. Maybe it will be easier for you to hear it from someone else in law enforcement so let me give you the name and phone number for an FBI agent in Seattle. In fact, I'll call him. His name is Special Agent Gary Fisher. May I call him for you?"

"Why I need to talk to him?"

"Because I'm being set up. Framed. He'll explain it to you since clearly you don't believe me."

Park continued to lean against the wall, arms casually folded across his chest, face expressionless.

"No. You tell me."

Jon took a moment to organize the story before starting with Lippmann's murder and the Avengers' threat. By the time he got to Feist's call to the hotel room earlier in the morning, it was clear from Park's face that he didn't believe a word.

In desperation, Jon said, "Please. Call Fisher. Hear it from him."

Park pushed off the wall, blocking the door.

"You just admitted you were at hospital early this morning."

This time Jon turned to the mirrored window to answer, making sure any recording captured his words.

"Fuck no, I didn't! I said I WENT TO THE EMERGENCY ROOM. I didn't go further into the hospital. The nurse and guard wouldn't let me get past the door because I DIDN'T HAVE ID. That was the only time since leaving yesterday late afternoon, that I was ever near the medical center."

"Why didn't you have your ID?"

Park's tactic seemed clear. Keep hammering and probing his story repeatedly from different angles mining for inconsistencies and contradictions until he trapped Jon in a lie. At this point Jon wondered if he should simply give up on making the afternoon flight, stop the interview and demand to speak to the American Embassy? Then, if he could convince Park he was innocent, he still had enough time to catch his flight. Once he was out of Korea…

He gave it one more shot with, "I was sound asleep when Dr. Lee called and said there was a problem and wanted me there. He hung up. That was it. By then I was upset and in a hurry. I got dressed and left. I didn't even think about the ID."

"When did you lose it?"

Jon realized this was a no-win interview, especially with his frustration building. He stopped pacing.

"I told you, I don't know. Just fucking call Fisher, all right?"

Park raised his eyebrows.

"He is here in Seoul?"

Park seemed to be intentionally badgering him now, trying to provoke him. He drew another deep breath and shook his head.

"I already told you that, too. He's in Seattle."

"Then how can he tell me you were not in the hospital?"

"That's not the point. The point is he can tell you who killed the patients."

"Ah, so you admit patients are murdered?"

Stunned, Jon stared at Park. The anger of a moment ago suddenly turned to raw fear as what just happened clicked into focus: instead of a fact-finding interview, Park intended this to be a confession. Jon raised a palm, the interview had gone far enough, he needed help.

"We're done here. Before I say another word, I want someone from the United States Embassy in this room with me."

Park shot his sleeves and straightened his suit coat.

"Why you want that? You do something wrong?"

"What don't you understand about what I just said? I want to talk to the United States Embassy."

Park raised his palms in mock innocence.

"You refuse to cooperate with an important investigation into the death of two Korean citizens?"

Jon turned to the mirror again and spoke slowly and clearly.

"I want it on record that I am a United States citizen being held against my will. I have requested to contact the United States Embassy. Before I say another word, I want to talk to someone from our Embassy. Also, for the record, my passport has been forcibly taken from me by Detective Park. There must be something in the Geneva Convention to cover this." Then, pointing at Park. "I will be happy to answer this man's questions once a representative from the US government is present."

Detective Park asked, "Mind if I smoke?"

"Yes I— "

"Is okay? Good."

Jon heard the metallic clink of a lighter lid, the scrape of a flint wheel, the hard snap as the lid closed, followed by a deep exhale. He smelled fresh cigarette smoke as he continued to face the mirrored window, his back to Park. He could see Park's reflection in the window, still blocking the door in an arrogant posture.

Park said, "I know many things about your business in Seoul, Dr. Ritter. Many things. If you refuse to cooperate, I will make things uncomfortable for you."

Jon suspected Park intended to egg him on into more statements to use as contradictions, so decided to not answer.

After a moment of silence, Park said, "You not think so? I know you come to Seoul to experiment on innocent Korean citizens. This you do because the FDA forbids you do the same experiment in your own country."

"Not true." Jon started add more but stopped.

Don't say another word.

"I know you do this work without hospital okay." Park paused to let this new bit of information sink in. "I know you put something in those patient's brain. I know the patients now dead." Another pause. "These are things you want American Embassy know about? I think not."

Park stepped closer, pointed a finger at him.

"For these reasons you must consider your situation very very carefully. Very carefully." Park gave a self-satisfied nod. "I come back in few minutes with cup of tea. This give you time to consider. I not be so patient next time. Oh yes," he pointed to the paper on the table. "Read confession carefully. You sign. Things will go much better when you sign." His English was worse, as if trying to make Jon believe he had trouble with it. "You sign, I make sure you treated good and tell American Embassy you here."

Jon heard the door open, then footsteps. He looked up to see two muscular guards enter.

Park said, "Oh, yes, security guard in Emergency Room remember you very well. He sign statement he see you in hospital. Westerners in a hospital in middle of night are very obvious."

The door latch clicked shut. The guards assumed parade rest, one to each side of the door.

Why were they here in a room this small and secure? There was no need for even one. But two?

Shit!

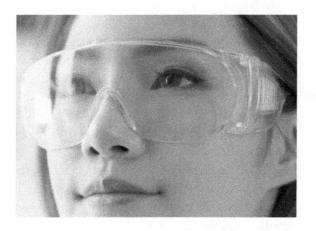

Chapter 34

THIRTY MINUTES LATER Park opened the door. The guards stepped out so he could enter. They closed the door, leaving Jon and Park in the cramped room. Park looked at the unsigned confession on the table.

"You refuse to sign?"

"You're not listening, so I'll say it again: State Department. I'm not doing anything until someone from the State Department is standing here to advise me. And a lawyer. Maybe both."

Park gave a what-do-I-care shrug.

"You wait long time, then. Day. Week. Month. No matter. I wait too."

Without another word, Park left the room and closed the door. This time taking the guards with him.

Now alone in the room with his back to the two-way glass, Jon fished his cell phone out on the off chance something had changed since the last time he checked. So far he hadn't been able to get a signal and suspected the room was shielded.

Maybe he could get a signal from a different room...maybe

a bathroom? Worth a shot.

He tried the door but, as suspected, it was locked. He pounded on it with the flat of his hand. No answer. Pounded again with more insistence. Several seconds later the door cracked open and a guard peeked in. Jon pressed both hands against his stomach and moaned.

"I need to go to the toilet," and pointed to his groin to clarify the point.

The guard studied him a moment before grudgingly opening the door wide enough for him to step into the hall and glance around. To his amazement, the other guard wasn't there, leaving just him and the one guard alone in the hall. The guard motioned him to go left, and Jon began slow crouching steps as if in pain. Muttering Korean, the guard shoved Jon's shoulder. Jon stumbled into the wall, glanced back at the guard, noticed a matte black gun in a hip holster. Without a second thought, he knew what he should do. Gave another moan and twisted around, knees bent and butt against the wall, hugging his gut.

"How far?" he asked.

The guard pointed to a door with a sign in Korean characters, then stepped away, eyeing him with suspicion. Grimacing, Jon gasped. The guard grabbed him by the collar and tugged him toward the door. Using the momentum of the tug, Jon lunged, wrapped his right arm around his shoulder and, putting all his weight into it, drove him hard into the opposite wall, heard a grunt and gasp of air leaving his lungs and the guard went down onto his knees, but not before Jon had the gun out and the barrel against his head.

He pointed at the door.

"Open it."

Eyes wide, the guard nodded.

"Inside."

The guard stepped in. Jon shut the door and flipped the latch, started trotting down the hall, dumped the gun in a trashcan and kept going, frantically trying to reconstruct the route to the basement. But he'd been in a mental fog when Park brought him up to this floor so had no idea which way to go. He continued along the hall looking for an exit sign or elevator. The hall dead ended into another. Jon turned left and ended up face-to-face with a uniformed cop coming the other direction.

Without missing a beat Jon asked, "Where's the elevator?"

The cop stopped, sized him up, replied in Korean.

Jon gave him a friendly tap to the shoulder.

"That's okay. I'll find it," and kept moving, fighting the urge to run, but knowing that would only draw attention.

At last, an elevator. He punched the down button.

Come on, come on.

Footsteps approached. He froze, face forward, eyes on the crack between the elevator doors. The footsteps stopped. He could feel the presence of someone next to him.

Have to do something.

Jon turned to a lanky, weathered face in horn rims and charcoal gray suit. Jon nodded.

"Morning."

The man returned the nod just as the elevator dinged. The elevator door clattered open and Jon nodded for the man to enter first. Two uniformed cops already inside, stepped aside to make room. Sweating, Jon followed him in and checked the panel of buttons. The ones for floors one and minus one, which he assumed to be a basement, already glowed. He faced forward and waited for alarms to start ringing or shouts. The doors closed and the cage started down.

The man asked, "You American?"

Mind racing for an excuse, Jon turned to him, hand extended.

"Jim Laing, Seattle Police. Sorry, didn't know if you spoke English."

They shook hands.

"Yung, Chen-Wa, Seoul Metropolitan." He eyed Jon a moment. "Your badge, where is it?"

Jon stared back at him in a bewildered moment, thinking, game over. Felt all three sets of eyes now drilling into him now and sweat streaming from his scalp. It clicked...should be wearing an ID badge, probably with VISITOR on it. Jon looked down at his lapel, felt along his neck, checked his blazer pockets. "I...don't...know...it was here..."

He probed his neck again in case they gave issued lanyard rather than clip-on tags.

"Who you with?"

Shit!

Gave the only name he could think of: "Park. Detective Park."

The cage jerked to a stop and the doors slid open, exposing a marble and glass lobby with a ceiling of tinted glass and armed uniformed guards manning a pair of metal detectors similar to those used in airports. Jon's stomach knotted.

Now what?

He stepped out and asked Yung, "There a Starbucks near by?"

Yung scratched his jaw contemplatively.

"Out the front door, go right. Two blocks down."

Jon smiled, "Thanks."

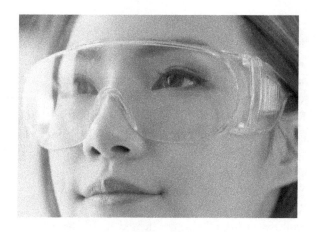

Chapter 35

JON HURRIED TOWARD the first door he saw as if late for an appointment, brushed past the first, then the second guard, then was pushing through the heavy glass doors into heat and smog. Just in case Yung was watching, he turned right and picked up pace.

How soon before Park discovered his escape?

Surely, by now, he knew.

Why no alarm?

Soon as he thought he was out of sight of the lobby, he started trotting, scanning the area dead ahead for a subway station or taxi, saw nothing, so just kept on moving. A half block later he noticed a cabstand across the street. The traffic light changed, giving him a break in traffic. He broke into a flat-out run, crossed over and headed for the first cab in line, threw open the door, jumped into the back seat.

"Airport! Hurry!"

He stabbed a finger at the street to make sure the cabbie understood, slammed the door, glanced back the way he came.

The cabbie, arm draped across the top of the seat, turned

207

to him.

"Kimpo, Incheon?"

"Incheon." Jon struggled to keep panic from his voice. *Shit!* "C'mon, let's go, I'm in a hurry."

Jon slid down in the seat and dialed United Airlines on his cell. From this compromised angle he could see trucks and busses passing in the opposite direction. Bad time of day for trying to leave Seoul. Traffic was already beginning to coalesce into the usual quagmire.

A female answered in Korean.

"United Airlines?" Jon asked.

"United Airlines," she confirmed in English. "May I help you?"

"What's the next flight from Incheon to the United States?"

"What city?"

"Doesn't matter…LA, San Francisco, whatever."

"Hold, please."

He became aware of a siren approaching from behind, slid left to peek between the seats at the rearview mirror but couldn't see the cabby's eyes.

If he pulled over …

As the siren grew louder the driver edged the cab to the curb and slowed to a crawl. Jon moved across the seat to the curb-side door, figuring if they got stopped by the cops, he'd run for it.

"Sir," the telephone voice said.

"Yes."

A police car, blue lights flashing, shot past, not even slowing. Jon craned his neck and watched it disappear into traffic.

"—flight leaving for San Francisco in sixty minutes. Are you at the airport now?"

"No, but I'm heading there."

"If you intend to take this flight, you'll need to check in at least thirty minutes before departure. Don't forget you need to deal with Security."

Jon gave her his name, asked her to hold a seat, thanked her and disconnected, leaned forward and prodded the driver's shoulder.

"Hurry!"

The driver nodded, then, to assure Jon he understood, turned into the outside lane, cut off another taxi and gunned it while the other driver leaned on his horn.

Time raced on with minutes slicing to a fraction of normal, the illusion magnified by repeatedly checking the minute hand of his watch as they hit one obstacle, then another. He could feel his heart beating anxiously in the center of his chest. Any hope of catching the flight would be impossible at their present rate of non-progress. Forty-seven minutes until the 747 shut its doors. Fucking Seoul rush-hour traffic...no way. But, he assured himself, there was always another flight out. He'd take anything. How soon before Park notified the airlines? And what would the airlines do if he tried to board a flight?

They hit a red light.

And waited.

Just as the light changed to green the flatbed truck directly in front stalled. The truck driver goosed the engine but flooded it. Next came the sound of the truck's starter grinding away without the engine catching. Horns honked. Angry shouts. The cabby shot a glance over his left shoulder, yelled something Korean to the truck driver, cranked the wheel left, peeled rubber into the oncoming lane, blew through the intersection just as the light was going red again.

In spite of himself, Jon checked his watch. Forty-five minutes to go and still not clear of the downtown core of congestion. No way in hell they'd make it now. He called United once more and asked for the next flight, found one to Denver departing one hour after the San Francisco flight. The next one after that was his Seattle flight, as if it made any difference. Right now, he just wanted to be airborne before airport security closed the door to him—if they hadn't already.

Finally, they hit the six-lane east/west highway but the three lanes out of Seoul clotted into one mass of bumper-to-bumper steel, exhaust fumes, and frayed tempers. Engine idling, they waited for traffic to start again.

And waited.

Forty minutes until the Denver flight.

Jon prayed to the god of air travel.

The taxi brushed the curb in front of the international terminal ten minutes before the flight's scheduled Denver departure. Jon threw enough *won* into the front seat to cover the trip plus tip, bailed, and started running for the door.

A large display in the main departure lobby showed the flight on schedule, the words BOARDING NOW flashing next to a gate number. Five minutes to make it. He decided to shortcut the ticket counter for the departure gate, hoping somehow to get through the security checkpoints without a boarding pass and buy a ticket at the gate.

Ahead, an impossibly long line of travelers was clearing the security body scanners one by one. He cut into the front of the line and spewed profuse apologies to the irate businessman he bumped. But instead of waving him into the scanner the security cop, a dour faced airport cop stepped in front of the entrance and raised his hand.

"Passport."

Jon glanced around as if the officer was addressing someone else, which was ridiculous, because the cop was staring right at him. Jon swallowed. He handed items to him.

"I lost it. Look, here's my picture ID and driver license."

The cop held up a hand.

"No good. Passport please."

Jon grappled frantically for a convincing story to allow him through security.

"Officer, please. This is an emergency. My flight's leaving.

I can't afford to miss it." Once more offering it. "Here, check out my ID."

The stern-faced cop motioned him to move away from blocking other passengers.

"Step away from the line."

Jon didn't move.

"Please, listen to me."

He glanced through the scanner at the people streaming toward the departure gates and, for one insane moment, considered making a break of it.

Could he become just one more traveler in the crowd?

"Step away," the officer repeated, this time harsher.

Fifty feet down the hall, an unmarked door in the wall few open and two police with Kevlar body armor materialized, heading straight toward him. One put a hand-held radio to his lips as the other popped the strap on his sidearm.

"Step away from line!"

Jon took off running the way he'd come.

Allen Wyler

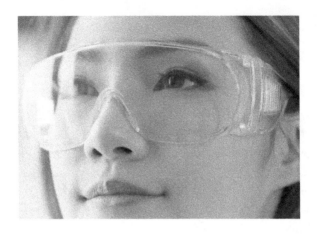

Chapter 36

METAL SQUEALED AGAINST metal along with the hiss of escaping gas, as the packed commuter train decelerated to a stop in a brightly lit subway station, one Jon hoped was in, or near, Yeonhee's neighborhood.

He'd never seen her apartment, nor knew its location, but for some vague reason believed it was either in or near the business district. With another belch of gas, the doors slid open and he was swept out of the train in a crush of passengers, allowing them to stream around him and across the platform to two banks of up escalators.

He side-stepped, freeing himself from the crowd momentum, moved next to the white tile wall for a look at the schematic map of the subway system and downtown Seoul. The long platform reeked of stale body odor, stale urine, and grease. The map of consisted entirely of Korean characters, so was of absolutely no help.

The flux of commuters quickly petered out, the slower ones finally vanished up the escalators, leaving a heavy echoing silence in their wake. Except for two passengers on the platform across the tracks, this level of the station was deserted, making him feel completely alone and helpless in spite of narrowly escaping the airport police.

After one final unsuccessful glance at the map for a hint of his location he looked at the escalators at each end of the platform, trying to decide which way to go, but even the small green exit signs were in Korean.

At least he could read the digits on the clock suspended from the ceiling. It was now almost an hour since the flight departed for San Francisco. God, he wished he were on it. His hatred for Park grew darker. But he couldn't dwell on that now, so headed for the escalator to his right.

The first flight dumped him into a cavernous station of white tile walls, maps, ticket machines, with determined commuters hurrying toward various escalators and stairs. This had to be the main level for this stop. With nothing to guide him, he randomly chose one of several exits and started up and was soon deposited outside on a sidewalk of a major street. He moved away from heavy pedestrian traffic to the front window of what looked like a bank, checked his cell's bar graph, and was ecstatic to see full strength.

He dialed Wayne.

"Where are you?"

Having Wayne's voice so loud and clear was comforting, almost as if he had his friend there with him.

"Oh, man, am I glad to hear your voice. I'm in deep shit and need help."

"Are you on the flight or what?"

"No, that's the point, I'm still in Seoul."

He quickly summarized the arrest and Park's insistence he sign a confession. Then explained how he escaped from the police station—something which in retrospect seemed too easy. And that, in itself, made him suspicious Park had set it up.

"I don't get it," Wayne said. "Why would he do that?"

"I'm no lawyer, but I don't think he had enough evidence

to nail me for the murders. But now, he certainly has enough evidence to get me on escaping custody, or whatever the charge would be. There's no question I did that."

"Jesus, Jon, get out of there."

"What do you think I'm trying to do?"

He realized he forgot to include the part about Park confiscating his passport, so explained that too.

Wayne asked, "What about Fisher, can he do anything to help with this?"

"Don't know. Haven't talked to him yet."

"Well, hell, what are you calling me for? Do it now. He's going to be more help than I can."

Jon checked the battery icon on the Droid. Only about half a charge remained.

"Don't worry, got his cell on speed dial. But before we hang up, I need you to do something for me."

"Absolutely. What?"

"Call around, find the best criminal defense lawyer in town and contact him."

"I assume you're talking Seattle, not Seoul, right?"

"Right."

"I'm on it. But just so I'm clear about what I'm doing, what good's a lawyer going to do you from here?"

Good question, one he had no answer for. But having someone lined up would be a comfort.

"I don't know. What I do know, is I'll feel better if I have someone lined up, whatever happens."

Wayne muttered agreement.

"Okay. Now call Fisher."

Fisher answered immediately with, "Don't tell me you're not out of there. Please, don't."

Having just recited the story to Wayne, he summarized the details succinctly and in chronological order. Fisher listened, breaking in occasionally to clarify a point.

When Jon finished, he asked, "You say Park claims to have

a witness who can place you in the hospital earlier than you were actually there?"

"That's the thing. He claims the computer records show that my badge was used to enter the main building. I don't think he said someone visually saw me. But maybe to them we all look alike."

"Okay, so Feist—or anyone, for that matter—could've used your ID and the computer wouldn't know the difference. When was the last time you know for sure you had possession of if?"

Jon thought about it again but couldn't be certain.

"That's the thing. I can't remember. When I got to the hospital, I realized I didn't have it. That's why they wouldn't let me past the ER waiting room. When I got back to the hotel room, I looked for it but it was gone. I guess I could've dropped it in the dressing room, but I know I didn't leave it in his locker because, now that I think about it, both Jin-Woo and I both looked there before he closed the door. The only thing still in there were the Nikes he wears in the OR."

"Man, that doesn't sound good. Someone really set you up." Fisher paused, muttered something. "The only thing I can possibly do from this end is call Park and explain the Avenger angle. Maybe if he hears it from me, he'll lighten up."

"Anything you can think of to help get him to ease up is good. I tell you, his mind's made up. He wants to pin those murders on me and move on."

Scary just thinking about it again.

Bad enough to be falsely accused of murder but add to the mix being in a foreign country…he felt helpless and alone. Having phone contact with Wayne and Fisher did help. Slightly.

Fisher asked, "Know anyone in Seoul? Other than your friend, Jin-Woo?"

He was about to mention Yeonhee, but stopped, wondering if his cell could be monitored. The fewer people who knew of her, the better. Not that he didn't trust Fisher, but one slip of the tongue…on the other hand, she was his only hope and he desperately needed help. Decided he had to trust somebody, why not Fisher?

"His lab tech."

"No one else? You see the problem, don't you?"

No, he didn't. At least not at first.

Now that Fisher mentioned it…

"You're thinking if Park presses Jin-Woo hard enough, he'll tell him about her?"

"Exactly. Wouldn't you?"

Yeah, maybe.

"Man!"

When Fisher didn't say anything more, Jon asked, "What?"

"I didn't want to mention this, but something's seriously changed. They found Phelps. He's dead."

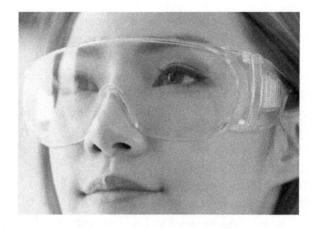

Chapter 37

YEONHEE LOOKED AT the computer screen but didn't make sense of the words, her mind elsewhere. She clasped and unclasped her hands, stood, walked over to the thermostat. 22 degrees, the same as the last time.

Went back to the computer, pulled up her email account. Nothing new since the last time.

She debated writing an email to a girlfriend but had nothing to say. She dialed Jin-Woo's cell again, but like the last four tries, it rang until finally rolling over to voice mail. So unlike him. He always answered. And if he was in surgery, he had someone in the OR answer.

When she'd arrived at the lab a few minutes after seven this morning Jin-Woo and Jon weren't here. Well, that was okay, she figured. Chances were they were probably in the hospital checking the post-op patients. Not being a physician or nurse, she never ventured onto the wards alone.

But today was different, there were two patients with freshly implanted stem cells, so it'd be okay to check too. After all, she was working with Jin-Woo and Jon. More importantly, the future of Jon's research depended upon the results.

What a breakthrough it'd be if the implants worked as they planned.

So she'd walked over to the hospital to look in on the patients, arrived at the first patient's room but found it empty, the bed freshly made, no personal items or family members waiting. A bad feeling blossomed inside her.

Same thing with the room across the hall in the second patient's room.

The bad feeling grew worse.

She hurried to the nursing station, directly to the first nurse she saw, asked, "Where are Dr. Lee's patients, the fresh post-ops?"

"I'm sorry. Are you a relative?"

"No. I work with Dr. Lee. In his lab."

The nurse glanced away, fidgeted.

"We're not allowed to give out information."

Yeonhee held up her ID for the nurse to read.

"Look at this. I work here in the medical center. I am involved in the patients' care," which was a stretch of truth. "I need to know where they are so I can record data."

Now telling a flat-out lie.

The nurse glanced from the ID to Yeonhee's face, as if weighing what to say or looking to see if she was lying.

Finally, "They're downstairs. In pathology. Waiting for autopsies. They died early this morning."

Yeonhee knew she should be shocked, but for some reason had already steeled herself for this news, probably because so many unusual little things had already gone wrong this morning.

"And Dr. Lee?"

"The police have him. They took him this morning; around the time I came on shift. They're saying the patients were murdered and that the American is responsible, and Dr. Lee helped him."

"That's ridiculous! He didn't kill those patients."

She had to do something to help. But, what? Neither Jin-Woo nor Jon answered their cells.

Nothing the nurse had said made any sense. What could Jon possibly gain by killing the patients? Just the opposite: he had everything to lose. The Avengers, on the other hand....

The first day Jon was in the lab he told her the story of the Avengers. Immediately afterward she'd Googled the name, brought up their website, and almost vomited at the sight of Jon's information there. Post a person's name on a website for crazies and you never knew what might result. Some real psychos inhabit this world. A reality she knew too well from dealing with her brother.

She was an excellent judge of character and believed Jon was a good person and superb scientist. Knowing little about actual surgery, she couldn't judge his skills as a surgeon. When first meeting him, his fixation on Alzheimer's—a nonsurgical disease—seemed a little, well, weird for a surgeon. So one day when she and Jin-Woo were in Jon's lab, she asked Jon why he was so interested.

For a moment he looked at her eyes, as if questioning her sincerity.

Then said, "My grandmother died from it."

He went on to describe her insidiously worsening forgetfulness, the waning interests in bridge club, sewing, and birdwatching, the deepening depression. How she'd fly into a rage over the least little ripple in her daily routine.

"It got harder and harder to care for her," he'd said. "Finally I had to put her in an assisted living home. The place was awful, but, well, we couldn't afford anything better. She never forgave me."

"How long did she live?" Yeonhee had asked.

"Six weeks. Two weeks after I put her in the home, she went into a coma. Never came out." He seemed to be staring at something far away. "She died like that."

She eventually learned that his quest for a cure of

Alzheimer's Disease had an even deeper motivation. There is an inheritable form of the disease: a gene that produces the protein apolipoprotein E. Everyone, even normal, non-demented people, have this protein because it transports cholesterol in the blood. The problem is, the gene has three forms: one protects a person from the disease whereas another does just the opposite, making a person more susceptible.

Jon's grandmother died relatively young, at an age more likely to indicate the inheritable form. Jon was deeply worried that he might have it. Without having tested his grandmother, the only to way know was to simply wait for the first signs of a rapidly developing disease.

On the other hand if he could find a cure...

Suddenly a loud banging started on the door to the hall. She jumped, her body a taut tangle of nerves and spun around to look. A face filled the narrow vertical window above the doorknob. More banging.

Heart beating wildly, she thumbed the intercom button.

"Yes?"

On the other side of the window stood a man in a suit.

From the intercom came, "Police. Open up!"

She reached for the stainless-steel handle, but then stopped, her mind spinning through several scenarios. Had something bad happened to either Jon or Jin-Woo? Both? Was she in trouble? Had her brother injured her mother? Then she remembered: the patients...

She cracked the door only enough to converse with him.

"Yes?"

A large man, early forties in a cheap suit and a mean determined expression, pushed the door open, shoving her back far enough to step into the lab, then backing her up even further to get out of his way as he started inspecting the room.

"Lee, Yeonhee?"

"Yes?"

His tone carried an implied threat.

"The American, where is he?"

Immediately she felt protective and defensive toward Jon.

"Who are you?"

The words seemed to surprise him, as if he didn't expect a lowly lab tech, especially a woman, to question him.

"Detective Park, Metropolitan police."

His surprise steeled her confidence.

"I'd like to see some identification please."

This time Park didn't bother to hide his irritation. But she knew her rights. Besides, a uniformed officer was witnessing this from the hall. Reluctantly, Park pulled a wallet from his suit coat, held it up to her.

She waved it away without a glance, happy at the small bit of control it gave her and the shift of dominance in the interaction.

"I don't know where he is."

Park continued inspecting the lab, checking closets, looking in sink wells. He eyed her suspiciously.

"The last time you spoke with him, when was that?"

She saw no reason not to answer truthfully.

"Yesterday."

"What time yesterday?"

"In the morning."

He rounded the bench in the center of the room heading back to the door, dropping a business card on the corner of the counter as he passed.

"If you see him, call me. You understand? Anytime, day or night."

She resented the arrogance and condescension but something unstated in his attitude seeded enough fear of him that she exchanged a sarcastic reply for, "Yes, I will."

Never in a thousand years will I help you.

Inspector Park glared at her from the doorway.

"For your sake, I hope you do."

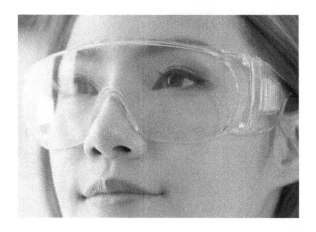

Chapter 38

JON DECIDED IT would be too conspicuous to hang around one place for long so pushed off the concrete wall and moved a half block. A Westerner in a city of Asians might draw unwanted attention, especially from police. He stopped to survey the area once again, hoping to see a familiar landmark, but saw nothing but generic big city buildings, pedestrians, vehicles, and neon.

Another half block and he stopped to fish the scrap of paper from his wallet with Yeonhee's cell number.

Again, no answer.

Where was she? Jin-Woo too?

By now his battery indicator showed only one segment, so he powered off the cell, replaced it in his pocket, walked another block to the corner and glanced up and down that street for a familiar landmark.

Although he'd visited Seoul previously, he hadn't had reason to learn the city from a pedestrian viewpoint. Most of his time had been spent inside the medical center or the hotel, on the outskirts of the main business district. As he now faced a multi-lane street of bumper-to-bumper traffic, a whiff of food caught his attention.

Half a block away, a street vendor sold what looked like chunks of chicken on a stick. When had he last eaten? Breakfast at the hotel? Seemed like days ago, yet he didn't feel hungry.

Well, hell, couldn't just stand here, had to go somewhere. At random, he turned right and resumed walking, figuring that a street this wide stood a good chance of intersecting with another major avenue so if he walked a mile or so he might spot a familiar landmark.

Yeah? Then what? What good will that do? You still won't know where you are.

True, but seeing something familiar would be comforting.

One corner and three blocks later his logic paid off: directly ahead was the Seoul Intercontinental, towering over the neighboring buildings. Jin-Woo had driven him past the hotel several times.

An idea formed: a hotel this large should provide sufficient anonymity for a day, maybe two, depending on how aggressively Park hunted him, to be able to work with Wayne and Fisher and the Embassy on obtaining a new passport that would get him out of the country. For the moment, having a plan rounded off the edges off his anxiety.

He dodged a cab exiting the driveway, hurried past a taxi with a trunk full of luggage, and followed an elderly Asian couple through the main revolving door into a cavernous lobby of maroon oriental rugs, huge Chinese vases, and chairs.

To his left, two rows of chrome stanchions linking red velvet rope formed a switchback to the registration desk. He stood in line behind two men in expensive looking business suits and Tumi attaché cases. As he waited, he discreetly scanned the lobby for police. To his relief, there were none.

After a couple minutes wait, his turn came, and a clerk at the counter motioned him over. When he got there the clerk continued to click away on a keyboard. For a minute Jon waited patiently until the receptionist finally glanced up.

"May I help you?"

"A room for one or two nights."

His eyes immediately went back to the computer screen.

"Name on the reservation?"

"I don't have one."

He adjusted wire-rimmed glasses, typed, waited for a moment.

"Smoking or non-smoking?"

Still no eye contact, which, on second thought, might be best.

"Non-smoking."

The keyboard started clicking again.

"One or two nights?"

He considered two, but decided to move to another hotel tomorrow.

"Just one."

The clerk studied the screen a moment, nodded, flashed a toothy smile at him.

"Credit card and passport, please."

Jon handed him his Visa card and driver's license.

"Passport's a problem. The airline lost my suitcase and it's inside. They said to go ahead, check in and they'd deliver it sometime this evening."

The receptionist's polite smile dissolved to a frown.

"Sorry, but we're not allowed to issue a room without a passport."

The clerk's face left little doubt this wasn't negotiable.

"But——"

"Sorry."

Back on the sidewalk, Jon tried calling Yeonhee again. No answer.

Try the lab?

Sure, he could do that, but what were the chances Park had

it under surveillance? Better not. Instead, he shut off the phone to conserve the battery.

What now?

Just then, his peripheral vision caught movement and he instinctively turned to look. A cop was stepping out of a patrol car, eying him intently. Jon continued walking to the corner, picked up the pace slightly.

A man's voice yelled, "Stop!"

Jon glanced back at the cop who was now pointing a finger at him.

"You. Stop!"

The cop started running his way, right hand on his holstered weapon. Jon broke into a flat out run, weaving through a group of pedestrians, danced around a trash bin, pushed two spaced-out ear-budded teenagers aside, frantically searching for a less obstructed path even though he had no idea where to run.

Just run!

Ahead, at the end of the block the traffic light was turning red. He bolted into the intersection, cutting diagonally across, dancing between fenders as horns honked and brakes screeched. He worked through six intersecting lanes of traffic, moving fast as possible, fighting the urge to turn to check on the cop because it would waste a half second.

A Mercedes screeched to a stop directly in his path. He put out his hands, did a western roll over the left front fender, his momentum carrying him forward, hit the pavement and kept on moving. Reached the opposite curb at a dead run, caught sight of a subway entrance, bee-lined for it, reached the top of the stairs and started flying down two at a time, out of control, shouldering people out of the way, muttering apologies.

He blew into a white tile cavern of ticket machines, noise and commuters, slowed enough to see two tunnels down and three sets of exit stairs up. Without a second thought, he headed for the furthest exit, ran the stairs up and out onto the sidewalk, rounded to the nearest corner and immediately slowed to a brisk, less conspicuous walk, and melted into a cluster of pedestrians.

Only then did he chance a quick glance over his shoulder, but the cop wasn't chasing him. He ducked into an alley, the air thick with rotting garbage and stench of urine, stopped to catch his breath, calm down, and think. His chest ached, the soles of his feet stung from running in leather street loafers.

Can't stay here, move...

Cautiously, he returned to the entrance of the alley, glanced right, then left. Coast clear. Half a block down the street a taxi pulled to the curb, the back door opened, and a couple stepped out.

Jon ran to it, jumped into the back seat before the man could close the door and ordered the driver, "Quick! Tyasami Medical Center. Emergency!"

The driver calmly accelerated back into the thick traffic. Gasping and sweating, Jon slumped back against the seat, thought, *What next?*

He thought about what just happened. A cop spotting him so easily could mean only one thing: Park released his description at least to the police and perhaps to the press, making it very more risky to be seen in public, and even more critical to secure a safe hiding place where he could work on getting a passport. Which raised the question: even if he had a passport, would it get past airport security? Had to think about that...and this cab, had Park notified the taxi companies? And if so, did the driver call it in? Not knowing the language kept putting him at a huge disadvantage.

Four blocks later, at a randomly selected stop light, Jon tossed a handful of *won* into the front seat, opened the door, darted into a group of pedestrians in the crosswalk. He waited for the cab to cross the intersection and disappear into traffic before deciding on which direction to go.

He realized he was still in the major business district—and

still lost. Across the street, on the front of a shop, hung the familiar green Starbucks mermaid logo. The sight of something so American and familiar brought a wave of relief. It didn't make sense, he knew, but at least he'd *feel* safer being inside and off the street.

Maybe with a few moments rest, he could calm down, regroup, come up with some sort of plan, maybe even reach Yeonhee.

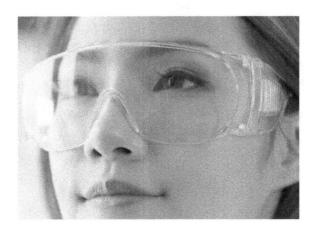

Chapter 39

JON SAT AT a small table for two nursing a latte, wondering what to do if he couldn't reach Yeonhee. Or, what if she refused to help? With frayed nerves already putting him on edge, he didn't need the caffeine but decided the drink was the price of admission for taking up a table.

He jotted down various options on a napkin, then carefully considered each one, regardless of how crazy they might seem. Twice he'd worked through the list, revising three, crossing out two, yet no one option outshone the others.

Call Jin-Woo?

Definitely not a good idea. Park knew he was Jon's main contact in Seoul and would lean on him to give Jon up.

Call Wayne?

He could do that, but without some sort of plan, it would accomplish nothing more than provide some moral support. Besides, until he located a charger for the Droid, he needed to conserve the remaining energy.

Fisher had nothing for him yet.

He considered going to the American Embassy, but

worried Park might have it under surveillance. It was probably best to reach them first by phone. For the moment, it seemed wisest to find a place to stop and get a reasonable plan together.

He checked his watch again. It had been ten minutes since trying Yeonhee's cell. He might as well try again. This time she picked up.

"Jon? That you?"

Only three words, but said with enough concern to be instantly comforting.

He asked, "Do you know about the patients?"

"Yes," she said without a hint of incrimination.

There was so much he wanted to say, and even more that he needed to know. Mostly he needed help, but could he trust her?

He said, "I don't know what you've been told or what you believe, but I had nothing to do with their deaths."

"I believe you."

What a relief.

"And Jin-Woo…what does he say?"

"I don't know," she said with alarm. "He didn't come to the lab, and I couldn't find him on the wards and he doesn't answer his cell. I'm worried because that's not like him."

He cupped the phone with his free hand and turned away from the other customers.

"When did you talk to him last?"

"Yesterday. When I came to the lab this morning it was empty, so I went to the ward. The nurses say the police took him away early this morning, right out from one of the patient's rooms, it seems. It's very embarrassing for everyone."

"Has a Detective Park talked to you yet?"

"Yes and he is not a good man."

Couldn't agree more.

"He talked to me as well. Look, here's the deal. I'm in serious trouble and don't have anyone I can turn to. Do you think you might be able to help me?"

"No problem. Anything. What can I do?"

It dawned on him: involving her—even slightly—would make her an accomplice. The last thing he wanted was to cause her to be arrested. And what about Feist, did he know who she was? Would he use her to get to him? Worse, would he kill her as retaliation? Suddenly his head filled with all sorts of problem he hadn't considered until now.

"Jon?"

"The patients...have you heard anything about their cause of death?"

"No, nothing. They were gone from their room by the time I went to the ward. It was awful. People are saying you..."

So there it was: convicted of a crime he didn't commit.

"Do you have any idea why they think that?"

"No. And I can't think of any reason either. If anything, you had so much invested in them doing well. I just can't believe you did anything to them. What can I do to help?"

Having her believe him and offering to help lifted a weight from him.

But at what price?

He glanced at the other customers, as if they would somehow advise him what to do.

"Jon?"

"Yeonhee, look...on second thought, this isn't a good idea. If Park finds out you helped me in any way, you'll be in serious trouble. But you don't know how good it makes me feel to just have you offer."

He'd have to figure out another way to get help, and most likely through the Embassy.

This time her tone was stronger and more determined.

"Where are you? I can come get you."

Go ahead, accept. She knows what she's doing. You don't know anyone else here other than Jin-Woo. Maybe a couple hours...just enough time to contact the Embassy to come up with a way of getting out of Korea.

"You sure you're really okay with this? Maybe just a few hours? At the most."

She didn't hesitate at all.

"Where are you?"

"Don't know. I'm totally lost." He glanced out the window again but saw nothing changed since the last dozen times he'd looked. "Somewhere in the business district."

"Find a cab. Take it to the Ritz-Carlton. I meet you in the lobby. Hurry."

Across the street, a taxi pulled to the curb, the third in a row of cabs outside a small hotel. He was out the door and across the street, the cell back in his pocket, thinking if he got out of here, he'd find a way to repay her.

The driver gunned the engine to drive up the steep winding driveway to the Ritz's front entrance. Jon reached between the front seats to pay the driver as a tuxedoed doorman opened the rear passenger door.

"Welcome to the Ritz-Carlton, sir. Any luggage?"

"No. Thanks."

Jon brushed past him, on through a revolving door into a lobby of marble, oriental carpets, vaulted walnut ceiling, and the lingering hint of cigar smoke. Stately, yet surprisingly non-threatening, as if those who could afford a room were immune from police suspicion. Ridiculous, he knew, but comforting in a way. Looked for Yeonhee but didn't see her.

For a moment, he stood just inside the entrance glancing around the lobby, feeling exposed and obvious, yet unsure of where to go or what to do. Then noticed his reflection in the glass doors. Unshaven, pitted rumpled shirt, an aura of panic. In short, an attention magnet. Across the lobby, next to the gift shop door, stood a polished glass display case with shelves of Mont Blanc pens, designer perfumes, and horribly expensive Hermes scarves.

Perfect.

Trying for the Ralph Lauren look, he threw his blazer over his shoulder and wandered to the display, peered in for a moment before turning to scan again for Yeonhee. Still not here. He sat down on a sofa to wait.

A bellhop materialized at his side.

"Checking in, sir?"

Shit, the guy was looking straight at him.

Jon glanced at the door.

"Soon as my wife arrives."

"Very good, sir."

The bellhop drifted back toward the registration desk to rejoin two other staff.

Still no sign of her.

He became increasingly nervous. Had he missed her? Had Park detained her for questioning? An accident? Were there two Ritz-Carltons in Seoul? Or had he heard her wrong?

Ten minutes later, Yeonhee—stunningly beautiful in a black linen blazer, cream silk blouse, black pants and flats—hurried through the revolving door, stopped long enough for a quick hair primp while casually scanning the crowd.

He caught her eye and started for her, relieved and exhilarated by the sight of a friend.

As they hugged he whispered, "Thanks for coming. You don't know how much I appreciate this."

She cast a nervous glance at the door.

"No problem. Let's get out of here."

"What's the matter?" he asked, alarmed.

She tugged his hand and headed toward the side door.

"Outside."

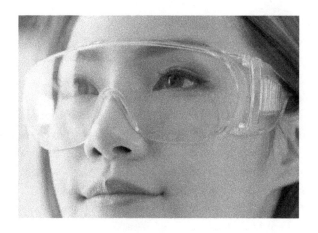

Chapter 40

HE FOLLOWED, STEALING a final glance to see if anyone was watching them but no one seemed to give them a second look.

Then again, so what? Would they be obvious about it?

Yeonhee was moving with purpose, making him hustle to keep up.

"What's wrong? Someone following you?"

"I don't know. But that detective, Park, knows I know you. I don't trust him. He made me nervous…creepy, I guess would be the word for it."

They went from hushed soft air-conditioning into muggy noisy warmth, down the steep sloping brick drive to the shadowy side street of concrete pavers, moving quickly, yet not on the cusp of trotting, side by side.

"Where're we going?" he asked.

"My place."

He stopped, put a hand to her shoulder, but she shrugged it off and tugged at him to keep moving.

"Come."

He took her hand and held firm.

"No. Wait a second. Let's think this out."

She looked past him, back toward the hotel driveway.

"Okay, but around the corner."

Yeonhee led him into an even more shadowy side street with taxis queued along the curb, awaiting the Ritz doorman's summons. Two drivers sat against one cab front fender, smoking and chatting while others waited in their vehicles. She was right, a random patrol car would have a harder time spotting them here. They continued walking, but at a normal pace.

She asked, "What were you going to say?"

He kept his voice low.

"Here's the thing, like you just said, Park knows you know me. What's to keep him from watching your place? I go there, game over. He nails me."

She nodded.

"I thought about that. My girlfriend, Gayeon," pronouncing it Ki-yon, "lives the across street. We go to her place, not mine. Come, we need to get you off the street."

Jon gently stopped her.

"Wait. I need to make a call first," and held up his cell.

She cocked her head to one side while finger-combing her hair.

"Who's so important you need to call right this minute?"

"The American Embassy. I should talk with them before the cops find me. They can help get me out of here."

And the sooner he removed any risk to her, the better.

She nodded agreement.

"Good idea, but right now we need you off the streets. Call from Gayeon's place. It's not all that far."

Again, she was right. As they continued walking, he took her hand, thinking it made them appear more like a couple. Especially with the cops searching for a lone male. She responded with a slight but definite squeeze, sending a tingle up his arm. He couldn't help wonder if his strong attraction to her was due, in part, to his reliance on her? No, he'd always felt this way about her.

As they continued on, he again was struck by how little he knew about the layout of Seoul. What would happen if they were forced to split up? He'd be right back in the same helpless situation.

He asked, "Where are we?"

"This district?"

"Yeah. For starters."

"This is Kangnam, the business district. My street is Yoksam-dong." She pointed at a street sign in Korean characters. "See?"

As if he could read them.

Five minutes later, they turned off a brightly lit six-lane avenue into a narrow one-way alley smelling of rotten garbage and lit only by a single mercury vapor lamp. Cars were parked at various haphazard angles, squeezed into every possible inch of available space. Yeonhee pointed.

"That's my building."

In the dim light Jon could make out a five-story brick building.

"I thought the plan was to go to Gayeon's?"

"It is. First I need some things. It will only take a minute."

"Wait." He gently drew her deeper into the shadows next to a brick building across the street from hers, whispered, "How long do you need?"

"Only long enough to call her, see if she's home and pick up a few things. You call the Embassy from there."

He didn't like the idea of entering a building Park might have under surveillance.

"Why not call her from here?"

Meaning, out in the street.

Yeonhee nodded, "Good idea," and pulled a cell from her purse, thumbed in a number, listened, frowned. "She usually picks up by now. Maybe she's with her boyfriend and just not picked up, or maybe she's out."

Figures!

He studied the building, thought of Park.

What were the odds he'd have it under surveillance?

He pointed at her building.

"Go ahead, check it out. If no one's inside waiting for you, text me." He held up his cell. "Ringer's off."

She leaned close, "Third landing," kissed his cheek, then was off, weaving between parked cars, trotting across the street, up the stairs, through the double glass doors, her approach triggering motion sensitive fluorescents in the small vestibule.

He watched the vestibule lights time out and die and expected to see a light appear in an apartment window when she entered, but the random pattern of dark and lit glass along the front of the building didn't change.

Well, maybe her unit didn't face the street.

The cell vibrated. SAFE appeared on the screen.

From the outside, the building looked new. Inside, the hallway smelled of freshly poured concrete, bonding agents, fresh paint. No wall marks, no floor scuffs. Surprisingly, the front door of the building remained unlocked and there was no sign of a security system or intercom. Unimaginable for any condo in a major US city. Up a narrow flight of gray granite to a small landing for three doors, one of which was open with Yeonhee waiting in it.

The dominant color of her apartment interior was yellow. Yellow-striped curtains, a yellow futon with a large matching pillow on blond hardwood. In one corner a small electric stove with a teapot on the single burner. A free-standing rack fashioned from bare pipe and right-angle fittings was crammed with clothes on brightly colored plastic hangers. The only bedroom contained a small wood cabinet serving double duty as storage cabinet and vanity. Louvered doors hid a closet, a standard door opened to a bathroom.

"Have a phone book?"

"Phone book? Are you kidding?"

She dropped onto the bed, laptop on thighs, and started typing. A few keystrokes later she proudly displayed the number for the American Embassy, which he programmed into his Droid.

He nodded at her cell phone, "Why don't you try your friend again while I call the Embassy?"

His nervousness increased as each second ticked past. At any moment he expected a hard knock on the door and the echo of boots on the stairs. Melodramatic and blown out of proportion, for sure, but regardless, his anxiety kept increasing. The sooner they were out of here the better.

Could Park have the phone company triangulate his cell?

Now that he thought about it, the cell was GPS enabled, which was all the more reason to keep it off.

While Yeonhee made a call on her cell, he dialed the Embassy, heard it click and switch to a recording: "You have reached the United States Embassy, Seoul Korea." After listening to a menu, he pressed "1" for the American Citizen Services section. Another recording clicked on: "The section closes at 3:30 P.M. Please call back during business hours. For an after-hours emergency, please call 8324517."

Shit!

He also programmed this number into the cell then dialed it.

"Citizens Emergency Center, Sunny speaking."

Sunny had a Korean accent.

Finally!

"I lost my passport. Who should I talk to about replacing it immediately? I have an emergency at home and need to get back soon as possible."

"Oh, a lost passport. That happens all the time. You need to speak with one of our Consular officers. I'll contact the night duty officer and ask him to ring you back. Is this your number?"

Obviously, her phone had caller ID.

He checked the battery icon again. Lower.

"Yes, but my battery's about dead. Can I call you back in a couple minutes? How long will it take?"

"You're in luck. I just checked the roster. The officer of the evening is Clark Bundy. I'll page him, see if he's still in the building."

The line clicked to hold.

Yeonhee smiled.

"I go see if Gayeon is home and just not answering. She does that sometimes when a boyfriend is over. Okay if I leave you here for a few minutes?"

He had momentary panic.

"Just across the street, right?"

"Yes."

"If you're not back in ten minutes I'll wait outside. Same place as before."

A deep, resonant voice came over the line.

"Bundy here. To whom am I speaking?"

At last! Someone in authority who could help.

"Oh, man, am I glad to talk to you. I just lost my passport and have an emergency at home. I need to fly out soon as possible."

"No sweat. Happens all the time. You'd be surprised how often."

The sound of papers rustling in the background along with an East Coast accent caused him to picture Bundy at a perfectly organized desk, ballpoints and paperclips in an Ivy League school coffee cup—Dartmouth perhaps—a career diplomat, product of wealthy State Department parents. A slight echo in Bundy's voice made it sound like he was on speakerphone, probably so he could take notes while speaking.

"By any chance have you previously registered with our agency?"

"You mean the Seoul Embassy or the State Department?"

"Either. But it'll be quicker if you registered with us."

Then a tap-tap-tap as if Bundy was aligning a sheaf of papers.

"No. The only contact I've had was with Homeland Security when I applied for my passport in Seattle, years ago. Does that count?"

"Then this just a short visit? You don't work here?"

"No, just a short visit."

"Right. Well then, here's what you need for a reissue. Proof of US citizenship, a couple of two-inch-by-two-inch color photographs, and fifty-five bucks to cover the application fee. Can you handle that?"

He mentally ran the list. Photos and money shouldn't be a problem.

"Proof of citizenship...well, that could be a problem. Will any photo ID do? I have a bank card, driver's license? I mean...I have a very serious problem at home. I need to get back soon as possible."

The clink of a pen being dropped into a desk organizer.

"No, nothing short of your birth certificate will do. Have someone stateside overnight it and we can start the process tomorrow."

A knot formed in Jon's gut. By now Park probably had the entire Seoul police force searching for him. He needed to get out of the city tonight, not in two or three days.

"That'll take at least two days. I don't have that kind of time."

"Sorry, these are Federal regulations. No exceptions. Especially since 9-11."

A wall of bureaucratic bricks and mortar was just built.

"You mean to tell me there's not some sort of emergency visa you can issue so I can go home? Can't I supply the papers after I get there? Look at it this way," he said, scouring his mind for some shred of persuasive argument. "All those documents should be on a computer somewhere from when I was issued the original passport. And when I arrived and went through passport control. Can't you find the record of that?"

Bundy didn't respond, making Jon afraid this conversation was doomed, so he added, "Also, I have the return portion of my airline ticket. Think about it. The airlines checked my passport before they let me come over. Right? Doesn't that prove I had my passport a couple of days ago? Can't you do some sort of computer check, make sure one was issued to me?"

"Sorry Mister...?"

"Ritter. Jon Ritter."

"Mr. Ritter, I can't bend the rules."

Jon sucked a deep breath and decided to come clean.

"Okay, let me explain something. I'm a surgeon. I was invited here to advise on a medical matter. Which I did, but unfortunately some problems were encountered, and the patients died. I have no idea what happened, but the police now accuse me of murdering them. They tried to force me into signing a confession. I didn't sign because I'm innocent. But they're trying to railroad me. I beg you: help me out here."

The heavy silence from Bundy's side of the call cinched the knot in Jon's gut tighter.

"Look, verify this. I'm being set up for something I didn't do. Neither one of us has time for all the details, so call Special Agent Fisher at the Seattle FBI field office and he'll verify everything I said. I'll give you his number. Got something to write with?"

"I have news for you, Dr. Ritter. Bad news. We already know all about the incident. Park contacted us immediately upon your escape. That alone, by the way, makes you a felon in the Korean justice system."

"But I—"

"Before you get worked up any further, let me explain the facts of life. Park has issued a warrant for your arrest."

Jon was floored. Then immediately realized he shouldn't

be. What had he expected?

"On what charge?"

"Our equivalent of First-Degree Murder."

Blood drain from his head, making the room spin. He leaned against the wall for support and slid slowly to the floor.

Bundy added, "You have a huge problem. Park isn't stupid. He knows you can't leave the country without a passport, and he probably notified Immigration the minute you escaped. Then he notified us. He probably figures we're the first people you would contact, so he demanded we notify him the minute you do."

"If you talked to him, you know exactly the type of person he is. I swear he's trying to close the case by pinning it on the first person he can, regardless of what really happened. That's me."

"Personally, I believe you. But the fact is we can't reissue a passport without the proper paperwork. With you being a fugitive now, there's nothing we can do that might be construed as obstructing their legal system. And that includes issuing you a passport even if you were able to submit the proper documents."

Jon felt like vomiting. He tried to think of a persuasive argument but knew that a government bureaucrat had little flexibility when it came to bending the rules. And without knowing any possible legal loophole to apply to his situation, Jon couldn't think of an argument to change Bundy's mind. He punched the pillow next to his right hip.

"You're saying you won't raise a finger to protect a U.S. citizen in a foreign country?"

"No. What I'm saying is that until your situation is resolved, we can't help you flee the country. End of story. Being in a foreign country, as you are, you're subject to the laws and justice system of that country. There's nothing we, meaning the State Department, can do to change that. Certainly, we won't smuggle you out of Korea in a diplomatic pouch if that's what you're asking."

Self-righteous prick.

"Why not? I mean, you do it all the time for spies and political dissidents. Why not an innocent citizen?"

"C'mon, you can't be serious. Your situation is entirely different. You're *not* an intelligence operative, for one. In addition, you *are* a U.S. citizen who happens to be a murder suspect and, to make matters worse, several hours ago you engineered an armed escape from police custody. All we can do is work within our parameters to protect your legitimate interests and insure that you are not discriminated against. We will, of course, provide you with a list of local attorneys for your defense. We can visit you and will certainly contact your family and friends back home. But that's as far as we can, and will, go in this matter."

An even stronger wave of nausea hit.

"This call...are you tracing it?"

Bundy gave a sarcastic snort.

"Hardly. We're State, not CIA, and we're certainly not on the payroll of the National Police. So, no, we aren't."

"Are you recording this?"

"I was until I learned who you are. Apparently the machine developed sudden mechanical difficulties and stopped working, maybe, oh, five minutes ago. Damn Samsung equipment."

This lessened Jon's anger at Bundy.

Perhaps he wasn't just being an asshole.

"Look, here's the deal: I'm not about to turn myself over to the police. Not after what I went through earlier. Park isn't interested in facts. All he wants is a fall guy for a murder I didn't commit. I know who did and told Park his name, but he won't listen. Give me a break, tell me what to do."

Bundy audibly inhaled.

"Listen carefully, Ritter. You tell anyone you heard this from me I'll deny it." Bundy lowered his voice. "What kind of connections do you have here?"

"I'm not following."

"I'm referring to go-to people who can get things done that might not quite be kosher."

Jon's frustration spiked again.

Had Bundy not listened to a word?

"That's the point. I don't know anyone here who can help. That's why I'm calling."

"Sounds to me like what you need is a passport. Not necessarily from the State Department."

Took a second to click.

"Got it."

Bundy said, "Let me know if you want that list of lawyers," before hanging up.

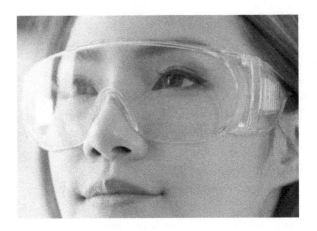

Chapter 41

SEEMED LIKE IT took an act of the United Nations to finally get through the bureaucracy, but finally the translator handed Fisher the phone, saying, "He's fluent."

Fisher thanked him, held the phone to his ear.

"Detective Park, Special Agent Gary Fisher. Thanks for taking my call."

Park spoke with obvious irritation.

"What is it? I'm very busy."

Given the watery quality of his voice and what sounded like vehicular traffic in the background, Fisher figured he was on a cell.

Fisher intended to reveal as little as possible, hoping to draw out more information from Park that way.

"This is about Dr. Ritter. He called me about the situation there."

"Fisher, is it?"

Hadn't his position been made clear by the translator?

"Yes, Special Agent Gary Fisher, Federal Bureau of Investigation, Seattle field office."

"There is no *situation*, Agent Fisher. And I would appreciate you not trying to meddle in Korean affairs. Are we clear on this?"

Fisher was taken aback, momentarily at a loss for words. "Hold on just a second, I—"

Park cut him off with, "There is really nothing to discuss. Goodbye Agent Fisher," and hung up.

Nigel Feist stood a sidewalk in front of a plate-glass window with bright red and blue blinking neon sign that read Karaoke Bar in English and Korean. Earlier in the day, after verifying the police had Ritter safely in custody, he moved from the Sheraton to the Ramada Seoul to be able to monitor the situation more closely. Less expensive there also.

He planned to hang around only long enough to assure Stillman that Ritter was never leaving Seoul, then dump this job, get the hell out of fucking Korea forever, and begin his retirement and fantasy road trip. Figured a week, max.

Then the situation took an unexpected turn.

He dialed Stillman as four laughing twenty-year-olds opened the bar door, momentarily blasting him with a bad rendition of a vaguely familiar country western song. He plugged his free ear to listen to the connection.

"Stillman."

"It's me," he said crisply, turning toward the street.

"And?"

Stepping further from the bar, "Your friend's bloody well gone walkabout."

"What?"

"Escaped. Your boy's escaped."

"Escaped? From the police?"

"Right-right."

Stillman spoke in an accusatory tone, as if Feist were responsible.

"How the hell did he manage that?"

"How the fuck should I know? One minute he's in custody, the next minute he's gone. Everyone's mum about what happened. I suspect it's 'cause they're too embarrassed to let on."

He was talking too loudly, he realized, and quickly glanced around, but saw no one in earshot, thank God. Indeed, half the people passing by had their own cell phones to their ears continuously. A few more generations and people will probably come straight out the womb a cellphone instead of earlobes.

"You said everything was arranged, that Ritter was signed, sealed, and delivered. How could you let this happen, goddamnit."

Feist lowered the phone and glared at the display.

Just say 'fuck it' and disconnect?

Better not. Tempting as it was, the fee for finishing this job through would add a tidy sum to his 401K. Finish this and he'd never have to deal with the likes of Stillman again. He returned the phone up to his ear and spoke calmly,

"He escaped from fucking jail, mate. How the fuck am I expected to be responsible for that?"

"If he'd simply been eliminated, we wouldn't be in this mess."

True. But the geezers were old, on their way out anyways.

That's why he'd chosen to do them instead of Ritter.

"Right, but that would draw attention, now wouldn't it. My way would've worked if he hadn't escaped."

"Point noted. Now here's *my* point. I can't afford him coming back here. If the Korean authorities can't keep him there, make sure he doesn't leave Korea alive. Do you understand me? Find and fix the problem."

"Don't get your knickers in a knot. Got me a lead."

Stillman gave a sarcastic snort.

"Do the police still have his passport or did he pick that up on the way out the door?"

Feist spat on the pavement imagining Stillman there.

"According to my source, they do."

That source being the head of Tyasami Security, but how much longer that particular spigot would remain open was highly questionable. Not because of lack of cooperation, but because it was unlikely the police would share any additional information with a private security firm if Ritter no longer had business at the medical center.

"I assume that in order to leave the country he'll need one. How difficult is it to obtain a counterfeit? Something that will get him through Immigration."

"Depends. He doesn't strike me as someone with the right connections for that, so he'll have to sort that out. Assuming, of course, the coppers don't catch him straightaway. You tell me, you know him better than me. What do you think?"

Stillman grunted what sounded like agreement.

"Far as I know, his only connection is Jin-Woo. But he's been to Seoul before, so might have other friends. A girlfriend, maybe. I don't know."

"Right-right. Coppers had the slant doctor in for questioning, last word I got. Figured I'd check on him in a few hours. Should be out by then. Got himself a condo not too far from here. Who knows, maybe Ritter is holed up over there as we speak. Which raises an interesting point. Supposing I find him—Ritter, I mean, not the slant. What exactly you want done?"

He wanted it clearly spelled out so there'd be no debate over the appropriate fee.

"Exactly? That's up to you. Depends on the situation."

Not enough clarity.

If things played out as he suspected they might, he'd have to kill Ritter. The original contract covered one snuff, but the two geezers used up that fee.

"Just so we're straight, best case is him in jail with the death penalty or life without parole. Right-right?"

It was his preference too—didn't much fancy killing

Ritter. Seemed like too good a man. Real bastards, now that was a different matter. Real bastards, well, they were expendable and usually deserved what they got. Mostly though, it boiled down to risk. Didn't want to jeopardize retirement, what with his heart set on it now.

"That's one way of putting it."

Feist asked, "And if that's impossible?"

"We've already discussed this. See to it that he doesn't come back here. Does that give you enough clarity?"

"All right then. But just so it's understood, that happens, I'm owed my premium."

"Understood."

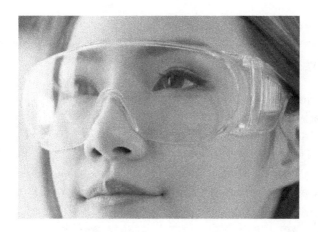

Chapter 42

YEONHEE DROPPED ONTO the floor cushion next to Jon, crossed her legs, tossed her head back and finger combed her black hair in one fluid movement.

"The Embassy will not help you get a passport?"

"No," he answered bitterly. "Not with the police after me."

"How can I help you?"

The walls of the small apartment seemed to close in on him.

"I can't stay here. I do, they'll find me for sure."

"My friend isn't home, so I talked to her on her cell. She'll be home later. We can wait here until then. Or," her face brightened, "you still owe me dinner."

A quick check his cell charge showed the battery critically low. He also worried about his appearance. By now, every cop in Seoul had probably memorized a detailed description of him. Which, now that he thought about it, probably explained how the cop spotted him so easily outside the Intercontinental. He held up the cell.

"I need to find a charger for this. And, I need fresh clothes.

Know any stores open this time of night?"

"No problem. There are several close by." She jumped up and held out her hand for him. "Let's go."

In a small dressing room Jon pulled on a pair of denim jeans and a black polo shirt.

A perfect fit.

He'd already selected a fairly good Ralph Lauren knockoff of a black shirt with epaulets. He undressed, removed the price tags, and redressed. Jon also bought a pair of Nike running shoes, a disposable cell, a charger for his Droid, and a small black gym bag to store everything. He was surprised at not thinking of getting a new cell sooner. He opted for one that gave him 200 minutes of international calling time. If that didn't last until he got out of here, well...

Now packed, he opened the dressing room door and headed for the cashier, Yeonhee falling in beside him. Initially, he worried about paying by credit card, but figured Park already knew he was still in the area so what difference did it make?

Holding Yeonhee's hand and acting like a couple, they walked back to the apartment from the restaurant. For the first time since meeting her at the Ritz-Carlton, she seemed relaxed.

She said, "Come, we go to Gayeon's apartment now."

"Hold on, let me make a call."

"No. It can wait until you're off the street."

Good point.

He slid the cellphone back into his pocket.

Gayeon's apartment was slightly bigger than Yeonhee's, a one-bedroom affair with a double bed. She worked as a secretary at a large company, Yeonhee told him. She was thin and strikingly beautiful, a few inches shorter than Yeonhee with a flatter face with pronounced cheekbones and equally large innocent almond eyes. Oversized glasses gave her a studious appearance.

As Yeonhee introduced them, Gayeon smiled, bowed and blushed.

"She speaks less English than I do," Yeonhee explained.

"Thank you for sharing your apartment," he said to her.

She put perfectly manicured fingernails to her lips and glanced at Yeonhee with a giggle.

Yeonhee muttered a stern reply in Korean. Then to Jon: "Make your calls now, okay?"

Wayne answered immediately.

"My God, Jon, you okay? I've been worried sick when I didn't hear back from you. Get hold of Fisher or the Embassy?"

"Yeah, but I'm getting jammed. Park notified the Embassy before I called so the guy I talked to—Bundy something—says there's a warrant out for my arrest, which, according to him means there's no way they can help."

"Aw, shit, this just keeps getting better, doesn't it?"

Yeonhee whispered to Gayeon as both of them sat on floor cushions, watching him.

"How about you? Do any better on finding a lawyer?"

"At least that's good news. I called around. Remember that thing a year or so ago with Tom McCarthy?"

McCarthy, another Seattle neurosurgeon, had been falsely accused of stealing classified material from the military.

"Yeah?"

"Figured he might know someone, so called him. He recommended a guy named Palmer Davidson. I got hold of him and explained your situation. He said there's nothing he can do in Seoul, that you'll have to find someone there, but went on to say that if you can figure out a way to get back home, he's happy to represent you. He made a point of saying to get out of there with or without a passport. Meaning if you have to, find a way to get one illegally. Way he sees it you wouldn't be heading back to Seoul any time soon, so screw 'em."

"Bundy basically said the same thing. I just haven't had time to do anything about it. And really don't know where to start."

"That anything Jin-Woo might help you with? You'd think with all those cousins of his, one of them would have a connection."

Seemed like Jin-Woo had a cousin in every business they'd ever discussed. He'd already considered and rejected that possibility.

"No good. I don't want to contact him. Park had him in for questioning earlier today and for all I know, he may still be there. And you better believe that before they release him, Park will lean on him to give me up the moment he hears from me."

"You're probably right." Wayne made a little humming sound. "Know what? Somehow, I can't believe the State Department would completely abandon a U.S. citizen, regardless of the circumstances. Thought of trying someone other than Bundy?"

"Yeah, but only if nothing else works. Bundy pretty much convinced me they're not about to help."

"Damn!" Made the little hum again. "So how do I reach you if something happens here? The number showing up isn't your cell."

"Figured that'd be too easy for Park to track, so I picked up a disposable. I plan to keep my regular cell turned off in case Park has any way to trace its GPS."

He had Yeonhee specifically check with the salesclerk to make sure his new one didn't contain any GPS function.

"Got it. Be careful."

He punched off and spent a moment reconsidering Wayne's suggestion to call Jin-Woo.

Was there any way to enlist his help and still dodge Park?

Maybe he did know someone who could help him obtain a counterfeit. He dialed Jin-Woo's cell, heard it ring until finally flipping over to voice mail.

Worrisome.

Maybe he was correct about Jin-Woo still being questioned by Park. Nevertheless, it was worrisome.

Chapter 43

SOON AS JON put the phone down, Yeonhee said, "You look like you could use a drink."

Gayeon stood and moved to a cupboard above the sink.

Not a bad idea.

He'd done about as much as he could tonight. They'd had only tea at the restaurant, so a drink might relax him and, in turn, help jog loose an idea or two about how to find a counterfeit passport. If Park was able to track him down tonight, there wasn't much more he could do to prevent it. Being out on the street or checking into a hotel probably carried more risk than staying here.

"Sure, why not."

A thought hit.

"Does Jin-Woo know you and Gayeon are good friends?"

Gayeon was pulling down glasses and a fifth of Johnnie Walker Green Label from the cupboard when she paused to shoot a questioning look at Yeonhee. Yeonhee thought about it a moment.

"Know what? I don't know for sure. I may have mentioned

her to him at some time, but there's no reason that he should remember it."

"So, you haven't talked about her a lot?"

"No. Actually, I tell him very little about my personal life."

He trusted her judgment.

Gayeon served them each a glass of scotch, neat. They raised glasses in a silent toast, sipped, then sat on floor cushions, each absorbed in their private thoughts. Yeonhee suddenly looked up at Jon.

"My friend, Jung-Kyo has connections. Maybe he can help."

A twinge of jealousy tapped his heart.

He swallowed a large portion of the scotch, sending a burning ember down his throat on into his gut.

"The guy you're dating?"

Yeonhee blushed.

"Yes." Then quickly added, "He's an important man. Maybe he knows people who can take care of it."

Made sense.

More importantly, he didn't have a better idea.

"Worth a try." Then remembered her complaint the other night, of Jung-Kyo's jealousy. "Is that going to be a problem for you?"

For a moment the question seemed to embarrass her, but quickly vanished.

"If he can do it, he'll do it for me."

Jon wasn't so sure it was a good idea, yet didn't see another option.

"Okay, give him a call and ask."

She dialed a number, listened, apparently got no answer, so dumped the cell back into her purse.

"He didn't answer his cell and it's too late to call his office. When he's out drinking with friends he doesn't answer or just can't hear the ring. I'll try his office in the morning when I know he's at work."

Gayeon stood and held out her hand. Yeonhee fumbled

through her purse a moment and came away with a set of keys she handed her.

Jon held up his hand to stop whatever was about to happen.

"Wait a minute. Where's she going?"

Yeonhee seemed surprised at the question.

"She stays at my place. We stay here."

Sort of what it looked like might happen.

"Not a good idea. The police already know about you. If Park came to the lab, he might come to your place too. They find her there, they'll know where to look next."

Yeonhee shook her head as if disappointed in herself for not having thought of this.

"Know what? You're right."

She rattled off a few words to Gayeon.

Gayeon glanced at Jon and smiled.

Jon was frustrated for being unable to understand one word they said.

"What?"

"She wants you to take the bedroom. We sleep here."

"Where?" He scanned the room, seeing nothing to sleep on. "On the cushions?"

Yeonhee laughed at him.

"Yes. On the floor. Koreans sleep on the floor all the time. Is not a problem."

"That's not right. She's our hostess. I'll take the cushion and you two take the bed."

Yeonhee shook her head.

"No. You're her guest. You get the bed. She already changed the sheets. To do otherwise would not be polite."

The cramped hot bedroom contained a double bed, dresser, small square bedside table with a thin black tensor lamp, CD player on it and barely enough room to navigate around the bed. It reminded him of the stateroom he and Emily shared on a cruise. Wearing only shorts, he stretched out on the top of the bed, turned off the small lamp and listened to the hushed voices of the two women chatting softly in the other room.

For the first time in what seemed like days, he could luxuriate with his thoughts. As he lay still, trying to relax and allow sleep to come, he became aware of other sounds. A toilet flushed upstairs, sending a rush of water down a pipe in the wall. Outside a dog barked.

A door slammed.

A jet passed overhead.

Soon, heavy fatigue dragged him into deep sleep.

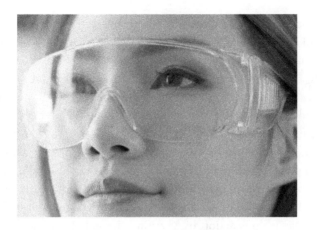

Chapter 44

YEONHEE CROSSED HER arms and leaned against the door jamb, watching Jon sleep. She debated how best to wake him, resisting the urge to do so with a gentle kiss on the cheek or by running her fingers through his brown hair.

Seeing him sleep seemed pleasingly intimate, a sight she would only experience if they were "involved."

What would it be like to be involved with him?

Would he be jealous, like Jung-Kyo? She thought not. He was more confident of himself than Jung-Kyo. Behind her, in the living room, Gayeon moved quietly, straightening up cushions and preparing the table for breakfast.

Before falling asleep last night, she debated the best way to approach Jung-Kyo about the passport. And now this issue still weighed heavily on her mind. No matter how delicately she worded the request, there was no way to actually get a passport without mentioning Jon's name. Eventually. As soon as she did, Jon would be at Jung-Kyo's mercy. Which would, she felt certain, be a problem...not to mention the things he'd accuse them of...

So, she decided to make the proposal in stages. First step would be to ask if he had the proper connections to obtain a false passport. If so, she would line everything up before actually giving him Jon's name. The passport picture would be the easiest part and could be done before that. And if Jung-Kyo pushed her, as she knew he would, there would be every reason to be evasive.

If he knew the document was for Jon—or any man, for that matter—he'd make a scene. *That*, she could handle. What worried her most was the possibility he'd notify the police immediately. And be totally self-righteous when he did it. Then justify his jealous action by claiming the police were, after all, hunting Jon.

Jung-Kyo was like that: always making excuses for what really amounted to petty jealousy. But, it was more than that. It was a control issue. He always had to be the one to control the relationship. If the tables were turned, if it were Jung-Kyo who needed help leaving the States, how would Jon react? Very differently, she suspected.

She settled for simply saying, "Jon, wake up," and not touching him.

When Jon came out of the small bathroom after washing up, Gayeon was at a two-burner hotplate brewing tea and cooking rice. Yeonhee, wearing a pair of back jeans and a Chicago Bulls sweatshirt, was dishing out three servings of kim chee with a set of long silver chopsticks.

Breakfast, Korean style.

They sat on cushions and ate at the low table but didn't talk.

Breakfast finished, Yeonhee began to straighten up the kitchen while Gayeon took her turn in the small bathroom. This gave Jon an opportunity to telephone the Embassy again. Last night—while waiting for sleep—he debated how best to approach the subject and decided simply to throw himself on their mercy. It required two separate conversations with low-level bureaucrats before finally being transferred to the consular officer, Warren Hamilton.

Jon started with, "Mr. Hamilton, Jon Ritter. Did Bundy tell you I called yesterday?"

"He did, and I'm well aware of your situation. As I understand it, he gave you some very *good* advice. Have you looked into his suggestion?"

A lead weight settled in his gut. Hamilton had just landed a pre-emptive strike. The man had no intention of helping Jon leaving the country.

"Are you recording this?"

"Yes."

"Good. Then, for the record, I didn't kill anybody. If the police have evidence to the contrary, I would love to see it. I'm being framed." His well-planned speech suddenly vaporized in a blitz of emotion. "Can we meet face to face? I need to tell you my side of this."

Hamilton spoke.

"Why? What good would that do? This is a legal issue that doesn't involve the State Department at all."

"At least give me a chance to explain my side of this. I didn't murder those patients. My whole research career was dependent on their outcome. The last thing I wanted was a complication. Okay, this sounds paranoid, but bear with me: an antiabortion group is trying to ruin me. They're responsible for this. You can verify this with one quick phone call to the Seattle field office of the FBI. Ask for Special Agent Gary Fisher. He'll confirm every word of this."

"Doctor Ritter—"

"No! Listen. Please. If those two patients *were* murdered the Nuremberg Avengers are responsible. They did it to destroy me and my work. Look at their website. Ask Fisher. They murdered Gabriel Lippmann when they attacked me a week ago. Fisher and the Seattle Police can verify this because it's true."

"Let me—"

Why wouldn't anyone listen to him?

"Verify it! Please! Call Fisher. He knows. He'll vouch for what I just told you."

"Hold on," this time even more emphatic, not giving Jon a chance to interrupt again. "Let me explain something before you go any further. None of what you're telling me matters."

The words floored him.

"Doesn't matter? What the hell you—"

"Let's cut to the chase. I may be a bureaucrat, but I'm not stupid. I know what you're asking. You want me to facilitate your exit of this country. In other words, commit a crime."

"Right. Exactly! I'm being framed for a murder I didn't commit. Why should I want to stay here and..."

What could he say to be convincing?

Jon continued, "You'd be asking the same thing if you were me."

"Let me explain a few facts. I work for the State Department. I, and all the other personnel stationed here, have nothing to do with the Korean judicial system. We cannot, and will not, interfere with their system in any way. Rightly or wrongly accused, you will need to deal with them on their terms. If this means you must stand trial in a court of law, so be it."

Abandonment, betrayal, and anger swirled through Jon's mind. Anger came out on top.

"Don't hand me that holier-than-thou shit. I remember a news story from several years ago...a U.S. Citizen working for a contractor in some place like Mongolia ended up charged with killing a man. I don't remember the exact details, but I do remember the government allowed him to return home until the trial. He later went back to that country to be proven innocent of any crime. Why can't you arrange the same type of thing for me?"

"I too remember that case. For your edification the dispute centered on whether the death happened to be an on-the-job accident. That's significantly different from your situation. In your particular case, the police claim premeditated first degree murder for which you were detained, but then you orchestrated an armed escape from detention."

Why isn't he listening to me?

"How could that possibly be? What could possibly be my motivation? Why would I do that? The only thing I did involving the patients was observe surgery. In fact, I never met either of them until the moment I walked into the OR and then they were under anesthesia."

Not exactly the whole truth, but he wasn't making headway otherwise.

"So you say. The Seoul police provide quite a different version. Correct me if I'm wrong but here's the official police version: you came to Seoul with the very specific intent of conducting research you were prohibited from doing at home. You pressured your friend Jin-Woo Lee into helping you. Then you instructed him to intentionally deceive Tyasami hospital personnel into believing you were conducting quite a different surgery than scheduled so you could conduct your research. You're saying this is all a pack of lies?"

Jon was speechless. Factually, Hamilton's version was closer to the truth than his version. But the way he told it made his actions sound so...slimy. And not even close to his intent.

Pressure Jin-Woo?

No, not at all. That was a lie.

Hamilton said, "Given these facts, you are hardly an uninvolved observer."

Jon had to say something to defend himself, to set the record straight.

"Even if what you say is half true—which it isn't—that doesn't mean I'm guilty of murder."

Hamilton gave an I'm-losing-patience-with-you sigh.

"I don't know how to get this across to you more clearly than what I just told you, so listen to me again: the State Department will not provide you with any under-the-table assistance in fleeing the country. Please resign yourself to that fact and move on. It's just not going to happen. Understand?"

"Please don't just leave me dangling in the wind."

"Doctor Ritter, listen carefully to what I'm telling you. You're in a foreign country and at the moment you're a political hot potato. So hot, in fact, we can't even consider bending rules for you."

Whoa, this is new.

"What do you mean, hot potato?"

"Don't be naive. Or have you not been watching the news?"

News? What news?

"What are you talking about?"

"You haven't followed the story of the rape? Up near the DMZ?"

Vaguely remembered hearing something on CNN…

"What does that have to do with me?"

"Then let me spell it out for you. Last week two American G.I.s allegedly raped a fifteen-year-old girl from a small village near the border with North Korea. The story hit the local news and then immediately went viral. Facebook, Twitter, you name it, it's there and the Korean press is having a political field day over it. They want to cut the dicks off those two service men and frankly, who can blame them?"

"What has that to do with me?"

"If you have to ask, you are not listening. The political climate in this country is not ripe for cutting Americans any slack. No matter what the circumstances. If anyone at State helps sneak you out of the country, we, meaning the United States government, could be in for a great deal of grief. We can't afford that now. Lest you ask, I'll give you one very good reason. Korean Air is on the verge of ordering thirty new Dreamliners. At the moment, they could go either way, Airbus or Boeing. And this but one example." He paused dramatically. "*Now* do you see the bigger picture, Doctor?"

Disgusted, Jon hung up, leaned back against the wall and blew between pursed lips.

What about Richard Stillman?

He thought about that a moment, sat bolt upright.

Why not?

The man was well connected. Maybe that meant he had some connections over here. He looked at Yeonhee, still straightening up the apartment. She seemed uncomfortable with asking her boyfriend to help, so why put her through the hassle if Stillman could solve the problem? Yeah, maybe he could help.

Worth a try.

He picked up the new cell phone and dialed.

"Yo, Jon!" Stillman sounded surprised. "What up, dog? When I didn't hear from you after surgery I tried calling. No answer. I've been worried sick about you."

Jon quickly highlighted the story starting with the phone call from Feist.

When Stillman heard the part about Jon's escape from the police he laughed and said, "Some cop probably got a new asshole for letting that happen."

Jon wasn't in the mood for jokes.

"Here's the problem. Park has my passport, and I can't board a flight without one. The Embassy refuses to help, so it looks like the only way I'm getting one is illegally. But I don't know anyone to ask for help. Any chance you might know someone in Seoul with the right connections for that?"

"Hold on, let me think." Stillman hesitated a few beats before, "Matter of fact, I do. There is this ex-pat friend who lives in Seoul. Bet he can help. Where exactly are you?"

At last!

A major wave of relief swept over him. Jon opened his mouth to answer when a sixth sense cautioned him. What possible reason could there be to tell him?

He hedged with, "Not sure. Downtown Seoul someplace. Why?"

Which was true.

"This your number?"

No sense lying about that.

"Yes."

"Give me a few minutes to make a call, see what I can arrange. I'll get back to you soon as I have something. One way or another. Give me, say, fifteen minutes, max. If I can't arrange something by then I'll let you know. Call you back soon as I hear."

Another spike of paranoia rippled through.

"No. I'll call you."

He planned to shut down the phone the moment they disconnected.

"Fine. Give me 15 minutes."

Jon felt stupid for not having asked Stillman before now. If he had, he might be on a flight this very minute. This was also best for Yeonhee. Not that he didn't trust her friend, but he didn't know him. Besides, the more options he had, the better.

"I can't thank you enough."

"No problem. Glad to help. After all, you're part of the Trophozyme team now."

Chapter 45

AFTER CLOSING THE office door, Richard Stillman returned to his desk with his back to the window and dialed Feist. For fifteen seconds he listened to dead space as computers and satellites magically ferreted out Feist's cell on the other side of the Pacific.

What was life like before the telephone?

He couldn't imagine.

Sounding annoyed, Feist answered with, "What?"

"We just had a stroke of luck. Our mutual friend called with an update. Sounds like things haven't been going well for him and he needs help. I offered to accommodate him."

"Bloody hell! Where is he?"

Stillman leaned back against the soft black leather, enjoying this situation. Mr. Bigshot Intelligence Agent needed his help locating the person he was being paid to keep an eye on.

"Wouldn't say, other than he's still in Seoul. But you were right, the cops have his passport so at the moment he's stuck. At least until he can get his hands on a fake. He asked if I knew someone who might facilitate finding one. Told him yes, that I'll arrange for him to meet you."

Feist laughed.

"Outstanding. Where?"

"You tell me. You're over there. Besides, I have no idea how you want to handle this. You name the place and time and I'll have him there. And listen, change of plans. It's not enough to just have him locked up, too many things have gone wrong. He's been too damn lucky. I'll set up the meet. You eliminate him and be done with it. Doesn't matter where or how, just as long as he never surfaces again. We perfectly clear on this?"

"If that's case, just about any place will do. Out in the open in a crowd would be best. I pop him up close, no one will see, and I'll be on me way."

Jon anxiously waited fifteen minutes to the second before calling Stillman back.

"We're in luck," Stillman said. "My friend says no problem obtaining what you need. But given the circumstances, he stressed completing this transaction soon as possible. The longer you're in Korea, the more likely you are to be caught. You ready to move?"

Jon couldn't believe it. Fifteen minutes ago he had no idea how to proceed. Now his problem appeared to be solved.

"Oh, man, I can't thank you enough."

He flashed thumbs up to Yeonhee who, he realized, was watching him with a worried expression.

"He said everything can be taken care of at once. They snap a passport photo then fill in the document. Name a place you feel is safe to meet and he'll be there."

"Hold on." Jon covered the mouthpiece and whispered to Yeonhee, "That big building on the next block. What's the name of it?" with a nod in that direction.

She glanced out the window.

"The Hyundai Building?"

Jon gave Stillman the name of the building but claimed it

would take thirty minutes before he could possibly get there.

Stillman repeated the name and the agreed upon time and added, "He'll meet you on the street outside the front door. You set?"

"Yes." Then, just before disconnecting, "How will I know who he is?"

Stillman laughed.

"That's the easy part. I'll e-mail him your picture. You're a westerner, so that makes you stand out. He'll be looking for you at the front entrance. What're you wearing?"

Once again, a chill of paranoia rippled down Jon's spine. He trusted Stillman, but could the Avengers monitor his phone? Could they find out another way?

He lied with, "Jeans, black tee shirt, black blazer."

"Got it. You think you can find it okay, or do you need more time?"

Jon looked through the window at the building a block away.

"No, thirty minutes should give me enough time if I start out now."

"Fine. He'll see you in a half hour. If, for some reason, he can't make it within thirty minutes I'll call back with a revised estimate." Stillman's tone became more personal. "I know I don't need to tell you this, but be careful, keep a low profile. And come home safely."

Jon reached for his coat and stood. Yeonhee stood too.

"I go with you."

At first he considered going alone but didn't want to risk getting lost even though it was only two blocks away.

"Great. I appreciate it."

She put her hand on the doorknob, ready to leave, but paused, looking at him closely.

"You trust this man?"

Good question.

The simple act of being questioned raised a flicker of doubt in him. And on second thought, if he really dug down into the depths of his feeling, he didn't trust him. So maybe that's why he'd been a little paranoid.

Why?

Because of a long-ingrained dislike for the man?

He pushed the doubts aside. After all, Stillman was bailing him out of a bad problem.

Wasn't he?

He shook his head, confused.

"Can't really say for sure."

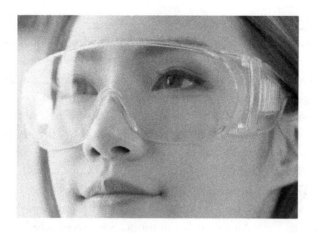

Chapter 46

JON TOOK IN Gayeon's small living room one last time, wondering what, if anything, to bring.

The black gym bag with his few possessions?

If he got the passport, rather than return, he'd catch the first available taxi and head straight for the airport. He slipped on his blazer, grabbed his bag, said to Yeonhee.

"Please thank Gayeon for me."

Yeonhee called something to her. A muffled reply came from behind the closed bathroom door.

"She says you're welcome back anytime."

Then they were out the door and moving down the stairs. Jon glimpsed his watch. Twenty-five minutes until the planned rendezvous. Certainly enough time to scope out the area and check for the presence of police before meeting Stillman's friend.

Before hitting the front door, he said to her, "I want to check this place out before we actually go there. Know anywhere we can do that without being seen?"

She approved of the idea.

"Easy, I show you."

He let her lead him along the narrow street fronting Gayeon's apartment, up a side street, across a wide, busy avenue, and down a cluttered narrow alley of back entrances and garbage cans reeking of rotted cabbage and spoilt milk.

She stopped at the back door to a shop, said, "A Chinese medicine shop. If we stand at the front, we'll be directly across the street from the building. Is good enough?"

"Sounds perfect."

The door opened noiselessly, and he followed her across a shadowy, dingy back room piled high with cardboard boxes giving off the odor of earth and mold. She parted a red curtain, stepped into the store crammed with rickety sagging wooden tables loaded down with wide-mouth jars and ceramic crocks smelling of cinnamon and other spices, giving the shop an exotic and soothing aura. A withered, skeletal man with white hair and a stained white tee shirt nodded at them from behind a glass display counter of powders and dried plants. If he was surprised at their entrance, he didn't show it.

Yeonhee bowed and said something. The old man turned stiffly, removed a lid from a jar, carefully sprinkled beige powder onto a tarnished brass scale. Satisfied with the weight, he dumped the powder into a square of white paper, folded it into a package, and handed it to her. In return, she paid him a 10,000 *won* note and bowed. The transaction finished, she led Jon through the front door but stopped in the small entrance under the shadow of the awning.

"What'd you get?" he asked.

She playful punched his shoulder.

"Ginseng. I tell him an older man like you needs good medicine for sexual power."

Jon felt his face redden and busied himself with scanning the sidewalk directly across the street. Yeonhee, standing shoulder to shoulder with him, did the same. The vantage point would be ideal if not for six lanes of two-way traffic obscuring the view. Only an occasional break in traffic provided a brief glimpse of the front steps and pedestrians.

"What are we looking for?"

"Police, for one thing. Other than that, I just…have this uneasy feeling…paranoia maybe, but I can't ignore it."

Yeonhee slipped her hand into his and gave a reassuring squeeze.

"You have met this person before?"

Holding her hand should've felt good, but instead, it seemed confining and intensified the butterflies in his stomach. He gave her hand a gentle squeeze before pulling free.

"No, never have."

He checked his watch again. Twenty minutes to go. Double-checked his cell to make sure it was turned off, scanned the area to either side of them, wiped both hands on his hips.

"Then how do you know who to look for?"

Good question, a point that was making him increasingly nervous.

"I don't. The plan is for him to find me."

He fidgeted and wiped his hand on his pants.

Another five minutes crept by.

Suddenly, the rhythm of traffic changed, providing a clear view at the sidewalk directly across the street. One man stood out, a Caucasian, buff, crew-cut, confident. Immediately, Jon recognized him as the soldier at Narita Airport, even though now he wasn't wearing the uniform.

Coincidence?

No. He suddenly knew it had to be Feist.

As if drawn by mental telepathy, Feist turned his eyes and immediately spotted Jon. A fresh onslaught of cars swallowed the momentary gap, hiding him. Then Feist appeared again, running, heading straight for him, ignoring screeching tires and honking horns as he barreled across the six lanes of traffic.

Jon grabbed Yeonhee's hand.

"Run!" He turned to run down the sidewalk, but she jerked

him back into the shop. "No. This way!"

They burst into the shop, dodging tables, weaving toward the red curtain, Yeonhee spewing sharp words to the shocked proprietor. They charged through the back room and out the door into the narrow alley. She cut right, tugging him, hit a dead run for twenty yards, cut left, threw open another door to a building and pulled him inside.

She shoved him toward stairs, then shot past, running up the dimly lit flight.

"Up here."

They stopped at the first landing, fumbled keys from her purse, sorted one out, unlocked a door, pulled Jon inside, slammed and locked the deadbolt.

Jon stood in a commercial-grade kitchen gasping for air. Hands on his hips, he dropped into a crouch.

"Where are we?"

Panting, Yeonhee leaned against the doorjamb, still clutching the key ring as if it were her life.

Between gasps whispered, "Shhhhh," and pushed off the door, came over, put her lips next to his ear. "A restaurant. An auntie owns it. They not open yet. Too early."

She coughed softly into a fist, patted her chest, silently returned to the door to peek through a fisheye security lens.

"That man, who is he?"

Less winded now, Jon began to look around.

"Don't know for sure, but I bet he's Nigel Feist. The one who killed Gabe."

The only light in the windowless kitchen came through a half-open door to a hall. Yeonhee backed away from the door and motioned him closer to the hall, put a finger to her lips and waited.

A moment later he heard footsteps growing louder from the stairs they'd run up a minute ago.

He leaned toward Yeonhee, whispered, "You lock the door?"

"I think so." But didn't sound convinced. They both looked at the door but didn't move. She asked, "Maybe we should go out the front now?"

Jon thought of the second man in the garage the night of the attack and wondered if Feist had a partner here too?

"No. He might have someone watching it."

He glanced around for a weapon.

Yeonhee put her hand on his arm to not move just as the footsteps stopped on the other side of the door. The glint of metal caught his attention. He craned his neck for a closer look. A heavy meat cleaver was embedded tip first in a chopping block. Without a sound, he levered it out, appreciating the substantial heft. Probably not the best weapon if Feist had a gun, but definitely better than nothing.

The doorknob rattled but the door didn't open.

Next came heavy pounding from the door with a muffled, "Open up."

Jon heard the soft padding of bare feet approach from behind them and turned to look. Yeonhee quickly kicked off her shoes before noiselessly running a few steps down the hall to intercept and whisper in an older woman's ear. The woman's eyes widened. For a moment she started at Jon, then nodded to Yeonhee, turned, and vanished.

More pounding from the door, followed by several seconds of silence. Finally, heavy footsteps descended the stairs.

Yeonhee whispered, "Auntie is watching from her office. She has a video security system and can see if he really leaves the building or is only trying to trick us."

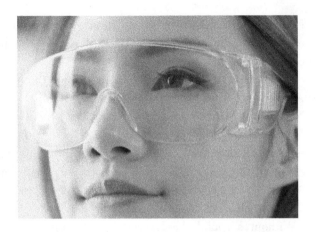

Chapter 47

YEONHEE ENTERED GAYEON'S apartment after Jon, closed and locked the door. They both slumped against the wall, Jon catching his breath again while trying to calm his raw nerves.

Yeonhee asked, "This Stillman...why would he do this to you?"

Jon dropped down onto a floor cushion and hugged his knees.

"I don't know. Nothing makes sense. Unless maybe the Avengers tapped his phone."

His instinctive distrust of Stillman was back now, stronger than ever, his mind running through several questions, coming up with serious doubts...

Gayeon padded from the bathroom in a terrycloth robe and a white towel turban, eyes darting from Yeonhee to Jon and back again. She said something to Yeonhee. Yeonhee chattered something in return before saying to Jon.

"She wants to know what's wrong. I tell her nothing."

Suddenly someone started pounding on the front door.

Seemed like all of Jon's muscles jerked in one massive startle response.

"Shit! He followed us."

Yeonhee and Gayeon looked at each other, eyes wide, neither wanting to answer or open the door.

More pounding.

Gayeon went to the wall beside the door, pressed an intercom button Jon hadn't noticed before, said something in Korean. A gruff male voice answered.

Yeonhee whispered to Jon.

"Quick. Hide. It's the police."

He started toward the bedroom, but she grabbed his arm.

"No. That's the first place they'll look."

He had no idea where else to hide in such a small apartment. The closet? Bathroom?

No, she was right, they check those places first.

There was no place else. He was totally screwed.

Gayeon motioned to Yeonhee who, in turn, shoved aside a rack of clothes, exposing French doors to a decorative, non-functional balcony. On closer inspection, it was only a wrought iron railing. The doors were probably intended for air circulation and light because they opened to a narrow alley with nothing but a brick wall on the other side. Yeonhee pushed him toward the opening.

"Quick, out here!"

Out where?

He grabbed the railing, leaned over, looked to either side.

What the hell was she talking about?

This side of the building was solid brick with a narrow ledge a half brick wide connecting similar balconies of the other two units on this floor.

"You kidding? There's nothing to stand on."

She pushed him again.

"Hurry!"

More pounding came from the door.

He peered straight down three stories to an alley of bricks, a few puddles, and garbage cans. His heart stopped.

Where the hell was he supposed to go?

A fall would kill him. His muscles locked up.

Yeonhee said, "Quick, quick! Go out there."

He couldn't…

"Jon! Detective Park is at the door!"

Great choice: Park or lying dead on stinking bricks in fucking Seoul.

He turned his back to the alley, stepped over the iron railing onto the narrow ledge, both hands in a death grip on the window jamb. She slapped his hands.

"No no, let go. Move away or they see you."

He sucked a deep breath and gripped the edge of the bricks at shoulder height, then edged to the left. Carefully, he studied each toehold while working inch by inch sideways, along the narrow ledge, his heart pounding in both ears. The moment he cleared the glass door it shut, trapping him in chilly morning shadows. The clothes rack reappeared on the other side of the glass, partially hiding him. But if he could still see over the top of it into the room, they could sure as hell see him. He inched further away to the left of the window.

Still not far enough.

Slowly, by first sliding his left foot a few inches, then repositioning his handholds one by one, he moved away from the French doors, finally decided this was far enough, no way was he moving one more millimeter. He'd take his chances right here.

Dizzy with fear, eyes clamped shut, fingers gripping brick, he prayed to God to not let him fall, pressed a cheek against a cool damp brick and drew a slow deliberate breath. How long before his legs suddenly buckled from the strain? In high definition slow motion he visualized the series of events that would ultimately kill him: the eventual loss of balance, the split second realization there was no way to compensate, the accelerating backward fall through space, slamming into brick, lying in a puddle of hurt as blood pooled from damaged organs into spaces reserved for lungs or intestines, the slide into shock, finally death in a stinking garbage-can-filled alley in fucking Seoul, South Korea.

Why?

You never knew when you'd die. Or how. But dying like this? Ridiculous! All because some fanatics didn't like the work or because Stillman....

Maybe both.

And that, more than anything, pissed him off.

In a moment of existential clarity, he wondered which emotions ruled: anger or fear? He vowed to survive—if for no other reason than to have the opportunity to fuck over Stillman.

Think!

He knew better than to look down, because his fear of heights would paralyze him and make falling a certainty.

Think! There had to be something to do.

From inside the apartment came a muffled gruff male voice. Yeonhee yelled something, followed by a burst of harsh words. Gayeon screamed. A male laughed. Doors slammed.

Hold on. Ignore the pain.

Every muscle in every finger ached. Same with his calves. His breathing came fast and shallow. A drop of sweat slithered into the corner of his eye, causing a blink, then another. He fought the urge to rub it with a finger. Instead, he pressed his cheek against the cold brick and blinked, diluting the salt, soothing the sting. He closed his mouth and purposely slowed his breathing, but this sucked dust up his nose.

He sneezed, the force pushing him away from the wall, almost to the tipping point. He teetered just shy of it, instinct saying to grip the brick harder as logic argued that if he did, his fingers might slip or fatigue out. He fought to not fall backward and remained suspended like this until his balance slowly shifted toward the building again, then stabilized to where he could pull back against the wall. He pressed against the brick, clamped his eyes shut and held on for dear life as time decelerated into a world of nothing but aching cramping muscles.

I can't take this any longer.

You have to.

He tried to distract himself by concentrating on deliberate deep breaths. Another drop of sweat stung his eye. He blinked, squeezed his lids tighter, and held on. Gayeon and Yeonhee yelled again. Another door slammed.

Fuck it!

He'd rather risk dealing with Park than endure another minute of this torture. Besides, he was rapidly reaching the limit of endurance. Too much longer and his fingers would give out. He started to inch back to the window, the simple change in position giving his muscles a much-needed sense of relief. He paused to listen, suddenly aware of a change inside the apartment as the voices faded. A door slammed followed by silence.

He inched closer to the French doors, reached the railing, slowly climbed onto the wider ledge, the surer footing giving his muscles and mind a huge relief. He waited a few seconds before knocking on the window. No response. He waited several more seconds before knocking again, harder.

The clothes rack jerked aside and Yeonhee opened the door.

"Jon, you okay?"

"Yes," he said, relieved.

He just wanted to be inside with both feet on something wider than half a brick. Careful to not slip or loosen his grip, he stepped onto the threshold of the door, both legs cramping from strain. For a moment he crouched, flexing his fingers, relaxing his calves before taking the final step over the wrought iron railing into safety.

Finally inside the room, he sat on a cushion, put his face in his hands and started shaking.

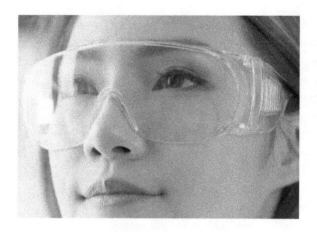

Chapter 48

JON REMAINED ON a cushion, back against the wall, Gayeon's laptop on his thighs, researching Richard Stillman and Trophozyme. An ugly suspicion shrouded his mind, making him nauseous.

What if Stillman's phone *wasn't* tapped?

What if Stillman had been orchestrating events from the beginning? There were too many coincidences to ignore the possibility, things like visiting him in the hospital the day after Gabe's murder. Or offering him the CMO job offer a month before his personal information and picture surfaced on the Avenger's website. Taken individually, none of those events amounted to much, but taken together...sure, it wasn't concrete, just a series of coincidences. But still, what was Stillman's motivation?

That was the easy part. The way the agreement read, if Jon didn't return from Seoul, the formulation would revert to Stillman. Emily always claimed he was too trusting, that one day he'd be taken advantage of. Well, maybe this was it.

"Jon!"

He glanced up at Yeonhee and Gayeon who were watching TV with the sound low. Gayeon started thumbing the remote, upping the volume as Yeonhee pointed at the screen. A news channel appeared to be reporting a breaking story, a reporter holding a wind-screened microphone just below her lips, police and gawkers crowding in behind her.

"What?"

She waved him silent, held up a finger. A moment later she turned to him wide eyed.

"It's Jin-Woo. He's dead. Murdered."

"Aw, Jesus..."

Then his own picture—the one on his passport—flashed on the screen with a voice-over. Gayeon rattled off a string of words and Yeonhee returned to the newscast. A wave of nausea hit. He knew what was coming before they translated. He checked his watch. Only 45 minutes until they were scheduled to meet Yeonhee's friend, Jung-Kyo, the Hyundai executive, the man with connections he hoped would secure him a passport.

He pushed the laptop aside and stood, knowing he had to do *something*. Although he wasn't sure what to do or where to go, he couldn't sit still another minute. Yeonhee pushed up off the floor.

"We should get going."

"It's only ten minutes from here. You want to take the risk of someone identifying you? Especially after this," referring to the news story.

One good thing about big cities, you could be anonymous in public. In that regard Seoul was no different than New York or Los Angeles. So the way he figured, a few extra minutes on the street didn't increase his chance of being arrested.

He picked up the New York Yankees ball cap he purchased yesterday.

"Doesn't matter. I have to get out of here and walk around, do something."

Yeonhee nodded agreement.

"Good idea. Give me a minute to get ready."

"I need to call Wayne anyway, so take your time."

The thought of getting away from the warm claustrophobic apartment already soothed his anxiety. On the other hand, meeting Yeonhee's jealous boyfriend was also making him nervous.

Could he trust him?

He decided that Jung-Kyo's reaction to seeing him with Yeonhee would be his only indication, and then it might be too late.

But what other option did he have?

He checked the cell phone battery, saw a full charge, unplugged it and dumped the charger in his gym bag. Done packing, he dialed.

Wayne said, "Sure hope you've got good news for me this time."

"Not exactly."

He summarized his narrow escape from Feist and the news about Jin-Woo. Lastly, he mentioned meeting someone who might be able to score him a passport.

"Do whatever it takes. Just get out of there as fast as you possibly can."

"Believe me, I'm trying."

Yeonhee shrugged on her black raincoat and pointed toward the door.

He held up a finger for one more minute and spoke into the phone, "Look, I need to go, but something occurred to me last night, so there's one thing I want you to do. There's a Trophozyme board member, Sandra Nolan. There's also a person on Council with the same name."

"NIH Council? The one that approved the human trial?"

"Exactly."

Wayne took a second to put it together.

"Son of a bitch. You thinking—"

"Yep. Check it out, see if they're the same person. Okay?"

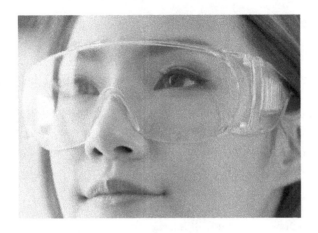

Chapter 49

YEONHEE'S IRRITATION GREW with each passing minute that Jung-Kyo kept them waiting. She saw it as another example of a passive aggressive attempt to control her.

Yes, he was a big-shot executive with important meetings on his schedule, but this was the only time she'd ever asked him to disrupt work for her. And she stressed the importance of the situation. He promised to leave the office immediately, but that was thirty minutes ago and the walk here shouldn't take more than ten minutes at most.

What would happen if the police caught Jon?

She was certain he hadn't killed the patients and knew for sure he hadn't killed Jin-Woo. Now, each minute he remained in Seoul increased the odds of his capture.

For the past half hour, they'd perched knee to knee on bar stools at a counter of a noisy hole-in-the-wall noodle bar, in thick steamy air smelling of grease, garlic, and ginger, pretending to eat, although neither she nor Jon had any appetite. They faced the window, Styrofoam bowls of a tasty, chilled specialty on the counter in front of them, the bill of Jon's New

York Yankees cap pulled low to hide his anxious tired face. He fidgeted constantly. She didn't blame him. She knew what it was like to be in a foreign country unable to speak the language. And knowing this only increased her sorrow for him and his situation.

She couldn't imagine being falsely accused of a crime for which the penalty might be death. She stabbed chopsticks at the noodles, silently cursing Jung-Kyo's juvenile jealousy.

How much longer could they sit here without attracting even more attention? Already, the proprietor was eying them with impatience, letting her know this was an eat-and-move-on type of place.

Jung-Kyo entered, roughly shouldering past a stooped weathered lady paying the cashier Won. Tall, lean, and handsome in a beautifully tailored Italian suit and perfectly glossed leather shoes.

She leaned close to Jon, her knees touching his thigh, whispered, "He's here."

They slid off the stools and came face to face with Jung-Kyo.

She pointed to the door, said, "We talk outside," and followed him out, Jon trailing. They moved away from the stream of pedestrians and next to the shop's window. She asked Jung-Kyo, "Can you get the passport for him?"

For several seconds he sized Jon up before saying in Korean, "What is he to you?"

"Please! We don't have time for this."

"The police are searching for him, aren't they?"

She looked directly into his eyes with no attempt to hide her anger.

"He hasn't done a thing wrong, Jung-Kyo."

With a scowl, he shook his head.

"That is for the police to decide, not you."

She finger-combed her hair and looked up at the small patch of blue sky between the tops of two office buildings, took a deep breath and considered her reply. Now wasn't the time to let the frustration with him cloud her thinking. Why had she hoped for a different, perhaps more mature, reaction, when in her heart she knew this would happen?

Slowly she brought her eyes back to him.

"Jung-Kyo, he is nothing to me. How many times must I tell you this? You know he and Jin-Woo are colleagues. They work together for years now. At the moment he needs help and Jin-Woo is not able to give it to him. This makes him my responsibility. Please, I am asking for your help because it will help me."

Jung-Kyo folded his arms across his chest, making a big deal out of watching an overweight woman walk a miniature poodle along the street, demonstrating to Yeonhee his power and control over Jon's destiny.

In that moment she realized how much he relished every moment of her dependency. Suddenly, she felt tired of the endless innuendos, the accusing looks, of having to explain every second she spent out of his sight. Her relationship with him simply wasn't worth the effort to save it anymore.

So, there was nothing to lose by giving him an ultimatum.

"Jung-Kyo, turn around and face me!"

He continued to watch the traffic as if she hadn't spoken a word.

She stepped closer to him and raised her voice, as if talking to a petulant child.

"Very well, then this is how it will be. Unless you help him secure a passport, I will never see you again. You have three seconds to decide."

He did not react, calling her bluff.

She took Jon by the hand and said in English, "Come. We'll find another way," and started leading Jon down the street.

Jung-Kyo caught up and grabbed her shoulder.

"Wait."

The photographer's tiny shop was filled with floor-to-ceiling color portraits: brides, gowned graduates with mortarboards, anniversary couples, families. Some smiling, some serious, others staring wistfully into the distance. A glass case held several cameras for sale.

Jung-Kyo introduced Yeonhee to the proprietor and then, without a word or glance at Jon, whispered something to Yeonhee before storming out the door. The studio, if it could be called that, was separated from the reception area by a sheet that doubled as the backdrop for portrait shots. Jon sat on a stool and stared into the camera lens.

The entire process took less than thirty minutes. The proprietor even accepted VISA, charging only five hundred dollars for the forgery and explaining that the charge would show up as a camera purchase. Jon ran his finger over the pages, marveling at the genuine look and feel, including a patina of travel wear and tear and immigration stamps from various Asian countries.

Yeonhee tugged his arm.

"Come. You must hurry. Jung-Kyo will give you two hours before he notifies the police. That's what he told me before he left, it's his way to regain control of me. Hurry."

Then she was moving him into the street, flagging a taxi, opening the door, shoving him in the passenger seat, shouting instructions at the driver as the cab began the race toward Incheon.

Jon watched utility poles flash past and tried not to think of what would happen if he made it to the airport only to be captured again. He reached over and took Yeonhee's hand in his. He wanted to tell her something, find some way to thank her.

She gave a slight squeeze but didn't look at him.

He wondered what she felt for him, if anything. But he settled instead on savoring each remaining second together in much the same way a death row inmate clings to each remaining minute of life.

A video monitor inside the international terminal listed flights in descending time to departure. A Singapore Air flight scheduled for Chicago in fifteen minutes. Too soon. Another one was going to Vancouver, BC in thirty minutes.

The next flight to North America would not board for another three hours.

Three hours: too much to risk.

A Cathay Pacific to Hong Kong outbound in 45 minutes: again pushing his luck to the outer limits. The moment Jung-Kyo reported the falsified passport to the Metropolitan police, it would become worthless. But the moment the aircraft left Seoul airspace he'd be out of their jurisdiction. On the other hand, if the authorities where he landed knew he was traveling under a false passport, disembarking might become a problem. But he'd rather face charges of traveling with false papers than first-degree murder in Korea.

Except for one agent, the Singapore Air ticket counter was deserted because the passengers for the next flight in several hours had already been assigned seats and were waiting at the gate. At the counter he handed her his credit card and passport.

He tried to appear casual, like a seasoned traveler simply moving up a flight.

"Any seat left on the Chicago flight?" he asked.

She glanced at her wristwatch.

"That is a problem. You might not make it through security, it's a bottleneck at the moment. I can ask them to hold the flight, but only for two or three minutes." Then with a charming smile, "Business or First Class?"

Hoping it would provide more incentive, he said, "First Class. But I'll take whatever's available."

She typed into the computer, swiped the bar code edge of his passport through a reader on the side of the monitor and waited. Ten seconds evaporated. She frowned, shook her head, shifted weight to the other foot. And waited.

What was taking so long?

Had Jung-Kyo already called the police? Do they cross check passports with Immigrations at the ticket counter? He turned to tell Yeonhee something but saw two airport police walking parallel to the counter, heading his way. He started to turn back to the agent but one of them made eye contact, so turning away suddenly would look suspicious.

Be cool. You don't know if they know...

After an appropriate pause he busied himself with filling out a baggage ID tag. Heard footsteps stop nearby and felt two sets of eyes bore into him. They were talking in Korean, their voices aimed at him, loud enough for Yeonhee to hear. Beads of sweat sprouted from his forehead. Yeonhee said nothing.

Finally, the airline agent said, "You're in luck. Are you traveling together?"

Jon shook his head and tried to smile.

"No, just me."

Seconds started flying off the clock even faster, rapidly evaporating any hope of making the flight. Maybe Yeonhee drew the cops' attention. Maybe they weren't even interested in him. Maybe...

Yeonhee clutched his arm in warning and whispered.

"Jon..."

The ticket agent pushed a VISA charge slip across the counter but kept the credit card to compare signatures.

"Please sign here, Mr. Ritter."

He felt the two policemen step closer, their eyes on the back of his neck. He picked up the ballpoint and scratched out a signature.

As the agent compared his VISA card to the slip, one of the policemen said something to her. As she answered Jon felt Yeonhee tense. The officer made another comment. After flashing a can't-be-helped smile at Jon, the agent passed the policeman Jon's passport. Jon turned to watch, as if only mildly interested, but quickly scanned the immediate area for an escape route. If need be, he'd make a run for it and hope for the best. The officer studied the document a moment before looking at Jon.

Time to say something.

"If you don't mind, I need to catch this flight. My wife is very ill and I need to get home as soon as possible."

With a nod at Yeonhee, he asked Jon, "Does your sick wife know about her?" then said something in Korean into the microphone clipped to his epaulet.

Jon decided to say nothing more until he had a better idea what might happen. The large clock on the wall showed only seven minutes until the flight would push away from the gate. Without a boarding pass there was no way he could make it. He shot the agent a questioning look.

Could she hold it at the gate?

She returned a regretful smile and shook her head.

"I'm sorry, sir. There's nothing I can do until he returns your passport."

With that, she busied herself with the computer.

Another minute blew past.

He leaned closer to Yeonhee and whispered.

"Anything happens, run. I go right, you go left. I'll either meet you at your apartment or call you on your cell."

She nodded almost imperceptibly.

Finally, the officer handed the clerk the passport and, without another word, turned and walked away mumbling something to his partner. The clerk flashed another regretful smile.

"Sorry, Mr. Ritter but the Chicago flight is ready to shut its doors. There is no hope of making it."

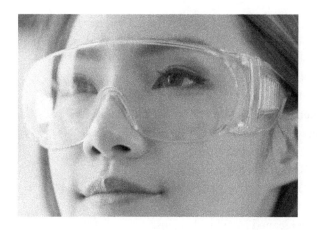

Chapter 50

FROM WHERE HE stood at the counter, he could see the lines at the security scanners growing longer, making him want to scream or pound the counter in frustration. He glanced at the nearest monitor for the next possible flight east, regardless of the destination, and noticed one to Vancouver.

"Any room left on the Vancouver flight?"

She typed a few commands.

"Aisle or window?"

He laughed at the irrelevance. He'd take a spot in the baggage compartment if it'd get him the hell out of here.

"Whatever's available. Just get me on that flight."

She reran the Visa and ticket, asked the routine security questions about baggage, explosives, and firearms.

"Any baggage to check?"

"No, just carry-on."

She handed him a boarding pass with stern advice to hurry if he intended to clear security in time.

His heart grew heavy as he and Yeonhee approached the first

security checkpoint. He stopped and took her in his arms.

"Thank you. I don't know how I'll ever repay you."

She pushed gently him away.

"Go! Or you miss your chance."

He held her tightly, nose buried in citrus-scented hair. She relaxed, allowing him a moment before pushing away one final time.

"Please, just two seconds."

"Go, Jon, or you miss the flight!"

"Yeonhee, if I make it back home safely, I want to see you again. Okay?"

He leaned in to kiss her lips.

She kissed him deeply before pushing away.

"Go! Good luck."

She turned and ran for the exit.

Jon settled into soft leather, fastened his seatbelt, relaxed against the headrest with both eyes closed. Essentially he was now trapped. If Yeonhee's fiancé tipped the police and they were monitoring the ticketing computers or had enlisted the airline's help, they would know he just boarded this flight. In other words, he was a sitting duck.

The only good news in this was the moment he entered the cabin the flight attendant shut and secured the door, and the captain gave the announcement to prepare for departure. Eyes closed, Jon listened, waiting to hear the cabin door reopen and the sound of approaching footsteps. Instead, the plane began moving backwards, stopped, turned and started forward, away from the terminal.

The trip to the end of the taxiway seemed to take forever, but finally the captain goosed the engines, taking the huge 747 through a lumbering left turn onto the runway, accelerated, nosed up for one, two, three seconds before magically starting to climb. The massive tires broke contact with the runway, precipitously dropping the cabin noise into the monotonous roar that would stay for the duration of the flight.

A huge wave of relief broke over him, making him suddenly aware of how tightly his jaws were clamped. He reclined his seat a bit, took a deep long breath, and considered his situation. From the armrest, he unfolded the personal entertainment center and rotated the screen to see their position, route, and miles to destination. For several minutes he watched the tiny plane icon rotate compass bearings until heading east over the Pacific Ocean.

He'd made it!

At this point it seemed doubtful they'd turn the flight back. On the other hand the odds were high that he'd have problems disembarking. Still, he'd rather deal with Canadian Immigration than the Seoul police. Best case scenario would be to somehow magically slip through Vancouver Immigration and hop a commuter flight to Seattle and be home in another twelve hours.

That remote possibility made him giddy. But he knew the odds of that actually happing were slim at best. The worse case scenario would be for Immigration to nail him.

Okay, so then what?

Would they dump him on the next flight back to Seoul? Or would they arrest him? If so, that was still better than returning to Seoul.

He needed to be pre-emptive, to stack the odds in his favor.

How?

Well, for one thing, he could use more information.

"May I bring you something to drink, Mr. Ritter?"

He glanced up at a male Asian flight attendant.

"A scotch would be wonderful."

The console between him and the window seat contained an Airphone. He swiped his VISA through the reader and waited, using the opportunity to discreetly check out the passenger next to him. He'd been so intent on getting seated that he hadn't paid much attention to the middle-aged Asian female in a business suit working furiously on a laptop. So far, they hadn't said one word to each other, so he didn't know if she was fluent in English. So he decided to shield his voice as much as possible.

A dial tone finally came up, so he dialed Wayne's number.

Wayne sounded like he was wakened from sound sleep. His free hand cupped around the phone, Jon turned away from his neighbor, lowered his voice.

"Do me a favor, okay?"

"Are you *finally* on a flight or something? I hear background noise."

"Yeah. On my way to Vancouver. But I need you to call..." he searched for the name, "Davidson? Is that his name?"

"Who? The lawyer? It's hard to understand you. Can you talk louder?"

"No, I can't," although he raised his voice slightly. "And yeah, the lawyer."

"Palmer Davison."

"Call him and lay things out for him. Tell him I'm flying to Canada, and I don't know what happens if the Canadian authorities arrest me."

"Christ, talk about living on the edge." Pause. "Okay, I'm on it. That's what, an eight-hour flight and you have how much left?"

"Not sure. We've been up maybe a half hour. How long you think you need?"

"How should I know? I've never been faced with something like this before...two hours maybe. I don't know how easy he is to get hold of. At the moment it's oh-dark hundred."

Jon realized the past hours were so intense, he totally lost track of time.

"Two hours. Got it. Thanks. Call you then."

The flight attendant extended the drink tray from the armrest and carefully placed a paper napkin and glass of scotch on it.

"Your drink, sir."

Jon swirled the ice in the glass and thought, step by step, through everything that transpired since the call from the parking lot the night of Gabe's murder.

Furious, Richard Stillman dialed Feist's cell. Not only had Ritter been lucky enough to escape custody, he was now fleeing the country. Lucky, that is for Ritter. Unlucky for him. If somehow Ritter managed to slip past airport security and make it across the border... Fuck! He didn't want to think about it.

Well, it would all be over within ten hours or so. He'd make damn sure the RCMP knew about Ritter's counterfeit passport. The increased immigration surveillance since 911 would guarantee they would catch him. Then, because of outstanding charges in Seoul, they'd be forced to stuff his raggedy ass on the next flight back to Seoul where Park and company could greet him with ear-to-ear smiles and a tube of K-Y jelly. But just in case....

Feist picked up.

"Yo, dog, we have a problem. Our friend just called Dobbs and he's on a flight to Vancouver. Chances are, he won't get out of the airport, but on the off chance he stays lucky and he manages to slip by them, I want you here."

"Indeed! I'm on my way."

Gary Fisher rolled over in bed, picked up the phone. "Yeah?"

A voice on the other end said, "According to Seoul Police, your man's on the move."

He recognized the agent's voice immediately.

"Where?"

"Caught a flight to Vancouver. His estimated time of arrival is six hours from now."

Sitting on the side of the bed now, phone in one hand, knuckling sand from his eyes with the other, Fisher began mentally sorting through options. His wife rolled over, propped up on an elbow, and raised an eyebrow at him. He motioned her to go back to sleep and headed toward the bathroom to close the door.

"How'd we learn this?"

"Apparently an anonymous friend dropped the dime on him. Claimed he's traveling under a forged passport. Our Seoul police started checking but didn't find out he boarded a flight until after it was airborne. By the time they could do anything about it, it was twenty minutes out and over international waters. The airlines told them basically to fuck off and to deal with it at this end."

With the bathroom door now closed and the light on, he checked his face in the mirror. Stubble and bags, more than ever with the bags.

"Do the Canadians know about this?"

"Unfortunately, they do."

"Shit!" The odds of Ritter reaching Seattle just zeroed out. "Thanks. Keep me informed."

Fisher hung up.

Bad news.

If the Canucks shipped Ritter back to Korea, his only viable lead for finding the Avengers would evaporate. He couldn't think of an argument that might change the Canadians' mind even if he knew who to call. For starters, laws concerning entering Canada under false papers were rigid. The fact that Ritter was charged with a capital crime and was fleeing custody only compounded the problem.

The only strategy he could think of was to somehow warn Ritter but had no way of contacting him.

Drive up to Vancouver International to meet the flight?

What good would that do?

Damn it.

Essentially, Ritter was hosed. Back in the bedroom he retrieved his wallet, returned to the bathroom and dug through it for the scrap of paper with Dobbs's phone number scribbled on it. If anyone knew how to reach Ritter it'd be him.

Dobbs answered immediately sounding wide-awake.

"It's Fisher. Sorry to call this time of night, but we have a problem."

"What?"

"You don't know any way to reach Jon, do you?"

"Why do you ask?"

"I just received word he's on a flight to Vancouver. Know anything about that?"

A tell-tale hesitation, followed by, "No. Why?"

Dobb's answer sounded like a flat out lie.

Why?

Just then his cell phone beeped for another incoming call. A quick check of caller ID showed it coming from an unidentified number. Let it roll over to voice mail? On the other hand, nobody called this time of the morning unless something was important.

"Hold on, got another call coming in."

He answered, "Fisher."

"It's Jon Ritter."

Whoa.

"Great timing. We have a problem. The Canucks know you're coming."

"Figured as much. That's the reason I'm calling. I need some advice."

"I'll do whatever I can to help."

"First of all, I got a lawyer lined up on your end. Will that be any help in this?"

"No. Because this is what'll happen: Canadian Immigration knows you're coming in under counterfeit paper. They'll have the Mounties take you into custody the minute you step off that plane. Once that happens, you're a dead duck and there's nothing no one can do to help you. The one catch however—and this is a legal technicality—until you actually pass through

Immigration, you're considered in international limbo, meaning you're neither in Canada nor Korea. Literally. This, in turn, means the Canadian legal system can't deal with you until you're legally in Canada. But what they can do—and this means they won't have to deal with the paperwork—is put you right on the next flight back to Seoul."

"But what about due process? I'll get screwed if I'm sent back."

"They couldn't care less about that. That's not their problem. You entering their country illegally is their problem."

"But—"

"But nothing. You're not listening to me. The key to this is to find a way to avoid the Mounties. Get it? And don't even think about asking for ideas because we never had this conversation. You got, what, maybe six hours to come up with something. Bribe a crew member, maybe. Hell, I don't know…just find a way to get off that plane and back to the States without getting caught."

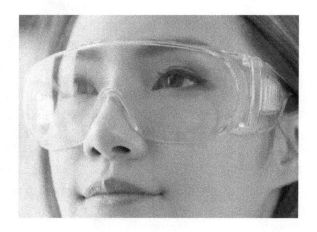

Chapter 51

FISHER'S NEWS WAS so unnerving, Jon almost forgot the purpose of the call.

"Wait, before you hang up. You still out to nail those assholes?"

"The Avengers? Absolutely. Why?"

"I think I have some things that might help."

He explained implications of Stillman setting him up to meet Feist, and then explained the suspected connection between Stillman and Sandra Nolan.

Fisher said, "Hold on. Maybe I'm slow, but I don't see how this fits into anything."

"Think about it. NIH knew about the Avenger threat immediately. How did that happen? Someone had to tell them. Who better than Nolan? She's on the Council."

"Council? What's that?"

Jon realized he was ahead of himself and backed up.

"When you apply for grant money from NIH, a group of independent scientists called a Study Section, reviews it. If it's good and makes the cut, Council decides who actually gets money and how much. The point is, Stillman knew we were approved before that information was ever made public. Meaning, he had to have inside information. The only way he could get that is if someone on Council leaked it to him."

Still not sounding sold on the idea, Fisher said, "Okay... "

"Then you have to ask yourself how NIH knew about Gabe's murder so quickly?"

"No problem there. It made national news."

"Right. But the point is, how did they link the murder directly to me? The only thing they might've known was Gabe Lippmann *may* have been murdered by an Avenger. Any other details were never released to the press."

"But they gave you the ultimatum and you must've mentioned it to people."

Ha! Precisely the point.

"I didn't and that wasn't in the papers. They should never have known."

Fisher thought about that a moment.

"Okay, I see where you're going with this and you might have a valid point."

"Okay, so humor me by checking Stillman's cell phone records, see if he talked with Nolan—cell phone, landline, whatever—but check it out. You have the date of the murder. See if anything corresponds to that date. Sure, she's on the Trophozyme board so could have a gazillion reasons to talk to from him time to time but look for calls around that specific date. Back that date up by two weeks and that's the date council awarded us funding. In addition, there's the Feist part of this. Look for calls between Stillman and cell phone numbers and then run those numbers. Feist has to be in there. Stillman must've called him a couple times these past two days in Seoul. Make sense?"

"We're already on that."

"I'll check with you later—if I get through Immigration."

"Here's hoping the Canucks get so bogged down in

bureaucracy you'll sail through before they can stop you. Good luck."

Fisher didn't sound like he believed it.

The thin Asian flight attendant who had welcomed him aboard hours ago smiled while handing him his black blazer.

"Mr. Ritter. Please put your seat in the upright position in preparation for landing."

Jon accepted the coat, thanked him, complied with the request, stood up and stepped into the aisle with a brief sensation of déjà vu from the flight over. The stern-faced attendant strapped into a bulkhead jump-seat jabbed a finger at his vacated seat.

"Sir, you must be seated. We're on our final approach."

Jon hurried past him.

"Sorry, but if I don't empty this bladder, we're both going to have a problem."

After a few seconds in the lavatory, he cracked the folding door and peeked out. The flight attendant remained strapped into the jump seat studying a checklist, paying no attention to him. Jon opened the door and slipped into the narrow aisle, hurried to the stairs to the 747 main deck and started down. At the bottom he stopped to glance round. First-class extended forward to the nose of the craft. Behind him was business-class with the economy section beyond a divider. Next to him, two lavatories and a galley separated business from First Class. A seated female flight attendant scowled.

"Sir, you *must* take your seat."

He nodded agreement and headed down the aisle toward the aft galley and rear toilets where the economy section appeared only half-full. The plane buffeted, throwing him off balance, slamming his right hip into a seat. He grabbed the seat back to steady himself and apologized to the occupant. Most of the passengers sat at the front of this section, so he continued to an empty seat at the rear of the plane next to the last emergency exit. His ears popped again as he sat down and strapped in. Being back here instead of upstairs in his assigned seat would only prolong the inevitable, but at least it would give him a few additional minutes to think.

Jon waited for the plane to come to a complete stop before standing up and moving to the aisle. By craning his neck and standing on a seat he could see past enough passengers to notice anyone entering the cabin before passengers began to deplane.

From the overhead speakers came, "Prepare doors for arrival." Then, "Will all passengers please remain seated. There will be a short delay before being allowed to deplane."

No one sat down and a grumble rippled through the crowd.

Uh-oh, here we go.

Mouth dry, palms sweating, he watched a flight attendant open the cabin hatch. Immediately, two suits and two uniformed Royal Canadian Mounted Police officers entered the cabin. The suits quickly disappeared up the stairs. The Mounties said something to the flight attendant before positioning themselves to each side of the cabin door.

The flight attendant picked up microphone and announced over the PA system, "Sorry for the inconvenience, but we have a passenger in need of urgent medical assistance. As soon as this is resolved, you will be able to deplane. For any passengers needing to make connections…"

Bullshit.

Jon mopped sweat from his eyes with the back of his sleeve, sidestepped to the emergency exit, thought about what he was going to do, reconsidered, then grabbed the red handle, took one final glance forward. The Mounties each had one foot on the first stair to the upper deck, looking upward, apparently exchanging words with the suits on the upper level.

Wait any longer and they'll search the entire aircraft.

Jon yelled, "Fire. There's a fire back here! Someone grab

an extinguisher."

Screams erupted. Passengers jammed forward into the narrow aisles. Jon tugged the red emergency handle but it didn't budge.

He noticed a switch labeled 'Manual' and turned it, then threw his weight into the emergency handle, pushing in a downward arc. The door swung open, ejecting a day-glow yellow chute from the fuselage. As the distal end dropped to the tarmac the chute inflated into a slide.

He called to the passengers jamming into the aisle behind him.

"This way! Let's get out of here!" before jumping feet first onto the slide.

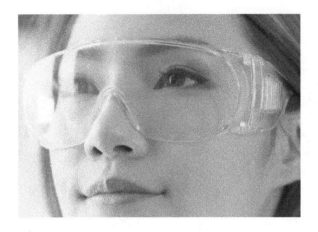

Chapter 52

JON'S FEET HIT the asphalt hard, then his butt, the momentum whipping his neck to the left and sending a momentary stinger down his right arm. For a brief moment he was too stunned to do anything but squint into the sun, so he sat still. Then the plastic chute jerked as another passenger jumped onto it. He scrambled to his feet and moved away just as a grinning teenager hit the ground in the spot he just vacated. Jon grabbed the kid's outstretched hand and pulled him to his feet.

"Move away from the chute!"

He glanced around frantically. He was on open tarmac and totally exposed to anyone watching from the plane or the terminal. On the other hand, the terminal contained miles of byzantine halls and potential places to hide. Fifty feet past the 747's nose wheel were two dented metal clad baggage cart doors to the ground level of the terminal.

He started running, burst through the swinging doors, ran a hundred feet before stopping behind a cement pillar to look around. Bare concrete halls led right, left, and dead ahead.

Which way?

Choose one and get going.

He continued straight ahead, picking up pace again for half a block, turned down another hall for another hundred feet to a door marked STAIRS, threw his hip into the horizontal trip bar and started up a bare concrete stairwell two at a time, shoes slapping metal, the noise echoing off the hard surfaces.

Christ, not too subtle.

He stopped at the first switchback, listened, heard nothing but his own heavy breathing and his pounding pulse. Satisfied that no one followed him into the stairwell he continued up at a normal pace while trying to calm his nerves and tuck in his shirt. He was sweating like crazy.

A half flight took him to the floor immediately above the ground level. He cracked the door, heard someone shout a command from down the hall followed by the sound of boots running on concrete. He shut the door and bolted back down the stairs, hit the ground level and was out the door he'd entered just moments ago. Around the corner off to his right came another voice. It sounded like it was heading his way. On his left, against the cinderblock wall, was an aluminum storage freight container. He slipped behind it, then used the side handles to pull it as close to the wall as possible, sandwiching him in the narrow space. He stood perfectly still and waited.

Footsteps approached and stopped.

A male voice said, "Delta tango niner."

There was no answer.

The male voice said, "Roger that. Am at sugar whiskey three zero. Negative for target."

Jon visualized a police officer with a microphone clipped to an epaulet and a curlicue wire to his ear. A moment later he heard the sounds of the police officer continuing his sweep of this area. Then he heard the bark echo off the hard concrete surfaces.

Dogs.
Shit.

He might be able to hide here from the patrolman, but a dog would sniff him out in a second. Quickly, he slipped off his shoes and then his socks, figuring they'd be a strong enough scent to distract the dog and give him enough time to try the stairs again. He slid open the door to the cargo container, draped his socks on the edge, and then replaced his shoes. Without shutting the container door, he pushed it against the wall, then he was back in the stairwell he'd exited a few minutes ago.

He ran up the stairs to the first landing, paused to catch his breath, then cracked the door and peeked into a deserted hallway. He widened the crack for a better look, saw no one, darted into the hall, letting the door click shut behind him.

Pausing for another deep breath and taking another second to calm down, he wiped his face with his hand then dried his hand on his pants. Two more big breaths and he had it together enough to continue. The names and titles on the doors indicated this was an administrative area rather than public but gave no clue as to which way to go, so he chose a direction at random and continued while wracking his brain for a story to spin if he ran into someone.

After a series of Immigration and Security offices he came to an exit door at the end of the hall.

But where did it go?

Stairs back down to the baggage level? Into one of the concourses? Regardless, he needed to look like he belonged.

He opened the door and without hesitating, entered a major concourse; travelers and flight attendants flowing past in both directions. Without stopping to look for signage, he melded into a clot of passengers, walked with purpose for another hundred feet before splintering off to stop next to the wall and try to figure out where he was. The ceiling signs told him he was heading toward Concourse B instead of Baggage Claim so he reversed direction, rounded a corner into the main lobby and stopped.

Mounties patrolled the area, eyeing travelers, while additional Mounties were stationed at the doors to the passenger pick-up zone, paying particular attention to those exiting. He backed around the corner, spotted a metal fire-door door only ten feet away with a sign AUTHORIZED PERSONEL ONLY. Well, shit. In for a pound or whatever that expression was.

It opened into a cinderblock stairwell with steel stairs and brown tubular railings heading up to another level or back down to the basement. He walked up to the next landing, cracked the unmarked door far enough to peer into a cavernous lobby of retail shops, fast-food restaurants, travelers, white noise, and ceiling signs to various concourses.

The departure level.

Now what? Can't very well stay in the stairwell.

Again, he entered the lobby and stood by the entrance to the Women's toilet, playing the role of husband waiting for his wife, thinking this would give him an excuse to stand here a few minutes and think about his situation without being too conspicuous.

He figured by now the Mounties must realize the person who escaped the aircraft via the emergency door was him. The question was, how long would they search the airport before turning their attention to other, more pressing, matters? No way to know. But common sense dictated that eventually they'd have to turn to other priorities. The longer he stayed hidden, the more likely he'd drop from their immediate radar. Perhaps the best strategy would be to remain hidden in plain sight until they slacked up at the exits.

Where?

He glanced around with this in mind.

Maybe at a retail shop?

In a duty-free shop, he passed a display of soaps, perfumes, chocolates, and continued to the back wall with a floor-to-ceiling rack of newspapers and magazines. He knelt behind a rack of flannel gray Vancouver, B.C. sweatshirts, picked a *Road*

& *Track* at random from the bottom shelf and started slowly leafing through it while listening for footsteps and scanning the immediate area in his peripheral vision.

"Sir?"

Startled, he jumped, turned toward the voice and saw a salesclerk help another customer at the sweatshirt rack. He swallowed hard and returned to thumbing through magazines while his heart continued to pound in his chest.

A minute slowly died. Then two more. After several more minutes he realized that staying here much longer might, in itself, be an attention magnet.

Okay, so what now?

He picked out an oversized gray sweatshirt and a Canucks cap, took them to the cashier. With the hat on he felt a bit more secure, cutting a diagonal across the hall to the men's room, a rectangle of white tiles, two sinks, two urinals, and, luckily, two empty stalls. He entered and locked the corner stall and sat down to think.

So far so good.

He'd made it out of the plane without being arrested. Using Fisher's logic, by not clearing Immigrations, he wasn't legally in Canada in spite of physically being in the airport. Right now, he was in international limbo. With his forged passport now blown, any attempt to use it would be suicide. Yet somehow, he had to figure out a way to cross the U.S. border without being caught. He seriously doubted that once he was back in the States, Immigration would kick him out. Besides, at that point he could enlist the help of his new lawyer.

Okay, fine, now what?

Think!

Call Fisher again? Yeah, he could do that, but Fisher made it clear there was little he could do to help. Certainly, Fisher couldn't solve the immediate problem of how to sneak out of the airport. If he could just do that, he was certain it'd be easier to figure a way to cross the border.

Five minutes later he still didn't have any sort of viable plan.

Have to do something.

After making sure his blazer contained nothing to link it back to him, he wadded it into a ball and stuffed it in the trash. Same with his damp shirt. At least with the sweatshirt and ball cap on, he no longer fit his earlier description.

He burnt another two hours in the stall before he figured it was time to venture out again to check security.

He opened the stall door.

One man stood at a urinal, another at a sink washing his hands. Both appeared to be travelers and not airport officials. For authenticity Jon flushed the toilet and pretended to cinch up his belt. At the sink, he washed his hands and splashed cold water on his face. The man at the other sink left. The one at the urinal zipped up and exited without so much as a second look. Jon decided to go out, maybe find another men's room, kill some more time. Every minute he wasted in here blunted RCMP attention.

About thirty feet into the hall the greasy smell of hot dogs caught his attention.

Jon dumped the change into a tip jar, carried the small plastic tray with two slices of pepperoni pizza and a medium diet Coke to a table as far from the hallway as possible. Back here, he wouldn't appear to be hiding, yet he'd be well away from the flux of people. And if someone did notice him, he was only one table from the rear exit, good positioning if he needed to run.

He ate slowly, like someone with hours to kill between connections, yet watching and listening for the slightest hint of someone recognizing him. What exactly that might be, he wasn't sure, but figured he'd know if it happened. Within minutes the tempo of his surroundings became routine: repeated warnings to not leave bags unattended, calls to a white courtesy phone, announcements for flight departures, the white noise of hundreds of passing conversations mixed into the rattle of luggage wheels on the floor. Behind the counter an ancient Sony boom box played Bob Dylan's *All Along The Watchtower* in direct competition to Neil Diamond's *Sweet Caroline* from the overhead PA.

He wondered what Yeonhee was doing. He hoped she was alright. And he really didn't like her boyfriend.

Would she really marry Jung-Kyo?

Suddenly, the semiconscious information processing part of his brain jolted him out of a daydream. Down the hall, to his right, two serious looking security officers were heading his way, slow walking, scanning people, casting occasional glances in retail shops. Casually, Jon shifted position, turning his side to them, head down, while still tracking them in his peripheral vision. They stopped, turned to watch a male pass, conversed a moment before resuming their meandering patrol in his direction.

Jon picked up a piece of pizza crust and began chewing, cupping his cheek in his hand, elbow on the table, turning further in his chair to where he no longer saw them.

And waited.

A few moments later they passed the dining area, still chatting with each other, never casting him a second glance. He relaxed. Maybe, just maybe, he could pull this off. Every minute undetected was a very good minute because soon security would relax enough so maybe he could get out of the airport.

Meal finished, he decided it would feel good to really freshen up more than just a face rinse.

On the way to the Men's Room, he stopped in a small shop and picked up a travel-size deodorant stick, a disposable razor, a small athletic bag, a book and a few magazines.

Again, the clerk paid more attention to making change than to his face.

At the sink, sweatshirt around his waist, Jon rinsed his face before using hand soap for lather, shaved, used a wad of wet paper towels to sponge a layer of dried sweat from his chest and arms, then dried off in a stream of warm air from a wall-mounted blower. He put the sweatshirt back on, finger combed his hair, replaced the ball cap, and for the first time in hours, felt half-way decent.

Now what?

He returned to a toilet stall to kill more time before making a serious attempt to leave the building. Sooner or later the police would assume he'd escaped and give up. For now, he was resigned to being stuck here.

He was turning a page of his book when the clatter of wheels became obvious, then grew louder, as if something was entering the room. He leaned forward to peer through the gap between the stall door and divider. A maintenance worker was positioning a pushcart with a black Hefty garbage bag on one end and two brooms sticking up from the other. After blocking the entrance with a yellow A-frame Wet Floor sign, he started emptying the trash bins and cleaning up.

"Going to be in there long?" the janitor called.

Jon marked the page with his thumb and leaned forward to peer through the slit again. The guy faced his stall with an annoyed expression.

Jon said, "Yeah, might be. Why?"

"Need to service the stall."

"Don't worry, it's clean."

"May be, but I need to restock the toilet paper holders and make sure the seat cover container's full."

Wonderful. An obsessive-compulsive.

"Give me a few minutes."

Jon found his place on the page and continued reading, figuring it wouldn't take long for the guy to get fed up and leave.

He didn't.

Page finished, Jon tore off a couple lengths of toilet paper for the sound effect, wadded and dumped them in the toilet, stood, used his foot to press the flush lever, and walked to the newly cleaned sink. The janitor watched him wash up and leave.

Back at the gift shop Jon studied the magazine rack until he saw the janitor push the cart back into the hall and collect the yellow A-frame sign.

A moment later he was back in the same toilet stall, reading.

"There a problem, sir?"

Surprised, Jon glanced up at the locked door. He hadn't heard anyone come in.

The voice was more emphatic, more demanding this time.

"Sir?"

Jon got an uneasy feeling. The voice carried too much authority to be another janitor.

"You talking to me?"

"Yes. Is there a problem?"

Jon checked his watch. Thirty minutes since coming back in here. He peeked out the slit.

Shit!

A Royal Canadian Mounted Police officer stood directly in front of his stall.

"Sorry, did you say something?"

The cop leaned closer to the door.

"There a problem?"

"Why do you ask?"

"Cause you been in here twice in the last hour."

Mind racing, he started sorting through likely excuses, searching for something at least half-way reasonable.

What?

Travel...something to do with travel.

"A problem? Yes. Nothing major though. Must've picked up a bug in Mexico. Touch of diarrhea...nothing serious."

Shut up. Don't overdo it.

The Mountie put his hands on his hips.

"That why you've been hanging around?"

Jon figured someone must've noticed him on a security video. The airport was full of ceiling-mounted CCTV cameras.

But so what? Travelers not infrequently endured lengthy delays between flights.

Jon rattled the toilet paper dispenser for effect.

"Is that a problem?"

"Matter of fact, it is. For security purposes we don't like travelers to loiter. Same reason we don't allow people to park in front of the passenger loading bays."

He didn't want to leave the stall and come face to face with the officer.

Would he give me a few minutes?

"Okay. I'll leave soon as I finish here."

"I'll wait."

Shit!

Jon flushed the toilet, stood, rattled his belt buckle, opened the stall door. The RCMP officer looked him over.

"Waiting for a flight?"

Jon moved past him to the sink to wash his hands. Anything to keep him from looking directly at his face.

"Not exactly." Mind racing again, searching for a dovetailing lie. "I was scheduled for a stop in Vancouver. A business trip. But my boss asked me to go over to Victoria first. My luggage didn't come off the flight, so I've been waiting to collect it before catching the Victoria flight."

He ripped off a paper towel, thought, *hey, that didn't sound too bad.*

"Sorry, but I can't allow you to loiter here. Either wait in town for your luggage or catch a flight, but you can't wait here in the terminal. While we're on the subject, I want to see some identification."

Oh, man, here we go.

"Not a problem."

Jon handed over the forged passport.

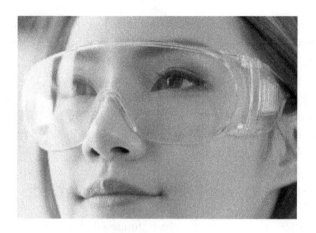

Chapter 53

THE RCMP OFFICER flipped through the passport, inspecting some pages, ignoring others.

"Travel a lot, I see."

Jon's legs felt rubbery, ready to collapse, so he put a hand against the wall for support, hoping the officer wouldn't notice his nervousness.

"I do. Business...a lot of business travel."

The Mountie seemed to take an interest in one page in particular and studied it a moment.

"Uh-huh. Know where the commuter terminal is?"

"No. Don't use this airport much. Matter of fact, I hardly ever travel in Canada."

Well, at least this was the truth.

"Here," the officer handed the passport back. "Victoria flights depart from the domestic terminal. Come with me, I'll show you."

Jon nodded more out of relief than gratitude.

"Thanks. That's very nice of you."

He followed him into the hall, turned left into the long

hallway, the officer falling almost into lock-step next to him. Halfway down the hall, the cop stopped and pointed ahead of them.

"See that, where the hall turns right?"

Jon did. A sign suspended from the ceiling had a left pointing arrow with the words, COMMUTER TERMINAL. Something only an idiot would miss.

"Thanks, you've been a great help."

"Well then, you're on your way, eh? I'll leave you here. Just don't let me see you back in this area. Understood?"

"I do."

After the turn, the hall funneled into a narrower, descending passage that seemed to extend forever without an exit. Meaning, of course, he was now trapped like a rat. His gut tightened as he kept moving, trying to think of what to do if caught here. Probably the best thing at this point was to clear the hall as quickly as possible, so he increased pace without breaking into a trot, like a typical pedestrian in New York.

The descending hall finally leveled off at a point probably designed to serve smaller, lower aircraft. Another turn emptied from the hall into the domestic departure/arrival lounge. Filled with travelers, some milling aimlessly, some slouched in molded green plastic chairs, while others stood in queues feeding a variety of ticket counters. Just inside the entrance, a small concession cart sold a limited selection of beverages and prepackaged fast food.

To his left a mother sat rocking a baby in an infant car seat and next to her, a disheveled businessman with his nose in a book. No police. Not yet, at least. Best of all, no one took an interest in him.

He noticed a blinking light above an open gate. A slide-in plastic sign behind the ticket counter had the word: VICTORIA. A haggard flight attendant in a navy jumpsuit and maroon scarf was collecting tickets from a small line of passengers. Jon approached.

"Any room left on this flight?"

Only two passengers remained.

She accepted a boarding pass from the second to last and tore it along perforations.

She said, "You're in luck. One seat left."

"I'll take it."

She nodded.

"Soon as I finish here, I'll take care of you."

She inspected the final passenger's ticket.

Figuring a passport wasn't needed for a domestic flight, he pulled the VISA card from his wallet and set it on the counter.

His peripheral vision caught movement at the entrance to the hall he just came from. Head lowered, he turned just enough to look. From the corner of his eyes, he watched two uniformed RMCP officers survey the crowd.

Must've just walked in the door. Why?

Looking for him?

The hairs on the back of his neck stood up, snaking a chill down his spine that screamed for him to make a break for the stairs and the tarmac below.

Do that, then what?

Running would only draw attention, plunging him right back into a pursuit situation. No, better to stand pat and hope they don't notice him. Besides, they looked seriously fit, not the pot-bellied rent-a-cops manning the security gates.

Shit, they're armed.

"Will that be cash or credit card?"

He snapped back to the ticket agent, her fingers clicking the keyboard, unaware his credit card was already on the counter. With his fingers shaking badly, he simply nudged it across the counter and hoped she wouldn't notice.

"Visa. Here you go."

A moment later, she returned it. Instead of replacing it in his wallet, he simply stuffed it in his pocket. Did she notice his nervousness, and would it cause her to pay more attention to him? The urge to flee ratcheted up a few notches. Against his better judgment, he chanced another glance over his shoulder. The officers were split up now, covering opposite sides of the room, the female weaving slowly along the periphery of the chairs, checking out each person while the male with intense eyes and drooping black moustache slowly worked toward him.

"Here you are, sir. Seat 6A." The agent passed him a ticket stub. "Any baggage to check?"

"No. Thanks."

He smiled and stepped to the open door and sunshine beyond.

A voice behind him called, "Sir, wait a minute."

His heart seemed to stop as a wave of prickly heat swept over him as he turned.

"Yes?"

The flight attendant waved him back.

"You need to sign the charge slip."

"Oh, sorry." With a forced laugh, he returned to the desk. The approaching RCMP glanced over at him. Quickly, Jon scrawled a signature on the charge slip. "Sorry, didn't want to hold up the flight."

"Thank you."

Then he was moving again, out through the open doorway, onto the uncovered galvanized landing, down a flight of narrow metal stairs to black asphalt, one hand sliding along a cold metal railing. The moment his foot touched tarmac he exhaled. Another hundred feet to the portable stairs up to the open hatch of the waiting Air Canada turboprop.

A deep male voice called, "Sir?"

He turned to see the thin mustachioed RCMP officer at the top of the landing. No mistake, he'd been addressing him.

The officer called, "Hold it," and came clamoring down the stairs, tall and young, probably able to outrun him.

Shit!

He fought the instinct to flee. But there was no place to go out here in the open with only taxiway, planes, and baggage carts. Besides, it'd only delay the inevitable. Jon watched him approach. The officer studied his face a beat before holding out his hand.

"Here."

Jon looked at the slip of yellow paper between his fingers.

"What's that?"

"Your charge copy. You left it on the counter. Can't be too careful these days with so much identity theft."

Fuck me!

"Thank you, officer."

A close look at the imprint showed the name and card number too faint to actually read.

A moment later, he buckled into the hard, leather seat of the narrow-bodied commuter flight. Five minutes after that, with both engines screaming, the pilot popped the breaks and the turboprop accelerated down the runway.

As the nose lifted, the tailbone-jarring vibrations abruptly stopped, and along with it, a huge weight lifted from Jon's shoulders. He'd made it out of Vancouver!

But, he reminded himself, he would be landing on an island. Somehow, he still needed to find a way to cross the Strait of Juan de Fuca and the border.

Chapter 54

SIDNEY, BRITISH COLUMBIA, is a funky seaside
retirement town on the craggy west coast of Vancouver Island.
A patchwork of English-style rose gardens, manicured hedges,
pastel stucco houses, sheer curtains behind leaded-glass
windows, two marinas, and Victoria International Airport due
east across Highway 17.

Jon stepped from the shaded plane cabin into squint-
producing sunlight, clamored down the portable stairway,
crossed the tarmac, passed through a modest one-level terminal
to automatic sliding glass doors. Only one police officer stood
listlessly next to the baggage conveyer talking to an elderly
woman with a luggage cart. Maybe such casual security was a
ploy to lull drug smugglers into a false sense of confidence.

Two taxis waited at the curb outside Baggage Claim, the
drivers standing between the vehicles smoking cigarettes and
chatting up each other. On the opposite side of the access road,
a driver was handing a parking attendant money. No one in the
immediate area so much as looked his way.

He approached the first cab and asked to be taken to the

main marina.

After paying the cab fare he waited for the taxi to vanish around the corner before starting south along a street bordering the harbor, the tang of salt water and drying seaweed stirred memories of a weekend getaway here with Emily.

He followed the curving seawall for three blocks, realigning his faded memories with reality. Three blocks later, he reached his destination, hooked fingers through a high, razor wire topped cyclone fence, and looked down at two acres of trees, lawn, a weathered, peeling white clapboard United States Immigration building, and a road curving downhill to a dock. A Washington State ferry was loading a string of RVs, cars, and pickups. One by one they crept over the metal ramp onto the main deck.

He knew the boat made the two-hour run from Sidney to Port Angeles only once a day, so if he intended to board, it'd have to be now. He walked through the gate and headed to Immigration.

The waiting room was small with an American flag draped over a 7-foot pole, a framed color photo of the President, a large corkboard pinned with layers of overlapping notices, faux wood veneer walls, worn checkerboard floor, and a middle-aged woman in a white short-sleeve US Immigration shirt leaning on the counter reading *USA Today*.

"Still time to board the Anacortes ferry?" he asked.

She glanced up.

"If you hurry. Walk-on passengers boarded a couple minutes ago."

"One, please."

She reluctantly glanced at the page as if memorizing her spot and straightened up.

"Passport."

He handed it to her and forced himself to not look away. Or fidget. Or hold his breath.

She took it, flipped it open to the first page and studied the picture a moment too long, her lips squeezing together. Her eyes darted back to Jon before swiping the passport through a bar code reader.

"This'll take a few seconds. The computers are running slow today for some reason. But we'll get you on. I'll just make a call, be sure to have 'em hold the boat." Turning away from him, she raised a handheld radio to her lips and whispered.

The room turned deathly still. He heard idling engines outside, then a seagull cry. The floor joists creaked as she shifted weight uneasily. Five silent seconds ticked past.

"Something wrong?" he asked.

She smiled and nodded, smiling a little too much and looking uncomfortable.

"Nope, nothing at all. Just need to get the ticket agent up here. That's who I was calling."

On his toes now, Jon craned his neck for a better angle out the window in the direction of the dock. The line of boarding vehicles was now stopped, and a male Immigration officer came trotting toward the building, left hand clutching a similar radio.

Shit!

Jon smiled at her.

He said, "I'll wait outside."

She shook her head and glanced out the window.

"No, no, wait here so we don't waste no time. Got a schedule to keep, you know."

She lifted a section of the counter to step into the reception area, but Jon was already out the front door, running for the gate.

Chapter 55

JON RAN FLAT-OUT for three blocks through a residential neighborhood, cut left at random, flew down a sidewalk of curbed cars, took a right a block later to an alley, dodged an overturned recycle bin, passed a barking Rottweiler with its front paws four feet up the fence, and on out the other end at which point he slowed to a walk and thanked himself for replacing his loafers with running shoes in Seoul. Which made him think of Yeonhee again.

Lungs burning, shirt damp, he stopped to glance around and get oriented. One lot down, an older woman knelt in front of a stucco house, planting flowers in a well-weeded bed. Across the street a girl about nine or ten hop scotched a chalk course on the sidewalk.

Just then a police car shot by, light flashing, no siren.

Well so much for flying under the radar.

And, he realized, they had a description of what he was wearing. Well, he couldn't go back into the commercial area of town. Best to get out of the area as quickly as possible. He didn't recognize the neighborhood because he and Emily never really drove though residential areas, but he had a vague idea of which area of town this was. The main highway would be cutting diagonally east to west to the south. He started walking in that direction.

He'd gone half a block when he noticed a clothesline in the back yard of a small white house. He couldn't believe anyone still used one. A faded navy-blue sweatshirt hung from the line. Without thinking, he darted into the yard and crept along the side of the house, not looking around to see if he was noticed by a neighbor.

Quickly, he took off his shirt, balled it up and threw it in the bushes. Then, after one glance into the back yard to make sure no one was there, he ran over to the sweatshirt, pulled it off of the line, and put it on.

Back on the street, he continued walking at a pace that was quick but not fast enough to attract attention. Four blocks later he encountered the road he needed, waited for a break in traffic, then sprinted across. Walking backwards along the shoulder to face oncoming traffic, he held out his thumb. The third vehicle, a white F-350 pickup mounded high with dark brown beauty bark, slowed to a stop.

Jon ran to the passenger door, said, "Thanks," tossed in his athletic bag, climbed in.

The driver, a thin sunburned man with a straw cowboy hat and hatchet chin, nodded before pulling a white Styrofoam cup from the console to spit out a load of tobacco. He wore denim bib overalls and a faded plaid shirt with the sleeves smartly rolled past bony elbows. The radio was playing Toby Keith—a song about his favorite bar.

"Where you headed?"

Jon kicked aside an empty Diet Coke can so he could pull the door shut. The cab smelled of tobacco and creosote.

"Victoria."

"Might want to buy yourself a lotto ticket, seeing how this is your lucky day. I can haul you all the way into the center of town, you want."

The driver pulled the Ford over on Wharf Street across from Bastion Square. Jon jumped down onto concrete, slapped the door twice to let the driver know he was clear, yelled, "Thanks," and stepped back to watch the pickup merge into traffic.

For a moment he looked around while patching together memories of the city. Late afternoon sun angled off windows, the temperature a perfect seventy degrees in. But he reminded himself, *don't let it lull you into carelessness.*

Surely by now the RCMP throughout all of British Columbia would be looking for him. At least Victoria was a large town, making finding him more difficult than in Sidney.

If memory served, Harbour Square Mall was only a few blocks away. He headed in that direction, mentally refining a possible ploy to get across the border. Which raised an interesting question: what about Feist?

Was he already back in Seattle waiting for him?

The way he figured, Stillman probably contracted Feist.

But how far did that go? And if he could eliminate Stillman, would that get Feist off his back?

A plan started to take form and soon as he found a place to hide, he'd spend more time thinking it through. For right now his highest priorities were to buy a change of clothes and a clean cell phone, then find a place for the night.

Stillman and Feist...there had to be a way to take them both down....

Allen Wyler

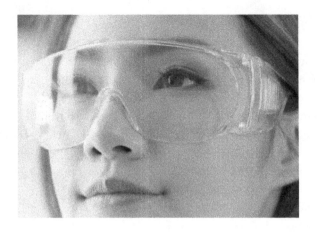

Chapter 56

JON WALKED OUT of the mall in a complete change of
clothes: navy polo shirt, blue jeans, tan windbreaker, and
baseball cap, the old set once again stuffed in a plastic shopping
bag at the bottom of the men's room wastebasket.

He exchanged the athletic bag for a rucksack and replaced
the few toiletries he'd left on the plane. Most importantly, he
purchased a throwaway cell with a two-hundred-minute card, a
number Stillman wouldn't know about. If his plan took more
airtime than that, he'd be in serious trouble.

Two blocks later he turned onto Wharf Street, a pretty
boulevard bordering the harbor, the air scented with drying
seaweed and mussels. He paused at a bulkhead half a block east
of the dock for the Victoria Clipper, a passenger/sightseeing
ferry connecting Seattle to Victoria. The boat sat idle at the
mooring, ready for the return trip to Seattle later this afternoon.

A straight shot to Seattle...hmmm, now there was an idea.

He resumed walking and saw a cash machine a half block
ahead. Almost certainly law enforcement agencies had an alert
on his bank card, but so what? Sidney Immigration had already

notified every law enforcement agency in the Pacific Northwest that he'd been seen on the island. Besides, he'd already used his VISA. He withdrew two hundred dollars for immediate expenses and would hit a different machine in the morning, depending on how he fleshed out the plan.

A few minutes later he came across the James Bay Inn just off the harbor on Government Street, a quaint, four-story historic hotel. He entered the lobby and went to the small reception counter.

A female voice from the room behind the counter, called, "Be right there."

A small TV on the counter was on and a broadcasting the local weather. That segment ended and the camera changed to a news anchor behind a desk. She said, "Authorities are looking for..." and his passport picture appeared on the screen.

Jon turned around and walked out.

He sat on a park bench across from the harbor, cap pulled low on his head, and put the final touches on his plan.

What were the potential flaws?

He didn't see any—which meant he was probably making a huge mistake. There were always things that could, and would, go wrong, even with the best conceived plans. Yet sooner or later you had to go with what you had.

He powered up the new cell and called Fisher.

Fisher said, "Don't recognize the number. Where are you?"

"I have a question for you."

The connection had a watery distant echo quality.

"Shoot."

"If the RCMP catch me, they ship me back to Seoul. Right?"

"Right. Unless they can be persuaded to ignore the extradition. And since you brought up the subject, did you attempt to use your passport to board the Sidney-Anacortes ferry?"

Trust him?

Jon decided if his plan stood any chance of working, he needed Fisher's help. Or, at least, his cooperation.

"Yes."

"This mean you're still on Canadian soil somewhere on the island?"

He was grateful Fisher hadn't asked exactly where.

"Yes."

"Okay, then this changes things in your favor. Slightly. But it's better than if they'd caught you at the airport. Now, if the RCMP find you, there has to be an extradition order from Korea for them to even think of sending you back. I'll check to be sure, but I don't think South Korea and Canada have an extradition agreement. But even if they do have one, the Canadians are notoriously hesitant to act on extraditions. My best guess is they'd incarcerate you until things get sorted out legally."

Good news. In a way.

He'd rather be in jail in Canada rather than in Korea.

"If I make it across the border what'll you do about it?"

Fisher laughed.

"Me personally or the FBI?"

"The feds. Immigration, customs, whoever handles this kind of situation."

"Same principle. If the Koreans want you back, they'd have to submit an extradition request to the State Department. Then, *if* State was inclined to honor it, they'd send the Marshals out to pick you up. Personally, I say do whatever you can to get back on US soil. Once that's done, we can start working on straightening this mess out. Based on what I know, I seriously doubt the feds would have any inclination to send you back."

The situation sounded better than before. Now to start setting up his plan.

"You checked Stillman's phone records yet?"

"Still working it. You were right, by the way. Calls *were* exchanged between his office and Nolan's on the days in question. Even more interesting is that during last week he had numerous calls between his office, home, and another cell. The thing that makes these calls so interesting is that particular cell was on international roam in Seoul."

"Got to be Feist. Which leads into my next question: have any idea where he is now?"

"Funny you should ask. He came through SeaTac a couple hours ago."

Well, that answered one thing.

"Back up. That cell, it has to be Feist's, right?"

"We think so, but we don't know for sure. We're having a problem ID'ing who it belongs to because the provider refuses to give us that information."

"You're kidding."

"They cite privacy issues."

Jon felt his blood pressure go up. He took a deep breath.

"When you say, 'calls were exchanged' what does that mean? You sounded hesitant."

"Simply stating the facts as they'd be argued by any good defense attorney. Even if we can prove it is Feist's, there no way to prove he was talking to Stillman when the calls occurred."

Frustrating.

"Give me more than that."

"I know where you're going with this. You want me to say there's enough to connect Feist to the murder of the two patients in Seoul. We can't say that. We don't have one piece of evidence to support that conclusion. We both *suspect* it, but as for direct evidence, there's nothing. With what we have now, a magistrate would laugh me out of their office if I asked for anything but a cup of coffee."

His head felt ready to explode, both temples throbbing.

"But aren't cases built on circumstantial evidence?"

"Sure. But not enough to prove a damn thing." Fisher let that settle before adding, "And before you ask, I have someone checking the manifest for flights to Seoul around the time you flew over, looking to see if Feist flew over."

Good.

He hadn't thought about checking that angle.

"Find anything?"

"Not yet. We had to file the proper paperwork with United before they'd release it."

At least Fisher was still working the case.

He changed subjects by asking, "It should be obvious Stillman monitored the calls I made while over there. Especially the ones to Wayne. Is there any way you can find out if there's a tap on Wayne's cell or landline?"

"I might. But tell me this, why? What are you thinking?"

Jon explained his plan.

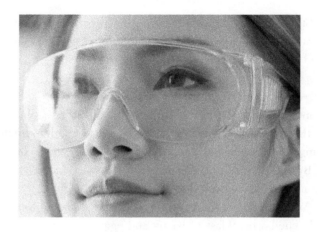

Chapter 57

A CAR DOOR slam woke Jon as he lay in a clump of bushes in Cridge Park. He opened his eyes but didn't move.

He could hear the soft chatter of a police radio and an idling engine and a gruff voice say, "Get up."

Jon looked in the direction of the voice. Not more then fifty feet away a scruffy male sat on the grass, his back against a tree, a bottle in hand. An RMCP patrolman stood in front him, hands on his hips, a patrol car at the curb with the back passenger door open. It was the middle of the night, Jon figured without looking at his watch. Probably close to 1:00 A.M.

"Why you gotta pick on me?" the man asked with the rasp of a smoker's voice. The man pointed toward Jon. "Why not him?"

"Because I'm talking to you," the officer replied without taking his eyes off the drunk.

Slowly Jon turned onto his belly and started to push up into a crouch.

"Aw, man, give a guy a break."

"I said, get up."

Still watching the officer, Jon moved back behind another tree, waited a second to make sure he hadn't been noticed, then turned in the opposite direction and started down the sidewalk.

At 11:32 the next morning, the brilliant sun felt soft and warm on Jon's face as he stood next to the iconic stone seawall that rims the city harbor—a welcome contrast to the long night of moving along deserted streets while mentally reviewing his plan.

By 5:00 A.M., the city began to slowly awaken, and the tension of hiding began to lessen.

Around 6:00 he found a café, used the restroom to freshen up, downed a breakfast of bacon and eggs with several cups of black coffee, and then headed back into the streets. He decided it was probably safer to go back to Sidney, which, would be the last place the RCMP would expect him. But he wanted to wait until traffic picked up so he'd be less conspicuous.

Satisfyingly stuffed, he headed back to Fort Street, turned north onto Blanshard, the city extension of highway 17, hung out his thumb at the passing cars and trudged north, away from the city. One mile later, a black Toyota Land Cruiser braked at the curb. Jon tossed his rucksack on the seat and climbed into an interior of stale nicotine and sweat and scattered fast food wrappers.

The driver, an obese man, maybe mid-thirties, said, "I'm heading north, up past Sidney. That work for you?"

"Sidney's perfect. I need to catch the ferry. Appreciate it."

The man checked his watch, "Lucky. Got yourself a ton of time, son," and pulled away from the curb.

The interior fell silent except for a "soft rock" station that dubbed itself "The Ocean." Jon preferred to listen than delve into any small talk that might draw attention to him or leave the driver with information helpful to the authorities.

Five minutes later the road transitioned into a highway and the driver kicked it up to 100 K/H.

On the radio a Phil Collins tune ended, and the female DJ

announced, "Turning to local news, an alert is still in effect throughout Vancouver Island for Jon Ritter, the Seattle neurosurgeon wanted by the RMCP for questioning. He's male, thirty-five years of age, medium height and weight, graying blond hair and was last seen wearing a gray University of British Columbia sweatshirt and tan pants. Police officials consider Ritter armed and potentially dangerous. Citizens are warned not to attempt to apprehend Ritter, but—"

"I certainly appreciate this lift," Jon said loud enough to mask the remaining description.

The driver laughed.

"Wonder what a neurosurgeon would do to get the police looking for him? Kill his wife?"

Jon forced a laugh. The man shot Jon a quick sideways glance.

"That description could fit hundreds of people. Even you."

"Yep, a *lot* of people," Jon agreed.

To the west the sun hovered just above the jagged tips of Douglas Firs as Jon scouted out the Van Isle Marina—a maze of slips, rust-stained corrugated-metal sheds, hull repair shops, parking spaces, and retail shops along Sidney's north shore. Most importantly, the development contained an excellent restaurant. On his walk over, he stopped at a tired, two-story, nineteen-fifties style motel a half block to the south, and paid cash for a room for one night.

Now, he approached the restaurant and stopped by the door to study the menu in the front window. Could be pushing his luck, being out in public like this, but on the other hand, acting confident might go a long way to deter suspicion. He was hungry again.

A wiry bearded *maitre' d* in denims and white shirt met him just inside the door with, "May I help you?"

Jon quickly scanned the tables, saw what he was looking for, said, "Dinner for one," and pointed at the table.

The *maitre'd* glanced at the obvious choice, nodded, "Certainly."

Before removing the second place-setting, the waiter handed him a menu and asked if he wanted a drink. Jon ordered a scotch rocks.

"Very good," and floated away.

Jon opened the menu as a ruse for a closer look at the older couple enjoying lively conversation over dinner. Both wore upscale casual clothes that radiated the affluent "boater look."

Perfect.

Jon shifted in the chair, crossed his legs, in a move that naturally turned toward them.

He took a moment to eye their entrées before asking the man, "Excuse me, but what's that you're having?"

The man glanced back with a friendly smile and laughing gray eyes that matched the color of a closely cropped beard.

"The veal. They do an absolutely amazing job with it."

He wondered if he was mistaken, that instead of boaters these were locals enjoying a dinner out.

"Really! You eat here often?"

"Whenever possible," he beamed. "This is our third day here," with a nod at the window and the marina beyond. After a chuckle, "We've eaten every one of our meals here."

Jon followed the glance to a view of sailboat masts in the evening sky.

"You guys sail?"

"Naw, we're power boaters. A forty-five-footer. Over in another site."

"Forty-five! Nice size for the two of you," offering his hand. "Wayne Dobbs."

The man set down his napkin to shake.

"Andrew Klein. My wife, Susan."

Susan simply nodded, dabbed at her lips with the corner of the white napkin, eyebrows in a suspicious furrow.

Alarm bells rang in the back of Jon's mind. That look...did

she recognize him from the broadcast descriptions?

Stay calm. Be cool.

Jon raised his scotch in a toast.

"Where you from?"

If pressed, his guess would be California. They looked the type to afford to moor such an expensive toy in a northwest marina year-round and jet up to enjoy a breathtaking cruise whenever their mood and busy schedules permitted.

Klein jutted his chin toward the other window.

"Lopez. Our excuse for coming over here is to use this marina for maintenance. I tell you, their work is top drawer. Turns out to be an amazing deal. But to tell the truth, the *real* reason we come over is to eat." With a laugh, he patted his flat stomach. "Got to watch the calories though." He glanced at Jon's empty place setting. "What'd you order?"

"Salmon."

With an approving nod and conspiratorial tone, "They do an amazing job on that too. One of my favorites, matter of fact. This is truly an amazing restaurant. Met the chef yet?"

"No. It's my first time here."

He sipped scotch and cautioned himself to not push too hard.

"Just a kid. In his twenties, I think. But absolutely amazing. The owner hired him right out from under some big-time Vancouver restaurant. A real coup. Expect to see him on Iron Chef one of these days."

"When you heading back? To Lopez, I mean."

Lopez was one of the major islands in the American San Juan chain, an archipelago sandwiched between Washington State and Vancouver Island.

"In the morning, looks like. Planned to head out tonight but turns out they couldn't get her prop on in time. So, of course, that gave us an excuse for one more dinner here."

He smiled at his wife who declined the obvious segue into the conversation.

Jon leaned closer to Klein.

"Mind if I ask a favor?"

His smile faded.

"Depends. What?"

"Any possibility I could hitch a ride to Lopez with you?"

Klein's expression lost the edge of friendliness. Susan Klein leaned over, whispered something in her husband's ear. Surprise flickered through his eyes.

Shit, she knew.

Probably heard about him on the news, maybe had even seen a picture.

Having anticipated this possibility Jon said, "Look, I'm in a bit of a jam and need help. Just hear me out. Okay?"

Andrew nodded. Susan folded the napkin over one leg with an I-Knew-It expression.

To defend himself, Jon briefly summarized what happened from beginning to end, including being held by police in Seoul, and then handed Andrew his cell phone along with Fisher's card.

"Here. Call him. Tell him you're with me and ask if it's okay for you to take me to Lopez."

Andrew eyed Jon suspiciously while Susan continued chewing slowly, her body language leaving no doubt where she stood on the issue. Klein glanced at her, weighted the offer a moment before picking up the phone and business card.

"Okay, but outside. Not in here where others can hear."

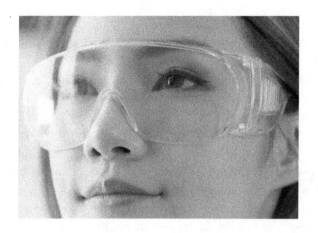

Chapter 58

JON FOLLOWED KLEIN out the door and along the sidewalk.

Klein stopped, scanned the area to make certain they were alone before punching in Fisher's number. He stood with the phone to his ear glancing just about everywhere but Jon's eyes.

Seconds later he glanced directly at Jon, raised his eyebrows briefly, and then spoke into his phone.

"Mr. Fisher? My name's Andrew Klein. I'm with a man who claims to be Jon Ritter and that he knows you...yeah, sure..." Klein studied Jon a moment. "Around thirty-five, I'd say about five-ten, slender, graying blond hair...yeah, he has the scar...we're in Sidney, BC. He wants me to ferry him to Lopez on our boat...okay."

He handed Jon the phone.

Jon asked Fisher, "We all set?"

"We are."

"I'll call you when, and if, I make it to Lopez."

Fisher said, "Excellent, but we never had this conversation. Understand?"

"Understood," Jon said.

"You have a way lined up to get from the island to the city?"

Jon wasn't about to tell him. Right now, landing safely on US soil was the most important thing in his life, so he didn't want to risk any problem.

"All taken care of."

As they turned toward the restaurant door, Klein put his hand on Jon's shoulder, stopping him.

"I'll tell you how we'll do this. Meet us here at eight in the morning. You buy breakfast, we run you to Lopez. How's that?"

For the first time since Detective Park detained him in Seoul, Jon believed he stood a chance of making it home.

He seemed so close now.

"You have no idea how much I appreciate this."

Jon's salad was waiting when he retuned to the table. As he settled in the waiter appeared along side the table.

"Another scotch, or would you like wine with dinner?"

Jon glanced at the salad, then back to his empty glass, a soft warm buzz carrying him to another place, numbing the accumulated fatigue and lifting the stress still weighing heavily on his shoulders.

"Better not. I still have work to do tonight."

The door to his motel room closed behind him with an anemic hollow thunk of cheap construction, the room air stale and warm with a faintly familiar residual of disinfectant and mildew. He pushed the button on the decrepit A/C window unit, and it coughed to life, clattering away, in a feeble attempt to exchange air. Next stop, the bathroom, to rinse his face. Returned to the bedroom, dropped down heavily onto the foot of the bed and, using his original Droid, called Wayne at home.

"Hey, it's me."

"Jesus Christ! Where are you?"

"Victoria," he lied.

"BC?"

"Yeah. Look, here's the deal. I need a big favor."

"Sure. Anything. What?"

"Immigration knows my passport is forged so they're looking for it under the reissue number. Only way I'm going to get back is to use a different passport. Park still has my original, but my old expired one is in the desk at home. Think you could get it for me and have Michael bring it tomorrow on the Clipper? If they don't look too closely, I might be able to slip through with it."

Wayne let out a long slow whistle.

"You honestly think they'll let you board with an expired passport?"

"Don't have a choice. It's my only shot."

"Man, oh, man. Well, hell, guess it's worth a try. I'll be happy to bring it."

His tone was not encouraging.

"No, have Michael bring it."

Wayne hesitated a beat.

"Why?"

Was the phone still bugged? It had to be for his plan to have any chance of working.

"Because the Avengers know who you are. Bet you they have no idea who Michael is."

Another pause.

"Got it." But still uncertain. "Tell me where to find it and how to get in your house. Michael will be there tomorrow."

Jon gave him instructions.

Just before saying goodbye, he added, "Be sure Michael has a cell phone with him just in case I'm delayed."

"I know you have this number, so I'll give him my phone instead."

"Perfect."

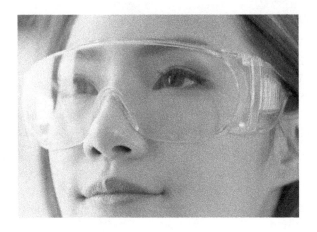

Chapter 59

NIGEL FEIST COLLECTED his change and round-trip ticket from the cashier before melting into the buzz of tourists.

Already the weather promised a gorgeous day for a water trip. Across Puget Sound, in the western horizon, the ragged white Olympic Mountain peaks towered above Bainbridge Island, spearing cloudless azure sky. Shrieking kids chased each other through scattered clots of adults.

Ahead of him, the little fag's partner, Michael, leaned on the tubular metal dock railing along side of the moored Victoria Clipper, a long white multi-deck boat with a bright Union Jack painted across the stern quarter. The fag had on black designer jeans, a tan cotton sweater over a white shirt, complete with a windbreaker draped over his shoulders like a fucking tennis pro in a Rolex ad. No socks, topsiders, a black Tumi messenger bag at his feet.

Well, at least the fag brought enough clothes. One thing Nigel learned growing up in a sea town was that no matter how warm a day appeared to be, it could get damn cold out on the water, especially in a moving craft. Best to err on the side of too many layers. In contrast, most of the tourists in the crowd—the ones toting cameras or holding maps—dressed too lightly. Five minutes after casting off, they'd be huddled inside the cabin complaining.

Nigel blended in well, he thought. Levis, a black tee shirt under a gray hooded University of Washington sweatshirt, Reeboks and a scalpel-sharp ceramic knife securely strapped to his right ankle. The beautiful thing about ceramic was the toughness of steel while being total immune to metal detectors.

A body scanner, on the other hand...

A crewmember unclipped the chain across the gangplank, allowing passengers to swarm aboard, racing for prime window seats. Nigel shuffled into line, making no attempt to gun for a good seat, figuring: best to not draw attention to oneself.

The *Million Dollar Script* was a beauty. Teak decks, blue canvas canopy over the flying bridge, all the expensive electronics a skipper might lust for.

After a quick tour, Klein advised Jon, "Stay below deck until we're well clear of the harbor. I'll call you when it's safe come topside."

Without argument, Jon moved into the main saloon and settled in on a blue cushion, content to listen to the idling engine and dream about setting foot on United States soil. The cabin carried that dry boat smell of overcooked vinyl and stale bilge water from too many days each year battened down without good ventilation.

With well-practiced harmony, Andrew and Susan cast off. Jon felt a subtle clunk as Klein shifted the driveshaft into reverse, followed by the initial movement as the boat slowly began backing away from her temporary slip.

Thirty minutes later Jon sat next to Andrew on the flying bridge, the wind whipping his hair as the sun warmed his face. Susan stretched out on a cushion on the forward deck reading a

Kindle, a wide-brim straw sun hat tied securely under her chin.

Jon asked Andrew, "Out of curiosity, what's the drill for clearing customs when you island-hop like this?"

"Pretty easy, actually. I have a special permit that allows me to call Canadian customs on my cell three hours before I arrive. Then, on the way back, I call U.S. Customs. They ask who's on board. I tell 'em. Simple." After a beat, he gave Jon another look. "Then again, they always have the option of inspecting the boat at anytime anywhere. Which is something they do at random, just to make sure. Lot of drug-running through these waters."

Jon decided to change subjects.

Although he always hated it when people asked him this question, he couldn't resist, "What kind of work you do?"

Andrew laughed, corrected the course slightly.

"Right now, nothing."

Jon watched the compass swing to the new heading and decided not to push for an answer.

Andrew continued with, "Actually, I'm taking what you might call a mini sabbatical. We escaped L.A. a couple years back. At the time, I planned on taking some time off. Six, maybe nine months tops. Turns out, I haven't worked in two years. But I'm getting ready to start back any day now."

An actor? Could be.

His face carried a handsome ruggedness but didn't look familiar. Susan appeared to be the quiet artist type, maybe a painter.

Jon was going to ask him if the boat's name meant what he thought it did when suddenly Andrew muttered, "Fuck, fuck, fuck!" and came close to pounding the wheel with a fist.

The sudden outburst startled Jon. He jumped.

"What?"

"Look to the port side of stern."

Aw, Jesus!

A white Coast Guard cutter, easily identified from the

diagonal red stripe across its bow was barreling straight for them in what appeared to be an intercept course. Susan Klein shot her husband an I-told-you-so look. Panic gripped Jon's chest.

He asked Andrew, "What do I do?"

Andrew thought for a moment.

"By now they've already seen you, so trying to hide will only raise suspicion. Guess we'll just have to see what they want. Stay put and try not to be nervous. Hey, look at it this way: they catch you, at least it's the Americans."

The Coast Guard boat throttled down and pulled alongside, perfectly matching Andrew's speed. From the bridge, a uniformed officer raised a red bullhorn to his lips.

"Cut your power and prepare to be boarded."

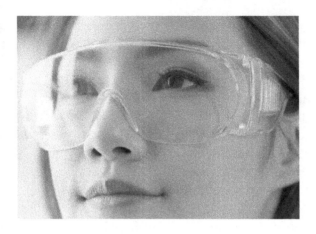

Chapter 60

ONCE HE WAS certain Michael whatever-the-fuck-his-last-name was had boarded the Victoria Clipper, Nigel snagged a window seat and relaxed. No sense following him around like a puppy dog.

Where the hell was he going to go?

Besides, wasn't worth the risk of being identified. Especially if the bugger was smart enough to check for a tail. But more than that, Nigel didn't want to look at his face just in case he had to kill him.

He didn't much fancy killing Ritter, but he knew he had to do it. Didn't much fancy killing Michael either. Neither one had actually done any wrong other than be the wrong person crossing paths with another wrong person. Which, in his business, was usually the case.

For reasons he couldn't identify, damaging people's lives began to bother him.

As a younger man, he didn't buy into the karma concept. Now, nearing retirement, the concept of 'what goes around comes around,' had begun to creep into his consciousness and resonate—especially during the increasing stretches of early morning insomnia when every little goddamn thing on your mind grows disproportionately important.

This definitely would be his last job. Snuff Ritter and be done with it. Might be a tad shy of the number his financial planner projected to maintain his present lifestyle the rest of his years, but close enough to suit him. Might mean one or two fewer trips to Vegas each year to get laid. But hell, the older you got, the less pussy you wanted anyway. Least, that's what he'd been told.

Temple pressed against the cold window, he stared out over the Strait of Juan de Fuca, breathed the pleasingly familiar smell of brine and boat oil as the rhythmic vibrations of the engine lulled his mind.

More and more lately he fantasized about long road trips on his maroon Harley Flathead. Nothing better to connect you with Mother Earth than being surrounded by the smell of cattle and freshly threshed hay, road heat, raindrops splattering your visor, surface imperfections in the road vibrating up through your spine.

Travel for miles, stopping only at appealing sites or towns. Stay one week or one hour depending on how it struck your fancy. Yeah, soon as this fucking job ended....

The Victoria Clipper's scheduled arrival was 11:15 AM with a 5:30 PM departure. By 8:30 this evening he'd be done with this job and back in Seattle. First thing tomorrow he'd be at the airport to catch the first available shuttle to LA. Soon as he was home, he'd start preparing the Harley for his first retirement trip.

Yeah, he'd really do it.

A road trip.

Jon remained on the flying bridge as Andrew and Susan climbed the stairway down to the main deck to help two Coast Guardsmen and one German shepherd board.

He heard one man introduce himself as Lieutenant Cosgrove and ask, "Sir, you just embarked from Sydney, did you not?" Jon's gut tightened.

Andrew answered, "Yes."

"Sorry for the inconvenience, but we need to do a quick search of your vessel."

"If you don't mind, what are you looking for?"

"Explosives and firearms, sir. OHS just put an increased threat level into effect. Now, if you don't mind, the sooner we start, the sooner you'll be under way."

Andrew pointed to the cabin.

"No problem. Have at it."

A few minutes later an African-American male Guardsman came up the ladder, said, "Excuse me, sir. I'll be out of your way in a moment." Glanced around the flying bridge, opened the only compartment, rummaged through flares and three life vests. Apparently satisfied, he secured the door. "Sorry for the inconvenience," and climbed back down.

Nigel Feist made sure he cleared the gangplank well before the queer did. Slowly, he walked the pier toward a stone retaining wall and the looming Empress Hotel, watching for Michael to pass him.

And that's exactly what happened.

Feist was leaning against the wall at the shore end of the pier when the little bugger pranced by. Nigel fell in behind him and followed. In a few minutes they'd meet Ritter, and the job would be finished.

With the same alacrity and precision as in Victoria, Andrew and Susan moored the *Million Dollar Script* at a large marina on Lopez Island.

With four bumpers in place and all lines cheated, Andrew told Jon, "This is as far as I take you. Man, if you get busted on your way to the ferry it isn't going to be in *my* car."

Jon shook Klein's hand.

"Thanks. I think you realize just how much I appreciate this." He paused to swallow the emotional lump in his throat. "You have my name. Next time you plan to come down to Seattle, call. I'd love to take both of you to dinner."

"Have to think about that one." Andrew laughed. "First, I figure to play it safe and let some time pass, make sure you're not being hunted by Al Qaeda or some other group before being seen with you."

Jon put a hand on Andrew's shoulder.

"Thanks."

"Ciao."

Jon jumped to the concrete dock and stood still a moment, legs adjusting to a stable surface.

He breathed in warm salt air. Creosote and drying seaweed never smelled so beautiful in his life. In fact, at that moment the marina seemed to be the most beautiful place in the world.

He started walking slowly along the dock toward the parking lot, fighting to control the emotions bubbling up from within.

The moment he reached shore, he dropped to knees, bent down, and with tears streaming from his eyes, touched his forehead to the warm asphalt.

Home at last!

"Wow, guess you weren't kidding when you said you're happy to be back."

Shielding his eyes from the sun, Jon squinted up at Andrew's silhouette. He swallowed, cleared his throat.

"You have no idea."

Klein offered his hand.

"C'mon, you convinced me."

Jon waved away the help, preferring to stand on his own power. The police could arrest him now. He didn't care. At least he'd have a fighting chance to defend himself.

"I'll drive you to the ferry. Hell, no one's going to risk picking you up looking like that." He chuckled. "They'll peg you for some sort of a psycho trying to hijack their car and probably run you down instead. Then it'd be on *my* conscience. I don't need that kind of grief. Besides, the dock is on the other side of the island. Way too far to walk." After a quick glance at the pier, he added, "Give us five minutes to close up the boat."

Struck dumb for words of gratitude, Jon settled for, "Thank you."

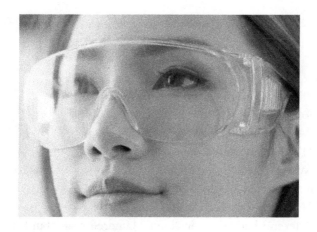

Chapter 61

JON STOOD ON the porch to The Landing, a shanty of rough-hewn siding and moss-laden shingles perched on a curvy hillside road snaking down to the ferry landing.

The small building played dual service as short-order café and waiting room for walk-ons. The clock behind the dusty window showed thirty-minutes before the next scheduled boat to Anacortes, the small ferry terminal town on the mainland.

Once again, he mentally reviewed the plan in play.

What flaws was he missing?

Would it backfire?

Well, he'd find out.

He opened the new cell phone purchased in Victoria and dialed Fisher.

Jon asked, "Did Wayne get the new cell phone?"

Fisher said, "He did."

"What's the number?"

After Fisher recited the number Jon programmed it into his system, said, "So far, so good. How about your end?"

"Perfect."

"Call you later." Jon disconnected and promptly dialed Wayne's new cell.

"Where the hell *are* you?" Wayne demanded.

"I'm going to catch the ferry to Anacortes in about an hour. It is possible for you could meet there?"

"Absolutely, but what the hell's going on?"

"I'll explain when I see you."

Wayne sighed, said, "Okaaaayyy. You want me to meet you at the ferry dock?"

"No. How familiar are you with Anacortes?"

"Haven't been there in about a hundred years, but I suspect I can find it. It's somewhere north on I-5 and south of the Canadian border. They haven't moved it, have they?"

Jon laughed, still giddy from crossing the border without being arrested.

"No. It's still there. Here's the deal, there's a marina on the east side of town right off the main drag as you come in. There's a marine supply and yacht sales office in the complex, lots of boats. Meet you there."

"Lemme see…should take about two hours to make it there, especially with afternoon traffic and all. What time do you think you'll be there?"

Jon checked the schedule taped to the inside of the store window. Four o'clock.

He told Wayne, "Five o'clock."

In a Starbucks down the street from the Empress Hotel, Nigel Feist nursed a latte and watched Michael read a paperback on a park bench facing the harbor.

Now mid afternoon and not a goddamned thing happened.

What the fuck is going on?

A suspicion began to nag, a feeling of having been in this situation before. Not déjà vu really. Rather, a misgiving…of being set up and fucked with.

If Ritter were meeting Michael, he should've shown by now. He checked his watch again, then looked back at Michael. The little bastard slowly turned another page, uncrossed his leg, and crossed to the other one.

Fucking color-coordinated faggot.

Checking the contents, Nigel rocked his cup back and forth. Only dregs.

Now what?

Can't very well sit here for fucking ever.

The Anacortes Ferry slip led to a long curving road on the western shore of Fidalgo Island with slightly over three miles of two-lane asphalt that connected the landing to the town's central business district and marinas. Jon caught a taxi outside the terminal and asked to be dropped two blocks north of the marina entrance.

Now, sitting at a wood table with a thick coat of Verathane in a fish and chips dive, he stared through greasy glass. Across the street a Cyclone fence enclosed a large rectangle of cracked asphalt packed with boat trailers and vehicles.

For the past fifteen minutes he nursed a cup of abysmal overcooked coffee while monitoring the minimal activity in the lot. No suspicious vehicles or people entered the lot. At the far end two men power sanded a cruiser hull up on blocks. They'd been working when he arrived and paid little attention to anything else going on around them.

Time.

He slipped from the booth and out the door, crossed the street, into the fenced-in lot, worked his way between parked cars and a random assortment of empty rusting boat trailers looking for a good spot to watch and wait. Found one behind a dented green dumpster reeking of garbage and fresh paint, the location providing an unobstructed view to the front door of Fidalgo Yacht Sales fifty yards away.

At nine minutes to five, Wayne's silver Mercedes e320

slowly turned into the parking lot and crept directly toward the yacht brokerage. The sight of Wayne sent a wave of relief through him. Had to force himself to stay put and watch, to make certain Wayne hadn't been inadvertently followed.

Wayne parked the car and waited patiently inside. After several minutes he stepped out and slowly turned a complete circle. Apparently puzzled, he walked to the sales office, cupped both hands to the sides of his eyes and peered through the window, shrugged and returned to the car, climbed in and closed the door to wait. After all, he was a few minutes early.

Convinced Wayne hadn't been followed, Jon trotted over to the car.

Wayne saw him coming and jumped out again, cocked his head to one side, looked him up and down, said, "My my, don't we look like a complete mess."

Jon gave him a quick hug.

"Not one of my better weeks. Thanks for coming." He quickly scanned the area one last time and, to his relief, saw nothing changed from a minute ago. He opened the passenger door to climb in. "Now, let's get the hell out of here."

If his plan was working, Feist was safely in Victoria. And if Fisher had done his part, an RMCP undercover officer was keeping a protective eye on Michael.

Wayne sighed.

"Well well, aren't we in a hurry." He fired the ignition but hesitated before engaging the transmission. "Just for the record, not that I'm going to leave you stranded here or anything, but am I about to get arrested for harboring a fugitive?"

"Not unless you brought the police."

"Rats! I've always wanted to be a cellblock wife."

With a dramatic sigh, he shifted into reverse, glanced over his shoulder, turned the car around and headed onto the street.

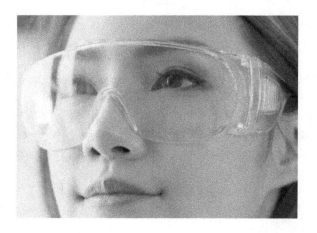

Chapter 62

BY 9:35 P.M. THE western horizon, seen from the ninth-floor conference room in the Federal Building, became a huge black void instead of sky, mountains, and islands. The smell of overcooked coffee and copier toner hung in the uncomfortably warm stuffy air. Gary Fisher, Jon's new attorney, Palmer Davidson, Wayne, and Jon were discussing options.

It seemed to everyone present that Stillman orchestrated both Lippmann's murder and NIH's withdrawal of the clinical trial on the assumption that unless Jon and Wayne resigned themselves to losing ten years of work, their only options would be to sell their technique to a biotech company or find an innovative source to fund a small stem cell trial. Both options were extremely limited and, as Stillman had correctly predicted, Jon came to him for help. Considering his prior job offer to Jon, allying with Trophozyme was the most obvious and logical course of action.

It infuriated Jon to realize how easily he'd been manipulated by Stillman. As a result, he now blamed himself for the murders of Gabe, Jin-Woo, and the two patients in Seoul, to say nothing of his living hell of these past weeks.

Why didn't he see through it? How could he have gone against his initial gut instinct and actually trusted Stillman?

Not only did the guilt demoralize him, it embarrassed him to think how stupid he must appear to everyone involved, including Stillman.

But it was also clear that the FBI had no hard evidence to support their conclusions. Meaning Stillman and Feist would get a free pass.

Furious, Jon turned to Davidson.

"You agree with Fisher that there's nothing we can do to Stillman?"

Davidson gave Jon the courtesy of appearing to contemplate the question in spite of having previously voiced this opinion.

"Every bit of information we have is circumstantial. Certainly, common sense leads one to believe he's the prime driver behind the events that have transpired, but no real evidence exists to warrant any formal charges. Certainly, we have nothing to persuade a prosecuting attorney to press charges."

"And Feist?" Jon asked, although they had discussed his complicity also.

Davidson raised both hands in a gesture of helplessness.

"We've been through this. It's exactly the same. Sure, we would have circumstantial evidence, but no smoking gun. Besides, most of these alleged crimes were committed outside the United States, giving us no jurisdiction. There's not a thing we can do."

Fisher cut in with, "I gave Park what we know and suspect about Feist. He's going to look again at the hospital security videos but even if they show Feist in the hospital that night, there is nothing to link him to the death of the two patients. The best we can hope for is to clear you."

Jon shook his head.

"Unbelievable!"

The room fell silent, everyone avoiding eye contact with Jon, sympathetic, yet legally powerless to do anything to alter the situation. For the final time, Jon mentally reviewed the last step of his plan. Would Stillman or Feist fall for it?

After inhaling a deep breath, he turned to Fisher.

"I need a word with you in private."

Fisher glanced at the others around the table.

"If you'll excuse us a moment."

Out in the hall, the conference room door closed, Jon asked, "Got it for me?"

Fisher pulled a folded slip of paper from his breast pocket to hand him.

"I suggest you call from the men's room."

Feist was checking the Australian team scores on Cricket.com, but was finding it difficult to concentrate, his mind continuously drifting back to the images of Victoria. The little queer, casual as hell, sitting on the bench flipping pages of the paperback, flashing that irritating smug expression. Like, he *knew* Ritter didn't intend to show.

That was the thing: he fucking *knew* it. And that bothered him. Greatly. Made him edgy to know he'd been had yet had no idea how. Nobody fucked with him like that. No question, he'd been played. Fucked over. No idea why, but it had to be true. Just couldn't see the angle...

He picked up the sheet of paper for a fresh look. The names Stillman, Michael, Ritter, and Wayne were printed in different corners, arrows connecting them from several directions. These were the only possible players except for...it dawned on him: the one name not there was the FBI agent. Hmmm...he jotted that one down too, figured this sheet was now too messy, so started over again on a fresh one.

Once again, how did this work? Stillman knew Dobb's partner, Michael, planned on taking the Clipper to Victoria to meet Jon Ritter...okay.

So?

Michael *did* go to Victoria. But once there, only thing he did was walk off the fucking boat and perch on a park bench to read until the return cruise boarded. No shopping. No sightseeing. No meeting. Just fucking reading. Then it dawned on him: a fucking decoy was what he was.

Either someone had fed Stillman intentional disinformation or sending him on a wild goose chase was Stillman's idea. Which begged the question why? Who would benefit by that? Certainly not Dobbs or his boyfriend. Leaving Ritter, Stillman, or the FBI. Nothing jumped out at him. And that was what was so frustrating.

Fuck!

Speaking of which, where was Ritter? One moment he's in Canada, next moment he's gone.

Very disconcerting.

His cell rang. Before he looked at the caller ID, a premonition struck, ill formed, yet dark and ominous. The only people to know this number could be counted on one hand. Ritter wasn't one. The display showed: UNREGISTERED. Hmmm...he put the phone to his ear and listened.

A voice he didn't recognize.

"You there, Nigel? C'mon, Nigel, you can talk to me. After all, we've been close these past couple weeks. Traveling together, meeting the same people, going to the same places. We should be old friends by now."

Aw, Jesus fucking Christ! How'd...?

Ritter said, "Okay, I can understand, you being a little caught off guard, maybe even upset, me calling like this. But I want to warn you."

Feist realized he was breathing too hard into the phone, so, angled it away from his mouth. No upside to tipping your hand. He rolled off the bed and stood, sweating now that he was on defense. Unfamiliar territory, it was. Unnerving too.

The little bugger, how'd he get his fucking hands on his cell number? Where the hell was he?

Ritter continued, "Stillman just cut a deal with the FBI; information for immunity. He agreed to turn state's witness and testify you killed Raymore Thompson. You remember Raymore, don't you? The dumb shit you brought with you the night Gabriel Lippmann was murdered, the one crime you committed in this jurisdiction. Wait, it gets better. He'll testify you hired out to the Avengers, to take care of me. So they're now looking into the possibility of linking you with those other murders. Pretty smart of Stillman, don't you think? Not really the guy you want to trust as your partner, after all."

Ritter stopped, clearly expecting a response, but Nigel knew better.

Fuck him.

He needed to think, regain the advantage, if possible, extract more information while walking a tightrope.

After several seconds, Ritter continued, "As you know, the FBI's been working the Avenger thing for months. What you don't know is that two days ago they busted their website. Guess who submitted my name and personal information?"

In a flash, Feist realized his mistake. He should've picked an internet café across the fucking country, say, Boston or New York instead of Stockton. Any big city would make it impossible to single out one user.

Wait!

If they narrowed in on a specific computer, so what? Didn't prove a thing. That Ritter...a sly little bastard, alright.

Almost canny enough to trip him up, trick him into saying something incriminating.

Ritter said, "But the FBI is smart. They figure you probably don't have any strong feelings one way or the other about abortion. I mean, you? C'mon. From what they say, you don't give a shit about kids and haven't set foot in church since being confirmed at St. Marks. So, I mean, why would you give a damn? Know what I'm saying?"

Fuck! They knew all that?

St. Marks, the church in Cairns his family forced him to attend.

How'd they learn something so miniscule, unless...did he ever mention it to Stillman?

"So they figure someone put you up to it. Makes, sense, doesn't it."

Severely tempting to say something, but he thought better of it. So far, speculation was the only thing to come out of Ritter's mouth. Proved nothing. Not a damn thing. Thought about that a moment...was this being recorded? Nothing more than a cheap trick to get him to say something incriminating?

"Heard of FinCen? Surely, in your line of work you know of them. They find bank records like you wouldn't believe. They know, for example, that Stillman's made several deposits in an offshore account of yours. I mean what a coincidence, huh?"

His breathing was back to normal now, the initial shock subsiding. Been in worse situations, he had, and always prevailed. Would this time, too. Just needed to know precisely what Ritter knew. The more the better. So best to keep the bloke talking.

Feist said, "I do business with any number of firms, mate. Means nothing."

"Perhaps, but bear with me. All the evidence just keeps getting better. Like you being booked on the same flight to Seoul as me."

"Coincidence, mate, pure coincidence."

"What about all the calls between you and Stillman?"

Feist laughed.

"If, as you suggest, I allegedly work for his firm, I just might have need to chat with him, now wouldn't I."

"True, but how do you explain your trip on the Clipper?"

Fuck! There it was. He fucking knew it. A set up.

Ritter said, "The reason I know about that is I was the one

who called Wayne last night to arrange it. No one else knew about that call. Unless, of course, Wayne's phone was being monitored. Soon as the call was over, you talked to Stillman. He told you to follow Michael to get to me. But it didn't work out that way, did it?"

Feist's mind was racing now, putting together details.

Ritter said, "I suppose you wonder how I know this. Well, the FBI followed Michael, using him as bait. They recorded you stalking him, everything from when you picked him up."

Feist said, "Know what, mate? This all sounds like a pile of rubbish. No fucking way the FBI would give you any real information on an active case. And if they did, why would you tell me?"

"Because, much as I despise you, none of it would've happened if Stillman hadn't put you up to it. I want that son of a bitch to fry for it. Understand?"

Feist knew better than admit anything to anyone under any circumstance.

"No, mate. I don't. Fact is, I don't know what the hell you're talking about. This conversation is over."

Feist ripped his coat from the hangar and bee-lined out the door.

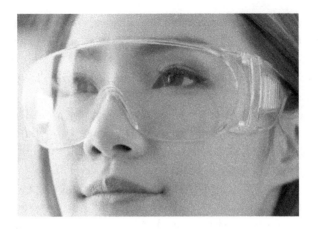

Chapter 63

NIKKI SHEPHERD WAS straddling Stillman, moaning and grunting all the guttural sounds that got him off.

Better yet, the doofus across the street was watching, making little attempt to be discreet about it.

Stillman had Nikki stretch out on the bed so he could sight past her left hip, out the open doors, over the balcony railing, across Third Avenue, to the darkened condo window where a glint of streetlight reflected off the binoculars.

Man, did he love watching being watched. Got him hard. A neighbor with expensive Bushnells trumped a palate of Cialis.

Not that he needed much when Nikki cranked him.

"Oh, gawd...."

The phone rang.

Nikki lunged forward, pinning his shoulders to the mattress, a drop of sweat dripping from the tip of her nose.

"Don't you dare!"

Perfect! Always the right reaction. Any other time he'd love it. But tonight he worried about not hearing from Feist all day.

Made him edgy in spite of great sex.

Had to be Feist.

"Hold that thought," he said, gently moving her aside.

She sighed and flashed a pouty face before immodestly spreading out on the sheet, giving doofus a full-on beaver shot.

Which, she shamelessly admitted, turned her on.

He picked up without a word.

Jon Ritter said, "We need to talk."

Interesting. Where the hell's he now? Canada?

Probably.

Couldn't have made it across the border…could he? So far, the little bastard proved more resourceful than he would've imagined.

This again, raised the question of Feist's whereabouts.

Hmm…how to handle this?

Especially with the handicap of not knowing what Ritter knew. Probably best to maintain appearances and act the role of friend.

Stillman said, "Yo dog! Am I relieved to hear from you! You okay? Where are you?"

"News flash, Richard: cut the crap. You know that I know you're lying. We both also know the only thing you're interested in is the formula."

Deny it? Probably best. Yeah, deny-deny-deny.

"Not so, I care about you. Don't forget I want you on our team here. But since you bring up the issue, yes, I want it. But that's not what *you* called about. What do you want to talk about?"

"A deal."

Maybe Ritter wasn't as dumb as he looked.

"Such as?"

"A trade. The formulation in exchange for Feist not trying to kill me. How does that sound?"

Ah, so Ritter did know…so, no use continuing the charade.

After all, the formula—and Trophozyme's salvation—was

359

the whole point of this little game. Time was running out. But no discussions about any of this over the phone. Especially with Ritter proving to be such a slippery little bastard.

Stillman said, "I understand how you might feel, ah, irritated...but all I can say is I had nothing to do with what happened to you. That apparently was The Avengers' work. However, you do raise a point worth considering: if we release a statement to the press stating that I now own the technique, perhaps those crazy bastards will give up and go away."

"Got to hand it to you, Richard, always looking out for self-interests. Well, whatever...just have Feist lay off."

"When can we discuss this in person?"

"I'm in Canada at the moment having problems getting across the border, but I think I found a way. It's going to take a couple hours. I can't possibly meet before...say seven tomorrow morning. Your office. Does that work for you?"

A deep-rooted distrust warned not to trust Ritter, that, impossible as it might be, he'd already made it across the border.

Call his bluff and demand he hand over the formula now?

But what if that was exactly what Ritter was counting on? What if this was nothing more than manipulation?

And what about Feist?

Why hadn't he heard from him? Something wasn't right...it definitely felt like a manipulation.

He began pacing, temples pounding.

Yes, he saw straight through Ritter's thinly veiled manipulation.

Or was it a manipulation? What if he really did want to trade personal safety for the method?

Then again, what if Ritter was trying to make him *think* it was manipulation so he wouldn't...yeah, maybe tomorrow would work best. Least that would give him time to track down Feist and clarify a few things.

But, what if...

No, that would be capitulating to Ritter, giving him the upper hand.

But was that what Ritter was counting on?

Stillman said, "No, not tomorrow morning. You want to talk with me, do it now. My choice of where."

"Then there's nothing to say. Any agreement needs to be done in person and I'm not there. I won't even have a passport for several hours. But I'm almost a hundred percent sure I can be there by morning. What's it going to be, your place at seven or nothing?"

Stillman's mind was spinning through options, rejecting some, refining others, honing down a plan, Feist being the wild card.

Needed to talk to Feist before any meeting took place, so maybe morning would be best.

By then a security company could sweep his office for listening devices, just in case Ritter's FBI buddy was somehow in on this.

Feeling more comfortable now, he agreed, "The morning then. 7 AM."

Not one minute after disconnecting with Ritter, the phone rang, and Feist's name popped up on the display. A wave of relief swept through him as he picked up: at least he could settle a few questions.

Stillman asked, "The fuck are you, dog?"

"Outside your building, mate. We need to have a little talk, you and I."

"Fine, I'll buzz you in."

"Bullocks. Outside. Now."

What?

Then he got it. And scanned the room, suddenly aware of all the places a listening device could be hidden. An empty feeling dropped into the pit of his stomach.

Fuck!

His condo was under surveillance. How long had it been

going on? Wait a minute...the voyeur...yes, of course, the binoculars...an image of the Asian's room formed in his mind: recorders, telephoto lenses, parabolic directional microphones with enough sensitivity to pluck conversations from incredible distances....

His discussions with Nikki, what exactly had they talked about? Fuck! Everything.

"Give me time to throw on some clothes and I'll be right down."

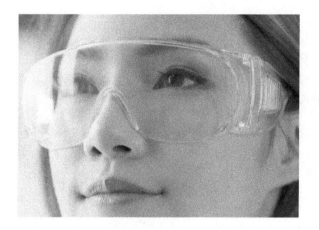

Chapter 64

STILLMAN STEPPED FROM warmth into chilly night air made worse by the harsh tint of mercury vapor lights and the empty streets at this hour of night. It took a moment to notice the figure across the street half hidden by a utility pole. He waited for a lone car to pass before jogging across the four lanes.

As he approached, Feist turned and started north at a leisurely pace, Stillman falling in beside him. Stillman was the first to speak.

"What the hell happened today? Why haven't I heard from you?"

Feist grabbed Stillman's shoulder, locked eyes with him. They remained like this a moment without blinking, Feist studying his eyes and face. Then, just as abruptly, Feist released him and continued along the sidewalk.

"Refresh my memory, mate. How'd you know the fag's little boyfriend would be taking the Clipper?"

Apprehension tingled Stillman, momentarily breaking his stride. Something in Feist's tone disturbed him.

He said, "What's your point?"

"Answer the fucking question."

Why the anger? What was he being accused of?

"Thought I was perfectly clear about this. Ritter called Dobbs, said he was in Victoria and needed Michael to bring up his old passport. Why? What's the problem?"

"The little queer went up there alright, but nobody ever came within ten paces of him. Spent the day on a fucking park bench, he did. So, you tell me what's going on."

Feist stopped, waiting for an answer.

Well, that's a relief.

Easily enough explained.

"So that's what all this is about?"

"All what's about?"

"This, this," Stillman swept his hand from right to left. "All this spy movie bullshit you insist on playing. Not calling...meeting outside like this...."

Feist said nothing.

"Ritter called just before you did. Just minutes ago..." letting it hang, waiting for his reaction.

Stillman rubbed his arms for warmth, the chilly night air creeping through his shirt.

"Wants to meet in my office, seven tomorrow morning."

Feist raised in eyebrow.

"About?"

"A trade. I get the formula if you leave him alone."

Feist cocked his head, a smile tugging the corners of his lips.

"Well then, that solves everything, don't it? You get what you want, I fold up the tent and leave. We're finished. Done."

Lowering his voice, Stillman leaned closer.

"No. It doesn't end here. You know as well as I do, our friend knows too much. And he's been talking to the FBI."

Licking the corner of his mouth, Feist glanced around.

"How're you so sure about that?"

Stillman recoiled.

"You joking, dog?" Frowned a moment, then shook his head, bewildered. "That motherfucker's been tight with them since the parking lot."

"Get to the point."

Stillman started massaging the back of his neck, working on the tense band of muscles, and stalling for time while he thought.

"Lift up your shirt, let me see skin."

With a laugh Feist, lifted his sweatshirt, exposing his chest. He let his shirt drop back into place.

"You know, if I was inclined to record this, I'd do better than something that archaic. As the person who hired me, you, of all people, should appreciate that. Now, as you were saying?"

"He needs to be eliminated. Long distance, Avengers style."

Feist scratched the edge of his chin, shook his head. "I don't know...had me heart set on retiring when I got back. Killing him's a risk I'm not sure I want to assume at this point."

Stillman said, "Why not? It's perfect. Far as anyone knows, he's still a target. Say he ends up with a bullet through the heart like those others? The media already knows he was involved in those implants. Damn, dog, makes him a better target than ever."

Feist looked down at the sidewalk a moment, rocking back and forth, considering it. Several seconds ticked past.

"Fifty thousand."

"What!"

Feist kept his head down.

"Don't play fucking deaf on me. I said fifty thousand. Take it or leave it."

Anger flashed through Stillman.

"Fuck you. You've been paid. The job was supposed be done in Victoria, but you backed out."

Feist looked up.

"And whose fault is that?"

Stillman interlaced his fingers and turned his palms out, cracking his knuckles, doing something to lessen the urge to choke him.

Fucking Feist!

Fucking blood sucker knew it was too late to hire someone else and was jacking him up for every damn cent he could.

Let Ritter go and take the risk?

No, couldn't chance it. The only sure way of controlling the formula was to kill Ritter by morning.

Stillman said, "It'll be in your account by six tomorrow morning, but with the stipulation that if he's not dead by 7:30 a stop payment goes into effect."

Feist nodded.

"He's due at your place at seven, is he?"

At least the bastard didn't gloat.

Chapter 65

NIGEL FEIST WAITED another three seconds before clearing his throat.

The desk clerk glanced up from the magazine discretely below counter level.

"Oh, sorry." His face reddened as he pushed out of the chair. "May I help you?"

"Room please," Feist answered with a noticeable twinge of Midwestern American in the double oo.

He wore black jeans, black leather jacket, a Harley Davidson cap, and polarized Oakley wraparounds in spite of the late hour.

The clerk nudged a computer keyboard closer.

"Smoking or non-smoking?"

"Tell you what, my friend," with a conspiratorial glance around the deserted lobby. "Third floor room, middle of the building wouldn't be available by any chance, would it?"

The young man shrugged.

"Dunno. Lemme check." A few keyboard strokes later and, "You're in luck. One's available." Then, more strokes. "How many nights you want?" As if this were a five-star hotel rather than a flea bag economy.

"One."

"Cash or credit card?"

Feist withdrew a wallet from his pocket.

"Cash."

"Okay, but I need to make an impression of your credit card for any incidentals."

Leaning closer, voice lowered, "Hey, bud, here's the deal. I plan on entertaining a special friend and I don't want to leave any trail her husband might track. Understand?" Straightening up, he pulled a $100 bill from the wallet, folded it lengthwise, handed it over. "I guarantee there'll be no incidentals. But you can hold on to this, just to be sure."

Up went a questioning eyebrow.

With a blasé nod, the clerk pocketed the bill.

"In that case, we can ignore the credit card for now."

Feist let the door click shut behind him, painting the room in weak streetlight shadows.

He stood motionless, waiting for his vision to adapt. Slowly the outlines of the bed and dresser became distinct. Without turning on a light, he dropped his heavy black duffel on the foot of the queen-sized bed, without a sound moved to the window, squatted on his haunches, sighted across the street at the office building.

A moment later, he returned with the duffel. Still working only in anemic streetlight, he assembled his favorite sniper rifle, a high powered SSG-2000 with noise/flash suppressor and telescopic sight.

Nothing better. Combat proven in Afghanistan.

He raised the window only far enough to poke the suppressor out and sight across the street. Although Stillman's office lights were out, enough streetlight filtered through the windows for him to see the faint outline of a desk and bookcase through high-grade telescopic sight.

He nodded to himself, satisfied with the angle this room gave.

Daylight would provide perfect illumination to take the shot. With a wry smile Feist withdrew the rifle.

Eight hours from now this clusterfuck would be done with and his first day of retirement would begin.

Allen Wyler

Chapter 66

IT'D BEEN ONE bitch of a night, Stillman mused, as he paced, waiting for Ritter to arrive. Last night, after his talk with Feist, Nikki was still spread over the sheet, waiting to finish what the phone call interrupted.

Fat chance!

The last thing on his mind by then was sex. When he didn't show any interest, she started nattering on, asking what was bothering him. Women! Always delving into relationships, emotions, and what ifs. All that Doctor Phil crap.

Why couldn't they just let things be?

Eventually, she stormed out in a snit.

Fine.

Gave him some peace and quiet, time to think things through.

Carefully, he worked back over the chain of events and still saw nothing that could even remotely link him to Lippmann or the Seoul murders. Sure, he'd signed a budget for a clinical trial, but so what? Far as the records showed, there hadn't been any clinical trial. Certainly not the disaster Ritter ended up with.

Lee Jin-Woo and Ritter enjoyed a well document association stretching back years so Ritter's visit to Seoul had nothing to do with Trophozyme. Now, if someone gunned Ritter down after a illegal entry into the States, so what? What did any of that have to do with him? As a matter of public record, Ritter was an Avengers target.

And as far as his association with Nigel Feist, Feist had an established security consulting business and worked with numerous corporations.

Why not Trophozyme?

One thing, however, did nag him: the possibility Ritter might double cross him by handing over an incorrect formula. How would he possibly know ahead of time if the formula was the real one? There was no way to guarantee results with tissue cultures. Even more troubling was that he never considered this possibility when negotiating the agreement? Okay, sure, the day Ritter embarked for Seoul, the formula was sealed in a safe deposit box that neither party could access until the terms of the agreement were fulfilled.

But what insurance did he have that Ritter placed the real formula in the safe? Had to rely solely on Jon Ritter's integrity for that. Then again, it seemed totally out of character for Ritter to be so devious. In fact, Ritter would be a set up for the perfect patsy. Jesus, he hoped to hell he'd made the right decision.

He came to the office at six but hadn't been able to concentrate enough to accomplish a damn bit of work. He settled for scanning the Wall Street Journal and the on-line news feeds.

Ritter and Fisher entered the building a 7:00 sharp, took the elevator to the fifth floor, exited onto worn carpet where a tall, lanky man in a loose-fitting suit stood waiting.

Jon didn't recognize him.

The man asked, "Doctor Ritter?"

"Yes."

The man looked past Jon, perhaps searching for anyone else accompanying them.

"I'm with Trophozyme security. Doctor Stillman is waiting for you." He turned to Fisher. "You are?"

Fisher proffered his credentials.

"Special Agent Gary Fisher. I'm with him."

The man nodded at the ID, apparently neither surprised nor impressed.

"This way."

Nigel Feist racked an amour-piercing jacketed round into the chamber, stabilized the rifle bipod on the window ledge, sharpened the telescopic focus on the corner of Stillman's desk before double checking the firing angle.

He covered approximately eighty percent of the office, the only reasonable areas someone might occupy. Stillman stood beside the desk, his back to the window, Jon Ritter slightly to Stillman's left, the two of them talking.

Feist didn't recognize the man just inside the closed office door, hands in his pockets, watching but not speaking.

As they entered the office, Jon saw Stillman push out of his desk chair and come around the desk, hand outstretched as this was a routine meeting, his smug arrogance infuriating.

Stillman said, "Good to see you, Jon." Then to Fisher: "I don't believe I've had the pleasure."

Not bothering to show credentials this time, Fisher stated, "FBI Special Agent, Gary Fisher."

Stillman nodded slowly, digesting the news.

"I see." Arms folded, Stillman sat on the corner of the desk. "I'm not sure I understand. What's with having the FBI present at a business meeting? Is there something I should know, Jon?"

Boiling anger suddenly blanked out the meeting strategy he and Fisher had discussed earlier, making it less than five seconds for Richard Stillman to punch his button. His mind went blank with furious raw anger.

He blurted, "You're an asshole," and immediately regretted the words as sounding so…immature.

Stillman laughed and rolled his eyes.

"I don't get it. You asked for this meeting, Jon. Perhaps Mr. Fisher can justify his presence at what should be a business agreement. If you are unable to do that," now looking directly at Fisher, "I suggest you leave us to our work."

Jon shook his head.

"No. I brought him as a witness, to make certain he hears what I have to say. You," pointing at Stillman's chest, "are responsible for Gabe's murder and the murders of two innocent old men in addition to my friend Jin-Woo. All for what, more money?"

Sitting cross-legged on a pillow, the SIG Sauer flash suppressor stabilized on the windowsill, Feist sighted, double checking the shot in case Ritter moved.

Things were heating up, he could see, with what appeared to be Ritter shouting, flailing his arm. Stillman pushed off the corner of the desk and squared his shoulders, his back filling the right half of the window.

Feist increased pressure on the trigger, ever so gently squeezing it while holding his breath to reduce any movement before completing the shot.

"Well, guess what, Jon shouted. "The day after I was discharged from the hospital, I sent a manuscript to *Science* that detailed the formula. You see, that's what Gabe would have wanted. When he was murdered, I wanted to leave something of his to be remembered and this was it. He despised your type, the way your greed contaminates academic research. You make me sick. People like you destroy medical research as a calling and make it slimy. You turn scientific objectivity and rigorous discipline into nothing more than a good business plan, deceptive marketing, and stock prices. Yes, I wanted to be the first to do this on humans, but my goal wasn't to make money.

"And guess what else, Richard. The manuscript was accepted. I'm sure you realize what that means for you, but in case you don't immediately see it, let me spell it out. The submission date was three days ago, which means that what I'm giving you today is already a matter of public record. And that invalidates any chance for anyone—especially you—to patent it. So go ahead, use it, here you are," throwing the papers into the air.

Stillman's face grew crimson over the several seconds it took to sink in. He stabbed a finger at Jon.

"No, dog, you're fuck—"

The window exploded, spider webbing into shards of flying glass. Stillman jerked forward, turned and fell across his desk.

Fisher yelled, "Get down," knocking Jon to the carpet.

Seconds passed with nothing but the sound of traffic outside the broken window.

Jon crawled to where Stillman lay motionless on the desk, saw an entrance wound in the back of the chest in what he expected would go straight through his heart. He palpated for the carotid artery but didn't feel a pulse.

He looked at Fisher.

"He's dead."

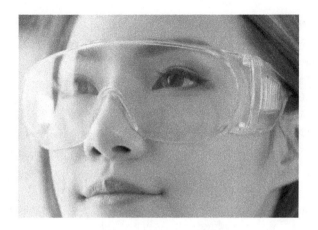

Chapter 67

One Week Later

THE KNOCK ON the door jarred Jon from staring out the window. He realized he was gazing at the same view as the night of Gabe's murder. Wayne stood in the doorway dressed in a dark suit, crisp white shirt, and sharp tie. Always the snappy dresser.

"How'd the call go?"

Jon sighed, leaned back in the chair, set his right foot on the open lower desk drawer.

"Not well. Seems that the funding was pulled before the money was officially awarded us, so it's gone. By now, a Grants and Contracts office at another university has it."

Wayne picked up manila folders on the only other chair in the office, dropped them on the floor, sat down, crossed his legs.

"That's depressing as hell."

"There are a couple bits of good news. Jin-Woo's medical center had enough political juice to squelch any publicity on our work there."

Wayne smoothed the pants over his knee, sharpening the crease.

"So, you're saying no one knows about it?"

"Correct."

Wayne sighed.

"And Feist?"

"Vanished. Hasn't been seen since he returned from Seoul. Fisher suspects he may have slipped out of the country on another passport and is back in Australia by no, but no one knows. Not that they have any proof of his involvement in the shooting. Like everything else, it just stands to reason."

"Fisher still thinks he intentionally shot Stillman?"

Jon nodded.

"From where I was standing—after all, Fisher should know—that's what their ballistics indicates. Especially with it centered so perfectly through the heart."

Wayne nodded solemnly.

"You said there were two bits of good news. What's the second?"

"Detective Park had their geeks enhance the video surveillance that was recorded the night the patients were murdered. They were able to verify that the person entering the building with my ID tag wasn't me."

"That mean you're cleared of the charges?"

Jon nodded.

"I'm cleared of the murder charges. Don't know if they've pressed charges for the escape."

Wayne asked, "Any way to find out?"

"Not for a while. Maybe never. Not unless there's a compelling reason to."

Jon checked his watch, realized he better get moving. He stood, shrugged on his sports coat.

Wayne looked puzzled.

"Where you going? Don't we have a meeting scheduled in

five minutes?"

"Sorry, forgot to tell you I need to cancel. I'm heading out to the airport."

Wayne's puzzlement increased. "What's up?"

Jon stood next an empty baggage carousel outside of Immigration, watching weary travelers file out of the sliding glass doors in ones and twos, some obviously familiar with the airport, others glancing around to orient themselves.

Then Yeonhee appeared, a black purse in one hand, a duty-free bag in the other. He waved. She caught his eyes with hers and beamed and quickened her pace.

He moved closer to the exit—then she was in his arms, hugging him. He hugged her back, then leaned down and kissed her without even realizing what he was doing.

She hugged him back.